just say yes

LENA HENDRIX

THE KINGS
BOOK 5

Copyright © 2025 by Lena Hendrix

All rights reserved.

No part of this book may be reproduced in any form or by any electronic or mechanical means, including information storage and retrieval systems, without written permission from the author, except for the use of brief quotations in a book review.

Without in any way limiting the author's exclusive rights under copyright, any use of this publication to "train" generative artificial intelligence (AI) technologies to generate text is expressly prohibited. The author reserves all rights to license uses of this work for generative AI training and development of machine learning language models.

This is a work of fiction, created without the use of AI technology. Any names, characters, places, or incidents are products of the author's imagination and used in a fictitious manner. Any resemblance to actual people, places, or events is purely coincidental or fictional.

Developmental editing: Paula Dawn, Lilypad Lit

Copy editing: James Gallagher, Evident Ink

Proofreading: Julia Griffis, The Romance Bibliophile

Model cover design: Echo Grayce, WildHeart Graphics

Model cover photography: Wander Aguiar

Discreet cover design: Sarah Hansen, OkayCreations

To any woman who thinks your inexperience makes you broken, Logan Brown—your consent king—is eager to prove you wrong . . .

LET'S CONNECT

When you sign up for my newsletter, you'll stay up to date with new releases, book news, giveaways, and new book recommendations! I promise not to spam you and only email when I have something fun & exciting to share!

Also, When you sign up, you'll also get a FREE copy of Choosing You (a very steamy Chikalu Falls novella)!

Sign up at my website at www.lenahendrix.com

AUTHOR'S NOTE

Just Say Yes is a look into how a shattered family picks up the pieces after their world is tipped upside down.

It contains discussion of parental manipulation, death of a parent, and a slightly coerced first sexual experience (not on page but discussed). For clarity-both parties consented, but instead of enthusiastic consent, one partner felt uncomfortable and later, nothing but regret. The other partner was also a post-coital dickbag, so . . . there's also that.

Please be kind to yourself when deciding if these triggers are too much.

I take all forms of domestic abuse (including sexual coercion) very seriously. If you or a loved one are experiencing any kind of unwanted sexual aggression or manipulation, please seek help by calling the National Domestic Violence hotline at 800-799-SAFE (7233)

MJ's book also contains explicit, open door sex scenes and a hot rugby player with an Olympic sized . . . heart. Logan is my consent king and is everything MJ (and you) deserves.

ABOUT THIS BOOK

Getting tangled up with an Olympic rugby player seems like the perfect way to forget about how my life is falling apart. Until I discover he's my **ex-boyfriend's best friend.**

Logan Brown walked into my small town with a charming grin and mischief in his eyes. He's a world-class flirt and his confident masculinity is almost as distracting as those rugby thighs.

Given my inexperienced history, I'm no match for our undeniable chemistry. I vow to keep him at arm's length. But with Logan, every lingering stare—every forbidden touch—awakens something inside of me I thought I had buried for good.

We both know we shouldn't cross that line, but I have spent my entire life being a good girl, and suddenly I'm tempted to be very, very bad.

Especially when Logan tells me to *just say yes.*

ONE

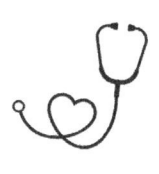

MJ

Due to recent personal events, I will be going off the fucking rails.

There was no other explanation for why I was slipping out of my comfy teal scrubs and into a skintight bodycon dress when my shift at the assisted-living facility wasn't even over. The tight quarters of the staff bathroom had me sweating. I balled up my scrubs and shoved them into my backpack.

Looking myself over in the mirror, I ignored the gnawing realization that I hadn't been on a *real* date in months. Not that it mattered . . . in a small tourist town my options were men I'd practically grown up with or tourists looking only for a good time. Neither option appealed to me—I was *over* men seeing me as one of the guys, and I still hadn't talked myself into being a one-night-stand kind of woman.

Yet.

Plus, it was damn difficult to date when you had four ridiculous older brothers who loved to insert themselves into your business.

A soft knock at the door rattled me. "One second!" I called and zipped my bag.

I haphazardly fluffed my mousy brown hair. It was flat and lifeless after my nursing shift at Haven Pines, but it would have to do.

I blew out a breath when a second knock sounded at the door.

I grabbed my bag and opened the door. Another nurse, Carol, stepped back with wide eyes and a surprised laugh.

I rolled my eyes. "Don't even ask."

She smirked and moved into the doorway. "I thought your shift wasn't over until seven."

"Abbey is covering the last half hour." I balanced in my heels.

Carol looked me over, waggling her eyebrows. "Hot date tonight?"

I smoothed a hand down my hips and tugged at the hemline that had somehow gotten shorter since I slipped on the dress.

I pinned her with a playful look. "Arthur Brown."

Carol tossed her head back and cackled. "Well, that makes sense. He's a charmer."

I pointed a playful finger at her and smiled. "He's a menace."

We shared a laugh as Carol disappeared into the staff bathroom. Arthur Brown was an elderly resident at Haven Pines, and in the few months he'd been with us, he had charmed a dinner date out of at least six other nurses.

I was lucky fool number seven.

In truth, Arthur was one of the sweetest residents at Haven Pines. He was polite, gracious, and wickedly funny. My shifts had become a bit lonely since my longtime favorite patient, Red Sullivan, had moved into one of the semi-independent houses on the outskirts of Haven Pines. I was so happy for Red but found I missed having a crappy cup of cafeteria coffee with him during my shifts. I made a mental note to swing by his place this week to say hello.

As my shoes clacked across the linoleum floor, the sky-high pointy heels pinched my toes. They were uncomfortable but gave me a few much-needed inches on my short frame. I lifted my chin and blew out an unsteady breath as I walked toward the nurses' station.

I slipped my badge from the pocket of my backpack. "Hey, Beth." I scanned the badge to unlock the hallway door that led to the corridor where Arthur's room was located. "I'll be in room forty-two if anyone needs me."

Beth didn't even look up from her phone, but she waved a dismissive hand and continued scrolling.

I gritted my teeth and stifled a sigh. Beth was new—and a pain in my side. She looked at her job as a stepping stone for something better. I'd overheard her making comments about how nursing at an assisted-living facility was beneath her and she couldn't wait to bag a wealthy neurosurgeon.

As far as I was concerned, she could take one.

I much preferred caring for the elderly—most were quiet, many were simply looking for a thoughtful ear, and they always had the *best* stories.

I loved my job.

Which was why, when Arthur sweet-talked me into having dinner with him, I couldn't say no. He also let it slip that he planned to dress up for the occasion. I found it endearing and figured faded, stained scrubs just wouldn't do.

When I reached his room, I gently knocked and cracked the door open. "Mr. Brown? It's MJ."

He pulled the door open and beamed at me. Arthur was

in his mid-eighties, short, and his shoulders stooped and rounded slightly. Despite his age, his eyes were bright and his smile was wide. His attention never left my face, and my heart swelled.

Old men are so much better than the ones my age.

"You are a vision, my dear." He shuffled his feet and moved to allow me to enter.

Like much of Haven Pines, each room was carefully planned to look less like a hospital and more like a studio apartment. The rooms were small, but each had a bed, side table with two chairs, and a comfy wingback for reading books or relaxing by the tall window.

On the side table, Arthur had arranged a round tablecloth, two place settings, and a pair of chairs. I had expected this, because it was me who had convinced the maintenance staff to have it set up for him.

"Come in. Come in." Arthur gestured toward the table with a smile.

"This is lovely, Mr. Brown." I smiled and walked toward the table. "Thank you."

"Please, call me Arthur." Arthur hurried behind me and scooted out a chair. "Allow me."

I obeyed and tucked myself under the small circular table. Arthur made his way to his side and sat down. His eyes twinkled as the papery wrinkles around his eyes deepened. Low music crooned from a bedside radio.

"How about we eat?" Arthur smiled again and removed the plastic lids from our dinner plates. It was the same Wednesday night supper that was on rotation at Haven Pines—marinated and grilled chicken breast, garlicky steamed green beans, and a dinner roll.

"You're awfully kind, humoring a lonely old man like me," Arthur said.

I looked across the small table at my dinner companion. I was so young when my grandfather passed away that I barely remembered him. My father, Russell King, had also been a difficult man—always controlling and emotionally absent. I had been happy to fly under his radar most of the time.

My father was awaiting trial for the murder of my mother, and suddenly my entire life felt like one big lie.

Yeah . . . this year had been a lot *to unpack.*

From the outside, I appeared strong and steady, but deep down I was aimless and floundering.

Maybe that was why I felt so at ease with the elderly residents of Haven Pines. Maybe on some level they served as the warm and loving grandparents I never had the opportunity to know.

I unrolled the paper napkin and placed it on my lap. "I wouldn't want to be anywhere else."

Arthur did the same, placing his napkin across his knees. When it slipped off and hit the floor, he struggled to scoot his chair backward.

"I've got it." I smiled and inched my chair out to retrieve his napkin. The space between the table and chair was small and dark. The constricting fabric of my regrettable dress made moving even harder. I stifled a grunt and tried to tug at my hemline while reaching for the napkin.

"Hang on," I said. "It slid all the way under the table." Unsure how I was going to manage, I finally gave up on being ladylike and dropped to my knees. On all fours, I scooted under the table and snatched the white cloth napkin.

"What the hell is this?" A deep, rumbling voice startled me.

My head whipped up, cracking against the underside of the table. "Ow, *fuck!*"

With one hand on the back of my head and the other bracing myself on the armrest of Arthur's chair, I looked up.

A man filled the doorway—not just with his size, but with a presence that was impossible to ignore, like a storm rolling in off the lake. My jaw dropped. He was tall—impressively so—with thick arms that crossed his chest. His wide stance showed off the thickest thighs I'd ever seen in real life.

Helloooo, stranger.

Even in the gross fluorescent lighting, he was undeniably handsome. His dark hair fell over his forehead, dipping down to dark eyebrows that cinched tight. His face was chiseled, and he had a mustache that stood out a little thicker than the rest of his scruff.

His mouth was set in a hard line.

The doorframe suddenly felt too small to contain him.

My attention bounced from the mystery man to Arthur and back again. I was on my knees, in front of Arthur, with my dress slipping precariously up my thighs. With Arthur's back to the door, I could only imagine what it looked like I was doing on my knees in front of him.

"Oh my god!" I struggled to maneuver out from under the table and onto my feet. The tight skirt of my dress restricted my movements, and my hemline crept higher.

Arthur looked at the man and grinned. "Logan." He sat up in his chair. "This is unexpected."

Logan.

The nurses were all abuzz over Arthur's broody and pestering grandson Logan. Apparently he called near daily wanting to check up on Arthur or demand to know the ins and outs of his grandfather's schedule. Rumor was that he was a bit of a princess and didn't like the fact that our residents had autonomy over their days. Arthur was free to do what he pleased, and we weren't required to get family approval before he tried pickleball or went to the local park to play dominoes with friends.

Maybe setting up dates with the nursing staff was a little left field...

Arthur stood and moved toward his grandson while I struggled to my feet next to the table, tugging at my dress and dusting grit from my knees. Logan accepted Arthur's embrace, but his eyes raked over me, lingering a second too long on the short hemline of my dress. I tugged at it again as I stood frozen.

Arthur beamed at the man. "There's someone I'd like you to meet." He gestured toward me. "MJ is my companion for the night."

I'm sorry—what now?

I had sputtered and attempted to speak when Logan let loose a deep, rumbling sigh. "Grandpa, we talked about this. You can't hire hookers to have dinner with you because you're lonely."

"Whoa!" I cut in, stepping forward with a hand on my hip. I wagged one finger in his direction. "First of all, I think the proper term is *escort*. Second—"

"Whatever." Logan cut off my rant just as I was gaining steam. He rolled his eyes, and my blood pressure spiked. "Grandpa, cut me some slack. We went over this. No hookers."

Arthur laughed, clearly enjoying the fact that his ridiculously handsome grandson was grossly misinformed. I couldn't blame him. He'd walked into the room to find me under the table, practically between his grandfather's legs, but I was still annoyed.

I crossed my arms in anger, until I realized the gesture pushed my boobs up even higher, and I quickly dropped them.

Arthur held out his hand to me, gesturing for me to step forward. "MJ, this is my grandson, Logan."

I gritted my teeth, then faked a smile and held out a hand. "Pleasure."

He eyed it before manners won out and he wrapped his gargantuan hand around mine. He shook, then moved his attention to his grandfather. "Are you done here? I thought we could talk before I have to leave for my match."

Annoyed, I cut in with a raised eyebrow. "Visiting hours were over at six."

His eyes flicked over my too-tight outfit again. "Then what's your excuse?"

My nostrils flared as Arthur simply chuckled. Clearly, the old man was enjoying himself. "Don't be rude to my companion, Logan."

I turned toward Arthur. "Okay, maybe stop calling me that."

Arthur blinked innocently. I snatched my backpack from the floor. "I think I'm going to go." Turning toward Arthur, I pleaded with my eyes, desperate to escape the entire incredibly embarrassing moment. "Thank you for the *almost* lovely dinner. I will see you next time."

I stormed past a brooding Logan, bumping into him when he refused to step aside. "Did you get paid?" he shot over his shoulder.

My high heels came to a screeching halt. "Wow!" I spun on my toes. "You really go all in when you step in it, don't you?" Fire was blazing in my chest. "Well, let me break this down for you, buddy." I emphasized every word with a jab of my hand. "I. Am. Not. A. Prostitute. I don't know who pissed in your protein shake, but I work as a nurse at Haven Pines, taking care of *your* grandfather. Something you would know if you had visited even *once* in the time he's been here. Your grandpa is a sweet man. He's funny. He is very charming. When he asked me to join him for dinner, I said yes. *As a friend* to a lonely old man—" I turned to Arthur. "No offense."

Arthur only laughed and shrugged. "None taken."

I turned my attention back to Logan. His brow furrowed, and I ignored the tiny spark that burned low in my belly. "Now, if you'll excuse me, I'm going to gather what's left of my pride and go home." I looked past Logan's broad shoulders. "Mr. Brown, I will see you tomorrow." My eyes flicked to a stunned Logan. I breathed deeply and smiled. "It is my sincere hope that I never, *ever* see you again."

At my back, Arthur hooted. "You really did it now, kid."

Logan grumbled something to his grandfather, but I didn't stick around to hear it. The night had been humiliating enough, and I didn't need the hottest man I'd ever seen to watch me fall apart.

I was annoyed that my pride could be so easily bruised by a handsome stranger. I should have known better. Men who looked like *him* meant only trouble.

I would know.

I sailed past Beth, not bothering to say goodbye. It was likely her fault Logan was allowed to disregard the visiting hours.

I considered changing back into my scrubs, but the last thing I needed was to come face-to-face with him again. My eyes flicked to the clock. It was five past seven, and my book club was just starting across town.

My feet ached, the back of my head throbbed from

where it hit the table, there was a knot in my shoulder from helping a resident out of bed today, and something pinched beneath my ribs anytime I recalled the dark, annoyed look in Logan's eyes.

I had to get out of there before I had to face him again.

If nothing else, the Bluebirds would understand.

TWO

LOGAN

Oh, yeah . . . I fucked up.

And not just a little. Full-scale, nuclear disaster fucked up. Implying the gorgeous woman who'd been kind enough to have dinner with my grandfather was a hooker? That wasn't just a red flag—it was an entire marching band of shame parading through my head.

To make things worse, she wasn't just gorgeous. She was fire. And I'd basically hosed myself down in kerosene.

Based on the fact my grandfather couldn't stop laughing, I had *really* fucked up.

I crossed my arms. "It's not funny."

My grandfather laughed again. "It's a little funny."

I pinched the bridge of my nose. "No, Grandpa, it's really not." I gestured toward the door. "I just called that poor nurse a *hooker*. Twice."

He smiled. "You're right. That was bad. MJ is so sweet too." He clucked his tongue.

I groaned, thinking back to the gorgeous brunette who'd been dining with my grandfather. "Don't make me feel worse."

He shrugged and sat in front of his dinner. "You're the one who made assumptions before getting all the facts."

I pulled my phone from the pocket of my jeans. "You're the one who texted me asking how much escorts earn nowadays."

Around a green bean, he said, "I saw a *Dateline* episode about sex workers." His shoulders lifted. "I was curious."

"Followed up by, and I quote, 'I have a date tonight and don't want to be rude.' I drove over to make sure you weren't getting taken advantage of or forking over your life savings, only to find a woman *under the table*." I looked at him expectantly, and he only took another mindful bite of his dinner.

"You know what? Forget it." I shook my head. There was no reasoning with him sometimes. Sometimes Arthur Brown just liked to be a shit-stirrer, and I should have seen this coming.

"Maybe you were just jealous I was having dinner with such a pretty girl." Grandpa waggled his eyebrows, his grin sly.

The image of MJ—the fire in her eyes, the way her dress hugged her curves—lingered longer than it should've. It was annoying that my grandfather was partially correct. "That is *not* true."

Okay, fine. Maybe it was a little *true.*

"Who was she?" I finally asked when curiosity got the best of me.

Humor danced in his eyes. "Best nurse they've got. She's sweet and always genuinely interested in the folks around here." He gestured toward the door. "Not like some of them who make me feel like they can't wait for me to shut up. MJ's one of the good ones."

Guilt rolled over me. I'd been a total prick to someone

who'd taken a genuine interest in my favorite person. I looked at my grandpa. "She said she works tomorrow. Maybe I can swing by to apologize."

He shrugged and rubbed his temple. "Don't remember. Memory isn't what it used to be."

I sat back on my heels and huffed. "Your memory is fine, old man."

Grandpa winked at me. "Ah, you got me there." He popped another green bean into his mouth. "You know . . . she goes to a book club every Wednesday night. The gentlemanly thing to do would be to hunt her down to apologize tonight."

"It sounds a lot less gentlemanly and a lot *more* stalkery when you use the phrase *hunt her down*."

He swatted a hand at me. "They like that nowadays. My friend Greta says the bookish ones are into *dark* romance."

I closed my eyes. "Please stop talking."

He hooted a laugh. "It's the Bluebird Book Club—downtown Outtatowner. If you hurry, you can still catch her."

Indecision gnawed at me.

"You can sit here moping, or you can find her. Women love a man who admits he's an idiot."

My eyes narrowed on him. "I don't think that's true."

Grandpa shrugged. "Worked on your grandmother. God rest her soul."

I was embarrassed that I'd assumed MJ was a sex worker—*and said that to her face*—but who could blame me? It wouldn't have been the first time my grandfather had pulled some wild shit because he got bored.

Still, I couldn't get the genuine look of hurt that crossed

her pretty face out of my mind. I pulled up the map app on my phone. "What was the name of it again?"

"Attaboy," my grandfather said. "Bluebird Books."

When the vague directions to downtown came up, I frowned.

"Go get her, son." Grandpa chuckled.

With a shake of my head, I left my grandfather behind looking all too pleased with himself.

∼

Outtatowner was the kind of coastal Michigan town I was familiar with. Having grown up in Western Michigan, it was the kind of place you visited in the summertime, fighting crowds of tourists for a spot on its pristine freshwater beaches.

After high school, my blossoming rugby career had taken me across the country, and it wasn't often I found myself back in my home state. Still, Michigan had always felt like home.

It was dark, but when I crested a small hill, the downtown strip of Outtatowner came into view. My truck slowed at the four-way stop. Off in the distance, about a half mile down the road, Lake Michigan's inky waters sparkled in the moonlit darkness. The roadway cut through the quaint little tourist town. Mom-and-pop shops dotted the sides, but nearly all the storefronts were locked up for the night. A bar on the corner had a few patrons coming in and out, but otherwise the town was quiet.

I scanned the app on my phone and noted the bookstore was just ahead. I swung my truck into a parking space, and my heartbeat ticked higher when I saw MJ, still dressed in sky-high heels and a tiny dress, stomping up the sidewalk toward the bookstore.

I didn't want to scare her, so I called out. "Excuse me!"

Her head whipped around, and her long hair tumbled down her back. When she recognized me, her eyes rolled toward the night sky. "You have got to be kidding me . . ." MJ moved to turn away.

"Wait," I called out. "Hold up."

She kept walking toward the bookstore. "Leave me alone." She yanked open the door, and I caught it with my hand.

"I just want a second." All I wanted to do was apologize, but the tiny firepot in front of me was making that all but impossible.

Her cheeks were flushed, and there was a dangerous spark in her hazel eyes. A spark I had no right liking as much as I did.

"How *dare* you follow me!" MJ's chin was high and her fists were clenched, like she was ready for a fight.

Inside the bookstore the lighting was dim. I followed MJ through the low stacks of books toward the back, where her book club seemed to be meeting. Women of varying ages were sitting in an eclectic assortment of plush seating arrangements.

Their jaws hung open as they watched me follow MJ deeper into the store.

"Relax, Thunder." A grin tugged at the corner of my mouth. "You might hurt yourself if you keep stomping around like that."

"Thunder?" she shouted, stepping forward. Because I was so much taller, her chin lifted higher, but she didn't back down.

Oh, I like that.

From the corner of my vision, I noted curious eyes peeking from behind the high backs of the chairs, staring directly at us and soaking up our interaction.

I scoffed and settled on my heels. "Yeah." I gestured toward her small frame. "You've got this whole storm-cloud vibe happening. It's cute."

When my gaze floated over her face, I licked my lip.

"Cute?" Fire danced in MJ's eyes. "You are absolutely unreal. Do you know that? First you skulk around an assisted-living facility—*after hours*, let me remind you—then you have the balls to insinuate that I'm a—a—a lady of the night!"

I was suddenly tickled by her account of what had happened tonight.

"You been thinking about my balls, Thunder?" Goading her was probably a mistake, but my grandfather's sense of humor was something I came by honestly. I shifted my stance as a few giggles tittered through the crowd of curious onlookers.

MJ threw her hands in the air with a frustrated growl. "You think this is funny?"

"Not funny. Amusing. There's a difference." I sighed. "I came to apologize." My voice was thick, but I hoped it sounded as sincere as I'd intended.

It was enough to stop MJ mid-rant. Her mouth hung open for a second before she snapped it shut.

Seizing the opportunity, I continued: "I had just gotten into town and wanted to say hello to my grandfather. The girl at the front desk said a quick visit wouldn't be a problem."

Her hazel eyes gazed up at me, and I stepped forward, drawn into her space. "Safe to say I was surprised to see a woman who looks like *you* having a candlelit dinner with my eighty-six-year-old grandfather."

MJ's fists clenched again, but the fire in her eyes had dimmed to a low smolder.

"You said your piece then." An older woman stepped beside MJ, placing a supportive hand between her shoulder blades. "You've disrupted our evening enough. Good night."

I looked around, and a sea of wide eyeballs were staring at us.

My grin widened as I raised my hand. "Hi." I chuckled and shook my head. The night could not have been more of a disaster. "Bye."

A few of the women waved back, stunned into a disbelieving stupor.

Before I walked out the front door of the bookstore, something stopped me. I looked back at MJ, who was still as pissed off as ever. "Maybe I'll see you around, Thunder."

MJ rolled her eyes with a huff and turned her back to me, walking straight toward her book club friends. "I need a drink."

You and me both, lady.

Amused, I made my way back to my apartment but couldn't shake the image of the pink in MJ's cheeks and the fire in her eyes. That tiny little spitfire was a lot less like a thundercloud and more like a tsunami.

I dropped my keys on the entryway table and plopped myself onto the couch with a huff. My temporary apartment was a few miles from Outtatowner, nestled between it and Star Harbor, another tourist town up the coast. As a kid from a no-name town in Michigan, when my star rose quickly in high school, my mom eagerly followed her only kid around the country. In fact, she and I had moved so much, it was hard to consider *anywhere* home. Somewhere along the line Mom had gotten tired of all the moving and settled back into our hometown.

I looked around the quiet, lonely apartment.

Just as good a place as any, I guess.

Fuck, I wanted a beer, but the image of my coach frowning popped into my mind. Only a few weeks off our recently successful Olympic run and I was still carrying around his voice in my head.

Apparently, even a gold medal didn't earn you a break.

A few of my teammates planned to keep up with their training in the World Rugby Sevens—international tournaments used to promote the sport. I'd had every intention to play, but one nasty concussion and a tweaked knee had pulled the plug on that plan. I needed the fall months to focus on a full recovery so I was prepared to show up in February at peak performance.

At thirty-four, I was already hearing the whispers—too old, too broken. Another bad injury and I'd be watching matches from the stands.

I needed focus. Recovery. Quiet.

Instead, I'd gotten thunder in stilettos, glaring at me like I was the worst thing to ever happen to her. And the part that irritated me most? I couldn't get her out of my head.

All I needed was to focus—any slip could mean losing everything I'd worked for.

Spending the fall and winter in Michigan with my grandfather and playing in a handful of exhibition games would be my life for the next few months until the real season started back up in the spring.

I stared at the clock as a minute, then two, ticked by.

"Fuck it." I pulled myself up from the couch and padded to the kitchen. When I yanked open the fridge, I made a mental note to head to the grocery store—wilted lettuce and a dozen eggs weren't going to cut it. I pulled a beer from the untouched six-pack and popped the cap.

With a deep pull and audible exhale, I closed my eyes.

Immediately the image of MJ flashed in my mind. She hovered above me, eyes glazed, mouth lax. Her lush lips taunted me as she looked down at me, her hands bracing her weight on my shoulders.

Damn, that's good.

I'm *pretty* sure I was referencing the beer and not the feisty brunette who was haunting my thoughts, but based on the way my dick was joining the conversation, I wasn't so sure.

I scraped a hand over my face.

I need a shave . . . and a life. Goddamn, dude.

Fantasizing about a woman I'd just met—a woman who hated me, nonetheless—was new.

What was it about her that I couldn't get past? In a few more chugs, I finished the beer and dropped the bottle in the recycling bin.

I could always find out tomorrow . . .

THREE

MJ

ROYAL

Whose ass do we have to beat?

> I'm sorry, what?!

ROYAL

I heard about some Olympic douche canoe harassing you at book club.

VEDA

Hey, now. You can't go spilling pillow-talk secrets.

> He wasn't harassing me. And thank you for telling my brother about that.

WHIP

For what it's worth, we all know about it.

> Fantastic.

ABEL

Do we need to take care of this?

JP

Sounds to me like we do.

> NO! Please pretend like this conversation never happened. I have to go to work.

WHIP

In that case, think you can get us an autograph?

> GOODBYE.

~

"WELL, DON'T YOU LOOK PRETTY!" Carol flipped a lock of my hair as she walked by.

I scoffed, smoothing a hand over the soft curls I'd added that morning. "What are you talking about?"

Carol leaned over the nurses' desk, resting her chin on her hands and blinking innocently. "I mean the fact you curled your hair and are wearing makeup. That doesn't have to do with a certain thick-thighed rugby player, does it?"

"Of course not. I couldn't sleep, so I had some time to kill this morning. It's nothing."

"Mm-hmm," she hummed, clearly not believing my obvious lie. "God, if I were twenty years younger, I'd give my left tit to take him for a ride."

A laugh erupted from deep within my chest. "I don't know, maybe he's into older women." I popped a fresh piece of mint gum into my mouth. I knew Carol was joking, but it still didn't stop the irrational spike of jealousy that poked at my ribs. "Maybe you should shoot your shot."

She sighed wistfully. "I wish." She narrowed her eyes. "Do you think my husband would understand?"

I giggled. "Poor Dub." Carol's husband, William—or as he was known in town, Dub—was the sweetest man. He literally worshipped the ground she walked on.

Carol clicked her pen and scribbled something as she spoke. "I'm telling you, Beth was absolutely *salivating* over him after he left."

I rolled my eyes. "I bet. I'm sure she saw nothing but Olympic gold-medal-size dollar signs."

Carol leaned in. "I think he only had eyes for you," she said. "After you left, he practically ran out of Mr. Brown's room, looking for you. I distracted Beth so she wouldn't ruin all your fun." She inched closer to whisper. "You're welcome."

I recalled our exchange the night before, and a tingle danced down my spine.

Carol's eyes went wide with glee. "He showed up, didn't he?"

I flipped through the chart in my hands, trying to forget about how all my friends witnessed our interaction and hounded me all night for more information. "Of course he showed up. Arthur is the most meddlesome old man I've ever met. We've talked about the Bluebirds before, so I'm sure he told his grandson where I would be."

She tapped her fingers in front of her and did a little shimmy. "Did he drag all that masculine energy up there, burst through the door like a starving man, and proclaim his desire in front of everyone?"

I looked her over and laughed. "You read too much."

Her nose wrinkled. "That's fair." She slapped a cardboard file folder onto the counter. "I'm just living vicariously through you. Dub's idea of romance is a bucket of fried chicken and a six-pack of Budweiser."

I smiled at my friend with a shrug. "I mean, at this point, I'd take that."

"See!" Carol encouraged. "You need to get out there. Meet a handsome stranger. Maybe go for a mustache ride and make a few bad decisions." Her eyebrows waggled, and her shoulders shimmied like bad decisions were the best part of the whole plan.

Trouble was, bad decisions had consequences. Like leading a man you'd been dating to think you were ready for more than you were.

I would know.

I turned to Carol, noting on my watch that I was already late for my rounds. "Look, I have no interest in Mr. Brown's grandson *or* his mustache rides."

Carol's smile froze.

Her eyes went wide as they flicked above me and back down again. My blood ran cold as a cavernous pit opened in my stomach.

I stared at her. "He's right behind me, isn't he?"

Her mischievous grin widened as she grabbed the folder from my hands. "I'll make these rounds for you!"

Before I could argue, she was practically skipping down the hallway. I took a steadying breath before closing my eyes and slowly turning around.

When I opened them, Logan was smoothing two fingers over the very mustache I was refusing to ride. "I mean . . . I'm not *not* offering," he said.

I scoffed. "You're a pig."

He laughed, totally unaffected by my insult.

I shifted my weight, hoping the stance made me appear aloof instead of entirely embarrassed he had overheard me. "What are you doing here?"

"It's visiting hours. I would know. I checked the website." He winked and his playful grin widened, showing off bright-white teeth and a small dimple in one cheek.

That dimple was very, very dangerous.

"Look," he continued. "I still feel bad about last night. I was a jerk, and I would like to make it up to you."

I eyed him warily. After he left the book club, Lark was all too eager to fill me in on Logan's status as a professional athlete. I was more of a reader than a television watcher, which had kept me completely unaware that much of the men's Olympic rugby coverage included Logan's prowess on *and off* the field.

He was practically a hometown celebrity. Nothing about him was safe, and my guarded heart was screaming at me to run in the opposite direction.

"Please?" His dark eyebrows rose.

I ground my teeth. It was the *please*, accompanied by the sincere, stricken look in his eyes, that made me crack. "Maybe."

His grin widened. "I can work with a *maybe*."

Logan reached over the nurses' station to grab a sticky note and a pen. He scribbled something down and handed it to me. "There's an exhibition match in a few days. Coming off the Olympic Games, the energy is still pretty high. It would be a great time."

He handed the sticky note to me with a time and an address. I looked down, then back up. "This is in Chicago."

Logan grimaced and dragged a hand across the back of his neck. "Yeah . . . there aren't a lot of small-town games, unfortunately. But you'd be my guest. I'd take care of everything. All you have to do is show up."

I gnawed on the inside of my lip as I considered his offer. Warning bells sounded inside my head. Logan was too charming. Too tempting. Too . . . *something*.

I knew men like him and had been burned before. My eyes flicked upward. "I'll think about it."

I might as well have said yes based on the way Logan

grinned. "That's good. Perfect." He headed down the hallway toward his grandfather's corridor. He stopped at the locked door and turned to smile at me. I pressed the button to unlock the door for him.

"See you around, Thunder." He turned, tossing a salute over his shoulder, and tiny butterfly wings tickled my stomach.

My carefully built walls were starting to show some cracks, and all it had taken were thick thighs and a rakish smile, apparently. I looked at the sticky note again before crumpling it in my fist and stuffing it into the pocket of my scrubs.

"You're going," Carol whisper-squealed from behind me.

A small laugh escaped and I shook my head. "I am not going."

"MJ . . ." She bumped my shoulder. "You're going."

My fingers toyed with the crumpled paper inside my pocket.

I was definitely *not* going . . . right?

"I've got my rounds." I plucked my stolen folder from her hands and grabbed the computer cart. "I'll see you in a bit."

I smiled, eager to escape Carol and her waggling eyebrows.

The rest of the morning was delightfully mundane. I administered medications, called family members, and checked on the well-being of my residents. When I rolled my cart up to room forty-two, I pulled in a deep breath before gently knocking on the door.

"It's open," Arthur called.

I pushed open the door and exhaled in relief to find him alone, reading a newspaper in his chair.

"Good morning," I said, pushing my cart to the side of the room.

"A pleasure to see you, as always." Arthur smiled and stood. He walked toward my cart, ready to take his daily medication.

I noticed that, despite the sunshine outside, Arthur's curtains were drawn closed. "It's a beautiful morning. Would you like those open?"

"With you here, I have all the sunshine I need." He smiled.

I smirked at him. "Don't try to butter me up now. I have a feeling our dinner last night was a setup."

Arthur gave me a sheepish smile. The man had known *exactly* what he was doing.

"Can you forgive an old man?" he asked.

I eyed him. Arthur was dressed in a cozy brown cardigan over a T-shirt. His slacks were neatly pressed, and his sneakers were as white as his eyebrows. If I could have conjured the most charming old man, it would be Arthur.

I exhaled with a smile. "Of course." I moved toward the curtain. "Now let's get some life into this cramped old room, shall we?"

Arthur nodded with a grin, and I walked toward the large windows. I snapped the curtains open, and warm morning sunlight filled the space. As I turned, a photograph of a man with a group of young boys, covered in mud, caught my eye.

Arthur came up behind me, plucking the frame from his desk. "Sometimes it feels like a lifetime ago." He held the frame out to me. "I coached Logan when he was first starting out. It was easy to see from the beginning that he was something special."

I accepted the frame and looked at the man in the

photo. Clearly, it was a much younger Arthur. The short stature was the same, along with the way his eyes always seemed to be smiling. His grin was wide as he stood, sandwiched between the muddy teenagers.

My eyes landed on the sweet, one-dimpled face of Logan. Mud streaked across his chest and legs. He looked sweaty and happy as his arm draped over the shoulder of his grandfather.

I scanned the other teenage faces.

My blood ran cold as I stopped on one face—standing next to Logan, with his arm around his waist, was a face I had hoped to never, *ever* see again.

Trent fucking Fischer.

The room spun, the air thick with the weight of a thousand memories I'd spent years trying to forget. The laughter, the lies, the cold silence that followed when he was done with me. And now he was here, smiling, charming, digging through the cracks in my carefully built walls.

I felt sick.

I swallowed hard as I tried to find my voice. "Was this your team?" I asked, pointing to Trent in particular.

Arthur nodded. "Some of them." He smiled down at the photograph, his eyes wistful with memories. "Logan's there." He then pointed to the other boys. "John played for a while but never went pro after college. Tim was a good kid—enthusiastic but didn't have an ounce of talent. Brent had a real shot but had a bad ankle break that took him out for good." Arthur's bony finger tapped on Trent's face. "Trent—too busy chasing girls and glory." He shook his head like he was disappointed. "I still tell him that whenever I see him."

"Oh, you . . ." I swallowed thickly. "You still keep in touch with some of them? That's nice."

"Trent and Logan stayed close. Best friends, even now."

Arthur was too busy looking at the picture and recalling memories to see the way all the blood had left my face.

Best friends.

When Arthur looked up, he must have seen the way I'd paled and misinterpreted it for disinterest.

"Well." He sighed. "You don't need me taking up all your time. You've got old people who need you."

I did my best to recover and fake a smile. "It's too bad you're stuck in here with all the geezers," I joked with a wink, hoping he didn't notice the subtle change in my mood.

Arthur laughed and clapped his hands together. "Don't I know it." Always the gentleman, Arthur walked beside me toward the door. "You have yourself a good day, MJ. And don't forget—my grandson is a catch. He might be worth a second chance."

I was still reeling from the revelation that Logan and my ex-boyfriend were *best fucking friends*, so all I could manage was a weak nod.

I stared at his back as he slowly made his way down the corridor toward the common areas.

My thoughts raced.

Trent's face flashed in my mind—his charm, the way he had pursued me, convinced me to trust him, to let down walls I didn't even know I had. And then the aftermath—the cold, empty silence, the texts left unanswered, the way he'd disappeared from my life like I was nothing.

He had taken something I couldn't get back and left me with nothing but regret. The pain was still there, lingering like an old bruise.

Trent had talked about his best friend, but he'd never given me a real name. He always seemed vaguely jealous of his friend. *Maverick* was just a ghost of a person I had always hoped to meet, and suddenly he was in my life—real, tangible.

That twisted the knife even deeper.

I fought the swell of disappointment that bloomed in my chest. Of course Arthur thought his grandson was a good guy, but I knew better.

Logan was best friends with my ex—Lucifer himself, he who shall not be named, the scourge of the earth—and the company you keep says an awful lot about you.

FOUR

LOGAN

The thud of my cleats hitting the hard concrete floor of the locker room echoed in my ears as I trudged toward my locker. The postgame buzz was subdued—understandable, given the way our asses had just been handed to us.

I shoved my bag onto the bench and ripped off my jersey, biting back the sting in my left knee that flared with the movement.

Thirty-four wasn't old—not in the grand scheme of things. But on the field, surrounded by a sea of twentysomethings with springs in their legs and no concept of limitations, it felt ancient.

A low whistle sounded, and I looked up to see Jack grinning at me. "Rough game, old man." He was a winger and a decade younger than me. A smirk was plastered on his face as he peeled off his muddy socks.

"Watch it," I growled, my tone sharper than I intended.

Jack was twenty-four, fast as hell, and one of the younger guys the team had brought on for exhibition matches. He was talented, sure, but the kind of player who didn't yet understand what he didn't know.

He laughed, shaking his head. "Relax, Logan. Just saying you could've used some WD-40 out there." He pretended to run in slow motion from the bench. "Grease the wheels a little."

I shot him a glare that shut him up, but the words stuck.

WD-40. Jesus.

I hated to admit that he might be right. Every ache, every slow recovery, every half-second hesitation on the field, made it feel like I might as well be dead and buried. Every twinge was a whisper of doubt.

Was this the year my body finally said enough?

I wasn't ready to listen. Not yet. But, damn, it was getting harder to ignore.

The loss stung more than it should have. Exhibition games didn't count for anything, but they mattered to me. I needed to prove to myself—and to everyone else—that I still had it.

But today I hadn't.

Since the age of fourteen, my entire life has revolved around rugby. My success and reputation meant everything —it was who I was. It was what got Mom and me out of poverty. One slip could mean losing everything I'd worked for, and if there wasn't rugby, what the hell else was there?

By the time I hobbled into my apartment later that evening, my frustration was a living, breathing beast.

The small space felt stifling, even though I'd barely decorated it. On the mantel were a few framed pictures of the Olympic team and one of me standing next to Mom as I hoisted a gold medal into the air. Their glossy surfaces caught the fading light through the window.

I dropped my gear by the door and limped to the freezer, grabbing an ice pack and wrapping it around my knee. The stiffness was worse today, but it wasn't just the physical discomfort that gnawed at me. It was the thought that maybe my body wasn't going to bounce back the way it always had.

The couch creaked as I sank into it, flipping on the TV for background noise. Some generic small-town news anchor droned about the upcoming fall harvest. I muted it after thirty seconds.

The contrast between this sleepy town and the electric pace of my usual life was glaring. No sprawling cities, no high-stakes tournaments, no constant movement across continents.

And yet the peace here wasn't entirely unwelcome.

I leaned my head back, closing my eyes, but the memory of a certain sharp-tongued nurse invaded my thoughts.

MJ's hazel eyes had a way of sparking with fire one moment and softening the next, like she couldn't quite decide whether to let her guard down or not.

She wasn't like most women I encountered. Usually they were eager, excited, quick to laugh at anything I said. MJ had been . . . different. She didn't fawn. She didn't try to impress me. If anything, she seemed hell-bent on resisting whatever pull we might've had.

And I liked it more than I should.

But the last thing I needed was a distraction. Especially one as unpredictable as her.

When the silence grew into the wrong kind of quiet, I found myself standing up before I realized what I was doing, tossing the ice pack aside and grabbing my keys.

The drive was uneventful, the sun setting in streaks of orange and pink across the horizon. By the time I pulled into Outtatowner, the town was alive with a gentle hum of activity. String lights hung like boughs across the store-fronts, glowing softly as people meandered from shop to shop. I parked my truck near Bluebird Books and stepped out, feeling like an outsider in a place where everyone seemed to know one another.

I wasn't sure what I was looking for, exactly, but I walked anyway, my hands shoved into the pockets of my jacket, taking in the town that felt both foreign and familiar.

The tattoo shop caught my eye first, its neon sign glowing in the window. Inside, a man with sleeves of ink leaned over a customer as they discussed a design. I lingered by the door, glancing at the drawings taped to the window—a mix of delicate florals and bold, edgy pieces.

"You thinking about getting something?" a woman's voice asked, pulling my attention.

I turned to see a petite woman with angular features and a confident smirk. Her hair was bleached icy blond, and she wore a leather jacket and short miniskirt despite the crisp September air.

"Not today," I replied, giving her a polite smile. "Just looking."

She tilted her head. Diamond piercings in her cheeks glinted as she studied me with a curiosity that felt a little too perceptive. "You're not from here, but also not a tourist."

I looked down at my jeans and jacket. "Is it that obvious?"

Her laugh rang out as she pulled a cigarette from her purse. "Very. You're the rugby player."

My brows lifted in surprise. "How'd you know?"

"Small town," she said with a shrug. The woman placed the cigarette to her lips, but didn't light it. "People around here like to talk, and you gave them plenty to talk about when you followed MJ into the bookstore."

I nodded slowly as the woman continued to suck on the unlit cigarette. "Do you need a light?"

"Nah, I quit." She smiled and gestured toward the shop. "It just annoys the boss that I still take breaks." The woman vaguely gestured across the street. "If you're looking for MJ, you're in the wrong place. She's working tonight."

"I'm not—" I started, but she raised a brow, cutting me off.

"Sure you're not." Her smirk widened as she stepped back and dropped the cigarette into her purse. "Good luck, city boy."

Before I could respond, she disappeared into the tattoo shop, leaving me feeling both amused and utterly confused.

I wandered aimlessly for a while longer, down to the end of the lighthouse pier and back up again. The sounds of laughter and clinking glasses spilled out from the town's local bar. It would've been easy to step inside, grab a drink, and blend into the crowd, but my heart wasn't in it.

I was restless, unsure of what I was even doing here.

My phone buzzed in my pocket, and I pulled it out, seeing Trent's name flash across the screen. I answered on the third ring, bringing the phone to my ear.

"Hey," I said, keeping my voice neutral as I made my way toward my truck.

"Hey, man," Trent said, his tone light. "How'd today's game go?"

I sighed, ignoring the fact I was still favoring my knee. "We lost."

"Damn. Thought you were the golden boy of the exhibition matches," he joked.

"Yeah, well, not today." I rubbed a hand over my face, fresh irritation prickling under my skin.

"Come on, man," Trent said, his tone turning vaguely patronizing. "It's just an exhibition game. You're not playing for a medal here."

"I know that," I snapped, the edge in my voice surprising even me. "I just . . . something isn't the same anymore, and I don't like it."

"Getting old sucks, doesn't it?" Trent joked, but there was an undertone to his words that didn't sit right. "Don't sweat it, though. You'll get through the offseason and be back to training before you know it."

"Maybe," I muttered, my grip tightening on the phone. Next season was starting to feel like a distant, fragile hope—a final chance to prove I wasn't done yet.

"Anyway," Trent continued, his tone shifting. "You're probably drowning in postgame groupies. We need to catch up soon so I can get in on that."

"Yeah," I said, forcing the word out. "Thankfully, there aren't really any groupies here."

There was a pause, and then Trent chuckled lightly. "Thankfully? You really are losing your edge. Where are you?"

"Outtatowner." I smiled, because even the name was quirky and charming.

He laughed again. "Well, you're in the middle of nowhere. What'd you expect? There's absolutely nothing memorable about that shitty town."

I harrumphed a noncommittal noise. I could feel my irritation growing, so I ended the call before I let my shitty mood ruin my best friend's night too.

When the call ended, I stared at the screen for a moment before slipping it into my pocket. I looked around the quaint little town. It really wasn't half bad if you were into blueberries, crappy diners, and nurses who were excessively hot and wanted nothing to do with you.

I chuckled because, let's face it, I just happened to like all three.

FIVE

MJ

This is stupid.
This is stupid.
This is stupid.

I held the sticky note with Logan's number in my hand as I paced across the wooden floors of my childhood home. You would think the opulent estate would be where many fond childhood memories were safely tucked away.

You'd be wrong.

Up until my father was arrested, the King estate was his kingdom, and he ruled with an iron fist. I was pushing thirty, living with my aunt Bug, with no clue what to do next. I looked around. My bedroom was my sanctuary, but maybe it was time to get an apartment—finally do something because *I* wanted to do it.

Trouble was, I didn't really know what I wanted. In the past, when I'd trusted my gut, things went terribly wrong. So I learned to focus on what was safe. If I put one foot in front of the other and kept moving, I wouldn't stumble.

Now I'd spent so long not stumbling that I just felt stuck.

I stared down at Logan's note, his phone number written in blocky, masculine handwriting at the bottom.

I knew he still wanted me to attend a match, but he hadn't pushed. A part of me hated that his confident, aloof attitude about it made me want to go to see what all the fuss was about.

The note had started to curl at the edges from how tightly I'd been gripping it. Logan's number stared back at me like it held some kind of forbidden mystery.

Calling him would mean stepping into something unknown. And unknowns had a way of biting me in the ass. I paced across the room, the wood creaking faintly under my sneakers, my thoughts tangling with every step.

A small knock sounded at my door. My pacing stopped as my heart skidded in my chest. "Come in."

The door cracked open, and Aunt Bug stepped inside. Her expression was tight, her eyes guarded in a way that made my stomach twist.

Something was wrong.

"Hey, MJ." Her voice was softer than usual, almost hesitant. "Busy?"

"Hey," I said cautiously, setting the sticky note on my desk. "Not at all. What's up?"

She closed the door behind her, leaning against it as though she needed the extra support. "I just got a call," she began, her fingers twisting the edge of her blouse. "It's about your dad."

My stomach dropped. "What about him?"

Her lips pressed into a thin line before she finally said, "He's dead, MJ. It happened over night."

The words didn't register at first. They hung in the air, sharp and impossible, like a punchline to a joke no one wanted to laugh at.

"What?" The word came out choked, barely audible. "How?"

Bug sighed, her shoulders sagging under the weight of the news. "He was stabbed at the county jail. Someone got to him with a shank." She hesitated, her gaze darting to the floor. "It was . . . Oliver Pendegrass."

That name. The recognition hit me like a slap. Oliver Pendegrass was a ghost from my brother Abel's past. Oliver had been Abel's roommate in prison.

"He killed Dad?" My voice was barely above a whisper.

Bug nodded, her mouth a grim line. "It sounds like he considered it a twisted kind of favor to your brother? I don't know all the details yet, but . . . it's done."

I sank onto the edge of my bed, the weight of the news pressing down on me like a lead blanket.

My father—dead. Stabbed in prison.

My mind scrambled to reconcile the man who had loomed so large in my life with this abrupt, violent end.

He was my dad. But he was also Russell King. A tyrant. A liar. A murderer. My feelings for him had dimmed a long time ago.

Still, a hollow ache spread through my chest.

"I don't . . . I don't know what to feel," I admitted, my voice cracking. "I feared him. But he was still my dad."

Bug crossed the room, sitting beside me on the bed. Her strong arm wrapped around my shoulders, steadying me in the storm. "You don't have to know what to feel right now, MJ."

A shaky breath escaped me. "It's just . . . I thought having him gone would feel like freedom, you know? Like I could finally breathe. But now . . ." I trailed off, my hands trembling in my lap.

Bug reached for my hand, her grip warm and grounding. "Russell made his choices, and those choices had consequences. You don't owe him anything—not your forgiveness, not your grief. Nothing."

I swallowed hard, her words both a comfort and a challenge.

Did I believe that? Could I let go of the guilt that always seemed to trail me like a shadow?

My gaze drifted to the sticky note on my desk. Logan's number. His invitation to the game. It was a sliver of something—something new, something outside the orbit of my father's influence.

Bug followed my gaze, her lips twitching into the faintest smile. "What's that?"

The note stared back at me, its significance dimmed by the events that had just unfolded. "It's nothing," I said, my voice flat.

Her eyebrows lifted. Bug rose, brushing a strand of hair from my face. "You've got a good head on your shoulders, MJ. Trust it. And trust yourself."

She left with a gentle pat on my shoulder, leaving me alone with my thoughts.

∼

THE DAYS BLURRED TOGETHER after Bug's revelation. I floated through them, doing the things that needed to be done—eating, working, existing. But everything felt muted, like the volume of my life had been turned down as I struggled to muster *any* kind of emotion regarding my father's death.

Was I some kind of heartless monster?

Bug took care of most of the arrangements, and for that, I was grateful. Neither my siblings nor I had it in us to make decisions about memorials or urns or any of the logistics that followed a death.

Not for him.

When I wasn't working or walking aimlessly through the house, I found myself obsessing over the sticky note on my desk, the edges curling just a little more each day. Logan's invitation still sat unanswered, and I hated the way it mocked me—bold and sure, as if stepping into something unknown wasn't terrifying.

But tonight wasn't about Logan. It wasn't even about me. It was about figuring out what came next.

For all of us.

A small knock sounded at my door. My pacing stopped. "Yep, come in."

The door cracked open and my sister Sylvie peeked through with a smile. "Hey."

I gave her a small, sad smile back. "Hi."

"Everyone's waiting downstairs." Sylvie, with her soft blond hair and dark-brown eyes, was the spitting image of our mother—not that I remembered Mom. I was only three when she left.

When he killed her.

I was still wrapping my head around the fact that my father had murdered our mother and let us believe she'd abandoned us all.

My intuition had always told me there was something dangerous about my father. It was what had warned me to quietly slip below his radar by overachieving and being pleasantly agreeable. I'd learned early that my father cared most about his reputation, and having a successful nurse for a daughter helped polish his image.

"It's strange," Sylvie said, looking around my room. "The walls feel quieter somehow."

I breathed in deeply, understanding exactly what she meant. "I think it's knowing he's not ever coming back . . . like the energy is finally at peace around here."

Sylvie smiled. "Now you're sounding like Hazel."

My brother's girlfriend, Hazel, was pretty witchy—she believed in healing energy and all kinds of natural remedies. She had healed my brother JP in countless ways, so it was hard to deny the effects of her methods, even if I couldn't really explain them myself.

The corner of my mouth turned up. "She did sage the fuck out of the entire place."

Sylvie breathed in a lungful of air and exhaled dramatically. "Well, I think it might have worked."

Together we laughed as I sat on the bed with my sister, resting my head on her shoulder.

"You okay?" she asked.

Unexpected emotion prickled inside my nose. "I don't know what I am," I admitted. "I'm almost thirty, living at home. All my siblings have found their purpose in life and someone to share it with. Even JP, which is actually mind-blowing. Sometimes I look around and wonder what the hell I'm doing. I don't even have a goldfish."

Sylvie's eyebrows bunched. "Do you want a goldfish?"

I laughed. "Not really."

"I think," she said, patting my knee, "if you want something different, do something you've never done. Find an adventure. No one is expecting you to be perfect."

My father's stern face flashed through my mind. Russell King expected me to be perfect, but he was gone.

My fingers slid across the crumpled sticky note before I handed it to Sylvie. "Logan gave me his number and asked me to watch him play rugby." I wrinkled my nose, trying to gauge her reaction.

Sylvie looked at the paper, and I could tell she was hiding a small smile. "That could be fun. You haven't really dated anyone in a long time . . ."

Since Trent.

Sylvie didn't need to finish her sentence for me to understand what she was saying. I hadn't shared all the details, but she understood that he'd broken something inside me. Trent had violated my trust and my body in ways I was still coping with.

I hated him—not only for what he'd done, but for how his actions *still* haunted me.

"Logan is Trent's friend." A sardonic laugh escaped me as I crumpled the sticky note in my hand. "What are the odds, right?"

Sylvie frowned but stayed silent.

I could hear people talking downstairs, so I stood and tried to brush my feelings away. "I'll figure it out." My words sounded far more defensive than I'd intended. Shame and guilt coursed through me.

Sylvie rose and squeezed my hand. "I know you'll figure it out. You always do. We'll see you down there."

With a gentle hug, Sylvie slipped out of my room. I stared down at the crumpled note in my hand.

My fingers itched to type in the numbers and accept his invitation. Besides, I kind of liked sports. Sure, I didn't really care who played or won, but there was always something magical and exciting about watching a game in person—the energy of the stadium, the crowd cheering, extra-cheesy nachos and a cold beer.

Plus, the people watching was fun.

With a resigned sigh, I dropped the sticky note into the drawer of my desk and shoved away the gnawing disappointment that Logan Brown was probably no different from the rest.

As I walked down the grand staircase, I followed the din of voices until I reached the solarium at the back of the house. Faded, golden light streamed through the floor-to-ceiling glass windows. The landscaped backyard stretched beyond the windows, and I recalled the bridal shower I had helped throw for Abel and Sloane.

My eyes landed on my oldest brother. He'd been so damaged and jaded after his time in prison, but his love for Sloane had pulled him out of his darkest days. All my siblings, plus Bug, moved to the dining room and sat.

Despite the crowd, the room felt too quiet, too still, considering everything that had happened.

The air was thick with unspoken words as we stared at the basic urn that held our father's ashes.

He was dead. We all knew that, but the weight of it hadn't settled yet. I looked at each of my siblings. The years of pressure and disappointment, and downright abuse served by the hands of our father, were palpable.

No one knew what to say. The past few years, cracks in my father's flawless mask had become caverns. Sadness washed over me as I realized he'd done so much irreparable damage to his own children that not a single one of us knew what to say.

My thoughts wandered to his other wife and adult children we'd learned about. His *real* family. I'd been stunned to learn that our mother was his mistress and that when she'd attempted to leave with us, he'd killed her. We'd lived our whole lives believing his lies—that she'd simply walked away from us because we were unlovable. He'd made himself out to be a hero, when really, he was a monster.

They can have him.

"I can reach out to his other family." My voice was soft but determined. "Maybe they'll want the ashes . . . his wife, or . . . someone."

The room went still as my words hung in the air. Every pair of eyes turned to me, some surprised, others relieved. I looked at the urn and swallowed hard. I didn't owe him anything. Not forgiveness, not kindness, not this. But maybe giving him to them was the only way to truly get rid of him —for all of us.

My brother Royal leaned back in his chair, giving me a long look. "You're a good person," he said quietly.

A tiny pang of guilt shot through me.

I wasn't doing it out of the goodness of my heart. We had suffered enough at the hands of Russell King. Our town revered him, and I couldn't stand the thought of anyone mourning his death.

Not after what he'd done.

Aunt Bug sighed from the end of the table, her hands nervously twisting the edge of a kitchen towel. "I always tried to keep you safe, you know," she said, her voice cracking with the years of weight she'd carried. "Even though I didn't want to believe he took your mother . . . I tried my best."

My heart twisted as the strongest woman I had ever known nearly crumbled.

"But you've always been our mom," Sylvie said, her voice firm, cutting through the heavy silence.

There was no hesitation in her words, no doubt. The rest of us nodded, and a chorus of agreement filled the room.

"Bug, you were more of a mother to us than anyone else ever could've been," Abel added, and for once, his usual gruffness softened.

Whip grinned despite the tension. "Yeah, you definitely fed us more sugar than was good for us. If that's not love, I don't know what is."

God, I loved him and his knack for cutting tension.

I sent him a grateful smile, which he returned with a wink.

Together we chuckled, the mood lightening, and Bug's eyes misted over as she looked at each of us, her makeshift children.

"Damn straight I did," she replied with a proud sniff. "And I'd do it again."

In that moment, as the laughter and warmth spread through the room, the weight of our father's death didn't feel quite so suffocating.

Abel was the first to leave, creating a ripple of disjointed goodbyes and awkward hugs. I sat, staring at the urn.

Why had I offered to see them?

"You okay?" I looked up to find my older brother JP frowning at me.

I wiped my hands across the tops of my jeans. We had been only five and three when our mother disappeared. Our other siblings had memories of our mother, and in many ways that had brought JP and me together. We'd bonded over the *lack* of her.

I looked at the urn again, taking a small, sick pleasure in knowing Dad would have hated how simple and unobtrusive it was.

"You think having him as a father was as horrible for them as it was for us?" I asked.

JP leaned on the back of a dining chair. "I don't see how it could have been much better. He was around a lot, which means he probably wasn't around much for *them*, you know?"

My lips twisted. "I guess."

"You know"—he leaned in—"you don't have to do it. I'll toss that urn in the garbage right now, and we'll never speak of it again."

A wry laugh burst out of me. "You're unhinged." I shook my head. "No, I think the guilt alone would eat me alive. I'll just hand it over and walk away with a clear conscience."

JP's hands spread. "Don't say I didn't offer." He flicked my ponytail. "I heard there's been someone giving you trouble at work. Any of that true?"

I groaned and rested my forehead in my hands. "Not you too."

I tilted my head to see JP smirking. He shrugged. "Hazel was *very* excited to tell me about it. I can't help that I'm a good listener."

I shook my head. "Logan Brown is a man-size child with an overinflated ego."

Who is also best friends with the worst human on the planet.

"Huh." I narrowed my eyes at my brother as he continued with a shrug: "Thought you were a better judge of character than that."

"Okay, you find *one* soulmate and you're giving dating advice now?" I teased as I stood.

JP grinned. "What can I say? I'm a changed man."

I returned the smile. "I always knew you were in there."

"Take it from me." JP gestured at his chest. "It's a lot easier when you stop fighting it."

With a quick hug, I said goodbye to JP and hoisted my father's urn onto my hip.

With no one around, I shoved it into a box in the broom

closet, locking it up along with every noisy, complicated feeling I didn't want to have.

SIX

LOGAN

Despite my grandfather's incessant matchmaking efforts, it had been two weeks and MJ still hadn't called. Hell, it was probably for the best. We'd lost another game, and my performance had been lackluster, to say the least.

I'd been in a piss-poor mood ever since getting back from a match in West Virginia.

While my ego could handle a little rejection, it still stung that the most gorgeous woman I'd ever set eyes on wanted nothing to do with me.

It had been far too long since I'd had to work for a woman's attention, and a sick part of me kind of liked it. I glanced over my grandfather's shoulder, hoping to catch a peek of MJ at the nurses' station.

"She's not here," Grandpa grumbled.

"What?" I tried to act like I didn't know who he was talking about.

"MJ. She doesn't work today. We're stuck with the bratty one who sighs so much she's starting to sound like a leaky tire."

"Mr. Brown . . ." a whiny voice sounded from behind us.

When I turned, a young nurse with too much makeup and a pissy look frowned at him. "You aren't supposed to be wandering around." She sighed, and I nearly cackled when it sounded frighteningly similar to a tire leak.

Her eyes flicked to me, and immediately her demeanor changed. "Oh, well." She smiled wider. "I don't think we've been officially introduced. I'm Beth."

She held out her hand, and out of politeness, I shook it. "Nice to meet you. Logan."

She giggled and smoothed down her straight hair. "Oh, I know who you are, Mr. Olympian."

"Oh, uh. Yeah, please don't call me that." I laughed uncomfortably.

"Okay." She rolled her eyes and giggled again. "Mr. Gold Medal." She purred the words, and I stifled an eye roll of my own.

Her sticky-sweet perfume overtook the space between us as she moved closer. Her eyes stayed locked on me, and the look in them was more than appreciative but not appropriate for anywhere outside of a bedroom.

I moved away. "Hey, Grandpa. Let's head out."

Beth blinked, stunned a bit by my abrupt change in conversation, but I'd seen and heard enough to know a swift exit was the best idea.

Without so much as a backward glance, I braced my grandfather's elbow and practically dragged him down the hallway.

Thankfully, Arthur Brown was still strong and nimble. When we rounded a corner, I stopped.

"Smooth moves, kid," he teased.

I glanced over his shoulder, half expecting Beth to have

trotted after us. "Just getting a little tired of all of the attention, that's all."

He scoffed. "Well, at least your head's not up your ass. That one is trouble. She looks at you and sees nothing but dollar signs and Division One babies."

A visceral shudder worked its way through me. Women and babies were the *last* things I needed, especially when I was struggling to keep my career from imploding.

All I needed to focus on was maintaining my performance and avoiding distractions.

Besides, there wasn't anything particularly enticing about Beth. I'd seen jersey chasers ruin promising careers and athletes throw everything away for the attention of a woman.

I was far too focused for that.

MJ's face flashed in my mind, and I pushed down the fact that the thought of her was becoming *dangerously* distracting.

Maintaining your focus took effort.

Oftentimes players were treated like gods—they could do no wrong. Many started at young ages, moving out of the house at fourteen or fifteen years old, like I did, to move to where a solid coach and team could elevate your skills. Many were given slack in school to focus on the sport.

A lot of men I had come to know in the sport had been brought up with inflated senses of celebrity and ego. They were used to getting everything they wanted . . . including women.

I was also lucky enough to have a grandpa who had a knack for bringing me back down to earth. "Well, *Mr. Gold Medal*," he teased. "Come on." He waved a bony finger toward the end of the corridor, toward the exit.

I smiled down at the man who had supported me every

step of my career. Even the awkward days when I couldn't hook the ball to save my life. He had been my first coach and the one to encourage me to find someone who could elevate my skills. He had stepped in when my father stepped out. Grandpa didn't just teach me rugby; he taught me how to stand tall, how to fight for something I wanted. Even when Dad wasn't around—and, honestly, even when Mom couldn't be—I always had Grandpa. If he wanted to spend the afternoon dragging me around town, I owed him more than that.

"Where are we going?" I asked.

"I know your mother didn't raise a liar, so you are taking me out. I'd like to swing by the bookstore and get Greta a new book, if that's all right by you."

Grandpa had been a widower for many years, and while I knew his love for my grandmother ran deep, it was nice to see him opening up to someone.

"Greta?" I teased. "Still striking out with the new girl?"

Grandpa smirked, and despite the lines on his face, it was easy to see that he had been a charmer in his prime. "Kid, you're not the only one pining over a pretty woman who hasn't called."

A pain squeezed my side, but I shook my head with a grin. "You're trouble, old man."

We successfully dodged Beth, and I let Carol at the nurses' station know I would be back later in the evening with my grandfather.

There was something that felt a bit wrong about checking him out of the assisted-living facility like some borrowed book, but he didn't seem to mind.

My mother loved him, but she had grown accustomed to following my rugby career and enjoyed traveling as much as I did. When Grandpa could no longer safely live by himself, he had been the one to suggest Haven Pines. If I had learned anything, it was that when Grandpa set his mind to something, there was no talking him out of it.

That hadn't stopped me from calling the facility behind his back to check on him as often as I could. I was sure I was a pain in the side to a few of the people who worked there, but I had done it all in the name of making sure my grandfather was comfortable and well taken care of. If it meant making a few enemies for his sake, well, then it was worth it.

On our way to town, we passed a sign for Sand Dune Art Barn. A beautiful old farmhouse with a large wraparound porch stood next to a gigantic old red barn that had been converted into what looked like an art studio. Signs encouraged tourists to stop in and create some art of their own.

Grandpa whistled as the art studio and the blueberry fields next to it whizzed past. "Sure has changed a lot around here over the years," he noted.

"Did you spend a lot of time in Outtatowner?" I asked.

"Here and there," he said. "Your grandma preferred a quiet country life, but I always thought the tourist towns had a buzz of energy that I couldn't quite find in the country."

I hummed in acknowledgment as we eased into the downtown area. Gone was the slow and quiet atmosphere of a small town shuttered down for the night. In the daylight, Outtatowner was bustling with people moving in and out of the shops and café and bakery. Even the local bar, the Grudge Holder, had an A-frame sign announcing its family lunch specials. From the lack of parking spaces, you would think it was still midsummer and not late September, creeping toward cooler autumn months. I glanced at the trees, whose tips were turning crimson and gold—the only hint of Michigan's slow transition to fall.

"Where to?" I asked.

"You telling me you don't remember where that bookstore is?" He raised one white, bushy eyebrow.

I shook my head and smirked, circling the block to try to find an open parking space. "Shit-stirrer," I mumbled under my breath.

Grandpa huffed a laugh. "That's what I thought." He reached over to pat my knee, seemingly pleased with himself. "Good boy. That's good." He lifted a finger. "I told you hunting her down was the smart move. Mark my words."

Once parked, I walked next to my grandfather down the sidewalk toward the bookstore, slowing my pace to match his and taking in all the people who flooded this small town.

"It's kind of charming," I noted as workers replaced dead summer blooms with vibrant bushy mums on the parkway.

We walked into Bluebird Books, and a flood of memories washed over me—MJ's cheeks flushed pink. The way the warmth of her hazel eyes blazed with a ring of golden, radiating sunlight. That perfect pink pout frowning just so slightly in my direction.

I cleared my throat and shifted to avoid the uncomfortable swell behind my zipper. As we meandered, I flicked a finger over the spine of a few books. "So what are we looking for?"

"Greta likes true crime, domestic thrillers, some blood and guts, that kind of thing." Grandpa scanned the racks.

"Well, that's comforting," I joked.

Grandpa shrugged. "She's a tough woman with thick

skin." He pinned me with a knowing stare. "But underneath it all, she's still a woman."

I smiled and shook my head. *The old bastard, still spitting game.*

Grandpa spoke with a young kid who worked at the bookstore, and he directed us toward a newly released domestic thriller. I beat Grandpa to the register, paying for the book, and the employee was kind enough to wrap it simply in brown paper.

"I think I could go for a cup of coffee," Grandpa announced, patting his still-flat stomach. While time may have robbed him of the bulk and muscle definition of his youth, he was still trim and well kept for his age.

I hooked a thumb over my shoulder. "There was a place we passed. The Sugar Bowl, I think it was called."

Grandpa nodded and led the way.

The bakery was busy, and as soon as we opened the door, the enticing scent of cinnamon and sugar filled my nostrils. My stomach growled. The whir and sputter of an espresso machine was the backdrop to the din of customers communing and laughing.

"Oh." Grandpa stopped short, suddenly flustered. He dragged a hand across the wiry white hairs on the top of his head. "I didn't expect to run into her so soon."

I looked from my grandfather to the line of patrons waiting to order. His attentive gaze was settled on a tiny little thing at the register. She was petite and appeared to be about my grandfather's age, with long silvery hair tied neatly in a no-nonsense knot at the nape of her neck.

Based on the rigidity of her shoulders and the wide-eyed stare of the kid behind the counter, the woman meant business.

My grandpa's hand gripped my forearm. "How do I look?"

I smiled. "Like a million bucks."

He nodded. "Now it probably won't come up since we're not townies and all, but if you're pressed, it's probably easier to just say that you're with the Kings."

I looked down at him, utterly confused.

"Old rivalry in town," he explained in a whisper. "The drama is all but dead now, but Greta is a bit old-fashioned. It used to be if you were a townie, you picked a side, Sullivan or King. And Greta has always been *firmly* planted on the Kings' side." His eyes shot to mine in warning. "Don't mess this up for me."

I started to laugh but stifled it with a cough when his piercing gaze held mine. "Yes—yes, sir," I muttered.

When the woman moved to the side to wait for her order, my grandfather stepped up, gathering his courage to greet her. "Well, Greta, it's a pleasure seeing you here."

The woman turned, and her hard features softened immediately. "Oh, Arthur, this is a surprise."

Her smile widened, crinkling her eyes at the edges. I couldn't help but smile back.

"Spending the day with my grandson, Logan." Grandpa's hand thumped on my back.

"How nice," she answered, holding out her hand for me to shake.

"It's lovely to meet you." I gently embraced her hand, surprised by her firm grip.

My grandfather stepped forward, holding out the wrapped book. "I happened to be in the bookstore and thought you might like this."

She looked down at the book, and I swear the stern old

woman actually blushed. Her hand fluttered to the golden locket around her neck.

"Oh my, Arthur. That's so kind of you." She accepted the book with a smile. "Thank you."

"Excuse me, Ms. Tiny? Your order is ready." A pretty blond woman with soft brown eyes held out a small white bag for her.

Greta nodded curtly and accepted the bag. "Thank you, Sylvie." She turned back to my grandfather and me and smiled. "Arthur, Logan, have a good day."

My grandfather watched Greta all the way out the door. I stared in awe of a lovestruck man.

I shook my head in disbelief.

I'd never been in one place long enough to worry about things like *long-term commitments.* Besides, there was nothing wrong with having a good time with a variety of people.

Live and let live—I'd learned there was a whole lot less collateral damage that way.

Finally, as Greta disappeared out of view, I cleared my throat. "Are you ready for that coffee?"

"Ah." My grandfather swatted his hand in the air between us. "No need. I'm good. Let's keep walking."

The rest of the afternoon, I enjoyed some much-needed time with my favorite person. Slowly the tension and frustration of a losing offseason started to wane.

Grandpa shared stories about the friends he had made at Haven Pines, the hot gossip down the hall from him, and how he had met Greta when she was visiting her older sister at the facility. It seemed everyone in town called her Ms. Tiny.

We walked at a meandering pace, stopping when

Grandpa felt tired, but it wasn't often. I was pleasantly surprised at how much energy he still seemed to have.

"Are you seeing any friends while you're around?" he asked. Grandpa knew that the offseason was often the only time I had to catch up with friends who weren't my teammates.

"Trent, Max, and Billy are around. We might get a few drinks later," I said.

He nodded. "That's good. You should always make time for friends."

I knew he was worried about my work-life balance, but what he didn't quite understand was that I was able to be at the top of my game *because* of my lack of balance.

During the season, rugby was my entire world. To be the best, there simply wasn't room for anything else. During this particular offseason I would have to train extra hard to maintain my skills while simultaneously giving my body a break—a feat that seemed nearly impossible.

When we reached the end of the lighthouse pier and turned back, he looked out wistfully at the beach.

It wasn't as crowded as I imagined it was at the peak of tourist season, but there were still a few brave souls in the water and even people bundled in light blankets, sitting on the sand. Some kids were throwing a football and laughing it up.

"Come on, let's live a little," I teased.

We ditched our socks and shoes in a haphazard pile on the beach. I knelt to roll up the bottoms of my grandfather's trousers and then cuffed my own. We walked along the sandy shores, letting the cold water lap over our feet. The water was brisk but refreshing.

As we walked along the shoreline, a football rolled in

front of us. A young kid who looked like he should have been in high school jogged behind it.

"Sorry! Excuse me," he called out.

"It's no problem." My grandfather reached down and picked up the ball.

The kid stared at me, stunned. "Oh shit, you're Logan Brown."

I smiled, shook my head, and held out my hand. "Nice to meet you."

He eagerly gripped my hand in his and shook. "I'm Seth. I'm a running back at Midwest Michigan University. Coach Sullivan has us review all your game tapes. Your in-game calls are absolutely unreal."

"No kidding? Thanks, kid." Rugby wasn't as widely recognized in the States as football or other mainstream sports. While being the fly-half on my team was kind of like a quarterback, it was fun to have someone *else* know what the hell it was.

Seth gestured toward the two other young men, who stared slack-jawed behind him. "You want to go for a round or two?"

I looked at my grandfather, who wrapped his leathered hand around the ball.

"Should I give it a go?" I asked him.

His mischievous smirk spread slowly as he gestured with his chin for me to get going. "Give him hell, son."

My grandfather pitched the ball sideways to me in a perfect rugby pass. The three kids cheered as they ran after me. My toes dug into the soft sand, and my calves burned as my legs pumped. My heartbeat thumped in time to their cheers.

I blew past their efforts to stop me, laughing when I reached the end of the beach. I had forgotten how fun it was to just let it all go and fuck around for a while. I wasn't winded, but I had to breathe through the slight pinch in my left knee.

It had still been giving me problems, and running through sand certainly didn't help matters. I braced my hands on my hips to catch my breath.

My heart thunked harder when I looked up and saw a smiling MJ standing next to my grandfather near the water, her hands planted on her trim little waist, mirroring my stance.

Her brown ponytail whipped in the breeze, a few loose strands catching the sunlight like they'd been kissed by fire. She listened intently to whatever yarn my grandfather was weaving as he pointed in our direction.

"Want to go again?" Seth asked.

I shook my head. "I'd love to, but . . ." I gestured with my head toward my grandfather and MJ. "I've got to go see about a thing."

Seth grinned. "Oh, I get it. No worries, man." He held out his hand to shake again. "Thank you, really."

"It was a pleasure." I shook his hand one last time before slowly jogging toward MJ and my grandfather.

As I got closer, my heart thunked harder. MJ was dressed in a loose pair of soft green sweatpants that swayed with the breeze. Her matching top was a quarter-zip sweatshirt. The zipper was undone, revealing tanned skin and the ties of a black bikini top. I imagined untying it with my teeth and reveling in the quick inhale of her breath as I took my time doing it. Her casual sweats made her look too relaxed, like she wasn't the single most infuriating person on the planet.

She was smiling as she spoke to my grandfather and

pointed to a small group of women who I assumed were her friends.

Sisters, maybe?

I shook the thought from my head. I had no idea why suddenly I wanted to know everything there was to know about the mysterious MJ King.

As I got closer, MJ started to slow clap.

"Very impressive," she said. "Annihilating a bunch of teenagers must do wonders for your ego." The teasing glint in her eyes forced my grin wider.

"They're in college," I said. "They're at least twenty." I glanced back at the young boys. "I think. What are you up to, Kitten?"

One eyebrow shot up. "Kitten?"

"You're the one who didn't like Thunder." I shrugged. "Just trying something else on for size."

"I like that less." Her eyes playfully rolled, and I could tell she was fighting a smile.

Damn, she was cute when she was trying not to give in.

MJ placed a gentle hand on my grandpa's shoulder. "Mr. Brown here was telling me you two have had quite the adventure today."

I grinned, loving the breeze and the crisp autumn air and the way the late-afternoon sun made her hazel eyes a riot of blue, brown, and earth tones.

"It's been a great day," I said. "Even better now."

A soft flush creeped up her neck. "Well." She cleared her throat. "I guess I'll leave you to it then."

"Hey, do you know what time it is?" I asked before she could run away.

MJ's brow furrowed slightly before she reached into her pocket to slip out her phone. "It's almost four."

"Oh, okay. Good." I gestured toward her phone. "I was

worried that thing was broken, since I hadn't heard from you yet about coming to a game."

A soft, teasing *ooh* from my grandfather only spurred me on as I rocked back on my heels.

MJ straightened her shoulders. "My phone is perfectly fine."

I tucked my tongue into my cheek. "I'm glad to hear it. We should get you back before dinner, old man," I said. "I'll see you around, MJ."

"Yeah," she replied softly.

Grandpa and I walked back across the sand. My phone buzzed, and when I saw an unknown number flash on the screen, I knew it was her. My grin stretched wide enough to hurt.

Four little words. Four words that shouldn't have felt like a win, but god, they did.

> **UNKNOWN**
> I'll think about it.

And just like that, my piss-poor mood evaporated. She was thinking about it. About me. And it made my whole damn day.

SEVEN

MJ

The crisp September air carried the scent of baked goods and spiced honey as I strolled through the farmers' market, the sleeves of my purple sweater pulled down over my hands. Stalls brimmed with pumpkins, squash, and the last of the summer blooms. Fall had officially taken over Outtatowner, and the locals were leaning into the season with jars of homemade jam, apple cider doughnuts, and bundles of cornstalks tied with orange ribbons.

I made my way toward my brother-in-law Duke's farmstand, where a line of customers admired baskets overflowing with plump blueberries and jars of deep violet jam. Duke, as grumpy as ever, stood behind the counter, his arms crossed over his broad chest.

Nowadays there was something softer about him as he handed a jar of jam to a small boy who beamed up at him before skipping off. My sister, Sylvie, had definitely worked some magic on him, and the thought made me smile.

"Hey, Dukey," I singsonged as I approached, slipping my hands into the pockets of my jeans.

"MJ," he greeted, his tone brusque but his eyes warm. "Come for the jam or just to hassle me?"

"Both," I said with a grin, scanning the display. "You still got that blueberry-lavender one? Bug's been raving about it."

"Last jar is yours if you want it," he said, reaching under the counter and pulling out a small jar with a neatly tied red gingham ribbon.

I wrinkled my nose at him. "You better stop being such a softie." I leaned in to whisper. "Everyone's starting to notice."

He harrumphed from behind his table, and I laughed. Teasing Duke made everything almost feel normal again.

"Fancy meeting you here." Logan's playful voice floated over my shoulder and I froze.

Duke's eyes narrowed as I stayed pinned in place.

When Duke married my sister and the King-Sullivan rivalry fell to the wayside, I'd somehow unintentionally inherited *three more* overprotective brothers.

But I'd be lying if I didn't say that at *this* particular moment, I didn't hate how intimidating Duke Sullivan's presence could be. I had no doubt my sister had filled Duke in on my embarrassing encounter with Logan at the bookstore.

I turned and acted confused. "Oh, I'm sorry, do we know each other?"

Unfazed, Logan laughed and reached a hand across the table to Duke. "Hi. I'm Logan."

Logan's eyes flicked to me as a casual smirk tugged at his lips.

His smirk was infuriating, the kind of grin that said he was used to winning, used to women falling at his feet. I wanted to hate it. I wanted to hate *him*. But the way my pulse kicked up every time he leaned closer told me my body wasn't exactly on my side.

He looked annoyingly handsome in a plaid shirt over a navy Henley that stretched across his broad chest and a pair of jeans that had definitely seen better days. His hair was slightly tousled, like he'd just rolled out of bed, and I hated that my first thought was wondering whether someone else had occupied that bed with him.

Reluctantly, Duke stretched out his arm and placed his hand in Logan's. I watched as their hands squeezed between me.

It was a bizarre and humorous display of masculinity that nearly made me giggle.

I placed the small jam jar into the knit shopping bag on my arm and raised it to Duke. "Thanks for the jam. I'll see you around."

Duke's expression softened as he nodded. Without looking at Logan, I left the Sullivan Farms stand and continued walking through the farmers' market.

Logan followed, a quiet shadow only steps behind me.

"Logan," I said, stopping short and fixing him with a look.

He tilted his head, that damn smirk still playing on his face. "Yes?"

He tried his best to look innocent, but I could see right through him. I shook my head and kept walking.

Logan fell into step beside me. "That color purple looks amazing on you, by the way. I think it just might be my favorite color."

"You're relentless," I muttered, glancing at him out of the corner of my eye.

"And you're stubborn," he shot back, his tone light. "It might mean we're a good match."

"We're not a match at all," I replied, tugging my sweater sleeves over my hands as the breeze picked up.

Can you imagine? A pro athlete with his choice of women throwing themselves at his feet and him choosing me?

A scoff escaped through my nose, but I think he mistook it for flirting, because he inched closer. "I think you see it too," he teased, his grin widening.

I stopped walking and turned to face him. "Logan, why are you following me?"

His grin was disarming, but his tone was casual. "Because you haven't told me to stop."

I fought back a smile. I hated that he was right.

With a half-hearted huff, I asked, "What do you want?"

His expression softened, the teasing glint in his eyes giving way to something more genuine. "My grandfather is an excellent judge of character, and he likes you. Plus, maybe I just like talking to you."

I opened my mouth to respond, but the words caught in my throat as the wind tugged a strand of hair across my face. Before I could brush it away, Logan reached out, his fingers tucking it gently behind my ear. The gesture was quick, but the warmth of his fingertips lingered, and I suddenly felt like the air had been knocked out of me.

Logan was Trent's best friend. My mind should not be wandering to the *what-if*s.

His hand dropped, and he stepped back slightly, giving me space. "You're really easy to fluster, you know that?"

"Maybe stop trying to fluster me, then," I muttered, though my voice lacked the bite I'd intended.

He chuckled, the sound low and rich, as he stepped closer. "Can't help it. I find you . . . fascinating, MJ."

I held his gaze with a defiant lift of my chin. "Fascinating because I'm not tripping over myself on the way to your bed?"

A laugh shot from him. "I wasn't thinking about that, but I sure as hell am now."

I snorted a laugh through my nose and glanced at the table beside us, pretending to study a display of homemade candles. "I promise I am the least interesting person in this town."

A deep noise rumbled in his throat. "I seriously doubt that."

Fighting a smile, I kept walking. "You've got a lot of nerve, you know that?"

"Nerve," he repeated, his voice tinged with amusement. "I'll take it as a compliment."

I playfully rolled my eyes and scanned a display of fresh flowers. "It's not."

"Sure it is," he said, leaning casually against the table, his eyes never leaving mine. "Otherwise, you wouldn't still be talking to me."

I sighed, trying to ignore the fluttering in my stomach as I picked up a small vase and pretended to inspect it. "You're insufferable."

I could feel his attention on me. "And you're adorable when you're annoyed."

I shot him a glare, but the heat in his gaze had my pulse racing. "Shouldn't you be somewhere else? Practicing? Putting that flannel to good use by chopping wood with your bare hands or doing something equally ridiculous?"

He laughed, the sound deep and genuine. "Trust me, I'm exactly where I want to be."

The sincerity in his voice caught me off guard, and for a moment, I forgot how to breathe.

He wasn't just casually flirting. He *meant* it. And that was more terrifying than anything he could have said.

I cleared my throat, shoving the vase back onto the table. "Well, enjoy the market. I've got things to do."

Before he could respond, I turned and walked away, my heart pounding in my chest.

"Are you still thinking about coming to a match?" he asked.

I couldn't help but glance over my shoulder one last time, fighting a grin. "Still thinking." I tapped my temple.

Logan stood there, watching me with that infuriating smirk, like he knew exactly what he was doing to me.

~

I STARED up at JP's secluded house in awe. It was tucked against the tree line, its black siding nearly disappearing into the forest behind it. The large yard was sprawling as it crept toward the sand dune cliff that led to Lake Michigan. Parked on the side of the house was Hazel's big white skoolie—a renovated school bus she'd used to travel across the country.

Behind me, Duke's truck rolled down the driveway and I smiled. Duke got out and nodded at me before getting their son from the back seat. Sylvie grinned and held up a covered dish.

I lifted the boxed pie I'd purchased from the Sugar Bowl and shrugged. When she stepped beside me, I turned back to JP's house. "He's *hosting*. Did you ever imagine?"

Sylvie's grin widened as though she'd known all along that JP would find his way. Her shoulder bumped playfully into mine. "Hazel's a witch, remember?"

I giggled and shook my head. We all knew Hazel was

the one for JP. She had a flair for the dramatic and a slightly witchy side, which should have sent JP running. Instead, she'd completely charmed him.

Teddy came barreling outside, launching his seven-year-old body off the porch steps. "Hi!" he shouted, without ever looking back. There was no denying that Teddy shared JP's DNA—everything about him reminded me of my older brother, right down to his uptight wardrobe. My chest pinched thinking about how little Teddy had finally found his place within our family.

Hazel followed behind him with a smile. "Hi!" Her smile was bright and friendly as she waved. Behind her, JP scowled, and the stark opposition of their expressions made me laugh.

"Teddy! Wait up!" She clambered down the steps. "That kid doesn't slow down for a second."

"You're not hanging around?" I asked, disappointed because I'd been enjoying getting to know Hazel.

She grinned. "Not tonight. Teddy was promised a play-date with Ben and Tillie, so Sloane and I are taking them to town." Hazel looked at the driveway. "No Bug?" she asked as she adjusted the strap of her purse.

I shrugged. "She said she was going to see a movie with a friend."

"Huh," Hazel said with a mischievous bounce of her eyebrows. "Sloane said the same thing about her granddad. See you later, alligators."

Hazel left me standing there, wondering when my aunt was going to finally admit she and Sloane's grandfather Bax were an item. Their friendly conversations had turned into daily coffee and walks on the pier. I smiled inwardly, and a soft noise rattled in my throat as I shook my head.

They always used his grandkids as an excuse, but I

knew he was the source of the blush on her cheeks whenever his name came up.

When Duke stepped up beside us with Gus on his hip, I frowned. "Hey, I thought Red was coming today."

Sylvie didn't meet my eyes, but she grinned up at JP's house. "He's behind us."

My face twisted. Ever since Red had moved to the semi-independent condos, I'd missed him. While the trial medication was doing wonders for slowing his early-onset dementia, there was no way he was able to drive himself to JP's house.

Sylvie didn't make it any clearer when she lifted her eyebrows and smiled before sailing past me and walking with Duke into the house.

As Hazel maneuvered her skoolie out of the driveway, she honked twice and waved out the window at another truck rolling down the drive.

This time, my heart dropped.

From the driver's seat, Logan grinned. Beside him was Arthur, and Red was in the back seat of the cab.

"What in the world . . ." I whispered to myself as I stared and watched Logan park his truck next to Duke's in JP's driveway.

I was rooted to the spot.

"MJ!" Arthur clapped his hands together after climbing out of the truck. "I was hoping you'd be here."

He walked up to me, planting his hands on my shoulders and giving them a squeeze.

"Hi, Mr. Brown." I looked directly at Logan. "This is a surprise."

Arthur chuckled as Red walked up. "Hey, kiddo. It's been a while."

Tears pricked at my eyelids as my heart swelled for Red Sullivan. "Hey, Red."

I wrapped my arms around him and squeezed. It was so easy to recall the bad days—the ones when he was confused and scared. So many times it seemed like I was the only one who could help calm him down and remind him he was safe and cared for. Now it was like he was a new man. There would likely always be a wary, confused suspicion in his blue eyes, but today they were bright and clear.

A good day.

He looked down at me. "I can't promise the coffee is any better at my place, but there's a cup waiting for you when you want to catch up."

I swallowed back emotion. "Next week. It's a date."

Red winked at me as Arthur gestured to him. "Let's go. My parole is up in a few hours. Let's cause some trouble."

A laugh shot from my chest as I leaned into Red's embrace one last time. The two men climbed the steps to JP's house, and my brother opened the door for him with a confused look. His eyes darted to me, and I lifted my shoulders. His stare darkened when he looked past me at Logan. I gave him the tiniest of nods to let him know I could handle myself.

Satisfied, my overprotective brother disappeared inside the house.

"How do I get one of those?" Logan's deep voice floated over my shoulder, and liquid heat followed in its wake.

"A date?" I asked, turning to him.

He crossed his arms and looked around JP's property. "A date. One of those hugs. I'm not picky."

I lifted an eyebrow and climbed the porch steps. "Be charming and handsome and over the age of fifty-five."

His arms spread as wide as his grin. "Two out of three ain't bad."

I rolled my eyes, looking down at him from the top step. "I'm serious. What are you doing at my brother's house?"

Logan sighed and slipped his hands into the pockets of his jeans. "Grandpa is very popular. He makes a lot of friends. Red invited him, and he needed me to break him out."

My eyes narrowed. "Convenient."

He sauntered up the steps, pausing when he got next to me. "Isn't it?"

Logan walked right into the house, folding himself into the fabric of *my* family.

I stood on the porch and steadied my breathing. I refused to let Logan get under my skin. The last thing I needed was another reminder of how disarming he could be.

With a resigned sigh, I carried my box of pecan pie into the house.

Dinner was surprisingly fun—Arthur and Red got along so well it was no wonder they'd formed a fast friendship. Arthur didn't seem to mind at all when Red repeated himself or slipped into an old story that made it sound like he was thirty and raising young children again. Together they never missed a beat, and hearing both of their laughter was soothing to my soul.

Sylvie poked and prodded JP about Hazel and Teddy. His face was stern, but I could tell he was hiding something, because the tips of his ears turned red anytime the woman in his life was brought up.

All the while I could feel Logan's eyes on me. He was charming and fit seamlessly into the patchwork quilt that was my family. While Duke and JP talked business, Logan never missed a beat. When Red reminisced about Duke's rodeo days as a bulldogger, Logan leaned forward, the roped muscles of his forearms flexing as he listened. After supper was done, Logan hopped up to help clear the table and start loading the dishwasher.

I watched as Duke, JP, and Logan worked together to clear dishes, like they'd done it a thousand times before.

Red stepped up beside me, leaning down to whisper. "It's not every day you get an Olympic athlete hanging around your workplace. Seems like a waste not to take advantage."

"Not helping, Red," I whispered through gritted teeth. My traitorous friend only chuckled beside me.

As if he knew we were talking about him, Logan looked over his shoulder. His eyes immediately caught mine, and he winked.

Heat flooded my system. It felt as though the room narrowed around me as a tingle raced up my spine.

I hated how easy it was for him to unnerve me, to peel back defenses I'd worked so hard to keep in place.

But would it really be so bad?

For as long as I could remember, I'd been the good girl who made safe choices. Something about the look in Logan's eyes made it all too easy to wonder what it would be like to be *bad*, just for once.

I took a deep breath.

It's just another day. Another dinner. This is nothing.

But the way Logan's gaze lingered, like I was someone worth figuring out, made me wonder if maybe *he* wasn't the problem.

Maybe the problem was how much I wanted him to try.

EIGHT

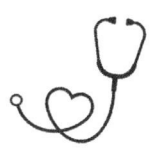

MJ

I'M NOT ENTIRELY sure why I finally decided I would go to a match.

Maybe it was the random pep talk from JP about not fighting my feelings.

Maybe it was because I wanted him to prove he was just like Trent, despite how sweet Logan was with his grandpa.

Maybe it was because he looked so *in his element* when he was horsing around with those kids on the beach.

Maybe it was to prove to myself that I wouldn't fall for another man's false promises.

Maybe it was that damn dimple.

Regardless of the true reason, I had finally driven the two hours to Chicago to attend a rugby exhibition match.

Logan had informed me that during the offseason, he'd be playing game one of a doubleheader with the Western Wildhawks, a team located in the upper Midwest. My butt hurt from sitting in the car, and I checked my outfit. I chose a pair of jeans and a hunter-green Henley, pairing it with gold jewelry. I adjusted the gold scrunchie on my wrist.

Finding gold and green to match the team's colors was a bit of a challenge at the last minute.

I curled my hair and applied a little bit of makeup. I hoped that it was true and that there would be tickets waiting for me at the box office.

I also prayed that I sat next to people who liked to talk. I had *zero* experience with rugby, so if I didn't have someone to help answer questions, I was sure to be lost.

I pulled a deep inhale through my nose, forcing a hit of bravery before climbing out of my car and heading toward the stadium. The Chicago wind nipped at me, and I pulled my jacket closed.

"*Shit*," I muttered. I would have to buy a team blanket or something so I wouldn't freeze to death before the first half.

Do they even have *halves in rugby?* I groaned inwardly. *Why am I even here? Oh, that's right . . . a freaking dimple.*

I walked across the busy parking lot. Much like I'd seen at football games, people were tailgating and celebrating before the game even began. Green and gold were in direct opposition to the blue and black of the Wildhawks' opponents. Fans cheered and called me over, offering a hot dog or a chance to play a beanbag toss game. I smiled politely and kept on walking.

When I reached the box office window, my nerves were rattling. "Hi," I said. "My name is MJ King. I think there might be a ticket for me?"

The woman in the booth smiled politely and typed into her computer. She paused, and then her eyebrows rose. "One minute."

My hand tapped against my thigh as I waited. The woman picked up a walkie-talkie and hit the button. "Hey,

Vince. I've got a special request from Brown. His guest is here."

Special request?

Vince responded with something I couldn't hear, and the woman smiled at me. "If you just wait here, someone will be down to fetch you in a minute."

"Thank you," I replied and stepped aside.

A few minutes later, Logan came into view. He was only half dressed in his uniform—protective shorts, socks pulled to his knees with slip-on sandals, and a white tank top that was sinfully tight. It showed off his thick arms and chest, which tapered down to a trim waist. My eyes nearly bugged out of my head as he jogged toward me.

For a split second, I thought about turning around and leaving. But then Logan smiled—that wide, boyish grin—and the thought dissolved into the cold September air.

"You came!" His smile was bright and wide.

I waved and pressed my lips into a small smile. "I'm here."

Up close, Logan smelled like mint and a fresh shower. The tips of his hair were damp, and heat pumped off him despite the cold.

"Come on," he said and gestured. "I'll bring you to the box."

"Box?" I asked as I followed behind him, sneaking a peek of his butt.

Logan had a perfect ass because *of course he did.*

In his uniform I could see how perfectly proportioned his thick thighs were with the round shape of his backside. A flash of me grabbing that ass as he settled between my legs startled me.

What the hell was that about?

Flustered, my steps faltered as we entered the small elevator.

Logan gripped my arm. "You okay?"

I hummed and nodded, trying to find my voice. He swiped a badge and pushed the button for the floor. Silence and tension filled the elevator. His masculine smell was all-consuming, and butterflies hammered in my belly.

Logan shifted and I was acutely aware of his every move. His forearm brushed mine, and warmth spread up my arm and across my chest.

"You were done thinking about it?" His voice was sultry and low.

I glanced at him and gave a soft smile. "Looks like it."

He turned, no longer facing the doors, but looking at me. He was standing over me, and his hand moved up to gently grip my chin. His eyes were hard on mine before they flicked to my mouth.

I inhaled, parting my lips, unsure of what would happen next.

"I'm glad you came." His husky voice was pure silk over gravel.

Mine was barely a whisper. "Your grandfather is very convincing. He told me how even when you're traveling you call every week, despite the time differences. I thought that was very sweet."

"I'm not always so sweet . . ." His thumb dragged across my cheek, igniting a path behind it. "But I can be."

My throat was parched and raw.

His fingers tilted my chin, and the world narrowed to the heat of his hand and the quiet hum of the elevator. His eyes flicked to my lips, and my breath caught, the moment stretching like a taut wire.

Was he going to kiss me? Did I want him to?

I stared up at him, waiting. *Willing* him to make the next move so I wouldn't have to.

The elevator dinged, and when the doors opened, I shook my head to clear my thoughts.

Beside me, Logan cleared his throat.

He'd felt whatever that was too.

When we stepped out of the elevator, my jaw dropped open. The entire floor was private and opulent. In front of me was a large, open room with a bar and various tables, chairs, and couches in comfortable seating arrangements. Beyond that, suites with walls of glass looked out onto the field. A few servers were talking at the bar and looked to be organizing trays of food and beverages before the game. Men and women dressed in team colors chatted and walked in and out of the suites.

He led me to a large, open suite. His hand pressed to the small of my back. "Here's where a lot of the WAGs hang out."

"Wags?" I asked.

"Wives and girlfriends."

My brows rose.

"Friends and family. That kind of thing," he said quickly. Logan dragged a hand through his hair and chuckled. "Everything is complimentary, so eat and drink whatever you want."

I looked through the glass, out onto the field, and frowned. The suite was almost too much—glass walls, plush seating, and an endless supply of food and drinks. It felt miles away from my reality, like I'd stumbled into someone else's life. Maybe I had. Maybe I'd stumbled into Logan's.

"What's wrong?" he asked.

I shook my head. "Nothing." I faked a smile. "This is great. Thanks again."

He stepped forward. "What is it?"

My shoulder bounced and my nose scrunched up. "It's just really far from the field. How does anyone see anything?"

He chuckled. "I guess a lot of people up here would rather have free drinks and a warm room than be close to the action."

"Oh." I laughed. "Right."

His green eyes narrowed. "You're not happy."

I shook my head. The last thing I wanted to do was hurt his feelings or seem ungrateful. "I'm happy. This is by far the coolest thing I've done all year. Thank you for inviting me."

Logan playfully rolled his eyes and gripped my hand. "Come on."

He gently pulled me out of the suite but didn't let go of me. My hand was swallowed by his, and the warmth of his touch flowed up my arm, spreading heat across my chest.

"You want front row? You're getting front row." With a determined line creasing his brow, I struggled to keep up with his long strides as he stomped down the hallway. Players nodded in greeting, but Logan was a determined man.

When we reached a lower level, he stopped in front of a security guard. "Tony, can you get her close? One of the open family seats, preferably. And please send down a team blanket to make sure she isn't cold."

Tony smiled at Logan and then at me. "Of course. That's no problem, sir." Tony stepped aside to make a call on his radio.

Logan turned to me, gently placing his hands on my shoulders. "I've got to get ready, but Tony will take care of anything you need. If you get chilly, head back up to the suite level. Otherwise, there's a server here for food and drinks. Anything you need. Understand?"

My mouth popped open. "I—this is—"

Logan grinned. "It's what you want, and it's perfect. Have a good time." With a gentle squeeze on my shoulder, he turned and jogged down the hallway until he disappeared.

"All set, miss?" Tony asked, gesturing at the doorway that led to the field.

I nodded in awe and followed. His massive frame shielded the sun as we walked toward the field. The area at this level was protected by a low wall. The seats were on swivels, and small, half-moon tables provided a place for food or drinks to be set down. There were even small screens to allow viewers to see close-ups of the action.

Tony caught the eye of a small group. "Got room for one more?"

A beautiful woman with long black hair wearing a green-and-gold jersey smiled and waved. "Of course! Send her over."

I pleaded at Tony with my eyes, but he just smiled. "You're in good hands." He stopped by the small group. "Maria, this is Logan Brown's guest . . ." He waited for me to respond.

"MJ," I said.

"She wanted to be closer to the action," Tony finished.

Maria patted the seat next to her. "That's my kind of girl. Have a seat."

Relieved, I exhaled and sat next to her. "Thank you."

"So . . ." She smiled. "Logan Brown, huh?" Her eyebrows waggled, and I could feel my cheeks heat. "We were shocked he wasn't competing in the Sevens, but having him on the exhibition team has made all these extra games much more exciting."

Sevens? I had no idea what she was talking about, so I simply smiled and nodded. Soon, a woman delivered a plush wool blanket in muted Wildhawks colors. Seats around me filled quickly with friends and families of players from both teams. I watched in awe at the friendly camaraderie of the fans. It was apparent that there was a sense of family and community that I didn't expect.

Maria wrapped an older woman in a fierce hug, and when she sat down, I leaned in. "Aren't we supposed to hate the opposing team?" I asked.

She smiled and laughed. "We let the men on the field do the battling. Around here, we're one big family."

One big family.

I liked that.

With a smile, I settled into my seat, wrapping the Wildhawks blanket around my shoulders just as the announcer started speaking.

∽

"LET'S FUCKING GOOOOOOO!" My voice was raw from screaming. Beside me, Maria was jumping up and down with her fist in the air.

The energy in the stadium was electric.

From this vantage point, I had a clear view of Logan as he prepared to go on the field again. He was rubbing his hands together, but his eyes were on me. He watched me scream from the seats before he tore his gaze away. His attention was laser focused, his jaw tight.

Fire raced through me.

In subtle ways, Logan had watched me the entire game.

I was surrounded by die-hard rugby fans who'd been more than happy to explain every detail, play, and position. It was way too much information for me to remember, but I loved feeling like I was a part of the crowd. The rush of adrenaline was unreal—like spinning out of control at the edge of a cliff with your arms spread wide.

Chills ran down my back, but I wasn't cold. I'd taken pictures and videos and asked Maria hundreds of questions. The grunts and slinging mud only added to the rush of the experience, and this was an *exhibition* match. I couldn't fathom what it was like during a seasonal game, let alone the Olympics.

Logan was unstoppable. A beast on the field. When the opposing team scored, it was like a switch was flipped. His intensity darkened and when he pointed and barked orders, I couldn't imagine a man or woman alive not listening.

He was sweaty, covered in mud, and the corded muscles of his thighs were one of the most impressive things I'd ever seen, but the team was struggling.

The score was against them, and every time they lost ground, Logan seemed to push harder, directing his teammates with quick, decisive gestures. Maria explained that in his position as fly-half, he was in the thick of it, constantly moving, setting up plays, and orchestrating the line.

It was like he could see the entire game three steps ahead of everyone else. He read the field as though every move was planned and rehearsed, even as the game moved faster than I could follow. He'd take the ball in hand, sidestep, pass, and slip through tackles, keeping his balance with a raw, honed power that seemed to pulse through him. The crowd was electric, roaring with every near miss and cheer, but I barely noticed them, too caught up in the way Logan took control of every play.

And yet, despite his best efforts, they were still down. I could feel his frustration. He wore it like an extra layer of sweat, jaw clenched, eyes focused and unyielding. Then, the moment he broke free with the ball, I couldn't breathe. Logan charged forward, cutting through the defenders, his determination blazing like a dare to anyone who could reach him.

He darted past one defender, then another, his moves almost impossibly quick for someone of his size. The opposing team closed in, bodies slamming into each other as they scrambled to close the gaps, but Logan slipped through each time, twisting and pivoting with an ease that left his opponents a step behind. Just when it looked like he was about to be taken down, he spun, offloading the ball to his teammate with a perfectly timed pass, setting them up for a break down the line.

The crowd roared, and I found myself leaning forward on the half-wall and screaming, heart pounding as I watched the play unfold. Logan was back on his feet instantly, racing up to support the drive as his teammate bolted toward the try line, defenders rushing to intercept. A tackle hit hard, sending Logan's teammate sprawling, but Logan was right there, scooping up the ball with hands that seemed remarkably steady amid the chaos.

He charged forward, now just a few yards from the line, and the crowd went wild. The tension in the air was palpable. Every breath I took seemed to catch in my throat. Logan's eyes narrowed, his focus laser sharp as he barreled toward the try line. Two defenders closed in from either side, but Logan didn't falter. He surged forward, muscles straining, teeth gritted as he pushed through, diving just as the opposing players slammed into him.

He crossed the line, the ball clutched in his hands, and

the whistle blew. Cheers erupted all around me, the noise deafening, but all I could hear was the fierce, victorious shout he let loose as he hit the ground. The team swarmed him, lifting him up, clapping him on the back, but even amid their celebration, his eyes found mine across the field. A flicker of something intense passed between us, an unspoken current that left me breathless.

Maria's arms wrapped around me as we screamed and celebrated.

The Wildhawks won, but it felt like more than that. Watching Logan on the field was a rush I'd never experienced before. After the final whistle blew, the team gathered in a line, shaking hands with their opponents, exchanging brief nods and claps on the shoulder. There was a camaraderie in it, a respect that lingered even after all the tackles and hard hits. As the Wildhawks turned to leave the field, Logan glanced back, his eyes sweeping over the stands until they landed on me. I felt the thrill of his victory radiating all the way from the field, igniting something deep and undeniable.

He jogged toward me. Something in his gait was off, and my nursing instincts screamed at me that there was something wrong.

Logan came to a stop in front of the wall that separated us. "Meet me outside the locker room." He glanced at Maria. "Can you show her where?"

Maria's smile widened. "Sure can."

He exhaled and winked at me before turning around to join his team. I turned to see Maria grinning. She gathered her blanket and flipped her long, black hair over one shoulder. "Well, you heard the man. Let's go."

My stomach bunched as I followed her out of the stands

and through a long corridor. Muffled cheers and excited chants echoed through the door.

"After their showers, he'll come out here. Want me to wait with you?" she asked.

I swallowed and shook my head. "I'm good. Thanks for everything today."

Maria leaned forward and wrapped me in a hug. "My pleasure. I have a feeling I'll be seeing you around."

We said our goodbyes, and my palms started to sweat as I waited for Logan. I checked my watch. It took two hours to get home, and it was getting darker by the minute.

When the heavy door opened and Logan appeared, my breath caught. Freshly showered, he looked just as intense as he had on the field, but now there was a softness in his eyes, a quiet pride that made my heart stutter. His damp hair fell just slightly over his brow, and he wore a hint of a smile, like he was just as reluctant to say goodbye as I was.

"Heading out?" he asked as we walked down the ramp toward the parking lot. His eyes landed on my car parked under a flickering light.

I nodded, wrapping the team blanket around my shoulders to hide my nerves. "It's a long drive, but I can listen to a podcast or something. I'll be fine."

But before I could even think about leaving, a loud crack split the sky.

Fat raindrops started slowly, then quickly turned to falling in torrents, coming down so hard I couldn't see past the first row of cars. "Shit."

Logan's face shifted instantly, protective and tense. I pulled out my phone, checking the weather app to see how long the storm was expected to last.

"I should get going." I showed him the screen on my phone. "It's supposed to last all night."

"You're not driving in this, not in the dark," he said, his voice firm, leaving no room for argument. He turned to scan the parking lot. "Wait here. Let me see if we can find you a room for the night."

I bit my lip, glancing at the sheets of rain pounding against the concrete, but before I could protest, he was already talking to the stadium staff.

A few minutes later, he returned, frustration flickering in his eyes.

"The team hotel is completely booked," he muttered, running a hand through his damp hair. "I'll drive you."

"That's ridiculous," I said. "Maria said you have another early game tomorrow. Besides, how would you get back?"

A heavy silence settled between us as he met my gaze, his expression unreadable.

His green eyes met mine, searching, as if he wasn't sure what I'd say. "You could stay with me." His voice barely rose above the sound of the rain, the words deliberate, quiet, and almost careful.

My pulse stuttered, and for a moment I couldn't breathe.

Staying with him in his hotel room was an option, one that sent a fresh surge of adrenaline through me. The rain blurred the parking lot into a smear of shadows and light.

Sure, I was more than capable of driving home in a rainstorm in the dark, but there was a part of me that didn't want to.

"Um. Okay, sure." I swallowed hard, my pulse racing as I tried to keep my expression steady, but every nerve in my body buzzed with anticipation.

NINE

LOGAN

Were there other hotels? Probably.

Did I care enough to check? Definitely not.

When we finally made it to the hotel room, the storm was still raging outside, a steady rhythm of rain against the window. From the door of my hotel room, we stared at the one bed sitting in the center of the room, mocking us both. It was just sitting there, all big and smug, like it knew damn well this was going to be a problem. I scratched the back of my neck, throwing a glance at MJ.

She lingered by the door, her arms crossed, the hint of a smirk playing on her lips as she looked at me with those watchful eyes, like she was waiting for me to make the first move.

"Just so we're clear, there's no way I'm sleeping on the floor," I said, keeping my tone light, though I could already feel the heat between us, humming like a live wire.

She raised an eyebrow, amused. "Wouldn't dream of it, Princess."

I chuckled at her calling me Princess.

MJ sighed. "So far you seem like a gentleman." She

eyed me. "I hope you're as sweet as your grandfather." She walked in and dumped her purse on the desk before slipping off her shoes. "The bed is big enough . . . probably."

"Probably," I echoed, giving her a small grin as I set my bag down. She stayed at the edge of the room, her fingers toying with the blanket in her arms, clearly hesitating.

"I'll keep to my side. Promise," I added, raising my hand in mock solemnity. But, truthfully, I was already feeling conflicted. MJ had this pull that felt half dangerous, half irresistible.

I wanted to know her—she was guarded, always holding back something just beyond my reach—but I wasn't about to pry. There were enough barriers in my own life to keep my head spinning without adding hers to the mix.

The bed felt softer than any hotel mattress should as I lay back, arms folded behind my head, sneaking a glance at her as she moved around the room.

"No plans to celebrate your win?"

I grinned. "The guys will go out, but not usually before a game day. We'll celebrate when we win again tomorrow."

A soft, disgusted noise rattled out of her nose. "So cocky."

I placed my hand on my chest. "I like to think of it as healthy confidence. Besides, us princesses need our beauty sleep."

MJ lingered by the edge of the bed, glancing down at her rain-soaked shirt, and I couldn't help but notice her hesitation. She pulled at the fabric a little, her eyes scanning the room.

"You could . . ." I started, my voice low, already wondering if I'd regret this. "You could wear my shirt if you want. Probably more comfortable than sleeping in that."

Her gaze snapped up to mine, a flicker of surprise

crossing her face. I grinned, maybe a bit too satisfied with myself, and stood. Reaching behind me, I pulled off the fresh team-branded shirt I'd tossed on after my shower. My name was printed across the back, along with the team logo, and something about offering it to her felt . . . oddly personal.

Still, I pulled it over my head in one motion, watching her reaction as her eyes darted over my chest and shoulders, pausing just long enough to tell me she noticed. She swallowed, her gaze dropping, but not before I caught her reaction.

Her lingering gaze sent a spark of satisfaction through me. For a moment I felt the air between us shift, heavy and charged.

I held the shirt out, and she reached for it, her fingers brushing mine in a quick, warm touch. "Thanks," she murmured, not quite meeting my eyes.

MJ slipped into the bathroom, and as soon as the door clicked shut, I let out a slow breath, scrubbing my hand over my face before walking toward the bed.

This was going to be rough. Sharing a room with her, sleeping in the same bed, all while pretending I could keep my cool? Not likely. She had a way of getting under my skin, and tonight I could feel it in every nerve. I was too aware of her, too drawn in by everything she was—and wasn't—saying.

And the thought of her in there, slipping into my shirt, her body wrapped in it . . . or, hell, maybe even my actual jersey, the fabric barely reaching her thighs—let's just say it wasn't helping my case to stay focused *or* relaxed.

My cock ached.

I shook my head, trying to push the image out of my mind, but the visual kept creeping back in.

Focus, Logan.

I heard the bathroom door click and looked up. When she stepped out of the bathroom, I forgot how to breathe. My shirt hung loose on her, the hem brushing the tops of her thighs. It wasn't just that she looked good—she looked like she belonged in it, like it was made for her.

And damn if that didn't do something to me.

I cleared my throat, turning back to fluff a pillow, hoping she hadn't noticed the way I'd frozen for a second there.

"It . . . uh, looks good on you," I managed, keeping my tone casual, though my pulse was anything but.

She shot me a quick, almost shy smile, tugging at the hem and tucking a lock of soft brown hair behind her ear. "Thanks."

We stood at the center of the room, neither of us acknowledging the empty bed. "So," she said finally, breaking the silence. "Why aren't you playing in the Sevens? Maria said it's what most of the pros do."

I felt the question settle in my chest, a familiar weight of pride and frustration. There it was—the thing I couldn't shake, gnawing at the back of my mind every time I thought about the team, about my body. I took a breath, choosing my words carefully.

"The thing is," I said, dragging a hand through my hair, "the body doesn't always bounce back the way you want it to. And when you're thirty-four, people start whispering about when you'll finally hang it up. I'm not ready for that."

She waited and I found myself opening up more.

"During the Olympic Games, I got a concussion," I said. "And I tweaked my knee. Didn't quite bounce back like I thought I would. Now I'm doing exhibition games instead. It's a temporary gig, just to stay sharp."

She was quiet, her gaze turned away, and I wondered if she could feel that tension in me. This was the reality—thirty-four years old and I was one of the senior players, no longer able to just shake off the wear and tear. The next Olympics would probably be my last run, but even that felt like a gamble now.

I'd lost count of the times I'd asked myself, *How much longer can I keep doing this?*

"Want me to take a look?" she asked.

I paused, considering her offer. "Is this within the realm of blood-pressure medication and enforcing visiting hours?" I teased.

She shot me a pointed look. "Very funny." MJ gestured to the chair tucked in the corner. "I'm an RN with an orthopedic nurse certification. I can show you my résumé, if you'd like."

"I believe you," I chuckled as I sat in the chair and pulled up the leg of my sweatpants.

MJ crouched in front of me, her eyes assessing my knee while I assessed her. A soft furrow creased her forehead, and her lips flattened.

"Hmm," she said. Her fingertips hovered over my bent knee. "May I?"

I nodded.

MJ's fingertips brushed the outside of my knee, sending tingles buzzing up my leg. Her touch was soft, yet efficient. Her eyes never left my knee as she extended my leg, then bent it again.

When she gently pressed on each side, I hissed.

She sat back on her heels, and I already missed her touch. "It's a little swollen. Feels a bit stiff. You should probably get it checked out to make sure it's nothing more serious."

I pushed my pant leg back down. "I'm sure it's nothing. I'll be fine by tomorrow's game."

MJ's eyes lifted, her expression softer, like she'd picked up on more than I intended to let slip. "Sure seems tough on the body."

"It's part of the game," I said, shrugging, trying to sound nonchalant as she stood. "You either keep going or you find something else."

She tilted her head, her eyes meeting mine, and I felt a jolt, that electric awareness between us kicking up a notch. "You don't seem like the type to just walk away."

"Is it that obvious?" I chuckled as I stood, but there was an edge to it, a heaviness. "It's hard to let go when it's all you know."

Our eyes held, and for a second, I forgot about the storm, the cramped room, and the fact that there was barely a foot of space between us. The silence stretched, thick with unspoken things. I tried to ignore the way her shoulder brushed mine, the warmth of her body radiating across that small, shared space.

It was distracting as hell.

"So what about you?" I asked, steering the conversation away from my troubles. "What's got you so guarded?"

She laughed, but it sounded strained. "Guarded? I'm not guarded." Her voice wavered, like she didn't quite believe it herself. Then she smiled, quick and practiced.

"Right." I let my gaze linger, daring her to challenge me. "If you say so." I slid into the bed, making sure to give her plenty of room on the other side.

She rolled her eyes, shifting to face away from me, but I saw the hint of a smile, the way her fingers fidgeted with the edge of the blanket.

I wanted to know more, to press her on it, but I could

tell from her expression that I wouldn't get anything real from her tonight. And maybe that was just as well.

We were strangers—strangers sharing a cramped hotel room during a storm.

MJ slipped under the covers, leaving me staring after her, my thoughts anything but innocent.

She pulled the covers up to her chin, eyes fixed on the ceiling. The storm outside roared, the sound making the room feel smaller somehow, more intimate. Her breathing was soft, steady, but I could hear every inhale, every exhale. The faint scent of her shampoo lingered between us, and I had to focus hard to keep my hands on my side of the blanket.

When she settled back against the pillow, the edge of her foot brushed mine under the covers, and she froze, glancing at me, her cheeks just barely flushed.

"Sorry," she murmured, pulling back, but the tension between us only thickened, that accidental touch lingering like an invitation I couldn't quite ignore.

I chuckled, lifting a brow. "Relax, MJ. I'm not gonna bite."

She gave a dry laugh, but I saw her lips curve. "I don't know . . . you seem like the type."

"Oh, you have no idea," I shot back, half teasing, half serious, and there was that smirk again, the one that drove me a little wild. She laughed, genuinely this time, and the sound made something twist in my chest.

"By the way," I said, adjusting my head on the pillow to get a better look at her. "I'm still deciding on the right nickname for you. You don't seem like a 'Kitten' . . . and 'Thunder' didn't quite fit either."

She gave me a skeptical look, her lips pressing together

like she was fighting a smile. "Why do I even need a nickname?"

"It's just a feeling," I said, shrugging. "Like I need something that suits you, something . . . perfect."

"*Hooker* wasn't good either?" she teased.

A genuine laugh cracked out of me.

She laughed with me and rolled her eyes, but I saw the slight blush rise on her cheeks. "You can call me whatever you like, Princess."

I grinned, loving that feisty edge in her. "Noted. But I can't make any promises, Peach." I looked at her and we both laughed. "Definitely not." I thought again. "Maybe . . . Lightning. Something powerful and impossible to ignore."

Her laughter was soft, but the tension grew only heavier, like neither of us wanted to break this thread connecting us, pulling us closer. We settled back, the silence between us charged, and every so often, I'd catch her glancing my way, her eyes filled with something I couldn't quite read—like there was something she wanted to say but kept holding back.

And I felt it too—that awareness, the electricity humming in the space between us. I'd never shared a bed with someone where *not* touching felt more charged than anything else.

Finally, I rolled onto my side to face her, my hand brushing hers as I shifted. Her breath hitched, and she went still, her gaze meeting mine with a spark of challenge and something deeper, something that had my heart racing.

"Stay on your side," she murmured, her voice low, teasing.

"Oh, is that a challenge?" I replied, feeling the grin stretch across my face.

She shrugged, her lips quirked into a half smile that was equal parts daring and shy. "More like a warning."

And there it was, that dare, the unspoken test hanging in the air between us, charged and almost electric. She looked away, but not before I caught the slight flush in her cheeks, the way her pulse flickered at her neck.

The tension lingered, neither of us willing to break the silence, and I could feel my body tense, every nerve lit up by the closeness, the warmth radiating from her.

For the rest of the night, we barely moved, both holding ourselves carefully, but every breath felt deliberate, every tiny movement loaded with something I couldn't put into words.

∽

When my alarm sounded and I opened my eyes, she was gone.

The bed was empty beside me, and I felt an odd pang of disappointment. Shaking it off, I got dressed and headed down to the field, ready for game two of the doubleheader, my thoughts still half on her as I warmed up. But I couldn't shake the feeling that lingered from the night before—that spark, that sense of something unfinished.

I shot her a quick text, making sure she'd gotten home okay.

The game was intense, faster than usual, and every time I caught the ball, the adrenaline surged, propelling me forward. My moves were quick, reflexes on fire, and everything clicked into place, like I could see the whole field with a clarity I hadn't felt in a long time. The roar of the crowd was thunderous, each play feeling like a surge of energy.

When we finally won, I couldn't help but search the

stands, looking for her. The rush of victory surged through me, and I barely noticed my teammate, Jack, clapping me on the back with a smirk.

"Man, whatever you did last night, do it again. You've got some serious lucky charm energy today," he joked, flashing a knowing grin.

I brushed him off with a laugh, but the idea started to take root. I showered, and at the first opportunity, before I even knew what I was doing, I pulled out my phone and fired off a quick text to MJ.

> Not saying you're my lucky charm or anything, but just played one of the best games of my life. You sure you weren't in the stands somewhere?

A moment later, my phone buzzed with her reply.

> MJ
>
> I had to get back early. Maybe your luck is because I'm NOT there. Ever think of that?

I chuckled, unable to keep from grinning as I typed back.

> There's no way. It's all you. I swear, you've got this weird magic going on.

> MJ
>
> Yeah, yeah. Keep dreaming, hotshot.
> Maybe you just needed a confidence boost from someone who doesn't even understand rugby

I could practically see the smirk she'd have as she typed that, and it hit me.

Maybe MJ wasn't so much a distraction as the lucky

charm I needed to get through the offseason. Jack had already proved himself the most superstitious on the team. He hadn't washed his socks a single time all season, and we were all suffering. He'd called it lucky charm energy, but the only change was *her*.

So that was it—I would need MJ to bring me luck.

The future of my career depended on it.

The drive back to Outtatowner was quiet, the hum of the truck's engine the only sound breaking the stillness of the night. As I turned onto the outskirts of town, something caught my eye—an old warehouse set back from the road. I eased off the gas, my gaze snagging on the boarded-up windows and peeling paint. It wasn't much to look at, just a weathered shell of what it used to be. But there was something about it, something that made me wonder what it could become if someone had the guts to try.

I shook my head and hit the gas, dismissing the ridiculous thought.

As I drove, I thought back to the game. The energy from the crowd, the adrenaline pumping through my veins—it was why I played. But something was different. When I'd glanced at the stands and saw MJ sitting there, her arms crossed but a faint smile tugging at her lips, it had felt like everything I'd worked for mattered in a way I hadn't realized before.

I gripped the steering wheel tighter, replaying the match in my head. Every tackle, every sprint, every moment the ball was in my hands—MJ was there, lingering in the back of my mind.

She was a distraction, but if she was also somehow a lucky charm, maybe I didn't need to shake her.

TEN

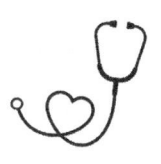

MJ

I'D SPENT the entire day trying not to think about Logan.

His stupid dimple. His stupid, cocky confidence. The way his shirt had felt soft and warm against my skin. The way *he* had made me feel safe and seen, which was entirely unfair. It wasn't supposed to be like this.

"Yoo-hoo, Earth to MJ."

I came back to life with a start, blinking when Carol's confused face came into view.

She waved a folder in the air before setting it in front of me. "What is with you today? It's like you're on another planet. Room seventeen is pissed because she spent her weekly cash at bingo but doesn't remember. Think you can calm her down?"

I nodded and swallowed hard, willing the memory of waking to Logan's masculine warmth beside me to go away. When I woke up in the hotel room, for a split second I had panicked—until I remembered.

Logan. Hotel room. The storm.

And, oh god, his shirt.

His shirt was soft, heavier than my usual sleepwear, and

it had still smelled like him, like faint cologne mixed with something inherently *Logan*. I'd stolen it on my way out of the hotel room, though I was still a little unsure as to *why*.

I remembered the way he'd looked when he handed it to me—broad shoulders, the shadow of soft hair dusting his chest, and a confidence that was somehow comforting and maddening all at once.

It was no surprise that he'd slipped into my thoughts all day.

I looked at Carol. "No problem. I'll head over there now."

A buzz in my pocket sent my pulse spiking again.

A text from Logan.

I hesitated, thumb hovering over the notification, half-wondering if opening it meant opening more than just a message. But curiosity was stronger than my caution.

> **LOGAN**
> Going to the Grudge Holder tonight. Care to join?

The audacity made me laugh, even as I felt my stomach flip. I hadn't seen him since I had sneaked out of the hotel room. Part of me wanted to stay home, curl up with a book, and forget Logan Brown existed. The other part? It wanted to walk into the Grudge, head held high, and prove that whatever I felt for him wasn't real. I tried to sound nonchalant in my reply.

> Celebrating?

> **LOGAN**
> A bit. We won.

> You know, townies just call it the Grudge.

His response was immediate, like he'd been waiting for me, and my stomach flipped.

> **LOGAN**
>
> Don't make me beg, Sweetie Pie.

> Sweetie Pie? Gross. Keep trying.

> **LOGAN**
>
> Noted. I also need to talk to you about coming to another game.

> Because I'm lucky?

> **LOGAN**
>
> Because I like having you there. (Also yes, I would like to test my theory.)

I rolled my eyes, suppressing a grin. I couldn't let him have the satisfaction of thinking he had me wrapped around his finger.

> I might be there, if only to disprove this ridiculous theory of yours.

> **LOGAN**
>
> The only thing ridiculous is you snuck out without saying goodbye.

> Goodbye, Logan. (Happy?)

His last reply came as I was putting my phone away and hustling toward room seventeen.

> **LOGAN**
>
> See you tonight, Pumpkin. 😊

I chuckled, pocketing my phone with a feeling I didn't want to name.

~

It was Saturday night, so not at all surprising that the Grudge was crowded. Despite the fact that the height of tourist season was over, the Grudge was the place for people to grab a bite to eat or a few drinks. I walked in with Sylvie and Annie by my side. I scanned the open bar and smiled.

It wasn't all that long ago that the Grudge was distinctly separated. The Sullivans, and those who aligned with them, on one side. My family and ours on the other. Since Duke and Sylvie crossed the invisible divide and even had a baby, Kings and Sullivans were mingling in the middle. It was a strange, but happy, mixture of my small town's rival families.

I waved to a few distant cousins huddled in the corner while a band was just starting their set.

Annie leaned toward me. "Lee is coming by once his shift is over. He said he could drive us all home if we needed it."

Sylvie smiled. "A goofball with a heart of gold."

Annie laughed. "That's my man."

I turned to my sister. "No Duke?" I teased.

"You mean my house husband?" she joked. "Not a chance."

We both knew her broody husband was more than happy to stay home with their son and never set foot in the Grudge unless he was forced by Sylvie or his brothers to be social. In reality, he was the perfect match for my quiet, selfless sister: grumpy, tenderhearted, and hopelessly devoted to her.

My nerves jumped as I scanned the crowd, trying to pretend like I wasn't actively searching for Logan. We hadn't discussed what *time* he planned to be at the Grudge.

I had invited Annie and Sylvie out with the hopes that I'd appear casually aloof and not overly anxious to see him, which was 100 percent the truth.

"Who are you looking for?" Sylvie asked as Annie ordered three lemon drop shots from the bartender.

Annie turned and laughed. "Probably her hot rugby boyfriend."

My attention snapped in her direction. "He's not my boyfriend. We're barely even *friends*."

I conveniently left out the part about sleeping next to him all night.

Annie leaned in. "You're telling me that you *haven't* imagined what it would be like to see him naked?"

"Leave her alone," Sylvie cut in. Her face softened when she looked at me and placed a gentle hand on my arm. "Virginity is nothing to be ashamed of."

The fuck?

"Is that what you think?" I looked between my friend and sister. "I've *had* sex."

Once . . .

They blinked at me like they didn't know what to say next.

I pinched the bridge of my nose and exhaled. "*Fine.* I may not be the most experienced woman in the room, but I'm not totally clueless." Their pitying glances were setting me on edge. My voice rose. "I know my way around a dick, okay?"

Annie sputtered a laugh as Sylvie's jaw popped open.

I lowered my voice and dismissed the curious glances. "I've had . . . *experiences*. It's just that whenever it comes to actual sex, sometimes I freeze. My head gets clouded with all the *what-if*s and reasons he won't call after." I snatched one of the lemon drop shots in front of me and threw it back. "I can have plenty of fun without . . . *that*."

Sylvie put up both hands. "Well, color me corrected. I didn't realize my baby sister was such a slut."

We all laughed, and I shook my head, easing the tension that had bunched between my shoulder blades.

"You know," Annie said as she shot back her drink, "there aren't any rules. You could have fun without all the extra pressure on yourself. No expectations, no heartbreak."

The idea immediately took root.

No expectations.

No heartbreak.

Was it really that simple? I think I was innately built for commitment, but what if I *chose* for things to stay casual? How could I feel used if *I* was the one doing the using?

I reached forward and gripped Annie's face between my hands and plopped an obnoxious, smacking kiss right on her lips. "Annie, you're a genius."

She laughed and bent her knees in a tiny curtsy. "Thank you, I agree."

"Excuse me?" A deep voice rumbled behind me and I grinned.

When I turned, my stomach soured, and the smile melted off my face at the sight of a tall stranger standing in front of me.

Whoops. Definitely not Logan.

I blinked up at him as he held out his hand. "May I have this dance?"

"Um . . ." I looked around for an easy exit, but Annie and Sylvie only smiled and nodded eagerly.

"Sure, okay," I answered before sliding off the stool. At the very least, he was offering an escape from even more embarrassing conversations about my limited sex life.

Out of politeness, I placed my hand in his and allowed him to lead me to the dance floor. It was an upbeat country song that was popular on the radio.

"Can you two-step?" the stranger asked.

I looked up and forced a smile. "I can try."

"All you've got to do is follow, darling." He winked, and my eyes searched the crowd again. When Logan used a nickname, it was silly, but I didn't love the way this man's eager eyes hovered a second too long on my face.

I looked over his shoulder as Annie gave me two thumbs up before miming an enthusiastic blow job. I fought past a giggle and focused on the other dancers as the man led me around the worn, wooden dance floor.

As he guided me through the two-step, his hand pressed low on my back, lingering in a way that made my skin crawl. He was too close, his grip too familiar for a simple dance between strangers. His cologne was sharp, almost overpowering, and it took everything in me not to grimace as he leaned down to murmur near my ear.

"You're good at this," he said, his voice smooth, but it only made my pulse speed up in the wrong way.

"Thanks," I replied, forcing another smile, but my eyes kept scanning the crowd. I caught Annie's gaze again, but she was deep in conversation, her attention elsewhere now, and I was left to fend for myself.

His hand slid lower than it should have, his cologne suffocating. I forced a smile, focusing on the other dancers, but my skin prickled with unease. When his breath hit my ear, murmuring something I didn't quite catch, I decided I'd had enough.

As the song ended, like a ripple in the air, I felt a change —a new presence close by, one that sent a strange, reassuring calm through me.

And then I heard his voice.

"Mind if I cut in?"

Relief flooded me, but it was tangled with something else—something that made my pulse race. The stranger's steps faltered, his hand loosening on me as he looked up in annoyance. I turned, and there was Logan, his stance casual but his eyes hard, exuding a quiet confidence. Logan wasn't just standing there—he was looming, his broad frame an unspoken warning that made the stranger step back without a word.

"I think we were just getting started." The stranger tightened his grip on my waist as I tried to pull away.

"Actually," Logan continued, his gaze never wavering, "I wasn't asking you. I was speaking to the lady. She's with me."

Without waiting for a reply, Logan reached for my elbow, his fingers curling around it with a strength that grounded me.

The stranger hesitated, eyes narrowing as he sized up Logan.

Mild panic itched in my throat. A muscle in Logan's jaw flexed. "You can start it," he challenged the man, "but I guarantee I'll end it."

The stranger paused, then shrugged and backed off, muttering something under his breath that sounded a lot like *prick*.

Logan's grip tightened slightly, his silent message clear: He wasn't letting me go.

"You all right?" he asked, his voice a low rumble, the warmth in his eyes undoing the last of my tension.

I nodded, a fresh wave of relief washing over me, and I looked up at him as my thoughts thumped to the beat of the music.

Casual.
Casual.
Casual.

Logan's hand slid to the small of my back, pulling me close in a way that felt nothing like the stranger's grasp. His touch was sure and steady, and the loud music and laughter around us faded, leaving just him and me, our breaths mingling in the small space between us.

His hand on my waist was steady, grounding me in a way that made me want to lean into him, to trust him. But that was dangerous.

Trust was a slippery slope.

"Didn't mean to interrupt," he murmured, his mouth quirked in a half smile that sent my heart racing for a completely different reason.

"Believe me, you weren't interrupting anything," I replied, my voice shaky but light. The words were meant as a joke, but the intensity in his gaze was anything but.

"Good," he said softly, his hand moving just slightly, almost teasing, but with that steady warmth that had my pulse pounding.

We fell into a rhythm, the romantic country tune now just background noise to the silent exchange between us. Logan's grip was firm yet gentle, his hand guiding mine in a way that made me feel like I was the only person in the room. His thumb brushed the back of my hand, and that one small movement sent shivers down my spine.

"Fair warning—I can't dance," he said, and the amusement in his eyes made my cheeks flush.

"Maybe we can just sway," I replied, feeling bolder now, relaxed in his arms as we moved to the slow, sensual music.

He smiled, a glint of something mischievous in his eyes. "I can do that." And he did, his steps steady and sure, swaying gently on the outskirts of the dance floor while more experienced dancers moved around us.

I barely had to think, his presence wrapping around me, his hand warm and possessive on my lower back, but not in a way that felt controlling, just . . . protective.

Right.

His hand shifted slightly, his fingers tracing a path that left tingling warmth in their wake. The air between us grew charged, the casual dance turning into something else entirely, something heavier, filled with possibilities.

"You know, I've been thinking about something all day," he said, his voice a low murmur just above the music.

I looked up in anticipation.

Logan's eyes flicked to my lips and back up. "I think I almost kissed you yesterday."

My breath caught, and I searched his face, unsure whether he was joking. But the intensity in his gaze was unmistakable.

"You think?" I managed, my voice barely above a whisper.

"Yeah." He leaned down, his mouth close to my ear, his breath warm. He reached out, brushing a strand of hair behind my ear, his fingers lingering just a moment too long. "If I'd had the chance . . . I would have started here." His thumb brushed the corner of my mouth, his gaze never leaving mine. "I would have gone slow," he murmured, his voice rough, almost like he was holding himself back. "Just enough to make you wonder."

He paused, his other hand tracing a gentle line along my waist. "I would have pulled you close, like this," he continued, drawing me even closer until there was almost no space between us, his body warm and solid against mine.

"And then?" I breathed, feeling every nerve in my body come alive.

He smiled, his lips dangerously close to mine. "Then I would have kept you waiting, just for a second, until you couldn't stand it. Until you needed it as much as I did."

The tension between us was thick, nearly electric, and it took every ounce of restraint not to close the distance between us.

His gaze dropped to my lips, and for a breathless moment I thought he'd actually do it. But he stopped, that wicked glint in his eyes back in full force.

"But not here," he said, his voice low and rough. "Not with an audience."

"Oh." I let out a shaky laugh, hoping it masked the way my pulse was racing, feeling equal parts relief and frustration.

"That kiss would be only for you," he replied, grinning, his hand lingering on my waist, holding me close a moment longer before finally, reluctantly, he stepped back just as the song ended.

I swallowed hard, my eyes bouncing between his. If I had any hope of being the kind of girl who kept things casual and feelings-free, I needed some space.

The secret that I'd been keeping—that I knew who he was and we had a shared history—gnawed at me.

"I know who you are," I blurted.

His brow creased. "And who am I?"

I blinked, trying to get my thoughts straight. "Maverick." My eyebrows rose, waiting for him to react.

He huffed a laugh and grinned. "It's a stupid nickname from childhood." His smile lifted. "Grandpa told you?"

My smile faltered, a strange knot twisting in my

stomach as the name lingered in the air. "No, it's . . ." I started, my voice hardening.

Even thinking about Trent filled the air in a way I didn't like, like a door creaking open to a place I had tried to lock away.

He must've noticed the shift in my expression, because his brow furrowed slightly, his eyes searching mine. "Are you okay?"

I forced a laugh, but it came out hollow. "Yeah. It's just . . ." I blew out a breath. "I knew someone who used to talk about a best friend with that name."

"Huh. Someone I know?" He leaned in, curious but oblivious, like he couldn't see the cracks forming in front of him.

"Yeah," I murmured, feeling my stomach drop. My mouth went dry as I searched his face for a trace of recognition, a glimmer that he'd know exactly who I was talking about. But his expression stayed open and unguarded, completely unaware.

"Trent Fischer," I said finally, my voice nearly cracking. "You're friends, right?"

For a split second, Logan's face lit up, the mention of Trent sparking a warm smile that twisted something deep inside me. "Hell yeah, we're friends. Trent's my best friend. I've known him since we were kids. Why?" He chuckled, clearly happy to share a story that, to him, was harmless.

But to me, his words landed like ice water doused over my head. The weight of it all hit me then, crashing over me like a wave. "Because I know him too."

I took a step back, the ground beneath me tilting, my throat tightening painfully. I suddenly felt the need to leave, to escape the reminder of everything Trent had taken from me. But Logan reached out, his hand brushing my arm, and the warmth of his touch rooted me in place.

"MJ?" he asked, concern flickering in his eyes. "What's wrong?"

I swallowed, my voice barely holding. "I . . . I don't know. I've known you were friends for a while. It felt wrong not to tell you."

Logan's brow furrowed deeper, his confusion turning to worry. "How do you know Trent?"

The irony was almost laughable.

His best friend didn't even know I had existed because Trent had been careful to keep me a secret even though we'd dated for *months*.

"Oh, I knew him," I managed, struggling to keep my voice steady. "He mentioned his friends, but apparently he left out a lot of details."

Like the fact that his beloved friend Maverick was Logan Brown, famous Olympic rugby player.

"Did he say something about me?" Logan's expression softened, a hint of protectiveness there that nearly broke my resolve. "I know Trent can be a little jealous, but he means well."

I didn't know if Trent was secretive about Logan's true identity because he was hiding *me* or if it was because Trent always liked to be the most amazing person in the room.

Logan's words tore through me, each one stinging more than the last. I could barely bring myself to look at him, but when I did, his face was open, honest—like he was still that guy I'd spent all this time with, getting to know.

The reality I had tried to ignore came crashing down. Now everything felt tainted, wrapped in the shadow of Trent's betrayal.

"I don't think you knew him like I did." I lifted my chin.

I was less than an hour into trying to be a new person—the kind of woman who didn't let an asshole ex ruin a potential good time.

Still, the memories of what he'd done poked at my ribs.

Logan's face fell, realization dawning slowly. "MJ . . . did something happen between you two?"

My laugh was bitter, empty. I looked away, the words spilling out before I could stop them. "We dated. And he . . . he wasn't exactly honest with me."

Logan's jaw tightened, a storm gathering in his eyes as he tried to process what I was saying. The warmth in his eyes was replaced with something harder—something that looked a lot like regret. "MJ . . . I'm sorry, but I have no idea what's going on. I swear. Trent never . . . Look, I travel a lot with the team and he never said anything to me."

The concern in his voice was real, but it didn't change the hurt twisting inside me.

The truth came tumbling out. "We dated for *months*. He didn't say anything because, to him, I was nothing. And now here I am, standing in front of his best friend, who didn't know who I was either." My voice cracked, the embarrassment of it all crashing down on me.

"I . . . I think I need some air." My voice was barely steady, and I took a step back, feeling like I was unraveling at the seams. I pulled away from him, every part of me screaming to get out of this place, away from him, away from the reminder of everything Trent had done. "You're his best friend. You've probably heard all about his conquests, his games, his lies."

Logan looked stricken, his face pale as he shook his head. "No, MJ, that's not . . . he's never told me anything like that. I swear, I didn't know he was like that with you."

The sincerity in his voice made me falter, my anger and

hurt warring with the part of me that wanted to believe him. But the memories were too strong, the wounds too deep.

"This was a mistake. I'll see you around, Logan."

Without stopping to say goodbye, I left Annie and Sylvie and walked outside.

I barely heard Logan calling after me as I pushed through the crowd, my chest tight and my vision blurred. The cold night air hit me like a slap, but it did nothing to calm the storm raging inside me. I wanted to scream, to cry, to disappear.

I wanted to be the kind of woman who could flirt with or sleep with anyone she pleased. I didn't want my feelings to get tangled up in a good time, because when it didn't work out, then I'd *really* be a mess.

ELEVEN

LOGAN

I watched MJ as she fled the dance floor.

I should've been relieved to find out MJ had dated Trent—it explained the weird tension between us. But the look on her face, the pain in her eyes . . . it was like a gut punch.

What had Trent done to her?

The question rattled in my chest as I stepped to the back of the bar and pulled out my phone to call him.

It wasn't just the fact that she had dated my friend. It was the pain that she tried to hide. He'd done something, and that settled like lead in my stomach.

The phone rang and rang, and I cursed under my breath when it went to Trent's voicemail. "Call me. Now. It's important."

I hung up and slipped the phone back into my pocket and dragged a hand through my hair. "Fuck," I exhaled.

Across the bar, the women MJ had been with looked concerned and confused. I rushed out of the Grudge and into the crisp night air after MJ.

She wasn't on either side of the sidewalk. "Damn it."

I opened my phone to call her, and it immediately went to voicemail. I tried to text her.

> We should talk about this.

"What did you say to my sister?" MJ's sister had her hands planted on her hips and looked ready to fight.

The redhead with her cut in, holding her hand out. "Hi, I'm Annie. I think you've met Sylvie." I shook it, and she grabbed a phone from her purse. "I can call her."

Sylvie crossed her arms, waiting for me to answer her question. I blew out a breath. "I'm not sure." My attention fell to Annie, who shook her head. "She didn't answer my call either."

Sylvie raised a finger and pointed in my direction. "If you did something . . ."

I liked knowing MJ had someone in her corner, even if her anger was directed at me for the moment.

I raised my hands as Annie exhaled. "If you're just here to make her cry again, turn around and walk away now. We've seen enough of that."

I hated the idea of someone making MJ cry. I stared down the sidewalk, willing her to come back.

"If she doesn't want to talk to you, maybe you should leave her alone," Sylvie said.

I nodded, knowing she was right.

This was exactly the type of drama and distraction I did not need in my life, but I couldn't stop from worrying about her anyway.

MJ's abrupt exit from the Grudge had left a curious knot in my chest, and I hadn't heard from her since. I had tried a few more times to text her, but they all went unanswered. So, a few days later, I found myself heading to Haven Pines early. Seeing Grandpa was the excuse, but MJ was on my mind more than I cared to admit.

As I walked down the main hallway, I caught sight of her up ahead, speaking softly to one of the residents with gentle patience. Her face lit up in a soft smile as she adjusted the blankets on an elderly woman's wheelchair, her hands moving with care.

For a moment, I just watched, trying to reconcile the woman in front of me with the one who had fled from the bar, wounded by ghosts of the past.

How the hell could someone like Trent leave this woman hurting after all that time?

When she turned and spotted me, her eyes widened in surprise. A flash of pink colored her cheeks, and I knew she was thinking about the other night.

"Hey," she said, her voice a bit unsure. "Didn't expect to see you here so early."

I offered her a small smile. "Came to check on Arthur . . . and you."

She glanced away, brushing a strand of hair behind her ear. "Yeah, about the other night . . . I'm sorry, I—"

"It's okay," I interrupted gently, moving a step closer. "Your sister is kind of scary," I joked. "But, really, I just want to make sure you're all right. That's all."

"I'm great." She took a breath, hesitating, her eyes drilling into me. "It's just . . . I knew you and Trent were friends, and things did not end well between us." She gestured between our bodies. "Whatever I thought this might be . . . is probably a mistake."

I nodded, settling back on my heels. "I totally understand."

Didn't I?

The truth gnawed at me. I didn't like thinking about MJ being with *anyone* else, let alone my best friend. Trent still hadn't called me back, and the more time went on, the longer it was festering in the back of my mind.

Her shoulders relaxed slightly, and she looked up, meeting my gaze. "Thanks, Logan. I appreciate that."

For a moment we stood there in uncomfortable silence, the busy hum of the nursing home a quiet backdrop. The hint of vulnerability in her eyes was raw, real, and it tugged at something deep and protective inside me. Best friend or not, I fought against the urge to kick his teeth in for putting that jaded look in her eyes.

After a beat, I cleared my throat, trying to lighten the mood. "You know, I'm still testing out nicknames for you," I said with a playful grin.

I was good at this—keeping things light and easy.

"Oh no," she groaned, rolling her eyes as we walked side by side toward my grandfather's room. "Do I even want to know?"

"Well, I'm open to suggestions, but I'm curious now," I said, tucking my hands in the pockets of my jeans. "You never did tell me what MJ stands for."

She hesitated, her cheeks flushing slightly. "It's, uh . . . Julep. My real name is Julep."

"Julep?" I repeated, testing the sound of it, letting it settle.

The name felt . . . right, fitting her in a way I couldn't fully explain. "That's a great name. Why doesn't anyone call you that?"

Her shoulder lifted. "My brothers thought it was funny

to call me 'Mint Julep' growing up, and it just stuck. Most people around here don't even know my real name."

"Do you like it?" I asked, genuinely intrigued.

"My name?" She laughed with a shrug. "Does it matter?"

My shoulders lifted to mirror hers. "It does to me."

MJ stared at me before smiling. "I do like it."

I smiled, a decision forming quietly in my mind. "Well, Julep," I said, letting the name linger with a sense of something just between us, "from now on, I think that's what I'll call you."

She blinked, surprised, her gaze flicking up to meet mine. "You don't have to . . . I mean . . ."

"It suits you," I replied softly, noting the faint hint of color in her cheeks. "Pure. No mixer."

She blushed again, and I found that I liked that shade of pink in her cheeks.

Though I didn't say it out loud, there was something about calling her by her real name that felt like a small honor, a privilege.

Her lips curved into a slight smile, a glimpse of the warmth she seemed to radiate from every pore.

The air between us settled into something easy, comfortable. I could still see the uncertainty lingering in her eyes, but there was also something else—a flicker of hope, maybe.

I wanted to nurture that, to see it grow.

Before I could stop myself, I cleared my throat. "I know this might sound like a terrible idea after the other night, but . . . would you still want to come to my next game? As friends. I promise the match will be a good one." I gave her a teasing smile, hoping to coax out that laughter I was coming to crave.

She hesitated, chewing on her bottom lip as she considered my offer. "I don't know if that's a good idea . . ."

"Come on," I coaxed, leaning in slightly. "We won two games. The team needs our lucky charm in the stands. They've been on a roll ever since you showed up. I don't think it's a coincidence."

She rolled her eyes, but I could see the hint of amusement there, the way her lips curved just slightly. "You're relentless."

"Only when I'm right," I replied, unable to stop the grin spreading across my face.

She sighed, looking like she was trying to convince herself more than me. "Fine. But only because I really like Maria. No expectations . . . as *friends*." She lifted a finger. "And no more sleepovers."

"Of course," I agreed, holding out my hand for her to shake. "No expectations."

If she noticed that I'd subtly left off the *no sleepovers* clause, she didn't let on.

MJ laughed, her shoulders relaxing, and the sound filled me with a strange sense of accomplishment.

If she wanted to be friends, I could do that. I was a fantastic fucking friend.

∽

Thankfully, the next game was in Central Michigan, so MJ only had a forty-five-minute drive before she arrived.

Before the game started, I couldn't help but search the stands until I spotted her, tucked in the middle of the front row. Maria had taken her under her wing, and for that I was grateful. Maria's arms swung wide as she chatted with MJ, pointing to parts of the field or other players and laughing.

Just knowing she was there sent a jolt of energy through me, my focus sharper, my movements faster. Maybe Jack was right after all—something about having MJ at the game affected the energy on the field.

MJ really was becoming something of a lucky charm, and I wasn't about to question it. If having her in the stands gave me an edge, I'd fucking take it.

As the game started, MJ didn't seem to notice me looking at first. Her focus was on the field, eyes moving with the action, her hand coming up to her mouth in moments of tension.

I found myself sneaking glances at her whenever I could, drawn to her expressions, the way her lips curved when our team scored, or how her brows furrowed in concentration as she followed the game or leaned in to ask Maria something.

As the game went on, tension was high. I took a hit that sent a shock wave of pain down my left leg. I staggered, pulling myself back up, and as I steadied, my gaze drifted toward the sidelines. There she was, her eyes wide with worry, her hand almost reaching out as if she wanted to pull me from the field.

Our eyes met, and in that moment her concern felt like a balm to the ache radiating from my knee. She gave me a quick, reassuring nod.

Somehow that small gesture grounded me, eased the pain, and gave me the push to keep going.

Fueled by her presence, I threw myself into the game with renewed determination. Every pass, every move, felt sharper, more purposeful, and by the time we scored the final points, sealing our victory, I knew that part of that win was hers.

After the match, I made my way over to her, ignoring

the soreness pulsing in my leg. She was waiting by the sidelines, her arms crossed but her eyes filled with relief as she watched me approach.

"You okay?" she asked, her voice soft but laced with genuine worry.

"Just a bump," I assured her, grinning. "Nothing I can't handle."

She didn't look convinced, her brows pinching together as her gaze flicked to my knee. "Looked like more than just a bump from where I was sitting."

Her concern stirred something inside me, and I found myself reaching out, resting a hand on the wall between us. "I've got my lucky charm here. What could go wrong?"

"You're an idiot." She rolled her eyes, but I caught the faintest trace of a smile as she glanced up at me. A faint mixture of guilt and satisfaction rolled over me. I *was* an idiot on the field sometimes—you couldn't get the rewards without a little risk. Still, there was something about her genuine concern that lit a fire in my gut.

For a moment it was just the two of us, standing close, the sounds of the crowd fading into the background.

"Thanks, Julep," I said, letting her real name slip off my tongue, savoring the sound of it. "For coming today. I know you didn't have to."

She looked down, her cheeks tinged pink. "Yeah, well . . . I like Maria. Plus, it's for the team, right?"

"Of course," I said with a grin. Though, really, I wasn't sharing her with anyone. If MJ was anyone's lucky charm, she was *mine*.

As I walked toward the locker room, I rubbed the little achy spot that bloomed in the center of my chest.

Goddamn.

TWELVE

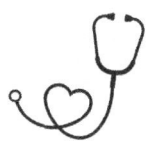

MJ

I SAT at the large picture window of the Sugar Bowl, enjoying my steaming cup of peppermint tea and daydreaming about a particular hot, sweaty rugby player, when Annie's wild red curls came into view.

After she saw me, her blue eyes lit up and she waved. Her face twisted into crossed eyes and puffed cheeks, pulling a hearty laugh from my chest.

The bell clanked against the glass door as she entered, and I stood to greet her with a hug.

"Hey, stranger!" She squeezed me tight. "Feeling any better?" Annie smiled and perched herself atop the high stool beside mine.

I held the white ceramic tea mug and let it warm my hands. After my not-so-graceful exit at the Grudge, I was so embarrassed that I'd gone dark and ignored their calls and only texted to reassure them that I was fine.

Annie and I had become close over the last couple of years, and I had confided in her how hurt I'd been after what Trent had done. She knew that sometimes I struggled, even now, to trust again when it came to dating.

But I was the cheerful one—always quick with a joke or a kind word. I didn't need my friends to start worrying about *me*.

The sooner I fessed up to what I was feeling, the sooner we could talk about something—and someone—*else*. "Hey, I'm really sorry about ditching you guys the other night."

Her hand found my back as she rubbed. "We were just worried, that's all. Are you sure you're okay? Just tell me if we're supposed to hate him and I will."

"Thanks. You're a girl's girl, you know that?" I leaned into her. "No, it turns out that Logan not only *knows* Trent, but is his best friend."

Her eyes went wide. "Oh, shit . . ."

I shrugged. "What are the odds, right?" I pressed a hand to my chest. "If you're me, pretty good, apparently."

Annie frowned as I watched her try to wrap her mind around it.

I shook my head. "It's fine. There was really nothing between Logan and me anyway."

Her eyes sliced to me. "MJ . . . it's okay to admit that you kind of liked him. It's okay to be disappointed. Besides, who knows . . . maybe it doesn't matter at all that he knows Trent. No expectations, no heartbreak, remember?"

No expectations, no heartbreak.

I repeated her words like a mantra. "I promise, it's fine. We had a few flirty moments, that's all. I think I just liked the *possibility* of him. I doubt very much he'll be interested in dating his best friend's ex-girlfriend. I think there's a bro code about that or something. Besides, I don't even know how *I* feel about it. It all suddenly seems . . . gross. We agreed that being friends is best."

Annie nodded in solidarity. "I get it. But maybe this was

a good thing. Maybe it means you're ready for something more."

I sat quietly and nodded. Logan was nothing like Trent . . . but that was the problem. He was better. And that made this whole thing feel even more dangerous.

"Bummer about those thighs, though . . . what a waste." Annie sighed, and I couldn't help but laugh.

"I'll cheers to that." I lifted my cup and took a sip of tea, letting its warmth spread across my chest.

"I think the next time you see him, make sure *he's* the one who's flustered." My brow pinched down so she continued. "Next time you see Rugby Jesus, just flip your hair and pretend like he doesn't exist. His ego won't know what hit him."

I cackled, drawing curious looks from patrons at the bakery. My hand clamped over my mouth as I giggled. "You're ridiculous."

Annie only winked and bumped her shoulder to mine. "All right, let's go."

I swallowed the last bit of my peppermint tea. "Go? Where to?"

Her hand slapped the white countertop as she hopped down from her stool. "I'm kidnapping you."

I shook my head. Annie was always full of mischief. "Kidnapping me?"

She stood and tucked in the stool. "Yes, I'm kidnapping you. Lee is finishing up his shift at the fire station. And you already said you weren't working today."

I looked at my empty cup. "Don't *you* have a job?" I teased, hoping she wouldn't pick up on the fact I was still in the middle of a self-pity party.

Annie folded her arms. "I'm an artist and an entrepreneur. I make my own hours. Plus, my muse is a fickle bitch, and right now she's telling me that my next art project is *you.*"

My face twisted. "Me?"

Annie grinned and flipped her curly red hair over one shoulder. "Okay, in fairness, I did watch *The Princess Diaries* last night." She exhaled a wistful sigh. "It has an incredible makeover scene, and I am dying to re-create it."

I fought a smile. "And you didn't think to make over yourself?"

She blew a raspberry with her lips. "Myself? Well, that's no fun." Annie's lips rolled as excitement buzzed through her body.

My eyes narrowed on my friend. "There's something else, isn't there?"

Annie squealed like whatever secret she was keeping came clawing out of her. "Okay, fine. I was also hoping you might go on a double date with Lee and me."

"A double date?" My eyes widened.

Logan's handsome face flashed in my mind. Sure, I was itching to try on this new bad-girl persona, and we'd agreed to *just friends* . . . but I also had zero desire to get set up with another man right now.

I shook my head. "No way, not a chance, Annie. I know all about the blind dates you set Lee up on."

Annie tossed her head back and cackled. "This is totally different. Kenny is a fun guy. I actually want you to be happy."

I pouted at the insinuation. "I am happy," I countered.
Right?
It wasn't really a lie. I mean, I was *mostly* happy.
Annie was practically dancing out of her skin.
I exhaled. "There's no way I'm getting out of this, is there?"

Annie's lips folded in as she shook her head. "Nope."

I tilted my face to the ceiling and let out an audible groan before looking down at my crew neck sweatshirt and jeans.

"And what's wrong with dating me just the way I am?" I asked.

Annie grinned, probably because she knew I was seconds away from caving. "Absolutely nothing. I'm just also looking for an excuse to go shopping. It's a win-win."

Annie's blue eyes went big and round. "Please," she pleaded.

Agreeing would make Annie happy, and that tugged at me.

It's one stupid date. It doesn't have to mean anything other than a night out of the house.

I huffed and held up one finger. "Fine. *One* dinner."

Annie clapped. "Eek! Okay, let's go."

∽

I STARED at my reflection in the dressing room mirror. The skirt was too tight and the top was cut way, *way* too low. "Remind me again why I agreed to this?"

From behind the curtain, Annie said, "Because you love me. Also, I thought a lot about what you said the other night."

I laughed, looking myself over. "You mean the part where I screamed *I know my way around a dick* in the middle of the Grudge?"

God, how many times had I replayed that scene in my head? *Me and my ridiculous mouth.*

Annie laughed. "Exactly. You're entering your Hot Girl Era." Her arm thrust through the curtain, holding an olive-green dress. "Try this. And," she continued, "because fuck Trent *floppy dick* Fischer and every one of his hot, rugby-playing friends. You're better than that."

I bristled at the mild insult toward Logan, though I couldn't help but laugh at her nickname for my ex. Typically I opted for being the bigger person and used colorful insults only in my mind. To be honest, it was a bit of a relief to share my hatred with someone else.

I slipped out of the clothes and looked at myself in the mirror. Part one of *MJ's Magical Makeover* was a brand-new, matching set of bra and panties. Annie had insisted that the secret to feeling flawless in any outfit was a pretty set of matching underwear.

I stared at the lacy, orchid-purple undergarments I had chosen. The memory of Logan telling me my purple sweater looked good on me and that purple was his new favorite color had drawn me to this particular set.

Why do I even care that purple was his favorite? Stupid brain. He probably exudes superhuman pheromones or something.

The bra cut low across my breasts, propping them up, and the see-through lace was delicate and feminine. The matching French-cut panties had a lacy edge that made my ass look fuller and sexier than it was.

It was impossible to deny—Annie had a point about matching underwear.

With a smile, I slipped into the olive-green dress. It hugged my curves and scooped low enough to be sexy, but not too revealing. I turned to see what it looked like from behind.

Huh. Not half bad.

With a pair of tights and some cute boots, I could definitely pull this off.

Annie handed me yet another outfit—this time it was a gray oversize cashmere cardigan and black leather pants.

"We said one dinner. Why do I need all this stuff?" I slipped off the olive dress and eyeballed the cropped leather pants.

Annie poked her head between the curtains of my dressing room, and my hands immediately crossed over my chest.

"Retail therapy." She disappeared again and I exhaled.

Well, I had been in actual therapy for as long as I could remember, so I doubted therapy of the retail variety could do any harm.

With a deep breath, I tugged on the pants and slipped on the cardigan. It was the softest material I'd ever worn. A small smile lifted at the corner of my mouth as I looked at my reflection.

"You're awfully quiet in there," Annie called. "Let's see it."

With a grin, I pulled open the dressing room curtain and turned.

Annie clapped once. "Hot damn! That's definitely it." She stepped forward, adjusting the neckline so it clung dangerously close to the edge of my shoulder and unbuttoned the top button of the cardigan. "Tuck in the front?" Her artist's brain was whirring as she examined me, and I did as I was told. Annie sighed. "It's *perfection*."

When I looked over my shoulder in the mirror, I couldn't help but smile. It *was* perfect. The outfit was chic and edgy but, somehow, still *me*.

My heart raced. No one could look at me and think *little sister*.

I still hated that Logan kept popping into my mind. I

also hated that Annie was trying to set me up, but I could be what she needed me to be for a single dinner.

I was good at being who people needed me to be.

With a smile, I looked at Annie and hoped I sounded genuine, despite wanting nothing to do with her setup. I sighed. "So tell me a little more about Kenny."

∼

Twirling Fox was a brand-new ramen restaurant that had opened over the summer on the outskirts of Outta-towner. I hadn't had the opportunity to try it out, so dinner with Annie, Lee, and Kenny was as good a time as any.

Sadly, the tonkotsu ramen was the only drool-worthy part of the evening.

Sure, Kenny was conventionally attractive with his swooping blond hair and devilish grin. He was handsome, but *boy* did he know it. He was also the funniest person in the room—don't worry, he'd tell you.

Call me too picky, but from the moment I met Kenny, I knew there wouldn't be anything beyond this pathetic setup.

He was too brazen.

Too loud.

Too . . . *young.*

My mind immediately caught on the memory of the tiny streaks of gray hair that were forming at Logan's temples. I wondered if he even knew they were there or if they bothered him.

They certainly *bothered* me, but not in the way they should.

I shook away the thought. Kenny was *my* age. It was ridiculous to think he was too young for me.

Still, I couldn't deny that there wasn't even the tiniest heart palpitation. When it came to Kenny, I was flatlining. Biting the dust. DOA.

Bad girl or not, I needed to feel *something*, even if I was planning to keep any potential relationship casual.

"Am I right?" Kenny's gentle nudge thrust me into the present. I looked around, having no idea what we were supposed to be talking about.

I hummed and nodded, hoping that was an appropriate response to whatever tale he was telling, and took a hearty bite of ramen so I didn't have to talk again.

"But you've talked to him, right?" Kenny nodded expectantly as I stared, struggling to catch up. "Logan Brown." Kenny shook his head and laughed. "It's so cool there's a gold medal Olympian in our midst."

I could feel my ears get hot as I swallowed. "Oh, uh . . . yes. His grandfather lives at Haven Pines, where I work." I looked to Annie for help.

She gently cleared her throat and tried to divert the conversation. "So, Kenny, why don't you tell MJ about the award you received. Chief's Company is a big deal."

Pride swelled in his chest as he droned on about the prestigious award he'd been given. As a firefighter, Chief's Company was a hand-selected group of men and women who received the honorary titles as a reflection of exemplary service.

I forced a smile. "The best of the best," I said. "Impressive."

Kenny leaned over, draping his arm casually on the back of my chair. His fingertips brushed against the exposed area at the back of my neck, and I wanted to crawl out of my skin.

"I'm glad you think so." His voice dipped low, and I

fought the urge to instantly recoil. "Most women can't resist a man in uniform."

I stifled a gag. *Uniforms are great—especially if they come with the ability to stop talking.*

I cleared my throat and placed my napkin on the table. "If you'll excuse me, I need to use the ladies' room."

I stood and glanced at Annie. Her brows were up as she nodded, as if to ask, *Need me to come too?*

I smiled at her and jerked my head, silently letting her know that I was fine. I pushed my chair in and excused myself.

When I turned, I was stunned into place by Logan's hard, assessing eyes. He was sitting across from a man who, from the back, looked like Wyatt Sullivan, but Logan's attention was pinned on me. His expression was anything but friendly. A hard line formed between his brows, and my stomach jumped.

The weight of his stare settled on me like a challenge, daring me to look away first. My cheeks betrayed me, heating under his gaze, but I lifted my chin higher.

I'd win this round.

I held his stare as I walked across the crowded restaurant toward the bathrooms in the back. I didn't break eye contact until I sailed past him and disappeared into the ladies' room.

I braced myself at the sink and took a deep breath. Logan's stare had been intense and mildly angry.

Why was that so fucking hot? Why did one look from him make me feel like I was teetering on the edge of something I couldn't control?

I checked my makeup and readjusted the cardigan to make sure it was placed exactly like Annie had told me to wear it. My lipstick had all but disappeared while I ate, so I touched it up before fluffing the soft curls in my hair.

After a reassuring breath, I determined I'd let my hips swing, just a tiny bit as I walked past Logan again. With a sly smile, I exited the bathroom and came to a screeching halt.

Logan was in the dimly lit corridor with his arms crossed and a pissed-off look on his face.

I lifted my chin. "Hey, Logan," I greeted.

"Who's the dickbag?" His voice rumbled across me, and a hum fluttered low in my belly.

The heat in Logan's eyes sent my pulse skittering, but I forced myself to remember our agreement.

Friends. Just friends.

Even if his intensity was starting to unravel every bit of resolve I had.

My nose crinkled. "Kenny? He's Lee's friend—Annie's attempt at matchmaking." I flicked my hair over my shoulder to settle my nerves. "He's nice."

Tension narrowed the corridor between us. "Nice doesn't put that look in your eye."

I scoffed and crossed my arms, trying to erase whatever look Logan thought he saw. "And what look is that?"

One eyebrow crept up his forehead. "Like you're trying not to laugh every time he opens his mouth."

A smile twitched at the corner of my lips. He wasn't entirely wrong.

Logan's eyes landed on my collarbone, hovering there before they moved across my shoulder and up my neck to meet my eyes.

"He's nice enough for you to get cozy with, I noticed." Annoyance simmered on the edge of his words.

I bit back my own annoyed response. Logan Brown

didn't have the right to act jealous. Not when pursuing something with his best friend's ex was completely off-limits *and* we had just agreed to keep things platonic.

"I should get back." I had stepped past him when his hand caught the crook of my elbow. Instead of dropping it, his fingers slid around, encircling my arm.

His grip wasn't rough, but it held me in place, and his eyes burned with something I couldn't name. Was it jealousy? Possessiveness? Whatever it was, it sent an infuriating shiver up my spine.

His hand was warm, firm, and for a moment I forgot how to breathe. My body leaned into his touch before my brain kicked in and alarm bells blared.

His voice was dark. Intimate. "I have another game coming up. I could use a little luck."

And there it is.

It wasn't attraction. It was his ridiculous hunch that I was somehow lucky to the team.

I pulled my arm from his grasp. "I need to get back." Anger crept into my voice. I walked away, and my hips swayed as I left him in the dark hallway. I paused and looked at him over my bare shoulder. "I'll think about it."

I'd think about it, sure. And while I was thinking, I would pretend that the heat of his stare wasn't still burning holes in the back of my cardigan.

THIRTEEN

LOGAN

I WAS LOSING my goddamn mind.

My hands scrubbed across my face as I watched MJ saunter back to Kenny the Close Talker.

Man, fuck that guy.

Every time Kenny leaned closer, my fists clenched tighter. He had no idea how far out of his league he was. And he sure as hell didn't deserve her attention.

I watched MJ like an unhinged stalker until she sat at the table. When she scooted her chair ever so slightly away from Kenny, I grinned.

Good girl.

Wyatt was waiting for me when I returned to our table. He watched me closely, and I wondered if he caught on to the fact that I'd all but chased after MJ King and cornered her in a dark hallway.

"Sorry about that," I said, clearing my throat. "Where were we?"

If Wyatt had noticed, he didn't let on. "My senior running back Seth won't shut up about you. I think that pickup game on the beach altered his brain chemistry."

I chuckled. "They were good kids. I was surprised he even knew who I was, to be honest."

Wyatt lifted a shoulder. "You're a big name, and not just in this small town. A lot of people will be watching what you do once you transition out of the sport."

"Out?" I sat straighter. "What do you mean by *out*?"

His hands rose. "I didn't mean any offense. I'm sure you've got a lot of solid years ahead of you . . . but I know from experience that it pays to start thinking about what comes next."

Next?

The only thing I needed to focus on *next* was the upcoming match. I couldn't get into my own head about the upcoming season, let alone retirement.

Wyatt nodded as if he knew exactly what was running through my mind. He had been an NFL quarterback, so maybe he knew a little about how I was feeling.

Didn't mean I had to like it. The truth was, I didn't let myself think about it too hard, because rugby was all I knew. There was never a plan B.

My jaw tightened. My eyes flicked to MJ, and my annoyance multiplied.

Our server quietly placed the black server book on the table, and I swiped it. "I got it," I said to Wyatt as he reached for his wallet.

He held out his hand. "I asked you to this dinner. I'm paying."

I flipped my credit card into the black leather folder and balanced it on the edge of the table. "Not a chance. Although you never did get to the point."

Wyatt laughed. "I tried. All I am saying is if you're looking for something beyond rugby one day, call me. The football program at MMU could use a coach like you. They could learn a lot."

I scoffed and sat back. "Coaching? Football?" It was ludicrous. "While I appreciate your faith in me, that's never going to happen."

Wyatt and I stood and he offered his hand, his grin easy but his tone firm. "There are all kinds of ways to stay in the game, man. You don't have to hang up your cleats completely. Hell, you've probably got a dozen ideas already."

I let out a dry laugh.

"You've got time to figure it out. Just never say never, my friend. Take it from someone who lived it—one day, you'll want to be part of something that lasts longer than a season. Coaching could be that thing."

We shook and Wyatt left the table. I glanced over to where MJ had been sitting with Annie, Lee, and Captain Creeper. Their table was empty.

My attention flew to just beyond the restaurant window. MJ was bundled up against the cold fall air, and my vision narrowed in on the way Kenny's hand ran dangerously close to her ass.

That hand had no business being anywhere near her, and every nerve in my body screamed to do something about it. Kenny didn't deserve to be near her—not when I could tell she was just being polite.

My molars ground together as they disappeared down the sidewalk.

The server processed our check at the table, and I quickly signed the slip before tucking the credit card back into my wallet.

I hated thinking about what may come after my rugby career ended—almost as much as I hated not knowing if MJ was headed home or if the group would extend their date after dinner.

The thought gnawed at me.

My feet were moving before I could talk myself out of it. I exited the restaurant, looking around the sidewalk to see whether I could spot their group. When I couldn't, I immediately headed in the direction of her house.

Sure, I'd subtly coerced my grandfather to confirm that she lived at the King estate.

That wasn't creepy at all.

And checking up on her was simply to make sure she'd gotten home safely.

Besides, it was what a friend would do.

MJ and her friends had left before me, and I circled the block but didn't see any cars I recognized at the Grudge.

Shit. Maybe he'd taken her straight home.

I broke nearly every speed limit on the drive to the King estate. The long, winding driveway was dark, but I pressed on. Finally, the mansion came into view, and it took my breath away. The house was opulent and oppressive. It screamed *ostentatious* in a way that was at odds with how down to earth MJ was.

I parked with a screeching halt, just as Kenny was approaching his car.

I exited my car, and his eyes went wide. "No shit. Logan Brown? Oh, man."

He held out his hand, and I gripped his with far more force than necessary. I didn't like this guy from the moment I saw him, and his cocky grin didn't help.

"Great to meet you, man." He looked back at MJ's house. "What are you doing here?"

I didn't answer but just stared.

"Uh, well . . ." he stammered. "You were amazing in the

Olympics—a real killer on the field. Think I can get an autograph?"

My voice was hard. "No."

He blinked at me. I had no idea why I was being such a prick, but I wasn't about to give him a goddamn autograph after I had to watch him paw at MJ all evening.

I stepped forward. "Listen to me. That girl in there . . ." I pointed over his shoulder to the house. "If I find out you hurt her, you make her uncomfortable, you so much as make her a little bit sad, you'll be answering to me."

Kenny took a step back. "Chill, bro. I was hoping for an easy lay, but she's practically frigid. I didn't touch her—not that she'd be worth the effort."

My fists clenched, and a low growl formed in my throat. "Get in your car—*now*—and get the fuck out of here. *Bro.*"

With a confused eye roll, Kenny disappeared into his car. I didn't bother watching him leave and instead took the front steps to MJ's house two at a time.

My fist pounded on the door to her home.

"Kenny, I—" MJ swung open the massive oak door, and the annoyed words died on her tongue. She blinked once. "What are you doing here?"

I crossed my arms. "How was your date, Julep?"

Her eyes narrowed on me as she crossed her arms and leaned against the doorway. Her gray cardigan slipped over one shoulder as her tits were pushed higher, and it made it impossible to think clearly. My eyes betrayed me, flicking to the curve of her collarbone, the soft rise of her chest. The thin fabric did fuck-all to hide the fact that her nipples were hard and pressing against the soft fabric.

Taunting me.

Goddamn it, Julep.

"What are you, jealous?" she asked with a snort, and the

question immediately pissed me off. "Because if you're going to play caveman, at least commit to the role and grunt or something."

Of course I was jealous.

I knew I had absolutely no right to be. MJ had dated my best friend, and there was clearly some history there. Not to mention she was a distraction of the worst kind—the *tempting* kind. The kind of distraction that made you forget all the years you'd worked, and suddenly you'd be happy to throw it all away just to see her smile every morning.

I ground my teeth together, refusing to answer her question.

Her eyes rolled because she could sense I was acting like a child.

"My dinner is none of your business, Logan." She straightened, ready to shut the door on my face.

Anger and frustration coursed through me. The woman in front of me was goddamn infuriating. My hand planted on the door, not letting her get away so easily.

She sighed. "What? You have a big important match coming up and you need a little lucky mojo?" Her words dripped with sarcasm. She shoved an arm in my direction. "Here. Rub my arm for good luck or whatever it is you think you need from me."

My brows furrowed. She had no clue what this was about. Hell, neither did I.

When I didn't make a move, MJ shook her head with a laugh. "Okay, good night, Logan." She pushed the door closed, and a pit opened in my stomach.

I should've left. That was what a sane man would do. But as I stared at the closed door, the thought of walking away felt impossible. Like losing a game I hadn't even started playing.

Oh, hell no.

My fist rose as I pounded on the door.

The door didn't move. My fist hit harder this time, rattling the heavy oak. "Julep," I said, my voice low and firm.

I wasn't leaving until she opened this goddamn door.

FOURTEEN

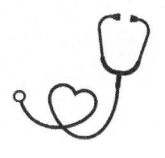

MJ

The butterflies in my stomach jumped when his fist landed hard against the thick oak door. I stifled a yelp and shook out my hands. I should have let him knock himself out and walk away. But the sound of his voice, the force behind it, had every nerve in my body sparking like a live wire.

I wanted to tell him to leave. I wanted him to stay. Hell, I didn't know what I wanted, except maybe him.

"Julep." His voice was frustrated. Raw, it danced over my skin, making the need in my stomach coil.

I was annoyed with him. Frustrated with the universe over the fact that he was completely off-limits thanks to my scumbag ex. Hurt by the reality that his interest stemmed from a superstitious need to win at rugby.

Logan Brown was temptation personified—a walking contradiction to everything I thought I wanted. He was trouble, wrapped in a charming, dimpled grin and a body that could make even the most composed woman forget herself. And yet here I was, teetering on the edge of giving in, knowing I could get hurt all over again.

All of the pent-up frustrations simmered beneath my skin and bubbled to the surface.

I could yell at him or lose myself beneath him. For the first time in years, the idea of being touched—really touched—didn't send me spiraling into anxiety. With Logan, it wasn't just about lust—it was about control. I wanted him, yes, but I also wanted to own that moment, to claim it for myself.

The shocking, primal image of him hovering over me, pressing himself between my thighs, had my temperature skyrocketing. Something about Logan made me feel powerful.

Alive.

Protected.

His knuckles pounded on the door again.

Bracing myself, I yanked open the door and set my jaw, ready to fight.

The sight of him took the air from my lungs. His jaw was tight, his chest rising and falling like he'd run a marathon, and his eyes—*god, those eyes*—pinned me in place. For a second, neither of us moved, the space between us electric, a thousand unsaid words hovering in the air.

He stared at me like no man had ever stared before. His hair was wild, like he'd run his fingers through it too many times. His eyes were intense, hard green orbs that bore into mine.

Based on his tone, I thought I would see frustration, jealousy, or irritation. Instead, staring back at me was something I'd never seen before. Logan looked like a man who was about to snap, if only I spoke the word.

Yes.

His dark brows were heavy and straight. His chest rose and fell with the same shallow breaths as my own. His broad shoulders were firm and set. One arm propped on the doorway, exposing the long, bulky muscles in his biceps and forearm.

His body was a fine-tuned, athletic machine, and all I could think about was how he could use it . . . *on me.*

If I let my feelings get involved, Logan Brown would ruin me, especially if I gave in to the clawing need growing inside me. Long seconds stretched between us as we stared, both unwilling to cross some invisible divide between us.

His eyes were dark in the dim lighting, and his face was unreadable. I was confused and horny, and entirely pissed off about it.

Hell, he was the one who'd come pounding on *my* front door.

I lifted my chin, praying my voice didn't betray me. "Are you done here?"

"No, we are not done here. I'm not going to let you walk away just because you're scared."

His words rang too close to the truth, and I steeled my expression.

"Do I think you bring me luck? Yes, I do. But that isn't why I came here. I watched you on a date all night." He paused, his jaw tightening as if the words were harder to admit than he wanted to let on. "I didn't like it. Watching him touch you, even just being near you . . . you're not his to have."

He had watched me.

A sick thrill danced up my spine.

"I came here to make sure you were okay," he continued. "I came here to see with my own eyes that you walked inside that house *alone.*" Logan jabbed a finger at the house behind me.

Intensity rolled off him, and heat flooded my cheeks.

"Thank you for your concern." I swallowed hard, unsure what would come next. "I'm home and I'm fine."

Logan stepped forward, crowding my space until I could feel the heat pumping off him. "Tell me to leave." His voice was a low growl that sent the butterflies fluttering in my chest. "Tell me to get in my car and drive away."

Tension was obvious in his neck and jaw. I stared up at him, his frame towering over me. He made no move to reach for me, but when his eyes dropped to my mouth, all thoughts of wanting to be friends with Logan Brown evaporated.

Maybe I really could do this—enjoy him while he's here. No expectations, no heartbreak.

"I think I have a better idea." I stepped forward as his eyes held mine. My heart was racing, my skin burning, but it wasn't fear. It was something exciting and unfamiliar, a need so powerful it eclipsed my doubts. For once, I wanted to stop thinking and just feel.

I didn't want to hold back or weigh the pros and cons of every decision. For once, I just wanted to feel—raw, unfiltered, and completely present. And Logan? He was the perfect storm I wanted to lose myself in.

"I want to try something." I gripped the collar of his shirt in my fist and pulled him forward.

His breath hitched as I pulled him to me, and for a heartbeat we just hovered there—so close I could feel the heat of his skin, the brush of his breath against my lips. Then his mouth crashed into mine, and every coherent thought evaporated in a wave of need as I arched into him.

Logan paused for half a second before his arm banded around my waist, lifting me from the ground and pressing my back hard against the doorjamb. His kiss was rough and demanding. I melted against him.

I moaned into his mouth as his tongue swept forward, sliding over mine. He tasted like mint and desire and *mine*.

He kissed like he knew what he was doing. Confident and sensual. I was certain he fucked like that too. There was no way a man like Logan didn't know how to please a woman. There'd be no fumbling. No uncertainty.

My leg hitched over his hip, silently begging for more. His hips ground into me, and fire burned low in my belly. The sheer clarity in my head was refreshing. The only thing I could think about was the fact that one hand was gripping my ass and the other was sliding up my neck.

With a rumble in his throat, Logan broke the kiss and pressed his forehead to mine. "Tell me to stop."

I shook my head, unable to speak through the fire burning through me. I kissed his neck, just beside his Adam's apple, and I felt it bob. I kissed again, letting my tongue taste his hot skin and feel his stubble.

"*Fuck*, if you keep doing that, I'm not going to be able to stop," he warned.

A low, dark giggle formed in the back of my throat. Part fear, part anticipation, a war waged inside me. He was too close. He felt too good.

For the first time in as long as I could remember, I wanted *more*.

I looked up at him. All I had to do was give in and he would push past my barriers. I could finally—*finally*—break past them.

His hand kneaded my ass while his brow furrowed. "Tell me. What's going on inside that pretty little head of yours?"

I shook my head, embarrassment clawing at my throat. My fingers tangled in his hair as I tried to deflect. "It's nothing. Don't stop touching me."

His hot breath fanned against my cheek as he set me on my feet. He lowered his gaze to look me in the eye. "I won't stop if you don't want me to, but you need to tell me how to make you feel okay with this. You set the pace."

His eyes searched mine, not with impatience but with a quiet intensity that melted some of my fear. His words wrapped around me like a warm blanket, grounding me in a way I hadn't expected.

My heart skittered. Without me having to express it, Logan understood something was a bit off.

"Kiss me," I said, licking my lips and begging him to keep touching me.

"Yes, ma'am." With a smirk, Logan lowered his mouth to mine. Softer and slower this time, he tasted and teased.

I moaned into him, pulling him deeper into the entryway and letting the door close behind us. The house was empty and dark. The warm wood beneath my bare feet grounded me in the moment, reminded me that I was standing in the foyer, making out with a man.

But not just any man. The man I'd lost sleep over. The man I'd fantasized about since we'd met. The man who could break my heart and shatter my trust all over again if I let my feelings get involved.

A man like him could get attention from any woman he wanted, and I had had sex only *once* in my life.

But stopping now would be pure torture.

"Hey," he said, moving his hands over my face. "Where'd you go?"

I swallowed hard. "In my head, I think."

"Stay with me." His voice was low and smooth. "Just keep talking. Tell me what you need."

What I need? A stiff drink and your stiff cock oughta do it.

His dick was hard against my stomach, and a fresh sizzle of electricity throbbed between my legs.

"Come with me." I turned, guiding him through the house toward my bedroom.

My aunt had gone away with friends on a fall foliage driving tour up to Traverse City, so I knew we'd be alone in the house.

Still, I sought the comfort of a closed door. A sanctuary where my mind couldn't get the best of me. Logan quietly followed behind, never breaking contact. His fingers tangled with mine, and his other hand stayed firmly planted at my hip. His lips brushed the top of my hair.

When we reached my bedroom, I turned on a small lamp at the bedside and sat at the edge of my bed. He stood, his thighs between my legs as I stared up at him.

"Tell me," he commanded.

I swallowed hard. *How the hell was I supposed to articulate what I wanted when the hard edge to his voice scrambled my insides?*

I leaned back, spreading my knees wider.

"Tell me," he said again as his hand moved up my thigh toward my waist.

Gathering my courage, my voice was soft. "I want you . . . whatever this is. But I need to go slow."

My eyes bounced between his, unsure if going slow would disappoint him or make him realize I wasn't worth the effort.

Instead, the corner of his mouth hooked up. "I like slow," he drawled.

"You do?" I asked, a bit wary and unsure.

Logan nodded. "Oh yeah. Slow is good."

My chest swelled, my tender, bruised heart about to burst. My hands shook as I unbuttoned my cardigan, but it wasn't from fear. It was something new, something thrilling. For the first time in years, I felt bold. I felt powerful. I wasn't just letting him see me—I was showing him who I was.

I allowed the fabric to gape open and expose the lacy purple bra beneath it.

His eyes latched onto my breasts. "You are full of surprises, Julep."

Julep. Somehow Logan insisting on calling me by my name felt special.

Intimate.

A hot blush crept over my cheeks. "It's new."

He hovered over me and nipped at my lower lip. "I hope you weren't thinking of showing it off to anyone else," he teased.

My head shook, and a sly smile took over my face. "You said you liked purple, remember?"

Logan gave me a wicked grin, and his dimple flashed, causing my pussy to clench desperately around nothing.

His body moved over me as he cupped my breast, his thumb stroking my taut nipple. "I like purple on *you*."

His fingers moved to the button of my leather pants, but stopped. His eyes met mine, waiting.

"Yes," I answered.

Logan undid the button and slowly pulled down the zipper.

Every touch, every kiss, was a revelation. For the first time, I didn't feel small or unsure. I felt bold, desired, and utterly in control. Logan wasn't just taking from me—he was giving, building me up with every whispered word.

I shimmied as he removed the pants and discarded them on the floor. His attention landed on the space between my legs, where my matching lacy underwear had been wedged between my pussy lips.

A tiny part of me wanted to shy away, but his gaze was intense. Comforting.

There was something powerful about being on display for him. Logan *liked* what he saw.

My knees opened farther.

His fingertips brushed over one breast, down my stomach, and across my pussy. His fingers brushed my skin like fire, sending sparks dancing across every nerve ending. The room felt hotter, the air thicker, and every thought I'd clung to dissolved under the weight of his touch. My hips moved on their own, begging for more pressure.

"I want to taste you." Logan licked his lips as he adjusted himself. His hands gripped my hips, kneading the flesh as he waited for my answer. "Do you want that?"

My brain scrambled. Nerves tickled my belly. "I—you don't have to. I know guys don't like that."

"Julep, I don't know what kind of loser boys you've been with, but *men*? We love it. I love it. Let me show you."

My teeth pressed into my lip as I watched Logan lower to his knees.

"I've never . . . done that before." *God, it was so embarrassing to admit that out loud.*

His eyes met mine as his strong hands gripped my hips and pulled me to the edge of the bed. Hooking his fingertips into the band of my underwear, he slid the lace down my thighs.

I sat, propped on my hands, watching him as he pulled off my underwear. His hands ran back up my thighs, and he brushed his fingertips across my bare pussy.

"If you let me, I'm going to enjoy every second of this."

His fingers slid between my lips, testing and teasing. "I promise I'll take good care of you."

Desire took over and I fell to my back, opening for him.

"Goddamn, you're wet for me. Do you like when I play with you?" His thumb circled my clit, and I nearly rose off the bed.

"Yes. *Please.*" He'd barely touched me, and I was already begging.

"Do you want more?" he asked, not going any further until I answered him.

"Yes. Oh my god, yes."

With a rumbling chuckle, Logan slipped one finger inside me. Pressure built, low and fast. It had been *ages* since I'd fooled around with anyone—so long that I forgot how different it felt to be touched by something other than my vibrator.

His fingers were thick and stretched me as he stroked in and out.

"More," I begged. My voice was quiet and raw.

Logan's breath was warm on my skin. He lowered his mouth, dragging the flat of his tongue against my pussy as he fingered me.

I squeezed my eyes closed as my hips moved against his mouth. His hand braced on my thighs, pushing my legs apart as he dropped his head between my legs. His tongue found and exploited every inch of sensitive skin, my body galloping closer to orgasm.

My thighs trembled, my belly hollowed.

When his tongue curled around my clit, I nearly dissolved on the spot.

"Logan," I whispered.

"Yes, baby. Tell me."

I wanted to tell him to fuck me. Flip me over and give

me all of himself, but, *damn it*, his mouth and hands felt too good.

"I'm close." It was the only two words my scrambled brain could pull together.

"Good," he answered. "When you come, I'm going to taste it—" He worked his mouth on me between words. "I want every fucking drop."

His words were lewd, and something feral and feminine blossomed inside me.

I was drunk on the power he gave me.

I wasn't afraid. I was protected. *Safe*.

The world narrowed to the points of contact between us—his lips, his fingers, his voice coaxing me higher and higher. I wasn't afraid anymore. I was flying, shattering, and when I finally broke apart, it wasn't just pleasure that coursed through me—it was freedom.

His voice rumbled across my skin. "Tell me what you want, Julep." His lips brushed against my ear. "All of it. Tell me you want to come."

FIFTEEN

LOGAN

"Yes."

That single word was enough to snap the last thread of my self-control. It wasn't just her answer—it was the confidence behind it. The way she owned her desires, like she was finally realizing how powerful she could be.

I could tell MJ was nervous. It was clear, based on what she'd shared, that she was a little inexperienced. Whatever fumbling assholes she had been with didn't matter.

I could show her how a woman deserved to be treated.

Every question was my way of checking for consent. Monitoring how comfortable she was with what we were doing.

Sure, I would have loved to slam into her, bending her in half and driving her into the headboard. I wanted to bury myself in her, to claim her in every way a man could. But this wasn't about me. Tonight was about showing her that she was worth every ounce of restraint, every second of waiting.

Right now, she needed slow . . . and I was a patient man.

My cock ached in protest.

I knew what she wanted and I could give it to her. My possessive streak had roared to life, and all that mattered was her pleasure. Her safety in that moment.

There'd be a time and place for making her scream my name as my cock drove into her. The urge to help her give in to the relief of an orgasm rippled through me.

Every nerve in my body was screaming to take her, to bury myself inside her heat and lose myself. But I held back, the ache of wanting her dulled by the need to prove she deserved more than just being fucked.

She deserved to be worshipped.

I feasted on her, and my thumb circled her clit, adding pressure as her thighs squeezed the sides of my face. Her hand tugged at my hair as she cried out my name.

"Yes," she sobbed as her pussy fluttered around my tongue. As promised, I lapped up every bit of her, enjoying every second of her orgasm.

Her body trembled beneath my hands, and I slowed my movements, giving her space to process every touch. I wasn't just watching her—I was learning her, listening to every unspoken cue.

I glanced up, appreciating the view as she lay on her back, panting.

Her chest rose and fell with shallow breaths, her skin flushed and glistening in the low light. She looked like a goddess—powerful and utterly unguarded. And I couldn't believe she was there with me, trusting me to give her this.

Her head lifted as I licked her taste from my mustache.

Her attention dropped to my mouth as her teeth sank into her bottom lip.

I smirked. "Do you want to taste yourself?"

Her eyes flew to mine as I stood. She scooted back on the bed, and I prowled over her.

MJ looked at my mouth again and nodded. I slowly lowered my mouth to hers, letting her experience how good she tasted.

We both moaned and I deepened the kiss, pressing my body into her. "You like how you taste?"

MJ smiled, a hint of embarrassment playing at the edges. "I like how I taste on you."

God, she was perfect—playful and sexy as hell.

It hit me like a punch to the gut that I wanted to be the only one who ever got to see her like this.

She tasted better than anything I could imagine. She was fucking perfect.

Satisfied, I rolled off her and exhaled. My cock pressed against the denim of my pants. Beside me, MJ propped herself up on her elbow. Her cardigan had disappeared, but her tits were still pushed up by that tiny little purple bra.

Her hand moved over my shirt and down to where my dick throbbed. The hesitation in her eyes was gone, replaced by something bold and sure. She was taking what she wanted, and I'd never been more willing to give someone everything they asked for.

When she moved to unbutton my pants, I gently caught her wrist. "It's okay," I assured her. "We don't have to."

She sucked in her bottom lip, and her eyes flicked to mine before lowering again. She was embarrassed, but I didn't entirely understand why.

Finally, she let go of the breath she was holding. "I still want to take things slowly—slow-ish, at least." She smiled as she undid the button and lowered my zipper. "But I do want this."

Her hand gripped me through my boxer briefs, and I sucked in a breath. "You can take from me whatever you want."

My cock. My heart. Fuck, I would have given MJ anything she asked for in that moment.

I watched her confidence build as the blush in her cheeks gave way to a sly smile. MJ slithered down until her face was beside my hips. Her bare ass was high and round in the air as she lowered my jeans and boxer briefs to free me.

I gripped the back of my collar and discarded my shirt in one pull, and she tossed my pants beside the bed.

"Holy shit," she breathed as she looked at my naked body. "You are unreal."

I flexed my abs, giving her the show she wanted, as pride stretched against my ribs. She grinned and gripped my length.

Her eyes whipped to mine. "I like when you talk me through it. Tell me what you like."

Jesus Christ, woman.

I brushed a strand of hair from her face. "I can do that."

Her smile grew.

"Open. Tongue out." I propped myself on the pillows to get a better look at her. She was on her knees, thighs pressed together, like she was begging for it.

I guided her head to my cock, gliding across her tongue into her warm, wet mouth. Her lips closed over me as she moaned. I felt like I was going to burst right there.

MJ may have seemed unsure of herself, but she knew what she was doing. Her other hand moved around me, squeezing me at the base while her mouth worked up and down my shaft. Her nipples, sharp points beneath soft purple lace, were begging to be pinched.

Her lips thinned as she took more of me, my cock stretching her mouth.

Fuck, how her pussy would stretch around me too.

Her head bobbed as she lathed her tongue around the head of my cock. She took more of me, further down her throat. I hissed a breath, willing my hips not to press deeper until she gagged.

Through gritted teeth, I commanded, "Eyes on me."

She obeyed, and I nearly came on the spot. I'd never experienced anything hotter than MJ staring up at me with her mouth full of my cock.

Her lips stretched around me, her wide, hazel eyes locked on mine. She was trusting me, giving herself over completely. The thought made my chest tighten even as the pleasure threatened to rip me apart.

When she gagged, MJ eased off me, a string of saliva still connecting us before she lowered again, stroking and bobbing on my cock.

"You're fucking perfect." I meant every word.

A tiny moan rattled in her throat as a curtain of hair fell into her face. I gently moved it away, but as soon as my hand touched her, she froze.

"I just want to see you, baby. You set the pace." I wanted to assure her that my hand on her head wasn't meant to startle her.

"You're doing so well." I could see her grin around my cock as she continued to work me. "Fuck, you're going to make me come."

She paused and looked up. "Tell me. Tell me when you're about to come."

"Where do you want it?" I asked as she brought me closer and closer to the edge. "Down your throat or across those perfect fucking tits?"

My control was threadbare, and the wet, sucking noises were almost too much.

"Tits," she answered.

MJ cupped my balls as she sucked, and it was game over.

In one quick move, I shifted, pressing her to the mattress and straddling her. With my hand wrapped around my cock, I stroked as she looked up at me with a sultry smile. Her hands pressed her breasts together and pinched her nipples as I erupted.

Hot, thick ropes of cum shot across her chest and up her neck. I groaned as I pumped out the last drops onto her gorgeous, flawless skin.

I was panting hard and braced myself on the headboard in front of me to keep the bulk of my weight off her.

Every muscle in my body relaxed, but my chest tightened all over again. It wasn't just the way she looked beneath me, flushed and messy and so fucking gorgeous—it was the way she made me feel.

Like I couldn't stop at just this, even if I wanted to.

A giggle shot out of her, and I looked down. She was radiant and irresistible.

"What's so funny?" I asked with a playful frown.

"You made a mess." Her soft laugh reassured me that she had enjoyed every second.

My fingers dipped into the cum on her chest, painting her—claiming her as mine.

My fingers stayed gentle as they wrapped around her delicate neck. "I'm just saying, you might need a tarp next time."

She smirked up at me, her hair splayed across the bed. "Next time? Confident, aren't you?"

I grinned. "Oh, there's definitely going to be a next time. Turns out I like making messes with you."

Before moving off her, I plopped a quick kiss on her mouth. "Stay in bed. I'll get you cleaned up."

Part of me wanted to take care of her while the other part was desperately trying to figure out why I not only wanted to take care of her but felt something dangerously close to a *need* to do so.

This was supposed to be simple. But every time I touched her, it felt less like something I wanted and more like something I needed. And that scared the hell out of me.

One thing I knew for certain: This thing with MJ King was dangerous, and I had no intention of stopping.

SIXTEEN

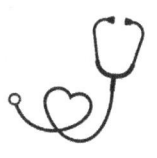

MJ

Lying on my side in bed, I stared at Logan.

My limbs were wonderfully numb. No man had ever made me orgasm before, and one hand-delivered by Logan Brown was absolutely earth-shattering.

I didn't know my body could feel this alive. Every nerve hummed like it had finally woken up, and it wasn't just the way he touched me, though that had been extraordinary. It was the way he looked at me—like I was more than the sum of my parts. Like I wasn't broken or hesitant, but whole.

Beautiful. Wanted. No one had ever made me feel like that before.

He didn't rush, didn't force it. He listened, read my cues, and perfectly delivered what I needed, wrapped in a tidy, mind-melting bow. Then he cleaned us up and wanted to cuddle.

The entire situation felt like a Hallmark fantasy come to life—if Hallmark included deliciously filthy mutual oral.

I laughed to myself. I still couldn't believe that Logan had followed me—after seeing me with Kenny, he had followed me home just to confront me. Maybe it was a big red flag, but I was quickly realizing that red may very well be my new favorite color.

I giggled at the thought.

I liked this new, unrestrained version of myself.

"What's so funny?" Logan brushed a loose strand of hair away from my face as he looked back at me.

"You," I admitted, searching his gorgeous green eyes. "I was just thinking about how grumpy you looked when you came pounding on my front door."

He frowned and my smile grew. "I just wanted to make sure you got home safe. That moron was pawing at you all through dinner."

"You were jealous," I teased and wrinkled my nose.

Logan's arm wrapped around my waist as he pulled me closer. His teeth nipped at my neck. "You're damn right I was jealous. I actually considered flipping the table."

"That would've been subtle." A giggle bubbled over as pleasure rippled through me.

His jealousy should have irritated me, but instead it made my heart flutter in a way I didn't know what to do with. It was probably a little toxic, but I liked the thought of him being jealous over *me*. It shouldn't even be possible. For a man like Logan Brown to care enough to be jealous—it was dangerous. Because it made me want more.

"He asked me for an autograph." His voice was laced with dark humor, quiet in the low lighting of my bedroom. "I almost punched him in the face."

I smiled. "I'm glad you didn't. Otherwise I would have had to pretend to be mad at you."

"Is he someone I need to take care of?" Logan asked.

I shook my head, silently liking this overly protective side of him. "No. Not at all. Dinner was awkward at best, and after I thanked him for the company and practically closed the door on his toes, I think he got the memo that I wasn't interested."

Logan inched closer. "I'm glad you didn't kick me out."

His arms were strong and warm, and I snuggled closer. "Me too."

"It turns out, you weren't lying . . ." His lips brushed the top of my head.

I adjusted so I could look at him. "Lying? About what?"

The corner of his mouth twitched. "About knowing your way around a dick."

Heat flooded my cheeks, and I buried my face in his chest with an embarrassed laugh. "Oh my god! Oh my god." I peeked up at him to see his eyes crinkled at the corners and a wide smile across his stupid face. "You heard that?"

A rumbling chuckle escaped him. "I'm pretty sure everyone at the Grudge heard you."

My hands flew to cover my face. "Nope. No, no, no, no, no." I playfully pushed at his chest. "Get out. You need to leave so I can die of embarrassment in peace."

He laughed and tightened his arms around me so I couldn't escape. "I'm not going anywhere. I'm still waiting to regain feeling in my legs."

I bit my lip to hide a proud smile. "It really was okay?"

His face twisted. *"Okay?* Hell, it was life-changing. You've ruined me forever."

I swallowed hard, struggling to find the right words. "I just didn't know if it was okay that we didn't . . . you know, go all the way."

"Hey," he soothed, his demeanor morphing from playful to serious. "I meant what I said. Slow is good. That way, if I ever do get to have you, I'll know I've earned you."

When he's earned me.

I liked the sound of that. There was honesty and safety in his words.

"Thank you," I whispered.

The energy in the room had shifted—from desperate need to playful banter to shy stillness.

I was well aware that I was out of my depth with Logan, but somehow he didn't make me feel bad for being less experienced. I felt empowered.

I closed my eyes and threw up a silent prayer that he genuinely meant the reassuring words he'd said.

Logan broke the silence by shifting topics entirely. "Hey, what do you have going on this weekend? Are you working?"

I mentally flipped through my calendar, though I knew exactly what was looming ahead of me. "I actually have to make a trip to Chicago. I'll be gone overnight."

"Oh, girl's night out in the city or something?" he asked.

I wish.

I shook my head. "It's a long story, but my father died. Someone needs to take his ashes to Chicago."

He hummed and nodded. "I'm sorry to hear that. Are you sprinkling them somewhere special, or . . ."

A wry laugh escaped. "No. Turns out he has a whole other family in Chicago—a wife, kids." The silence stretched between us, but Logan patiently waited for me to continue. "My father was not a good man—that we already knew. What we didn't know was that all those business trips were him actually going home to his real life. Turns out, *we* were his dirty little secret."

Tiny arrows of hurt and betrayal punctured my heart, but I still wasn't ready to admit the full truth out loud—he had also killed my mother.

How could someone be so good at faking love? Our father had smiled at us, sat at our dinner table, even provided the occasional hug when we were hurting. But it was all a lie, every last bit of it. And yet ... some traitorous part of me still wanted to believe he cared, even just a little. Maybe meeting them would finally kill that hope—or give it life.

I wasn't sure which was scarier.

Logan's protective arms didn't let me go. "Can't someone else take the ashes?"

I gently shook my head. "I volunteered, actually." I looked up, hoping he wouldn't judge me. "There's a part of me that's looking forward to meeting them. I'm *so* curious. My father was demanding and controlling—manipulative in ways that somehow felt like love. It's strange, but I feel connected to these people that I've never met. I kind of want to see what that's all about."

To not be alone in all this pain.

I hated my father for what he'd done to my mother, to us. But a part of me—a traitorous, yearning part—wondered whether meeting them would somehow fill the hollow spaces he'd left behind.

Logan nodded as a warm hand stroked up and down my spine. "That makes sense."

I exhaled in relief. He didn't judge me, even if he couldn't *fully* understand.

"Do you want company?" he finally asked. "We have a match on Saturday, and I was going to invite you, so I'll be in Chicago anyway. I can stand there for moral support or man the getaway car, if you need me to."

His words were simple, but the weight behind them wasn't. Logan didn't just offer support; he offered himself. And that terrified me almost as much as it comforted me.

A sharp sting pinched my nose. *Did he still think I was a lucky charm?*

It was only fair that we were both using each other: me to prove I could move beyond my past and him to get the luck he needed for a winning offseason.

A big part of me wanted to run away and forget all about my father's other life. An even bigger part needed to meet them.

Alone.

"Can I think about it?" I asked.

Logan pulled me close. "Of course. The offer is good—whenever you need it."

"Thank you," I whispered, feeling the heavy comfort of his arms as fatigue tugged at my eyelids.

All the reasons that we didn't make sense danced across my tired brain:

He's famous, out of my league.

We agreed to be friends.

Once the regular rugby season starts, he'll be gone, fighting off throngs of eager female fans.

He's best friends with the scum of the earth.

Girls like me don't bag men like him.

Ever.

Beneath my ear, his heartbeat thunked in a soothing rhythm.

There may be all those reasons, plus a hundred more, why starting anything with Logan didn't make any sense, but . . . right then and there, in the quiet stillness of my bedroom, he was mine.

By the time Saturday rolled around, I'd almost convinced myself that the vision of Logan between my legs was a figment of my imagination. The incessant, low throb was an erotic reminder that it had, in fact, happened.

Twice.

And it was freaking incredible.

I stifled a giddy scream and smiled as I crossed the street toward the Sugar Bowl. A piercing whistle caught my attention, and I found Royal leaning against a concrete planter on the sidewalk outside of King Tattoo. The collar of his coat was flipped up against the autumn wind that whipped across the lake.

"Hey," I called with a wave.

He pushed a finger against his lips and jerked his head. My eyes narrowed, and I scurried toward my brother.

"What are you doing?" I whispered, knowing Royal was definitely up to something.

He grinned and opened his coat, flashing an air horn hanging from the inside pocket.

I rolled my eyes and laughed. "What the heck is that for?"

His eyebrows bounced, and his eyes moved up the sidewalk toward the Sugar Bowl. It was then I spotted Duke, dropping off our sister and giving her a kiss that lasted long enough to make me blush.

When Sylvie turned to go inside, Duke swatted her butt and I smiled. "Don't be mean to Duke. He's a good guy."

Royal kept his attention on Duke as he sauntered up the sidewalk toward us. "I don't know what you're talking about."

As Duke got closer, Royal gripped his jacket, and I stuffed my fingers into my ears, waiting for him to blast the air horn and make Duke jump out of his skin.

To my surprise, Duke offered Royal a stealthy nod, and instead of blasting the air horn, Royal simply opened his jacket. Without a word, and in one smooth move, Duke pulled the air horn from Royal's coat and slipped it into his own.

"Morning, MJ," Duke called and kept his lazy pace down the sidewalk.

Royal grinned.

"What was *that*?" I asked.

My brother shrugged. "Like I said, I don't know what you're talking about."

I rolled my eyes and laughed again. "So you're working *together* now?"

Now that the Kings and Sullivans were one, big dysfunctional family, it was getting hard to know where the lines of the feud had blurred. My guess was they were gone forever, but the boys still had fun busting each other's balls with childish pranks.

Thankfully the label of *sweet little sister* typically kept me out of the crosshairs. I'd used it to my advantage only once or twice. Either way, I was taking any involvement to the grave.

Like the time Lee convinced me to look the other way when he slipped over-the-counter urinary tract medication into Royal's drink. The next day Royal's pee was neon orange, and he was convinced his wiener was going to fall off. Of course he'd come to me, and I'd had to convince him that it was completely harmless.

I chuckled at the memory.

"So who's got you floating on a cloud?" Royal finally asked.

I blinked up at him, hoping he couldn't see Logan's name flashing across my forehead. I tried to look annoyed.

"What? Ew." I watched as Duke disappeared around a corner. "Just happy to see everyone getting along."

"Mm-hmm." His stern, disbelieving eyes watched me. "Well, just know that if he breaks your heart, I'll break his legs."

A shotgun burst of laughter escaped me. It would be a tough match between Logan and Royal, but the sheer image of it was ridiculous. I wondered whether the rest of the King and Sullivan men would jump to restore my honor.

I had a sneaking suspicion they would.

"I'm good, but I appreciate the offer." I bumped my shoulder into Royal's.

He looked me over. "You're dressed awfully cute to go to work."

I looked down at my olive-green trench coat. Beneath it I wore a cream-colored knit sweater with a mock turtleneck, medium-wash jeans, and low-cut brown leather cowboy boots with a snip toe.

Maybe I should be offended by his comment, but my outfit was a lot more polished than my work scrubs, so I guessed he wasn't wrong. Truth was, I'd spent *hours* last night debating on the perfect outfit to meet the *other* Kings.

Something cute but effortless. Polished but that didn't look like I was trying too hard.

I shook my head. It still blew my mind that there was an entire group of people, related to us by blood, living only a few hours away and we had no idea.

"Today's the day." I sneaked a peek through my lashes at my older brother. "I'm going to drive out and deliver Dad's ashes."

Royal's hand landed on my shoulder, and he gave me a reassuring squeeze. "You're the best one out of all of us. I mean that. If it were up to me, that urn would have gotten lost on the side of a highway."

I shrugged, overwhelmed by sadness for my siblings. They'd experienced the brunt of my father's manipulations.

I was simply ... forgotten.

Not worth investing time in.

"It's the right thing to do," I said.

Royal had always been the one to shield me from the worst of Dad's bullshit. Royal had never said it, but I knew he saw me as something fragile, something to protect. And maybe that was why I couldn't bring myself to tell him just how much meeting Dad's other family meant to me.

Royal pulled me in for a hug. "It's still hard to believe we didn't see this coming."

I wrapped my arms around his middle and squeezed. When I stepped back, I lifted a shoulder. "I guess we would have found out eventually. His will was pretty explicit with who gets what."

He shook his head. "Still, people can be weird when it comes to money. Maybe keep your guard up a little."

I shook my head in return. Royal was just being overprotective. "I can't imagine they'll feel bad about getting half when it was so much money. I'm sure they'll feel the same way we all do." I looked at my watch and bit back a curse. "Yikes. I have to get on the road before traffic gets bad."

And Logan is waiting for me.

Just the thought of seeing him again sent a thrill through me, even as my brain screamed for caution. He was dangerous—not because he'd hurt me, but because he made me want things I had convinced myself I didn't need. Things like hope and happiness.

Things like *him*.

I gave Royal a playful salute. "Later, alligator."

Royal looked like he was going to say something more, but held back. He didn't say it, but I could see the worry in his eyes. My brothers had spent years sheltering me, and now I could feel the weight of their unspoken fears pressing down on me. They still thought of me as the baby sister who needed protecting. And maybe they weren't entirely wrong.

"Just . . . be careful," he said.

I was so sick of everyone treating me like I couldn't take care of myself. "I'll be fine." I jerked my chin toward his shop. "Get outta here and go tattoo a crucifix on someone's ass or something."

Royal chuckled and shook his head. "So judgy."

He winked and turned toward his shop. I turned in the opposite direction, heading toward the Sugar Bowl to load up on coffee and road trip doughnuts before I headed out of town.

As the Sugar Bowl's bell jingled behind me, I couldn't shake the mix of dread and anticipation coiling in my stomach. By the end of the day, I'd meet the people my father had chosen over us.

And, somehow, that felt like facing a ghost.

SEVENTEEN

LOGAN

By 8:00 a.m., I was rolling down the long driveway to the King estate and buzzing with energy. MJ had refused my offer of support to go with her to meet her father's *other* children.

I knew she didn't need me there. MJ was strong, capable, and perfectly fine handling this on her own. But damn if it didn't sit right in my gut. Something about the idea of her facing that family alone made me itch to be there—for her, if nothing else. And maybe for me, too, just to make sure she came out of it unscathed.

But MJ couldn't argue with the simple logic that we were both driving to the same place around the same time.

The day before a match was reserved for the Captain's Run—an hour-long practice run by the team captain instead of the coaches. I could do it in my sleep—a twenty-minute team meeting where I try to inspire my teammates, followed by a field workout. The team would do a warm-up, defense skill drills, plan attacks, passing and kicking, and lineouts. All in all, we were on the field for only about an hour . . .

just long enough to get our heads in the game but not long enough to get tired or injured.

The remainder of the day would be for rest, which I could happily spend tangled up in *her*.

When my truck came to a stop, MJ walked out of the front door with two to-go cups and a white bakery bag piled on a drink carrier. A small overnight bag hung from her shoulder.

She was bundled in a light olive-colored jacket and had on a knit hat. Her brown hair flowed in waves out of the bottom and tumbled across her shoulders. I could see her cream sweater peeking out from her coat, and the jeans and boots made her look casually chic, yet sophisticated.

I absently rubbed a tight spot in my chest.

Behind MJ, her aunt stood in the doorway, holding a white box and staring down at me.

I offered a wave, and the older woman only raised a stern, assessing eyebrow. The woman didn't even bother with the polite smile most people offered strangers. Her raised eyebrow and cool stare felt like a challenge.

Fine by me.

Winning over MJ's family wasn't going to be any harder than winning her over—both were proving to be the more satisfying fights of my life.

MJ waved back as she approached me with a smile.

I reached for the drink carrier. "Good morning, Julep."

I leaned forward slightly, going in for a casual kiss, but when MJ stiffened, I stopped myself. My eyes flicked over her shoulder to where her aunt was still watching us.

I slipped the duffel bag from her shoulder. "Ready to go?" I asked, opening the passenger-side door.

"One second." MJ turned and climbed back up the front steps. She accepted the box from her aunt. They exchanged a few words, and MJ wrapped her arms around her aunt. The woman softened and touched MJ's cheek as she spoke. She may come across as a hard-ass, but it was clear that she had a major soft spot for her niece.

I put the coffees and paper sack in the center console of my truck before holding the door for MJ.

"Need a hand?" I asked, gesturing toward the box.

She looked at the car, seemingly unsure of what to do. She lifted the box. "Logan, meet my dad. Dad, this is Logan."

Her awkward laugh made me grin like a fool. She could make hauling around an urn feel like a goddamn meet and greet.

I bent slightly at the waist. "Nice to meet you, Mr. King. Shall we?" I gestured toward the back seat of the cab, pulling open the rear door.

MJ looked at me with a soft smile.

I leaned in to whisper. "A ride in the truck bed seems a little rude, don't you think?"

"Thank you." She smiled again, and I felt like I'd won another gold medal.

"Of course." I nodded and carefully took the box from her, placing it in the back seat along with her duffel bag. The box was awkwardly placed on the seat, and I didn't want it just rolling around, so I pulled the seat belt across the urn and made sure it was secure.

MJ looked at me with her pretty, wide eyes. I gestured toward the front seat. "Hop in. Let's get you on the road."

Her shy smile bloomed, and I rounded the hood of the car, feeling like I'd done something to make her feel good, and I liked that. It wasn't just the way she smiled—it was the way she tried to hide it, like letting me see her happy was a risk. The more time I spent with MJ, the more I realized she was a walking contradiction: confident but cautious, sweet but guarded.

And all of it made me want her more.

I got behind the wheel and turned around in the wide driveway.

MJ picked up a coffee and took a sip. "Thanks for driving."

I nodded and eyeballed the paper coffee cup. She was being weird. "You know, we could have swung into town before we headed out."

Her eyes stayed focused on the road. "Oh, yeah . . . I don't know, I was up already so . . ." A nervous chuckle escaped her. "We're keeping things casual, right?"

I stifled a small laugh. "Are you *hiding me*, Julep?"

"What? No. I—" Splotchy pink marks flushed her cheeks, giving her away. "I thought we agreed that we'd be friends and—"

"Julep." My voice was low and stern as I leaned toward her. "I can't stop thinking about how pretty you looked with a mouthful of my cock. I know how you taste. If that's how you define friendship, I need to seriously reevaluate the friends in my life."

I counted the beats while her shock morphed into a sly smile as she crossed her arms. "You know what I meant."

"Mm-hmm," I teased, liking the playful banter between us. I shook my head. "Wow. I feel so . . . *used*."

MJ laughed. "*Fine*. My sister works at the Sugar Bowl, and I wasn't ready for all the questions yet. My aunt Bug already knows something is up, but at least she isn't a gossip. The rest of Outtatowner? *Woof*. Being a hot topic of conversation is the last thing I need right now."

As I came to a stop sign, I leaned closer to whisper. "Can I let you in on a little secret?"

She turned her face toward me, only inches away. My eyes moved from hers, down to her lips, and back up again.

"It's not gossip if it's the truth." I popped a quick kiss on her surprised mouth and sat back with a satisfied smile. MJ blinked as she stared out the front window. I pointed toward the radio. "Okay, as Passenger Princess, you're in charge of the music selection."

Beside me, she grinned. "I think I can handle that."

A few hours simply wasn't long enough. We cruised down the highway, making our way toward Chicago. MJ fiddled with the radio, and I learned she liked a mix of pop music, country, and eighties power ballads. We hit a bit of traffic crossing the border from Indiana to Illinois, but I leaned into the extra time it gave us.

My hand found its place on her thigh, and when she didn't move away, I let it creep just a little higher. "So tell me about your siblings—the ones you grew up with, I mean."

MJ exhaled. "Well . . . there's not much to tell, I guess. Abel is the oldest. He owns the brewery, mostly keeps to himself. He's married to Sloane, and she's got two kids, but Abel loves them like his own. Then there's Royal." She chuckled to herself. "He's always having a good time. Veda keeps him in line, mostly. Whip is a firefighter, and he's with Emily, our local librarian. I swear, they are the cutest couple ever." A wistful sigh escaped her lips, and my hand rubbed her thigh. "Sylvie married Duke Sullivan—you met him."

I nodded, remembering the protective stance he'd taken at the farmers' market. "He's definitely got older-brother energy."

MJ laughed. "He does. He's a lot like Abel in that way. But he brought Sylvie back to life. He loves her and the family they've made with everything he's got. JP is after her and probably who I am closest with, outside of Syl. He's always been a little misunderstood. Dad put a *lot* of pressure on him to carry on the family business. He met Hazel, and it was like a light was turned on inside him."

Her words settled over me. "I like that—a light. It's nice," I replied.

The way she talked about them made it clear they were her anchor. Every sibling, every story—it all painted a picture of a family who had weathered storms together and come out stronger. She didn't just love them, she admired them.

MJ smiled. "So that's them, I guess."

Something in the way she mentioned her father stuck with me. She had said before that her father wasn't a good person. There was more to that story, and I was curious to know what it was. "Sounds like your dad was kind of intense."

Her eyes flicked to the back seat as if he could overhear our conversation. "It's extremely complicated."

I nodded. "Most families are."

"We aren't most families." She gently shook her head and looked out the passenger window. "I should hate him—he was dismissive and cruel and he ki—" She stopped whatever she was about to say and cleared her throat. "I've learned he was not at all the man he pretended to be but . . . he was still my dad, you know?"

I swallowed hard. Her voice wavered, and I could tell she was holding something back. Whatever it was, it ran deep, like a wound that hadn't fully healed. I wanted to ask, to take that weight off her shoulders, but I didn't. MJ would tell me when she was ready—or maybe she wouldn't.

On some level, I knew what she was talking about. My

mother was a saint, but my father? The only memories I had of him were random weekends with random women. I saw the hurt in my mother's eyes every time there was someone new he wanted me to call *Mom*.

I still carried the shame that I'd done it, simply because I was a child who wanted his approval. It pissed me off, and I had spent my entire adult life secretly trying to make it up to her.

"What about you?" I asked, shifting the focus back to her. "Where do you fit in with all those personalities?"

"Ahh . . ." She chuckled and pointed to herself. "Resident baby sister. Part-time comic relief."

"*Really?* Huh." I watched her bristle out of the corner of my eye and tried to suppress a smile.

"What?" I could feel her stare boring into the side of my face.

"I don't know . . ." I lifted a shoulder and tried not to laugh. "It's nothing."

MJ turned in her seat, leaning against the door to look at me and crossing her arms. "Well, what is it?"

I did my best not to smile. "I guess you're just not all that funny."

A shrill, shocked sound erupted from her throat, and I finally cracked, laughing a hearty chuckle.

"I am *hilarious*, I'll have you know." Her pout was pretty fucking cute. "In fact, if it wasn't for me, Royal wouldn't even be all that funny. Nine times out of ten, he just overhears me say something funny and then repeats it louder . . . and everyone laughs and laughs at how he's the funny one."

It was me who was laughing now. "Maybe your delivery just isn't that great."

"Ugh, you're the *worst*." She tried to act angry, but she was fighting a smile.

My thoughts wandered to the day she had ahead of her and my grip tightened on the steering wheel. MJ was going out of her way to carry out one last act of kindness by delivering her father's ashes to a family who might very well hate her. I still couldn't wrap my head around the fact that MJ and her siblings were a secret part of his double life. It was becoming clearer how a forgotten girl had survived by being the funny, loyal little sister who did what she was told.

I leaned over, still watching the road, but wanting a kiss. "Hey, come here."

MJ's eyes narrowed into little slits before she gave in and moved closer. The kiss was quick, and I yearned for more. I had been honest with MJ that we could take things as slowly as she needed, but I wouldn't have minded if she needed my mouth between her legs a few more times before our trip was over.

"So let's go over the plan," I suggested. "We will stop at the field first to drop me off, and you can have the truck. Take as long as you need. When practice ends, I'll catch a ride from one of my teammates. Tonight we can meet up at the hotel and maybe get dinner? The night before a game I don't usually go out, but we can walk along the lakeshore if that's something you'd like to do. Then we can just chill in the room."

I could tell MJ was nervous about the day ahead, because she would alternate twisting her fingers and sitting on her hands. It hit me that maybe she wasn't as nervous about meeting her dad's family as she was about sharing a hotel room with me again.

Things between us had shifted since the last hotel, that was for damn sure.

I cleared my throat. "I made arrangements with the hotel for two rooms. There's no pressure to stay together if that's not something you want to do." Her eyes went big and round as I continued: "I would love for you to stay with me, but even if you do, there are no expectations. I want you to know that."

MJ's hand snaked around my neck, and her fingertips tangled in my hairline. "Thank you."

When she rubbed the base of my skull, I nearly groaned.

Her hazel eyes were warm in the morning sunlight as she smiled. "If it's not too late to cancel the extra room, I think I'd like to stay together."

"Yes, ma'am." I squeezed her thigh and focused on not driving off the road as my heart hammered against my ribs.

When we finally reached the stadium, I was more amped to play than I'd felt in *years*. There really was a lucky energy when it came to MJ King. We both climbed out of the car, and I grabbed my bag from the back seat, then slung it across my shoulders.

MJ stood in front of me, and I put my hands on her shoulders. "Remember, no matter what happens today, you're doing the right thing."

She swallowed and nodded.

I stepped closer, sliding my hand up her neck and into her hair. My other hand pulled her closer so our bodies could finally touch. Her head tipped back to look up at me.

"You're compassionate." I kissed her. "Kindhearted." Another kiss. "And even a little bit funny." I grinned and deepened the last kiss, moving my mouth over hers until her tiny moan filled my mouth. I eased her back against the car, pushing my hips into her.

Her hands fisted on my jacket, pulling me closer. My

tongue slid over hers. I'd missed her taste and the warmth of her lips.

When the kiss ended, I only wanted more. Her cheeks were flushed and her eyes were dazed. I went in for another taste. My cock thickened against her as she squirmed beneath me. If she'd have let me, I would have pinned her against the car and shown her exactly how a woman deserved to be treated.

From behind us, one of my teammates approached, and an obnoxious barking interrupted us.

I growled, shielding her with my body as I shot Jack a deadly look over my shoulder. "Fuck off."

Jack grinned. "Come on, Cap. You're going to be late for your own practice."

I looked down at MJ. "He's right." She patted my chest. "Have a good practice. I'll keep you posted on what I'm up to."

I swallowed hard. A major part of me wished I could just go with her. What she was about to do couldn't be easy, and I hated that she was going alone. Up ahead, Jack whistled at me again.

"Hey." I kissed the tip of her nose. "They're going to love you, Julep."

Her pretty smile carried me all the way through practice.

EIGHTEEN

MJ

Driving Logan's truck, I gripped the wheel and glanced at the map on my phone again. Elizabeth Peake's residence in Kenilworth was only about twenty miles from the stadium, but in city traffic it took me nearly an hour.

What was I even hoping for? A sense of connection? Closure? Maybe a little validation that the man who had abandoned us hadn't been all bad?

The questions swirled, tangling with the guilt that clawed at my stomach.

He didn't deserve forgiveness, and I didn't want to feel this hopeful.

The entire ride, I couldn't shake the heebie-jeebie feeling of Dad's ashes being casually buckled into the back seat. It was sweet that Logan didn't want to put the ashes in the truck bed, but, honestly, I wished he had.

The fancy North Shore community was gated, so I rolled to a stop at the guardhouse. "Hi. My name is MJ. I'm meeting with Elizabeth Peake?"

"Good morning," the guard answered as he picked up a phone. "I'll let her know you've arrived." The friendly guard smiled at me as he waited for someone to answer his call.

"Nice neighborhood." I smiled and looked at the mansions just behind his guardhouse.

"Luxury lakefront living at its finest. You'll—" He paused and spoke into the phone. "Good morning. Your guest has arrived. Yes, of course, madam."

Madam?

The guard hung up the phone and smiled at me. "Your identification, miss?"

I scrambled to grab my wallet and hand him my driver's license. If the guard recognized and was curious about my King last name, he didn't show it.

He handed it back to me. "You're all set. Follow the curve to the end of the road. The big blue house on the right. Have a wonderful day." He pressed a button, and the gate groaned as it opened. I tucked my ID away and exhaled before winding down the road toward my destination.

When the house came into view, my jaw dropped open. "*Damn.*"

The sprawling estate and pristine landscaping screamed of a life I could barely fathom. The King estate back home suddenly felt small, modest, even humble. The King estate in Outtatowner was considered large and ornate for such a small town, but this home was *unreal*. It was at least double the size and by far the largest house on the block. The lake shimmered aqua and white behind the house as I made my way down the driveway. Huge metal sculptures decorated the manicured lawn. High hedgerows lined both sides, providing privacy from prying eyes.

It was exactly the kind of multimillion-dollar home I would have expected my father to own.

When I came to a stop at the end of the driveway, my

palms were sweaty. I glanced in the rearview mirror at the white box in the back seat. "Here goes nothing."

Unbuckling, I rounded the truck and retrieved him from the back. The box was surprisingly light, and I tried not to think about the gruesome fact that the entirety of my father fit inside such a neat little package.

I rang the buzzer at the door and waited.

A man's voice crackled over the speaker. "Who is it?"

"Hi. MJ, um . . . King." *You know, the same person the guard just announced was here? Your long lost, half . . . whoever?* "I'm here to see Elizabeth?"

Without a reply, I was unsure of what to do next. Moments later, the door opened and an older gentleman in a well-tailored suit smiled at me. He had a short crop of salt-and-pepper hair, and his suit was beautifully starched and pressed. "Good morning. Ms. Peake is eagerly awaiting your arrival."

I stepped inside, grateful to be out of the chilly autumn wind. "Thank you."

The man gestured toward the box in my hands. "May I?"

"Um . . ." I held it out. "Sure."

I hesitated before handing the box over, my fingers reluctant to let go. It felt wrong, watching a stranger cradle the last remains of the man who had shaped so much of my life—for better or worse.

He accepted it with a sad sigh. "Oh, it's just so tragic, don't you think?"

I tried not to look completely confused as the man gazed wistfully down at my father's ashes.

I swallowed past the lump in my throat. "Yeah."

The clack of high heels echoed down the hallway and drew my attention. When my gaze lifted, I was stunned speechless. I had seen images of Elizabeth Peake on television after my father's arrest. She had vehemently denied any accusations against him, and while she had been pretty on camera, she was absolutely *breathtaking* in person.

Her tailored skirt swung in time with her dark hair. With her arms outstretched, she walked toward me.

"Welcome. Please come in." She stepped into my space, dropping air-kisses on either side of my head.

Elizabeth's smile didn't reach her eyes. Everything about her—from the tailored skirt to the way she pronounced *welcome*—felt like it had been rehearsed. She was perfect, polished, and utterly impossible to read. I couldn't decide whether she was welcoming me or sizing me up.

Her firm grip on my shoulders squeezed. "Thank you for bringing him home."

Elizabeth looked at the man as tears welled in her eyes. "Oh, Frederick." She waved a hand between them. "Just throw him in an upstairs closet"—her tone suddenly changed, dropping the mourning-wife routine—"but not in the blue room, one of the back ones. Maybe the east wing bathroom no one uses."

The fuck?

The woman who had defended him so fiercely on television now spoke about him like an old piece of furniture she no longer had room for. It was chilling, the way she could switch between grief and indifference.

Getting a read on these people was difficult. Was this just another role for her, or had she truly stopped caring about him long ago? Was she really the grieving widow she displayed on camera, or a woman who would toss her dead husband's ashes in a bathroom closet?

Elizabeth turned her attention to me. "Well, shall we have some tea to warm you up?"

My mouth opened for a second before snapping shut. "Sure. Thank you."

"Frederick, please bring it to the salon." She motioned toward a long corridor that led to a grand sitting room off the main hallway.

The butler nodded, whisking my father's ashes away. I swallowed hard as warring emotions swirled in my stomach. I hadn't even said a proper goodbye, yet I was also relieved.

As Frederick carried the box away, a hollow ache settled in my chest. I hadn't expected to feel this way—like I was handing over the last piece of the man who had caused so much pain but was still my father. Was this closure? Or just another door shutting on a life I could never make sense of?

I took one last look at the box as Frederick walked away. *Bye, Dad.*

I followed Elizabeth down the hallway. In the salon, high, thick beams ran across the ceiling, but they were the only hints of color. Everything else was a stark white—walls, molding, furniture. The entire space looked utterly untouched and unlived in.

Two women, not much older than me, stood behind the massive couch in the center of the room.

It was jarring to see two pairs of my father's eyes staring back at me. There was no denying these women were Russell King's children. Nerves bunched in my stomach.

Their eyes—his eyes—should have been familiar, but they weren't. They didn't hold the same weight of disappointment or fear I remembered from my childhood. Instead, they shone with curiosity and warmth, as if being his daughter had been a gift instead of a curse.

The taller of the two women stepped forward first. "Hi,

I'm Bianca." She gestured toward the other woman. "This is Blair. We are so thrilled to meet one of Daddy's children."

Daddy?

I limply extended my hand, desperately trying to make sense of the situation that was rapidly unfolding before me.

Elizabeth stood beside me, carefully reading the interaction. "I'm sure it's confusing, and maybe a little bit surprising, to hear that we now know about you and your siblings."

A weak laugh escaped me. "Yeah. A little."

Elizabeth sat on one of the chairs near the couch, and I did the same. They were as stiff and uncomfortable as they looked.

"Russell and I had an unconventional marriage. You see, I grew up not far from here. My father is a powerful, very influential businessman. I liked my life." She gestured around her as if to say, *Who wouldn't love all this?* "I was a hardheaded girl and had no intentions of marrying, but my father insisted. He hand selected Russell King. I kept the Peake name, of course. Russell received the money he needed to get King Equities off the ground, and I got two beautiful children."

A business deal that dealt in money and procreation.

"Oh," I said, glancing between Elizabeth and her daughters. But something else gnawed at me. "So you knew about his double life the whole time?"

Elizabeth's features softened as she looked at me. I recognized pity when I saw it. "Russell loved his hometown. I certainly had no desire to live there, and what he did with his time was his own business."

The way they spoke about him—like he was a charming, if slightly eccentric, husband and father—made my stomach twist. They didn't know about the manipulation, the cruelty, the lies. Or maybe they did, and they just didn't care. Either way, it felt like we were talking about two completely different men.

I leaned forward. "So you knew about his relationship with my mother, Maryann?"

Elizabeth's smile never faltered. "Russell had his fun and I had mine. It was better for the both of us if we didn't ask questions."

I still couldn't believe she was openly discussing her husband's long-standing affair in front of her children, and they didn't seem upset about it in the least.

My brows dipped down. "But you defended him—on television I saw you hold those press conferences and deny everything."

Her pitying glance was grating. "It's important for my girls, and the Peake name, to keep negative press to a minimum."

Question upon question zinged through my mind. One in particular kept getting stuck and I had to know: "Did you know my aunt Bug? Was she at your wedding?"

A flicker of confusion crossed Elizabeth's face. "Oh, no. Russell hadn't spoken to his sister Ruth Anne since they were young adults. If Russell chose to distance himself, I assumed it must have been for good reason."

Elizabeth may have been under the impression that she and her husband had a perfect, open relationship, but he had been keeping secrets from her too.

He made it so Bug could raise his children while he lived a double life. Elizabeth had no idea what he had been capable of.

Frederick broke through the rising tension when he entered with a white marble-topped cart containing a steaming teapot and several cups and saucers. A small porcelain box, also white, held a variety of teas to choose from.

I selected a sachet of peppermint tea as Frederick poured the hot water into my cup.

"It's so interesting to finally meet you." Blair sat on the sofa next to me, her eyes roaming over my face. "You really do kind of look like us . . . a little bit in the nose. The hair color, for sure."

I toyed with the ends of my hair. "Yeah, I guess so."

"It's still so sad to think he's really gone." Bianca's voice was laced with genuine grief as she fought back tears. She grabbed a framed photograph from the mantel of the fireplace and walked toward us.

Did they know the truth? Did they understand that he was killed in prison, in part, because of what he had done to my mother?

He had openly admitted that, years ago, my mother had planned to leave him and take us with her, so he had killed her—choked the life out of her and deposited her body in Wabash Lake.

In many ways, he had led each of us to believe that she had abandoned us because we were unlovable.

And yet these women mourned him.

I looked at the frame Bianca held out for me. My father's face was lifted with a wide smile. He was much younger. He looked happy. It was an action shot—him running behind a little brunette girl riding a bicycle down a tree-lined street.

Tears stung my eyes. Blair noticed and her hand gripped mine. "We miss him too."

They didn't understand at all why I was near tears.

I didn't have a clue who the man in the photograph was.

I certainly didn't know a father who laughed and ran beside me while I learned to ride a bike.

JP had done that.

These people didn't know the real him at all—only the role he played to keep Elizabeth and her father happy. They were blissfully unaware of the irreparable damage he'd caused my siblings and me.

They spoke of *Daddy* like he was their North Star, guiding them through a charmed life. But for me and my siblings, he'd been a shadow we couldn't escape, casting darkness over every attempt to grow.

The air inside that house was thick and choking. So many unanswered questions swirled in my brain, but I couldn't get past the image of my father—*their father*—being the kind of man who made happy memories with his children.

I had been so curious about his other family. A small part of me assumed I would have someone else who understood what it was like to have a father like mine. I never expected *this*. I was a fool to think that what I felt for them was connection. They were nothing at all like me.

I'd spent years wondering what kind of man my father could have been if he'd chosen differently—if he'd been a better father, a better husband. Meeting Elizabeth and her daughters confirmed what I'd always feared. He had been capable of love and joy . . . just not with us.

Every word, every smile, every glance, chipped away at the fragile image I'd built of him in my mind. I'd come here hoping for answers, but all I'd found were more questions—and the sickening realization that he'd been everything we feared he was and more.

The teacup trembled in my hands, the fine porcelain thinner than I'd expected. It felt like one wrong move could shatter it, much like the image of my father that had already begun to crumble.

Without bothering to take a sip of my tea, I set the cup and saucer to the side and rose. "I'm sorry, but I really should get going."

"Oh, but you just got here." Bianca's face creased with concern.

"It's a long drive and I should get home," I lied, already backing up toward the door.

"We'll do lunch," Blair offered with a nod. "Once Daddy is laid to rest, we can show you where in the family plot. That way you can pay your respects anytime you need to."

Elizabeth clicked her tongue. "You are so thoughtful, darling." She looked at me. "I'm sure you've had a long day, and this can be overwhelming."

I nodded as an internal scream ripped through me. I had let my curiosity get the best of me, and it had been a huge mistake.

It was somehow even more painful to know that my father's treatment wasn't because he was incapable of love; it was because it was *us*.

With a forced smile, I made a clean exit and nearly ran toward Logan's truck. My phone dinged, and I glanced at it to see a text come through from Sylvie.

> SYLVIE
> Please check in after you've met them. I'm worried about you.

More responses from the group chat flooded in as I enclosed myself in the cab of Logan's truck.

WHIP

What are "the others" like?

ABEL

Why do you care?

ROYAL

We shouldn't have let her go alone.

JP

Did they allude to the dissolution of King Equities? We're prepared to fight them if they try to come after what's left of the business.

SYLVIE

JP, I'm telling Hazel to smack you for being insensitive again. MJ, please just tell us you're okay.

ROYAL

I'm sitting next to him and slapped the shit out of him. You're welcome.

I read over their words, and a sob escaped me. I frantically wiped at my tears, hoping no one would come outside and interrupt my escape. Hot, angry tears streamed down my face as I barreled down the driveway and onto the main road.

I didn't know whether I was crying for him, for us, or for the life he'd built without us. Maybe it was all of it. Maybe it didn't matter. All I knew was that I'd given him to them, and now I had nothing left to hold on to. No anger, no answers, no closure. Just the weight of what he'd taken from us.

I barely looked at the guard as he offered a friendly wave and raised the bar to allow me to leave.

Escape.

By the time I pulled into the circle drive of the hotel, my

hands were still trembling on the wheel. The weight of the afternoon lingered, heavy and oppressive. I typed out a quick response before my brothers and Sylvie sent out a search party.

> I'm totally fine. They were surprisingly warm and welcoming.

I didn't have the heart to tell my brothers and sister how differently Dad had been with them—how we'd truly gotten the worst of him. Not yet, at least.

I took another deep, cleansing breath, willing the lump in my throat to dissolve. When I looked up, the sight of Logan stepping out of the lobby doors brought a thread of relief. He strode toward the truck, his tall frame relaxed, but his sharp eyes took one look at me and softened.

The second I saw him, the knot in my chest loosened. Logan didn't need to say anything—his presence was enough. The way he looked at me, steady and sure, made me feel like I wasn't alone in this.

For the first time all afternoon, I could breathe.

"You okay?" he asked as he pulled open the car door, his voice low and steady, like it was meant to ground me.

Relief flooded my system. I had gone into the morning knowing I would face my father's family alone, but something about Logan's presence made me feel better. I was grateful to have someone to lean on when my insides were so frazzled.

I nodded, swallowing hard. "Yeah, just . . . a lot to process."

He didn't push, didn't ask questions, just opened the door and took over. "I've got it from here," he said, his tone leaving no room for argument as he grabbed the keys from my hand and retrieved my overnight bag from the back seat.

He handed the keys to the valet. I followed him into the luxury hotel, the warm blast of air from the lobby's heaters hitting me in a way that made my shoulders sag. The staff at the front desk barely looked up as Logan handed me a key card and led me toward the bank of elevators.

I clutched my purse like a lifeline. My nerves hummed in anticipation, but whether it was from the overwhelming day or the thought of being alone with Logan tonight, I wasn't sure.

Maybe both.

The elevator dinged and the doors opened, the hum of tension stretching between us. Logan stood close, his presence a steadying force that made me feel both grounded and breathless. When the doors opened and he stepped aside, his quiet confidence was strangely comforting.

I let out a breath, silently hoping for something —*anything*—to take away the knot that had formed in my stomach.

NINETEEN

LOGAN

MJ looked like shit.

Not like *actual* shit—she was still stunning, but the red rim around her eyes betrayed her. Whatever had happened at that house had rattled her, and I had no clue how to make it better.

The slow elevator ride was fraught with tension.

Do I ask how it went, even though it's clear what the answer will be?

I was stuck in a weird limbo of wanting to offer comfort while trying to give her the space she might need.

Her silence sliced through me. Every instinct screamed to wrap her up and shield her from whatever had shaken her, but I couldn't tell if that was what she needed.

Our silence yawned and grew as the elevator stopped on the third floor to let in another passenger. The old man offered a polite smile and stood off to the side. I took a side step toward MJ.

We leaned against the back wall, side by side, not speaking. I ran my hands down my thighs and shifted her bag on my shoulder while some shitty instrumental music filled the small space.

The man must have also felt the tension in the elevator, because he started to whistle along with the music. When I realized the song was "Closer" by Nine Inch Nails and the old man was whistling right along to it, my jaw flexed to hide a smile.

MJ's gaze slid to me as I bit back a giggle. Her lips flattened, and I tried to breathe through my nose.

We reached our floor, and the elevator dinged before the doors opened to let us out. I extended my hand to gesture that she should go first. As we skirted past the old man, I acknowledged him with a nod.

"Evening," he responded and then went right back to whistling.

As soon as the doors closed at our backs, MJ doubled over with a laugh. I followed suit, dropping her bag and leaning against the wall.

"Holy shit, do you think he knew?" she asked, wiping tears from her eyes.

I looked at her. "He knew *every* verse."

My deadpan delivery made her laugh again.

"Oh," she exhaled. "I needed that." She stood tall, walked down the hallway, and started humming the song to herself. The throaty vibrations paired with what I knew the lyrics to be made me grin.

Given the chance, I'd fuck MJ like an animal in a heartbeat.

When we got closer, I gestured toward the end of the hallway. "That way and to the left."

Our room was nestled at the back of a long corridor. The suite was secluded from other parts of the hotel, offering an upscale and private experience.

I didn't know if a fancy room could fix a shitty day, but I figured it couldn't hurt. The second I saw the view and the plush bed, I knew it was exactly what MJ needed: space to breathe, to feel safe.

The team didn't normally stay at such a ritzy hotel, but I had made special arrangements. I'd wanted to give her something nice after what I knew was a brutal day. Maybe it was overkill, but if it made her smile, it was worth every penny. And sure . . . I wanted to impress her a little. The boutique hotel was ridiculously expensive, but for good reason.

Using my key card, I unlocked the door and moved aside to allow MJ to enter first.

"What the hell . . ." she called out.

I grinned and stepped in beside her. Floor-to-ceiling windows offered an impressive view of the city skyline and Lake Michigan.

The suite came with a private butler, who nodded with a subtle bow. "Welcome to the presidential suite, Ms. King. Mr. Brown."

I stepped past MJ's gaping stare and extended a hand. "Thank you. What's your name, sir?"

"Benedict, sir."

I shook his hand. "Thanks, Benedict. I'm Logan. This is MJ." When I looked at MJ, her mouth was open. With a grin, I used my knuckle to push it closed and diverted my attention back to Benedict.

"A pleasure," he said. "I can take that." He gestured toward MJ's duffel on my shoulder, and I passed it to him. "The other piece of luggage was delivered this morning, and I took the liberty of unpacking it in the primary bedroom."

"Thanks, Ben." I smiled and gently patted a shocked MJ on the back.

Benedict was completely unfazed by MJ's gawking. "May I prepare some coffee or tea? If you'd like, I can arrange for room service or a dinner reservation, if you prefer."

I smiled at him. "I think we'll take a minute to settle in. If we need anything, I will let you know."

Benedict bowed again. "Very well, sir. If you need anything at all, you can pick up the phone and dial nine-two-four. That is my direct line, or you can communicate with me directly via the hotel's app."

I held out my hand again. "I appreciate that."

Benedict shook my hand and disappeared into the primary bedroom with MJ's bag.

"Pretty nice, right?" I asked.

MJ turned and blinked at me. "Pretty nice?" She gestured around the room. "Pretty nice?"

I grinned. The suite was bigger than the apartment I was renting, and the atmosphere in the suite was cool and casual. The architectural details were evident in each space. The kitchen area was spacious and clean. There was a sitting area near a fireplace. One bedroom was to the left, tucked behind French-style doors, and another to the right. I may have canceled the extra room, but when given the opportunity to upgrade to the presidential suite, I took it.

Benedict silently exited, and I felt the knot in my shoulder release. I'd spent the entire day distracted with worry about MJ and how things were going for her. My head wasn't where it needed to be, but now that she was here, I could relax.

I watched as MJ explored the suite, her fingers grazing over the back of the chairs near the fire. She stopped by the floor-to-ceiling windows and looked out over Lake Michigan.

"Think we can see Outtatowner from here?" she asked with a wistful note to her voice.

The way her lips curved into that soft smile—god, it did something to me. For a moment the shadows under her eyes faded, replaced by this quiet hope that lit her up from the inside.

An undefined part of me wanted to be the one who kept that light burning.

I sidled up behind her. "I think if I squint really hard, I can almost see the lighthouse."

She hummed a laugh, knowing it was bullshit. My hands smoothed up her arms, hating the layers of fabric between us. I could feel the tension radiating off her, but she hadn't opened up about how her meeting had gone.

It felt too awkward to ask, so I figured distraction was the next-best option.

"So what do you feel like?" I asked. "The team dinner is at Nivori, a French-Japanese fusion restaurant. Or we can order something and hang out here. Lady's choice."

MJ considered my offer as she continued to wander around the suite. She pulled open the French doors and gasped. In the center of the primary bedroom was a massive four-poster bed. Off to the side in the primary bathroom, there was an oversize soaking tub and steam shower. Across from it was a grand walk-in closet.

The suite was definitely overkill, given we were staying only one night, but the look of shocked pleasure on her face alone was worth it.

"Dibs on this room." MJ laughed and launched herself toward the bed, bouncing as she landed on her back.

I walked toward her, latching onto her ankle and dragging her toward the end of the bed. My fingers slipped under the bottom hem of her jeans, seeking the warmth of her skin. She giggled and stared up at me.

"That's fine," I replied. "There's an identical one across the living room."

Her bottom lip jutted out as she shimmied to the side. "Hop up here. Let's see if it's big enough for the both of us."

The bed was massive, so when I turned and fell backward onto it with a thud, she barely jostled. Together, we stared up at the ceiling.

"Seems roomy enough," I said, trying to ignore the way my cock noticed the fact we were lying together on the bed.

MJ rolled toward me, tucking her hands under her face. "Are you too tired for the team dinner? Because if you're not, I think I'd like the distraction."

I wasn't tired. In fact, I wouldn't have minded getting *more* fatigued after a few rounds of my new favorite pastime: *Make MJ Scream My Name*.

I shook my head. "I'm not too tired." I slipped my phone from the pocket of my jeans. "I'll let them know you're joining us." I typed out the message to our manager, who handled all the reservations. "Maria will be thrilled."

MJ exhaled. "I really, really like her."

And I really, really like you.

My brows creased, as I tried to process what was happening between us. She swore she wanted things to be friendly and casual. That was good. It was what I needed, but I couldn't deny the invisible pull that was there, whether I liked it or not.

Breaking the silence, MJ shot out of the bed and walked toward the bathroom. "How much time do I have to get ready?"

I looked at the time. "About an hour, but take all the time you need."

She nodded and the door clicked closed.

I looked back at the ceiling with a heavy sigh.

Things with MJ were getting dangerous.

A serious part of me knew I needed to shove aside all my feelings for MJ. She was too sweet, too innocent. It was a real mind-fuck that she'd become some kind of gorgeous talisman I couldn't shake, but the reality was that she was also a major distraction. Once the season started back up, I wouldn't be returning to Michigan. I didn't need an image of her brokenhearted tears once I walked away.

I needed all my focus and attention to be directed at my next Olympic run.

Eyes on the prize.

My singular focus on rugby had been what garnered my success in the first place. No one worked harder than me.

Trouble was, I wasn't totally convinced it would be her heart that would be broken at the end of it.

***

I CHOSE to give her space and shower in the other bathroom while she cleaned herself up for dinner. The team dinner was semicasual, but I'd packed a cozy sweater with two thick, wooden buttons to pair with my dark denim jeans.

I wasn't sure why I couldn't rid myself of the simmering anxiety I was carrying around. Maybe it was because the impending game would be a tough one—the Red Rock Reapers were heading into the match undefeated, and my team was still getting its legs. Maybe it was also knowing the team would inevitably jump to conclusions when I showed up with MJ on my arm.

I was waiting for her when she came out of the primary

bedroom. Still dressed in the same outfit, MJ had curled her hair and freshened up her makeup.

Her hand still rested on the door handle. "I didn't have another set of clothes."

I shook my head. "You're perfect."

Her smile bloomed, soft and genuine.

I held out my arm. "Ready?"

"Let me grab my coat," she said.

I shook my head again. "No need. Nivori is inside the hotel."

With her hand tucked into the nook of my arm, we left our suite and rode the elevator to the mezzanine level, where the restaurant was located. I gave my name to the host at the stand, and we were escorted through the restaurant to a private dining area. Most of my teammates were already there, laughing and talking over one another.

MJ was shy at my side. I hadn't introduced her to any of my teammates yet, and when we walked through the door, all eyes shifted their attention to us. Thankfully, Maria cut the tension by standing and eagerly waving us over.

The way she smiled at Maria made my chest feel too tight. She was already weaving her way into the lives of the people around me, and I didn't know how to stop it—or if I even wanted to.

MJ smiled at me as I pulled out her seat and took the spot next to her.

The lighting was low and moody. Stars twinkled on an inky black sky through the panoramic windows. We were seated at one of two round tables, and another long table stood across from us. The sheer mass of a team of rugby players plus their spouses and guests made the space shrink.

I overheard a young teammate talk about plans for finding a bar or club after dinner. I leaned toward him.

"Take it easy tonight. Tomorrow's a big game. The Reapers won't be hungover, and neither should you."

The young fullback stifled an eye roll. "I'll be fine, old man."

Old man? The jab stung and I scowled. *When did I become the old man of the team? Cocky older brother, sure, but old man?*

I focused my attention on MJ, who was smiling and listening to a story Maria was telling. She didn't even realize how effortlessly she'd slid into the conversation, laughing at Maria's jokes and asking thoughtful questions. The team loved her already, and watching her charm them made my chest swell with pride—and dread. Trent had no idea what he'd lost, and the thought of him ever coming close to her made my blood boil.

The waitstaff offered drinks and appetizers—spiced edamame, pan-seared shishito peppers, and Japanese cucumber salad in a soy vinaigrette. Platters of ornate sushi, crispy rice, and thinly sliced Wagyu beef tartare were passed. Thankfully the staff understood the clientele they were serving, because the sheer volume of food consumed was staggering.

An hour flew by as conversations overlapped—stories of brutal injuries, heroic plays, and missed calls. Excitement and anticipation of tomorrow's game were palpable. I had done my job at the Captain's Run.

They were ready to kick some ass.

My phone buzzed in my pocket, and I glanced at it to see Trent's name flash across the screen. I'd been waiting to connect with him and MJ was still wrapped up in a story, so I stood, brushing my fingertips across her shoulder.

I silently gestured at my phone, and she nodded.

I took a few steps away from the crowd and answered. "About time, man."

He scoffed. "Don't bust my balls, Mav."

It was loud in the confined space, so I left the room in search of a quiet area. The fact that Trent had taken so long to call me back had grated on my nerves.

Was he avoiding me? Had he caught wind that MJ and I had—hell, I didn't even know what to call it—fooled around?

"What's up, brother?" Trent asked.

"Just checking in, man. It's been a while. What's new?" I asked, trying to gauge the conversation. It was loud wherever he was, and the din of chatter behind me wasn't helping. I stuffed a finger in my ear and tried to listen.

"Ah, the usual. Kicking ass and taking names. Heard your exhibition season was off to a rough start." His words were garbled, but I think I got most of it.

Frustrated, I pressed the speaker button on the phone. "Can you hear me?" I asked.

"Yeah, but I'm out," he shouted.

I rolled my eyes. Trent had called *me*, but it was nearly impossible to hear him over the background noise.

"What are you doing?" I asked.

"Do you remember that redhead, Stacy? The one with the huge tits." He laughed, and it was clear he'd already been drinking. I looked around, glad no one had overheard his crass comment, and slipped into a dark hallway that led to the bathrooms and staff area.

Trent didn't wait for my response. "Man, she is primed and ready. *Desperate*, you know what I'm saying?"

When did he forget to grow up? Had he always been like this? I exhaled. "Did you call me just to tell me you're getting laid?" I pinched the bridge of my nose.

His drunk laugh cracked through the speaker. "No,

man. I'm going to be at your match tomorrow. Make sure there's a ticket for me. Good seats too. Club level for your boy."

Panic spiked my heart rate. I had been trying to get ahold of my best friend ever since MJ had told me they had dated. He'd hurt her feelings somehow, and the thought of it gnawed at my insides.

I'd assumed MJ would attend tomorrow's match, but if Trent showed up and surprised her, it would be a complete shit show.

Loyalty to my longest friend warred with the hurt I could imagine in MJ's eyes. I needed to get to the bottom of it.

"Hey, I think I ran into someone you might know. She works with my grandfather and we got to talking . . . MJ King?" My ears buzzed as I waited for Trent's response. I wanted something—reassurance, I guessed—that while things between them may have ended, MJ was simply holding on to old hurts.

Distorted music thumped through the speaker. "Nah . . . doesn't ring any bells. Why?"

No way any man in his right mind would have dated MJ and not remembered. It simply wasn't possible. Maybe it was a case of mistaken identity? Could it be his name was bland enough to be a coincidence?

I ignored the headache building behind my eyes. "It's nothing, I guess. Look, I have to go. The team's waiting and—"

"Oh, wait! Fuck yeah, I remember her. The nurse, right?" Lead filled my gut. "I worked for *months* to get into her pants, but once she finally gave in, she lay there like a scared rabbit." His dismissive and cruel laugh sent me reeling. "Fucking waste of a virgin pussy, if you ask me."

The phone shook in my hand. Every muscle in my body tensed, ready to snap. My vision tunneled, the only clear image in my mind was Trent's smug, drunk face. He'd reduced MJ—my Julep—to some twisted punch line, and I wanted to destroy him for it.

Blood and rage whooshed between my ears. *Virgin.*

I squeezed the phone and wanted to smash it against the wall. Anger and confusion mixed as I played his cruel words over and over in my mind. Without even saying goodbye, I ended the call and clenched my fist.

When a text came in, I could only stare at it.

> **TRENT**
>
> If you get the chance, bang her and report back. Tunnel bros! And don't forget my ticket.

I gripped the phone so tightly I thought it might snap. Trent's words looped in my head, each one crueler than the last. How could someone treat her like that? How had I not seen this side of him before?

The walk back to the private dining room was slow and torturous. I finally understood why MJ had gotten so upset when she realized I was friends with Trent. His past conquests had never really been any of my concern, but now it was affecting someone I knew. Someone I was starting to care about.

When I got to the entrance to the room, I stared at her. My teammates were surrounding her, laughing and including MJ in their conversations.

She deserved so much more than Trent's careless cruelty. Hell, she deserved more than me. But the thought of anyone else having her, of her trusting someone who didn't see her worth—it twisted something inside me, dark and possessive.

Her hazel eyes lifted and met mine. A shy blush crept across her cheeks, and my throat itched like sandpaper.

The fact Trent couldn't have cared less about her was only the tip of the iceberg. He'd taken her virginity, and if he'd treated her anything like his past conquests, then when he'd lost interest, he had dropped her like a hot stone.

I barely knew what to do with that information.

As MJ's laughter floated across the room, I made a silent vow. Whatever it took, I'd make sure Trent stayed the hell away from her. He planned to show up at my match tomorrow, and for the first time I wanted to fucking kill him.

TWENTY

MJ

When my eyes lifted and met Logan's, something had shifted. Tension and frustration pressed on his shoulders like a bad omen. He looked miserable and handsome at the same time, with his brows pinched down and his large frame coiled tight.

When he settled in the seat next to me, I leaned over. "Is everything okay?" I whispered.

The silence between us wasn't just heavy—it was suffocating. My chest tightened with each second he avoided looking at me.

Did I say something wrong? Was he regretting inviting me?

My mind spiraled, searching for an answer.

His jaw was set, and he only nodded before taking a long gulp of ice water. I didn't want to pry—maybe it was nerves for the upcoming match. Logan took his job as captain seriously, and the rest of the team seemed like they were eager to have a wild night, despite their match in the morning.

Everyone was talking and having a good time, but Logan's silence beside me made me uncomfortable.

Maria gasped, and I looked up to see the waitstaff carrying in trays of little desserts. I'd already consumed my weight in sushi and teriyaki noodles, but when the server placed a small plate in front of me, I couldn't resist.

"Madagascar vanilla bean crème brûlée with calamansi gelée," the server announced.

I didn't have a clue what calamansi gelée was, but the dish in front of me looked like a standard crème brûlée. I hoped calamansi wasn't some kind of fish, but I plunged my spoon into the little white pot anyway. I quickly eyeballed the crème brûlée and gave it a quick sniff. It certainly didn't smell like seafood, but rather warm vanilla with a hint of citrus.

I bravely stuffed it into my mouth and moaned. A quick giggled followed as my fingertips pressed into my lips. "Sorry," I mumbled.

"Don't be." Maria laughed and took her own bite. "This is better than sex."

"Hey!" Maria's husband's face twisted at her comment. She had once explained that his position on the team was something called a *prop*, and Joe was absolutely massive.

Maria bumped into his gigantic shoulder. "Try it and tell me I'm wrong."

With a disbelieving scoff, he took a bite off his wife's spoon, and his eyes went wide. "Oh, damn."

Together we laughed, and I tried to lean into the moment, but beside me, Logan was still tense.

I gestured toward the untouched ceramic dish in front of him. "Not a dessert guy?"

He shook his head but didn't look at me. "Just not hungry."

He pushed the dish an inch toward me, and with a shrug I hooked my spoon onto the edge and pulled it toward me. The entire time I devoured my dessert—and his—Logan was still and quiet.

The second my spoon rested beside the crème brûlée pot, he leaned in. "Ready to go?"

I glanced around the room. Everyone was still mid-conversation, laughing and refilling their wineglasses.

I brushed the linen napkin across my lips and set it beside my plate. "Sure."

My hand found Maria's back. "We're heading out. See you at the game?"

Her eyes flicked from me to Logan and back again before she smiled. "Good night, you two."

A hint of playfulness in her voice made my cheeks heat. I waved and quietly said my goodbyes as Logan practically dragged me out of the restaurant. He was broody and tense as he stomped past the other tables and jabbed the elevator button with his finger.

"Are you okay?" I asked.

"I'm fine."

He was definitely *not* fine. Maria had warned me that professional athletes get moody and superstitious and weird before big matches. Maybe this was just how Logan dealt with the pressure.

Still, somehow it felt like his frustrations were directed at *me*, and I didn't like the sinking feeling it created in my stomach.

I definitely didn't need that second crème brûlée.

I rubbed my aching stomach, willing the tightness to go away. When the doors opened, I was relieved that we weren't alone in the elevator. I didn't want to say the wrong thing, but I also didn't feel like I had done anything to warrant the silent treatment he was dishing out. When the elevator stopped on the ninth floor, Logan's wide steps quickly outpaced my own.

"Wait up," I called, my annoyance stacking like angry little bricks.

Logan used his key card to open the door and held it for me with one hand.

I brushed past him, then turned with my arms crossed. "Did I do something wrong?"

Logan sighed and dragged a hand through his hair. "No."

My eyes narrowed. "Are you sure, because the whiplash I'm experiencing right now is really confusing?" He wouldn't look at me. "Was the phone call bad?" I stepped forward when a terrible kernel of a thought wedged into my brain. "Is Arthur okay?"

"*Fuck*," he muttered. His green eyes lifted to meet mine. "Arthur is fine. It was Trent. He was asking about tomorrow's game."

Hearing Trent's name fall from his lips was like a slap, angry and stinging. The walls of the room seemed to close in, squeezing the air from my lungs. I thought I'd buried him—buried what he did—but the sound of his name dug it all back up.

I had worked doubly hard to separate the two men in my mind.

In reality, I preferred to forget Trent ever existed.

He took one small step forward. "I would like to talk about Trent."

I would very much like to never *talk about that. Especially with you.*

My cheeks heated, and the walls closed in around me.

Even hearing his name out loud sucked the air from the room.

I lifted my chin. "There's nothing to talk about."

Logan shook his head. "Yes, Julep, I think there is."

Self-preservation and pride reared its ugly head, slamming a wall between Logan and me. I had worked too long and too hard to go back to that dark place. The air grew uncomfortable, and I inched back, my body screaming for me to run and hide. The last thing I wanted to do was flay myself open and admit the mistakes that had allowed Trent to do what he had done.

Anxiety clawed up my spine. Logan was staring back at me, his expression stricken. If I wasn't so frantic, I might almost think he looked *concerned*.

He took another step forward, and I retreated with my hand in the air. "Don't." I couldn't focus on him—my thoughts muddled and tripped over each other.

Logan's hands were in the air in silent surrender. "I spoke with him tonight. He remembers you."

A disgusted scoff rattled in my throat as tears burned my eyes. "Oh, well, that's a relief."

"Look," he said, and his stern voice had my gaze whipping up. "I'm not at all happy with the things he said, but it doesn't change the fact that you slept with my best friend."

Dread pooled in my stomach. I thought I could be the kind of woman who could keep sex and feelings separate. I thought I could do casual.

"This whole thing was a mistake." I wasn't entirely sure whether I was talking about the trip to Kenilworth, staying with him at the hotel, or whatever was blooming between us *everything*

My vision blurred with unshed tears. I needed to leave

before I shattered completely, before Logan saw how deep my cracks ran.

I brushed past him, heading straight to the walk-in closet, where my duffel bag was lying empty on the floor. There wasn't much to pack, so I quickly stuffed my clothes into the bag and hoisted it onto my shoulder. It was a long drive back home—far too long for a rideshare, but worst-case scenario I could call one of my brothers . . . not that I would look forward to *that* conversation.

I'll call JP. He can keep his mouth shut and knows how to clean up a mess.

And, fuck, this had quickly become a mess.

When I moved to leave the room, Logan was blocking the doorway. He looked down at my bag and stepped aside.

His shoulders were slumped, and a single, frustrated tear betrayed me. I wanted to be a hot, roll-around-together good-time gal . . . not the inexperienced sad sack who couldn't rein in her emotions.

"He was wrong." Logan's voice was low, but angry, and it stopped me in my tracks. "I don't even need to hear your side of it to know that."

I turned to see him, a tortured expression marring his handsome face. My chest tightened.

Logan stuffed his hands in his pockets. "He said some things . . . things I wasn't prepared to hear or accept." He let out a defeated sigh. "Look, Trent is an asshole. Deep down, I've always known that, but when you've got media attention and articles being written about you, it becomes harder and harder to know who really has your back and who is using you for your influence. Trent has been there from the beginning . . ."

Something in the way he trailed off made me wonder if

suddenly Trent wasn't sitting so cleanly in the *has your back* category.

His friendship with Trent, a relationship he trusted and valued, had changed because of me. Guilt slicked like motor oil in my stomach, and I felt sick. Logan was accustomed to being used, and I had lined up to do the same, just like all the others.

I shook my head. "You don't have to justify your friendship."

"No." He shook his head in return. "I think maybe I do." He looked angry. "Please stay. *Talk* to me."

My chin wobbled. He was the last person I wanted to know what had happened. It made me feel weak, used, and shameful. I pulled the duffel from my shoulder and let it plop to the ground.

His eyes were lost and confused.

"What do you want to know?" I finally asked.

"Only what you're willing to tell me. Help me understand what happened and why you're holding on to it so tightly."

I circled him and entered the kitchen to get cold water. Somehow standing behind the kitchen island helped me feel protected. The cold water did little to soothe my parched throat, but when I set the glass onto the granite countertop, I sighed.

"Trent and I met a few years ago when he was in Outta-towner for some bachelor party bar-crawl thing." It was then I realized that Logan could have been there. I shook away the thought. No way in hell I wouldn't have noticed *him*.

"Probably Randy's. I didn't go because I was playing," Logan offered.

"He hit on me at the Grudge and"—I sighed again and

let my hands drop against my thighs—"I was charmed. He was older, attractive. Funny and attentive—knew all the right things to say to make me feel special. We hung out that night and exchanged numbers. He lived a few towns over, so we started texting." I let the memories of those early days wash over me. To be fair, it had been fun and exciting to feel like the center of someone's universe.

"He would send flowers and sweet little *good morning* texts. We got together on weekends, always in my hometown. I started asking about meeting his friends, and it was always some excuse: *Mav's traveling, Randy has work, next Saturday is guys' night out.* I was so naive that it never dawned on me that he might be hiding me. I had dated before but never anything that felt like it could become serious. Our relationship felt so grown up and full of promise."

Logan shrugged. "He was into you. I get it."

A bitter laugh shot through me. "For months, he made me feel seen—special. I clung to his sweet words, the little gestures that made me believe I'd finally found someone who wanted me for me. And then, in one careless moment, he shattered it all. He was *so into me* that when we finally had sex, he left before I even had my pants on and never called again."

Logan shook his head. "Julep, that's . . ." He dragged a hand across his face.

Once I started, it felt like I couldn't stop. I needed to get it all out. "I tried for months and months. Calls, texts, driving past his work, circling his hometown in my car. I felt like I was losing my mind. Finally, I realized that what I thought we had never existed. And whatever made-up relationship I thought we had ended because of *me*."

"You?" His face twisted, like he didn't understand how it could possibly be my fault.

I flattened him with a look. *Was he really going to make me say it?*

I clenched my jaw. "Yes, me." I let out a wry chuckle. "I'm not really the girl that gets the fairy-tale ending. I'm not the main character—I'm the kind-of-funny sidekick. The best friend. The cutesy little sister."

Logan tried to interrupt, but I lifted my hand and barreled on. "It's fine. I've accepted it. I learned a very valuable, but hard, lesson that day."

His jaw ticced. "Fuck, that's—" Logan sighed. "I'm so sorry he—"

I gestured in his direction. "Please do not apologize for him."

A frustrated growl tore through Logan as he paced. "Well, what do you want me to do? Because right now the only thing I want to do is find him and tear his head from his shoulders. He's my oldest friend, and I can't stop thinking about how I could fucking *kill* him for what he did to you."

Logan's fists clenched, his knuckles white. The anger in his voice wasn't aimed at me, but it still startled me. He wasn't just angry—he was furious on my behalf. I wasn't used to this, someone fighting for me instead of against me. It scared me almost as much as it comforted me.

"It was *my* fault!" I shouted through angry, frustrated tears. "He knew I was inexperienced, but I didn't tell him the whole truth. I was too shy and embarrassed to admit that I had never had sex. He didn't know until afterward, when I had bled on the bedsheets. Then, he told me I needed to clean up my mess."

His voice rose. "It shouldn't matter if it was your first time or your fortieth. He knew and you deserved better. None of that is your fault."

Shocked, I looked at Logan. "He told you that he knew?"

A muscle in his jaw flexed. "Just tonight . . . based on what Trent said, he knew."

I shook my head. "It doesn't matter. I *wanted* to get it over with. I used him just as much as he used me. But he was smarter—he played the game and came out on top."

"He was cruel. And an asshole. Friend or not, he was wrong for how he treated you."

My eyes lifted to meet his. Logan had maintained a respectful distance, but I could tell he was itching to move forward. He was holding himself back because he wasn't sure what I wanted.

"Yes, he was wrong, but I let it eat me alive. I couldn't get over the sting of rejection. I let it fester and rot. Would you believe that I haven't been able to have sex since? The truth is, I'm broken." A sob escaped me as the painful truth came out. I buried my face into my hands.

Warm arms gathered me in a bundle, and I melted against him. My hot tears flowed as he stood in the kitchen, silently letting me fall apart.

For the first time, I didn't feel judged or dismissed. Logan didn't try to fix me or brush off my pain. He just held me, steady and unyielding, as if he could absorb the pieces of me that were breaking apart.

His soothing *shh* vibrated through me and I cried only harder.

Why couldn't it have been him?

TWENTY-ONE

LOGAN

Holding her as she cried shredded me. Every sob was a sharp edge, cutting through my chest and leaving behind something raw and unfixable. I wanted to fix it for her, to take away every ounce of pain, but all I could do was hold on and hope it was enough.

I held her until her gut-wrenching sobs morphed into soft sniffles.

"Hey." I leaned back, holding her face in my hands and using my thumbs to wipe away her tears. "Listen to me. You are not broken."

Her chin wobbled, but she didn't argue with me.

"I know just what you need." When I stepped back, MJ's brow crinkled. "Give me two minutes. Stay here."

I scurried around the island, disappearing into the primary bedroom. The four-poster bed loomed in the center of the room, but I skirted around it and went straight to the bathroom. Tapping the lights, I fucked with them until only a soft glow from around the mirror shone in the room.

I plugged the soaking tub and scanned the small bottles of shampoo and lotion until I landed on bubbles and a small round bath bomb. In a pinch, it would have to work. I dumped the entire contents of the bubble bath under the spray of the tub and unwrapped the bath bomb before dropping it in with a thunk.

I looked around. *No candles.*

Steam rose from the bath, and I checked the temperature and set out two towels for her. It was simple, but hopefully it would do. I listened for her but couldn't hear anything over the roar of the faucet. Satisfied that I'd done my best to make the lighting soft and the experience cozy, I turned off the faucet and went in search of her.

MJ was standing barefoot near the tall windows of the living room. Her curvy frame was so small against the massive blackness.

A protective urge danced through me.

Not wanting to startle her, I cleared my throat. "Hey, I think it's ready."

She turned, a small wry smile twitching at her lips. "What is it?"

"A hot bath." I raised my hands. "Solo. Just something to help make you feel better."

Her chin wobbled again and my mind raced. *How had I fucked this up even more?*

"Why are you so sweet?" she asked.

My smile cracked. "I have my moments." I held out my hand. "Come on."

MJ stepped forward, slipping her tiny hand into mine. I squeezed once and led her to the en suite bathroom.

She stepped into the dimly lit room and inhaled. "It's so fancy."

"I did my best." My fingertips brushed the hem of her sweater. "May I?"

She looked at me over her shoulder and nodded. As I

lifted her sweater, she raised her arms. My eyes flickered over the back of her cream-colored bra, but I pinned my gaze ahead. This wasn't about me or my dick.

It was about her.

I took a small step back. She didn't need my boner stabbing her as I undressed her.

She needed patience. Care. Tenderness.

My arms encircled her, stopping at the button to her jeans. "Is this okay?"

I watched the small muscles in her neck work as she swallowed and nodded.

My hands trembled as I unhooked her jeans, each brush of her skin against my fingers testing my control. This wasn't about me. It couldn't be. But every inch of her I uncovered was another crack in my restraint.

With an aching slowness, I peeled the denim down her hips. She wore a matching thong, and her ass was flawless in the soft lighting.

Fucking focus.

I lowered to my knees, pulling her jeans the rest of the way down her smooth legs. She stepped from them but stood facing away from me. My hands gripped her hips as I slowly turned her around.

On my knees, I looked up at her.

Her dark hair tumbled across her shoulders as she looked down.

Goddamn she is pretty.

MJ licked her lips, then reached behind her to grab the clasp of her bra. A better man would have stood and given her privacy, but my knees were rooted to the ground.

Her eyes never left mine as she removed her bra. Her nipples formed hard little buds, tempting me, only inches from my face. My hands kneaded her hips, stopping at the waistband of her underwear.

With a tiny nod, she granted me permission. A tiny sip of air moved through my lips as my cock groaned in protest. Slowly I hooked a finger into the band of her thong and lowered it.

She stepped from her underwear and stared down at me. From my vantage, she was strong and powerful. She was in control.

"Logan," she said, her voice breathy as her hand moved across the back of my skull. I could smell her arousal. I knew exactly what she wanted.

Still, I shook my head. "Your bath is ready."

A little smirk lifted her lips. "I'm already soaked."

"*Fuck me*," I exhaled. "How am I supposed to be a gentleman here when I can still remember the taste of your cunt?"

Her grip in my hair tightened as she inched forward, but her eyes were still red and glassy from crying.

My hands flexed on her hips as I steeled my resolve. "Tonight isn't about that. It's about getting the care you deserve. What you should have gotten in the first place."

She stared down at me in silent disbelief.

I closed my eyes. "Just let me do the right thing. Let me do this for you."

When I opened them, her hazel eyes had softened, glowing in the dim bathroom lighting.

I rose, holding on to her hand and guiding her into the massive tub. Her toes disappeared beneath the bubbly surface, and my eyes roamed over her naked body as she lowered herself. My fingertips dragged up her arm and across her shoulder.

MJ hummed as she sank lower into the water. She cracked open one eye. "You should get in."

I shifted, adjusting my hard cock and chuckling softly. "I don't think that's a good idea, Siren."

"Siren?" An eyebrow inched up her forehead.

I grinned. "Gorgeous women who lure sailors to their deaths. I know a siren when I see one."

MJ scooted forward, leaving room behind her. "Come on. I won't bite." Her eyes flicked up to mine. "I trust you."

Yeah, but do I trust myself?

I made quick work of pulling off my sweater and dropping my jeans. I hesitated only a second before stripping out of my boxer briefs and kicking them to the side. I slid into the hot water behind MJ. Her skin was warm and silky smooth against mine.

My dick was rock hard and pressing into her back. "Sorry," I grumbled.

MJ's soft giggle filled the air. "It's fine." She settled against my chest and let her head fall to my shoulder. My heart pounded against my ribs, and I focused on her slow, relaxed breathing.

Under the water, my fingers danced across her arms. She was nestled between my thighs, and her nails dragged delicate circles down to my knee and back up again.

"I'm sorry that I yelled at you," she whispered.

My fingers continued their slow path up and down her arms. "You don't ever have to apologize to me for being honest. Your emotions don't scare me."

After a long stretch of silence, MJ asked, "Is it true? What you said?"

Soothing heat eased my tense muscles. "Hmm?"

Our fingers tangled under the water. "That you still

remember what I taste like?" My chest squeezed and my cock twitched against her back.

She giggled. "I'll take that as a yes."

I kissed her wet shoulder. "Julep, I don't think I'll be forgetting anytime soon."

In the large tub, MJ turned, careful not to slosh water over the edge. Draping her legs over mine, we sat face-to-face with her arms on my shoulders and my hands beneath the water at her hips. Thick bubbles filled the space between us, obscuring her body from view.

She reached up and leaned in for a kiss. It was soft and sweet.

"Thank you for this." Her wet fingertips smoothed over my mustache.

I smirked. "I knew you liked the 'stache."

She flattened me with a stare, a smile twitching the corners of her mouth. "You know what I meant."

I stared into her hazel eyes, appreciating the way everything felt natural. Easy. "You deserve it."

You deserve everything.

"Now turn back around. I'll get your hair."

MJ sucked her lower lip into her mouth to hide her smile, but she did as I told her. I washed and conditioned her hair, and she told me about meeting her father's other family. I mostly stayed quiet, offering small noises of agreement.

"They were so . . ." She blew out a small breath. "Nice."

I smoothed my hands over her hair as I poured a cup of warm water over her strands to rinse out the conditioner. "That's good, I guess."

"You want to know the worst part?" she asked softly. I hummed to encourage her to continue. "One of the girls, Bianca? She had an old picture of my dad and her. He was teaching her how to ride a bike, and he looked so *different*. Younger, sure, but more like he was thrilled to be there. The only bike I ever got was a hand-me-down from Syl, and it was JP who'd taught me how to ride. We didn't get that version of Dad, that's for sure."

She let out a disbelieving grunt, but it was laced with deep sadness.

How often had MJ been forgotten?

The thought gnawed at me. It was no wonder her emotions were all over the place today.

I moved her wet hair away from her shoulder and dropped a silent kiss on her warm skin. "You are strong, resilient—"

"And tired." She sighed, letting her head fall back.

I kissed her again before moving her forward so I could slip out of the tub. I snagged a fluffy oversize towel and wrapped it around my waist before holding one out for her. MJ rose like a siren from forbidden waters, and my mouth went dry. Heat crept up my back and I looked away, still holding out the towel for her. When she stepped closer, I wrapped it around her.

Giving us both space, I walked into the bedroom to throw on a fresh pair of underwear. I stopped to stare at the bed. It was turned down with a small plate of chocolates on one pillow.

"I think we forgot to put the *Do Not Disturb* sign on the door," I chuckled, plucking a chocolate from the pillow.

MJ stepped up beside me. "Benedict is eerily quiet." She looked around the room and out the French doors before tightening the towel around her breasts. "Do you think he's still around?" she whispered.

I shook my head but grabbed my phone anyway. "Nah,

I doubt it, but I'll message him in the app that we don't need anything until morning."

She smiled and dressed in pajamas while I slipped into the bed. Her skin carried the scent of honey and lavender from the bath, and I pulled in a deep inhale.

She settled in beside me, her eyelids puffy from crying, but her smile was soft and her shoulders looked relaxed.

Satisfied, I leaned forward and brushed a kiss on her forehead. "Good night, Julep."

She blushed and closed her eyes. "Good night."

~

I couldn't shake the knot in my gut. Trent had been my closest friend for years, but now I wondered whether I ever really knew him. The things he'd said about MJ . . . I clenched my fists. There was no excuse for any of it. She deserved better. I wanted to protect her from that kind of cruelty, even if it meant reevaluating a friendship that had once felt unshakable.

I had played rugby at the Olympic level, pushed through injuries and bloody knuckles, busted lips, and swollen eyes. Still, nothing had ever been more difficult than sleeping beside MJ and not touching her.

Fine. When we woke up, tangled in each other, my hand was full of her left tit, but that barely counted.

"Mmm," MJ groaned and stretched against me. She sighed and rolled over to look at me.

"Morning." I tried to angle my face so my morning breath didn't totally kill the vibe.

She hid her mouth behind her fingertips. "Morning."

For a moment we just stared at each other, smiling. The

rapid beeps of my alarm stole the moment from us, and I reached over to turn it off with a groan.

She seemed lighter this morning, her laughter more genuine, though the shadows of yesterday still lingered in her hazel eyes. It wasn't like her pain had disappeared, but maybe she was starting to let herself breathe again.

"Big day today." MJ blinked at me with a sleepy smile, and it was easy to forget that anyone outside of that hotel suite existed.

Only they did. *Trent* did, and he was expecting to show up for my match. "Yep."

MJ stretched, her smooth leg rubbing against mine before she laughed. "What a waste of such a great room."

I knew she was talking about the fact we hadn't fooled around. "I don't know . . . I thought it was a pretty good night."

She grinned. "Me too. I hope the rest of the team didn't get too wild last night."

I rolled to my back and rubbed my eyes. "If they did, it'll be a lesson they won't soon forget. Taking a hit when you're hungover is punishment enough."

Beside me, MJ hummed, but a soft sigh followed closely behind it. "You'll have to let me know how it goes."

I propped myself up. "Why wouldn't you see for yourself?"

MJ looked up at me. "I just thought . . ." She blew out a breath. "With Trent going, I don't think it's a good idea for me to be there."

I frowned down at her. "He isn't going. He might *think* he's going, but he's wrong. I want you there."

The slow bloom of her smile squeezed my chest. "Really?"

I leaned down, not caring that both of us had morning

breath, and kissed her. "Yes, really. I need my lucky charm out there today. Now get dressed before we're both late."

I stared into her eyes, searching. Neither of us acknowledged that it was a hell of a lot more than some ridiculous superstition. Because it wasn't just superstition. With MJ in the stands, I played better, more focused. She grounded me in ways I hadn't experienced before. Her presence was a reminder of everything I was working for.

MJ set her chin and, with a tiny shake of her head, scooted out of bed. I knew she understood.

The frenetic buzz of pregame energy whipped through me, but now it was paired with the fact I'd spent an entire evening with the most irresistible woman on the planet and nothing happened.

The match wasn't just another exhibition—it was a chance to prove to myself, to the team, and to the press that I still had what it took. With every passing season, the whispers about my age grew louder. But I wasn't ready to let go. Not yet. And not with her watching.

We were too close to admitting things we shouldn't. For now, it was best if we kept up the facade that we were friends who occasionally fooled around rather than admit to myself how I was really feeling.

It was safer for the both of us that way.

TWENTY-TWO

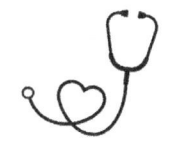

MJ

"Hey," came Logan's playful voice. "Try this on."

A bundle of fabric flew at me, and I caught it midair. When I opened it, I realized it was a jersey—*Logan's* jersey.

My eyes whipped up and he shrugged. "If you want to."

I grinned and disappeared into the hotel bathroom to slip it over my long-sleeved shirt.

A thousand butterflies took flight in my stomach.

Wearing Logan Brown's rugby jersey was not on my bingo card, but staring at my reflection in the hotel mirror, it was hard to deny that Wildhawks green and gold looked pretty damn good on me. I turned to look at my back and admire how *Brown* stretched across my shoulder blades.

If Trent showed up and saw me wearing it, would he care? Would I care that he cared?

A petty part of me wanted him to see me in it and get pissed off. I wanted Trent to realize that he'd messed up when it came to me. Maybe Logan was right and Trent would realize what he'd done was cruel and wrong and that what he had done had hurt me.

I shook my head. Trent's actions had proved to me that

he had the emotional intelligence of a gnat. The more likely scenario was that if he noticed, he would give Logan a hard time and rattle him before his match, or he wouldn't give a shit.

I didn't know which was worse.

"Ready?" Logan called from the kitchen. "I've got coffee to go."

I exhaled and fluffed my hair one last time. When I exited the room, our overnight bags were stacked neatly by the door, and Logan grinned at me with one paper cup in his hand. "Looks good."

I twirled, showing off the jersey with a laugh before accepting the paper coffee cup. "Nothing for you?"

He shook his head. "No caffeine before a match. I've got a pretty regimented plan on game days."

"Ah," I said, taking a small sip of the coffee he had made for me. "Another superstition. Remind me again how you think it's all bullshit?"

I stifled a laugh as Logan's flat stare bore into me. "Let's go, Clover, before I show you just how unsuperstitious I can be. Checkout isn't until noon."

A delicious thrill danced through me, knowing exactly what he meant.

Logan grabbed our bags, despite my offer to help, and together we walked out of the suite and toward the elevators. He filled the drive to the field with casual conversation. Small moments were *easy* with Logan. It made me feel like if we had met in a different timeline, things would be so much simpler.

Reality came crashing back when Logan hit the brakes and muttered *fuck* under his breath. I followed his gaze to see Trent and another man standing outside the box office, arguing with the ticket agent.

Logan threw the vehicle into park. "Wait in the truck."

Before I could even argue, he was gone. I stared in shock as Logan stomped toward Trent. I hadn't seen him at all, except for a few pictures online when I was still stalking his social media accounts, since he'd ghosted me.

It struck me as almost funny—his hair seemed to be thinning. He wasn't as tall as I'd remembered either. Something about him had lost its luster, and for that I was grateful. Sadly, the imaginary horns I always pictured him with were missing, but it had never felt like he was the one who'd gotten away.

It was more like I'd dodged a bullet.

From the truck, I gripped the edge of the seat, my pulse racing as Logan marched toward Trent like a storm about to break.

Trent's casual smirk twisted into something uglier as Logan pointed at him, his jaw tight. My breath caught when Trent's gaze sliced to me, his expression darkening with recognition.

The last time I'd seen those eyes, they'd left me feeling small and unworthy.

I could barely hear their words over the rumble of nearby engines, but the tension in Logan's shoulders said everything. The car was parked close enough that I could just make out the faint words through the glass windows.

"What are you doing here?" Logan's voice was clearly surprised and annoyed.

"May!" Trent went in for a hug, but Logan's back was stiff and he didn't return the embrace. Trent looked at him, confused. "What's the deal?" He hooked a thumb over his shoulder. "They're telling me there's not a ticket."

"There isn't." Logan gripped the back of his neck before

dropping his hand. "I texted you this morning. Today isn't a good day."

Trent's arms spread. "Come on. Don't embarrass me. I told Mikey that we'd have club level." The back of Trent's hand tapped Logan's stomach. "You can get us in."

"I said, not today. Sorry, man." Logan's head moved slightly as he glanced back at the car.

Trent's attention followed the movement, and I sat, frozen. I should have dove under the dash to hide, but it was too late.

"Seriously?" Trent gestured toward me. "Is this what it's about? I already gave you the green light to fuck her."

They had talked about me?

Heat crept up my cheeks. Logan stepped forward, dangerously close to Trent's face. I couldn't make out what he was saying, but his body language was clearly threatening.

With a shake of his head, Trent walked away, hitting Logan in the shoulder as he passed. Clearly he was pissed about what had happened, and his glare was directed at me.

I sat, frozen as he walked toward the row of cars. When he neared me, I could hear him, clear as day: "Fucking cunt."

In an instant Trent was on the ground. Logan had tackled him from behind, and I screamed.

I pushed open the car door. In the next space over, on the cold parking lot asphalt, Logan was straddling Trent, and a hard punch landed to his face. I screamed again as blood spurted from Trent's nose. Logan reared back, and another punch connected with Trent's rib cage.

Logan's fist connected with Trent's face a second time, the crack of bone against bone echoing in the chilly air. "Say it again," Logan growled, his voice low and menacing, as he pinned Trent to the ground.

Trent heaved and spat blood onto the asphalt. "All this for her? She's not worth it."

Logan's fury erupted, and he grabbed Trent's shirt collar, yanking him up. "You don't get to talk about her like that."

His knuckles had tightened, ready for another swing, when my panicked voice broke through.

"Logan, stop!" My hands were on his shoulder, my voice trembling.

My words seemed to pull him back from the edge. He glanced at me, his chest heaving, then released Trent with a shove that sent him sprawling.

Logan was on top of him again. "If I see you near her again, I won't stop next time."

I stepped forward but was shoved aside by two security guards as they pulled Logan off a moaning Trent. They could barely contain him as he shrugged them off and lunged toward Trent again.

"You keep your fucking mouth shut," he shouted at Trent.

Trent's angry gaze flicked my way as he wiped blood from under his nose.

"Don't look at her, you look at me." Logan was seething. "Go home."

As Logan was yanked away by the security guards, Trent stood and took a cheap shot, cracking him in the jaw.

Furious, Logan lunged forward, but the two guards barely held him back. By now a small crowd was gathering, and the scuffle had drawn everyone's attention. The last thing Logan needed was someone taking a video of him beating the shit out of his best friend in the parking lot before the match.

I stepped between them as Logan spat on the ground before taking a step forward.

"Stop." I pressed my palms into his solid chest and tried to shove him backward.

Trent stood behind me, laughing, as tension dripped from Logan. His chest moved with heavy breaths, but I couldn't get him to budge.

He pointed at Logan as I stood, helpless between them. "You are unbelievable, man."

Logan's stare was cold and hard as Trent turned and started to walk away.

"Mr. Brown." A man wearing a suit and looking entirely pissed off stared at Logan. "My office. Now."

Logan shrugged off the security guards and wiped the small drip of blood coming from his lip. My fingers moved to inspect it.

"I'm fine." His tone was cold and clipped. He watched as the man walked away and the security guards followed.

"Who was that?" I asked quietly.

"The club manager." He pressed a finger to his lip again and sighed. "Fuck."

I searched his face, but his expression was unreadable. When he started walking, I kept up but stayed quiet by his side. The guard at the entrance didn't bother asking for identification, and we slipped through the gate.

We walked down a long hallway until we came to a private set of elevators. An attendant used a key card to open the elevator.

"Hey, Phil." Logan tried to smile, but it was pinched tight. "The big boss wants to see me."

Phil nodded and gestured for us to enter. If he noticed the red mark on Logan's jaw or his bloody lip, he didn't mention it. Then he used his key card again to punch in our destination.

We rode in tense silence. When the elevator doors opened, we stepped out and Logan turned to me. "I should only be in there for a few minutes."

"Okay." I tried to sound supportive and hopeful. Logan's mouth was set in a grim line, and he only nodded before turning away.

I wiped my hands down the front of my jeans. The hallway was undecorated and windowless. I couldn't hear anything after Logan knocked on the large wooden door and slipped inside. Minutes ticked by, and I started to worry that he was going to get into serious trouble for starting a fight in the middle of a parking lot.

Would he be fined? Kicked off the team?

Each scenario felt worse than the last.

Still, I replayed in my mind the moment when Trent called me a cunt and Logan tackled him for it. A heady buzz moved down my back and settled between my legs.

It was unhinged, but also . . . really fucking hot.

No man—even the ones who were related to me—had ever stood up for me like that. A primal part of me found the sheer masculinity intoxicating.

When the door cracked open, I stood taller. Logan's green eyes were angry and intense as he stalked down the hallway and stopped in front of me.

"What happened?" I asked quietly.

I stared at Logan, stunned. He stood there, jaw tight, his lip bloodied, and yet he wasn't apologizing. If anything, he looked defiant.

"I'm benched," he bit out. "The team will have to play without me. The club has strict rules about fighting. To be honest, I'm lucky a one-game suspension is all they're giving me. If the owner finds out, I could lose my spot on the team."

"You're benched?" I asked softly, my voice catching.

"One-game suspension," he replied, his tone clipped. "Could've been worse."

A relieved whoosh of air escaped me. "I'm sorry."

Logan looked down at me. "I'm not."

My throat tightened. He'd risked his career—his reputation—for me. "Logan, I didn't mean—"

"I know," he interrupted, his eyes locking on mine. "And I'd do it again."

My breath hitched, his words knocking the air from my lungs. No one had ever fought for me like that. Not my ex, not my family—not even myself.

My insides liquefied at his words.

Logan glanced over my shoulder. "I need to get going, though. I'll stay to support the team, and we're about to take the field. I need to change clothes. You can take the truck if you don't want to stick around."

I shook my head. "I can stay. Maria will keep me company, and I'm finally starting to understand the rules."

A small smirk lifted the bruised corner of his mouth. "Okay. Let's get you to your seat."

∽

With Logan benched, the game wasn't as thrilling as it usually was, but I was still enthralled. From the bench, Logan jumped up, shouting instructions and pointing to his teammates. Despite the chaos of the morning, Logan was clearly in his element.

It also meant a clear view of his thighs, peeking out from his shorts, as he prowled down the sidelines.

My eyes kept drifting to Logan, his body coiled with energy as he barked instructions to his teammates. Even benched, he was commanding—his presence magnetic.

He caught me staring and quirked a small smile, the corner of his mustache lifting just enough to make my stomach flip.

My fingers toyed with the hem of his jersey. Every time the fabric brushed my skin, it reminded me of the man who'd given it to me. Not as a trophy, but as a promise.

For years I'd convinced myself I wasn't worthy of this kind of attention. But Logan's actions today—the way he fought for me, the way he looked at me—told a different story.

By the second half it was obvious we would need a miracle to pull off a win.

With the team struggling, Maria's knees bounced beside me. I rubbed my mitten-covered hands down my legs as we watched the team attempt to gain ground.

The Reapers scored and Maria threw her hands up, slamming her back into the seat. "Damn it!"

I pulled the blanket tighter around my shoulders. "This sucks and it's all my fault."

Maria grumbled but shook her head. "No, the team can't rely on just one player. They need to get their shit together. Besides, if it were Joe who punched someone for me, I wouldn't be upset—I'd be planning my celebratory striptease."

A white cloud puffed into the cold air as I laughed.

Maria laughed beside me. "It may be barbaric, but when a man fights for his woman, it's so hot."

I couldn't disagree with her. There was absolutely no denying that watching Logan defend my honor had my inner feminist showing herself out the door.

Maria nudged me with her elbow, her grin mischievous. "So, what's the plan, Lucky Charm? Gonna reward your knight in shining armor?"

"I don't think I'm his woman. He's just a nice guy."

Maria looked me over like she didn't believe a word I said. "Well, nice guy or not, I've never seen his jersey on another woman."

The thought that I was the first woman to wear Logan's jersey took root. Tickled by the thought, I sat back and watched the Wildhawks, all while a flurry of questions bounced around my head.

Why was I still letting Trent control the narrative?

What if one good romp with someone else was all I needed to get past it for good?

No expectations, no heartbreak.

Logan had more than proved he was a good guy—what was stopping me?

I laughed, but her words stuck with me. My whole life, I'd let people like Trent write the script—deciding how I should feel, what I deserved. But Logan was different. He didn't ask for control—if anything, he gave it back to me.

I glanced at the field, where Logan stood, his eyes scanning the players like a hawk. He'd done his part. Now it was my turn.

Straightening in my seat, I smoothed the jersey over my thighs and made a decision.

No more letting the past define me. No more holding

back. If Logan wanted me to be his lucky charm, then I'd damn well own it.

As I watched him from the field, our eyes met. The left side of his mustache ticced up, and he jerked his head.

Heat gathered in my stomach, spreading warmth to every corner of my body.

The only thing stopping me was . . . *me*.

TWENTY-THREE

LOGAN

"You're quiet." Beside me in the truck, MJ's eyes flicked from me back to her hands.

I shot her a half smile. "Just thinking about the match."

She shifted in the cab, angling her body toward me as I drove down the darkened highway. "A win is a win, right?"

I harrumphed as I mulled over her words.

The team had barely pulled their heads out of their asses long enough to squeak out a victory. Had it not been for a few very lucky calls in our favor, the match would have likely gone in a very different direction.

Half the team was hungover as hell, and the other half played like they didn't know a rugby ball from the ones between their legs.

I should have been out there on the field.

It was an odd sensation, the feeling of helplessness, as I shouted directions from the sidelines. But more than that, there was a strange sense of pride when I could see a play start to take shape. From the outside, it was like an orchestrated dance of flying mud and pained grunts.

I glanced at her again. The way MJ sat beside me in the

truck, her legs tucked up like she belonged here, made my chest tighten. She was burrowing under my skin in a way no one ever had before. Rugby was supposed to be my only love. But lately I couldn't focus on the game without picturing her on the sidelines, wearing my jersey, cheering me on. The thought both thrilled and terrified me.

The tip of my tongue touched the dried blood on my lower lip.

"Does it hurt?" she asked.

"No," I scoffed. "Trent punches like a man who sits behind a desk in a cushy office. I'm fine."

From the corner of my eye, I could see MJ suppress a smile.

Relief washed over me. We hadn't really talked about my scuffle with Trent, and a part of me worried that she thought my reaction was too over the top.

I didn't want to believe that my oldest friend would be such a prick, but I would be lying to myself if I said I was completely surprised by his actions. Trent had always been a little wild and self-righteous.

The sting in my lip was a reminder I wouldn't soon forget.

I steadied my breathing, slowly letting out an exhale and hoping it would relieve the tension that had settled in my neck. Without my usual physical exertion from a game, I was wound tight. My hands tensed on the steering wheel. I needed to focus on the dark highway and not on how good MJ looked in my jersey.

Fuck.

The thought alone shot straight to my cock, and I shifted in the seat.

"I think I finally have it figured out." MJ slipped off her sneakers and crossed her legs in the seat beside me. My eyes appreciated every inch of her denim-clad thighs. When my gaze reached their apex, I cleared my throat and refocused on the road.

"Figured what out?" I asked.

"Rugby."

Thankful for the distraction, I chuckled. "Oh, yeah?"

She grinned and nodded. Her hands animated the words as she spoke. "So . . . the big guys all run into each other, while the slimmer guys stand in a line and watch. Eventually the big guys get tired and pile on top of each other. The ball pops out of the pile, and the skinny guys kick it around for a while. Then the big guys get up and start running into each other again. Sometimes the referee will stop the play because someone dropped the ball, and that's a big no-no. Pretty much anything else goes. Sometimes one group of big guys pushes the other team of big guys over the line, and there's some manly hugging. After a while, they add up the score and someone wins."

My laugh filled the cab of the truck. "That is shockingly accurate."

Pride swelled in her as she grinned a cheeky smile that I returned.

"You make it sound like a bunch of toddlers fighting over a ball," I said.

MJ grinned, shrugging. "Am I wrong?"

"Yes, actually." I pretended to be offended. "It's a highly strategic sport."

She tilted her head. "Strategic toddlers, then."

I laughed, shaking my head. "Stick around, and I'll turn you into a fan. You might even learn the rules."

MJ snorted. "Doubtful."

Eventually the dark and winding highway gave way to the blueberry fields and farmhouses that dotted the outskirts of Outtatowner. I slowed the truck, stretching out the long drive just a little more.

When I turned down the driveway of the King estate, MJ sighed. "Thanks. For the ride and for . . ." She shrugged and laughed. "I don't know, defending my honor, I guess."

I smiled, bowing my head. "It was my duty and a privilege, m'lady."

MJ laughed and climbed out of the truck. I followed, grabbing her bag from the back seat and walking behind her to make sure she made it into the house okay.

MJ slipped a key from her purse and unlocked the door. She stopped before opening it and turned to me, a shy blush evident, even in the moonlight. "Do you want to come in for a little bit?"

I looked up at the huge house and grinned. "I'd like that."

Quietly, I slipped inside behind MJ. She flicked on a light in the foyer, illuminating the open space. "Bug," she called. "I'm home!"

We listened, but there was no answer. "Hmm." She frowned at her phone and typed out a message. "She must be out."

I looked around the grand house. It was eerily silent. "Maybe she went to bed early."

"Are you kidding me?" Her throaty laugh sent sparks straight to my cock. "Bug has a more active social life than I do." Her phone buzzed. "Ah, see. She's out and about with Bax." MJ dropped her purse on a small console table by the door. "Told you, she's the popular roommate."

MJ slipped out of her coat and hung it in a nearby closet. "Come on. I need a snack."

She took off her sneakers, and I put my shoes next to hers.

I followed her, walking quietly as she wound her way through the house toward the kitchen. My eyes settled on my last name, scrawled across the back of her jersey. Heat swirled in my stomach. Seeing her in my name, my colors, felt like a punch to the chest. It wasn't just about pride—it was about ownership, belonging. And that scared the hell out of me, because the more I wanted it to be true, the more I knew I could never let it happen.

But she looked damn good in my jersey. She looked like *mine*.

Suddenly my head was filled with possibilities. MJ at my games. Flying her out with us during the season to wherever our next match was. Watching her laugh on the sidelines or cheer beside Maria and the other wives.

But those possibilities only existed in an alternate universe.

My attention was on building my career. Sure, I was no saint, but I had never wanted to be the type of guy who had a woman in every city. I refused to be the kind of man my father was. Having a relationship when you were constantly traveling was damn near impossible.

So, instead, I focused on the game and never let myself get too distracted.

Or tempted.

But at that moment I was having a hell of a time remembering why.

When she flicked the switch, light flooded the kitchen, illuminating a large marble island. MJ disappeared inside a walk-in pantry. Moments later she was holding a bright-blue package.

"Cookies?" Her eyebrows bounced.

"Sure," I chuckled.

"I'll get the milk." MJ grabbed two short glasses and pulled a gallon of milk from the large stainless-steel fridge.

"Now," she asked as she poured milk into the glasses, "this is a very important question. Are you a dunker?"

Her fingers brushed mine as she passed me the glass of milk, and a spark shot straight to my gut. She didn't pull away, letting her touch linger, as if daring me to close the distance between us. "You're staring," she said, her voice soft but teasing.

I leaned closer, the air between us electric. "Can you blame me?"

I pinched a cookie between my fingers. With a grin, I shoved the whole thing into my mouth and started chewing. Then I grabbed the glass and washed it down. "Milk is strictly for post-cookie enjoyment."

Horrified, MJ slid the package of cookies away from me. "You're a monster!"

Her giggle was infectious.

I reached around her, trying to steal another treat, but she swiveled, keeping the cookies just out of reach.

"You're a shit," I said, gripping her sides and tickling her.

MJ squealed, scrambling out of my touch and holding the cookies above her head. Her hips pushed back into me, rubbing herself against my front as we wrestled. My already rock-hard cock sprang to life as she rubbed against me.

My grip tightened on her hip as my lips closed around the soft skin at her neck. Her laughter died, and her breathing morphed into a soft moan. Her hips pressed backward as the package clattered to the countertop and one hand reached up to get lost in my hair.

My hands moved to grip her shoulders and rub the muscles with my thumbs. "You look good in my colors."

MJ turned, facing me as she looked up, taunting me with one raised eyebrow. "You think so?"

Heat gathered at my spine. "Julep, I know so."

Without breaking eye contact, her fingers lingered on the button of her pants, but she didn't move right away. For a second she just looked at me, her hazel eyes searching.

My breath caught in my throat as I wondered what she saw. *Did she see the man I was pretending to be? Or the one who was falling for her, hard and fast?*

A sly smile spread across her pretty face. "How do you think these colors would look if I had nothing else on?"

This was it.

My last shred of self-control was dangling by a thread, and MJ's fingers on that button were the scissors poised to cut it. I wanted to pull her into my arms, kiss her senseless, and lose myself in her completely.

My hips ground against her, and a tiny whimper pushed through her lips. "Show me."

MJ's chin lifted as she shoved me back, anticipation glittering in her eyes.

Just as her hands undid the button of her jeans, a low buzz from my phone filled the air.

We both froze, the tension crackling between us. "You gonna get that?" she asked, her voice breathless.

I shook my head, stepping closer. "Not a chance."

I knew I was playing with fire. Letting her in, even a little, was a risk I couldn't afford to take. But standing here, watching her look at me like I was the only man in the world, I couldn't bring myself to care. For once, I wanted to forget the rules.

Forget the game and just get lost in her.

TWENTY-FOUR

MJ

There was a challenge in Logan's stare, but I was ready. Without breaking eye contact, I lowered the zipper of my jeans. Shimmying my hips, I slid the denim down my legs.

Logan's fingertips dragged up the side of my bare thigh, and an appreciative grunt rumbled in his chest.

With him, I felt confident and *alive*.

I reached behind me, unhooking my bra and snaking one arm inside the oversize jersey to slip my arm free. Logan watched as I pulled my bra through the armhole without removing the jersey. I held it to the side before letting it drop to the floor.

"Impressive." He smirked. Logan's hands flexed at his sides, but he didn't touch me.

Not until I give him permission.

I grinned up at him, hoping my nerves were well hidden. In a move I had hoped was sexy and not completely awkward, I slid my underwear down and kicked them to the side.

Every nerve ending buzzed with anticipation, but somewhere beneath the bravado, the old whispers of doubt lingered. *Was I enough? Could I really hold his attention?*

But the way Logan's eyes burned into me made every insecurity melt away. Right now I wasn't broken. I wasn't just the funny sidekick.

I was his.

Logan's jersey was oversize, brushing the tops of my thighs and just barely covering my ass. "Logan, I have a very important question."

His eyes moved over the hemline of the jersey before working his way up. His gaze paused at the spot where my nipples poked through the mesh fabric, then settled when he looked me in the eye. "Yes, Julep."

Nerves skittered beneath my skin. I had no idea how to seduce a man who was far more experienced than I was. I took a deep breath, hoping my voice didn't betray me. "Do you want to touch me?"

He inched forward, his hips barely brushing against me. "Do you want me to touch you?"

The masculine scent of his skin and cologne was intoxicating. Heat pumped off his huge frame, soaking into my bones.

My hand moved up his broad chest and behind his neck before disappearing into his hair. I hummed, arching my neck to allow him access, begging for him to kiss me.

His lips hovered above my skin, his breath warm on my neck. "You have to say it, Julep. Tell me you want me to touch you."

He hadn't moved yet, and the ache between my thighs became unbearable. His heat pressed against me, so close but maddeningly out of reach. My breath hitched, and I realized I was holding it, waiting for him to close the distance. When his fingers finally grazed my skin, it felt like the first spark of a wildfire.

"Logan, *please*. Touch me." My permission was all it took for him to snap.

He was everywhere.

Logan pinned my back to the island as his mouth covered mine with a low, deep growl. I moaned into his kiss, threading my arms around his neck, hiking the jersey even higher. He slid his hand up to palm my breast through the material.

His hands fisted the hemline of the jersey, pulling our bodies together. "Seeing you in this makes me fucking feral."

The way Logan's hands gripped my hips, possessive yet careful, made my stomach swoop. His gaze burned into me, and it felt like I was the center of his universe. I swallowed hard, trying to steady my breathing.

I didn't just feel wanted—I felt *claimed*.

I blinked up at him. "Green is my color," I teased, emboldened by the low octave of his voice.

Logan's jaw flexed. "It's not the color. It's my name on your back. It tells everyone what you are."

"And what's that?" I asked as my stomach swooped.

His nostrils flared as one hand moved to grip the back of my neck. "*Mine*."

My lips parted and his mouth hovered an inch over mine. "Say it," he commanded.

With barely a whisper, I gave in to what we both needed to hear: "I'm yours."

His kiss was rough, our teeth clacking when he pulled me into him. One hand held my neck while the other slid up my bare thigh. My legs parted, trying to maneuver to give him more access to me. He slid between my thighs, teasing my slick entrance with one thick fingertip.

My head dropped back, giving in to the sensation of being explored.

Worshipped.

Logan turned me, pressing my hips into the cold marble countertop. I bent at the waist, leaning over the counter and jutting my hips into his lap.

His nails raked up the backs of my thighs and I gasped, my pussy going wet in anticipation. "Yes, Logan."

He groaned as I pushed my hips backward. "You don't know how badly I want to fuck you right now."

I looked at him over my shoulder. "I'm ready."

He frowned, like his head and his dick were at war with each other.

I stood, arching backward so my back was flush with his front. I gripped his neck and pulled him closer. "I don't want to be treated like I'm breakable. This is what I want."

I gripped his wrist, guiding his hand lower. "Here," I whispered, my voice trembling but sure. "Right here."

The flicker of a grin on his lips told me he loved it when I took the lead, but the way his hand covered mine and held it steady reminded me I was safe to let go. One hand moved under the jersey to cup my breast. He pinched my nipple between his fingers.

"Yes," I moaned.

He made quick work of removing his pants, and he tore his T-shirt over his head. His boxer briefs were gone and he stood behind me, hard and toned and gloriously naked. He held me steady with one hand gripping my hip. The other fisted his cock and teased the seam of my ass.

I arched to grant him access, and just when I thought he would place the tip of his cock at my opening, he stopped.

I looked back at him. A deep line creased his forehead.

When our eyes met, he shook his head. "Not here. Not like this."

My chest squeezed as I turned. Logan licked his lip, and the dimple in his left cheek deepened. In a quick move he bent, then tossed me over his shoulder. My surprised yelp morphed into giggles when he stomped naked through the house, carrying me.

When we got to my bedroom, he kicked the bedroom door closed with his foot and deposited me on the bed.

I stared up at him, my hair fanned around me.

"I want to take my time with you." His hand moved across my chest, over my breast, and down my stomach before stopping between my thighs. "You're going to tell me exactly what you want, and I'm going to give it to you."

Logan's muscles bunched beneath my hands, his jaw tightening like he was holding himself back. The raw heat in his eyes made my stomach flip. He didn't say a word, but I could feel the tension radiating from him, the barely controlled desire humming under his skin. It was electrifying to know I had that effect on him.

Drunk on power and him, I grinned and spread my legs. "I want to feel you." My hand brushed across my wet pussy. "Right here."

Logan grinned and tugged my legs wider as he mounted the bed. Settling between my thighs, he fisted his hard cock and ran the tip through me.

"I've been tested." His focus was lasered in on the spot where his cock rubbed against my pussy.

"Me too." I squirmed beneath him, silently begging for more. "And I'm on the pill."

The hard length of his cock slid against my clit, and I nearly shot off the bed.

His hand settled at the base of my neck. "Tell me."

Our eyes met and I stared, unable to deny the *want* I had for this man. I wanted to be stretched. Filled. Owned.

"I want you." I swallowed hard.

A satisfied grin spread across his handsome face. I'd given him permission, but he hadn't filled me. Not yet.

My back arched and my head tilted backward. "Logan, *please.*"

I could hear my own desperate, needy plea, but I didn't care. My mind was lost in the moment—those delicious seconds of anticipation. I'd never experienced anything like it. My one and only time having sex was with Trent, and he certainly hadn't taken any time with me to make sure I was relaxed and ready.

And with Logan, I was so fucking ready.

My core lit up with desire as he took his time, teasing my nipples, sucking the pulse point that hammered at the base of my neck. His thick finger slid through me, adding gentle pressure.

He swirled it at my opening. "You're fucking soaked."

His words set me on fire, and my hips canted upward. My mind was already lost in the sensation of him touching me. When his finger slipped inside, my breath hitched.

One finger, then two.

Slowly he moved in and out, stretching me open. Priming me for his thick cock. His kiss was passionate and deep as his fingers moved inside me. My nipples puckered as a deep ache bloomed in my core.

"I think I'm going to—" The words died on my lips as he kissed me again.

"Show me," he commanded. "Show me how pretty you are when you come."

My hips moved in tandem with his hand as I rode

toward release. Pleasure seized my body, and my pussy pulsed around his fingers.

When the wave hit, it wasn't just pleasure—it was freedom. Every broken piece of me felt whole under his touch. My body shuddered as I cried out, his name on my lips, the only thing anchoring me to the moment.

As my orgasm crashed over me, Logan slipped his fingers from me, moving them to his mouth. I watched him suck my taste from his fingers.

"Now you're ready." The gravel in his voice sent delicious shivers down my back. Fisting his cock, he guided it between my legs.

Once notched at my entrance, he paused, silently checking in with me. I nodded and spread my legs wider.

God, yes. Now.

I held my breath, waiting in anticipation. Logan went slowly, stretching me as I breathed through the sensation of him finally entering me.

With a guttural moan, he slid in a little deeper. Propped on my elbows, I spread my legs wide. My eyes were fixed on the spot where his massive cock disappeared inside me. Logan braced himself on the bed, taking care to keep the bulk of his weight off me as he continued to slide in and out.

His movements weren't just deliberate—they were reverent, like he was discovering something sacred. Every thrust felt like a promise: *I see you. I want you. You're safe with me.*

And for the first time in years, I believed it.

My body reacted when I realized he wasn't even all the way in, yet I was already so full. I didn't think I could take any more.

My mouth hung open as another inch disappeared.

"Tell me you're okay. I won't hurt you." The pained

expression on his face sent a tug of emotion pulling at my chest.

Logan wouldn't hurt me. I could trust him.

"I want more." My voice wasn't my own. It was confident and sexy and all woman.

"Fuck, you're taking every inch." He slid out until just the tip remained inside, before sliding right back in again. "You're taking me so well."

His words buzzed through me, and I collapsed onto the bed. My fists gripped the sheets as his hips moved forward. With each thrust, Logan lit up every nerve ending inside me. I pulled my knees up, hoping I could take all of him as his hips pistoned.

The moment he was finally all the way in, an appreciative groan tore through his chest.

When his hips hit mine, I saw stars. Heat and tingles moved down my spine. Over and over he thrust, his deep grunts pushing me closer to another orgasm.

"Jesus, Julep. You feel so fucking good." He moved again, and sparks fluttered in my belly. "Being buried inside you is unreal."

His filthy words lit up my insides, stripping me of any insecurities and making me feel like a goddess.

His eyes never left me. He was assessing, making sure that I was taken care of. My heart squeezed. He watched as a fresh wave of ecstasy rolled over me. My hands gripped the muscles in his back in a desperate effort to pull him closer.

I cried out, screaming his name and wrapping my legs around him. He filled me again and again until his thrusts got jerky and erratic. His hips shuddered, and he stilled before his hands framed my face and our tongues tangled.

Inside me, his cock twitched as he collapsed on top of

me. The sheer mass of his body should have smothered me, but I was overcome, delighted with his weight pinning me to the mattress.

Relief flooded my system as tears pricked my eyes.

This is what it's supposed to be like.

When he lifted his weight, his cock slipped from inside me. Logan propped himself up beside me and stared down at me as the warm trickle of his cum seeped from my pussy.

A spike of panic raced through me as memories of *making a mess* played over in my mind. My legs started to close when he gripped my knee and pulled me open. His fingers swiped across my thigh, collecting the sticky mess. I inhaled as I watched him gently push it back inside.

Heat spread across my cheeks and neck as his appreciative eyes moved over my naked body. Sated and sweating, I buried my face against his shoulder. I squeezed my eyes closed, and I hoped he couldn't feel my grin. His heartbeat pounded beneath my ear.

Logan settled onto the mattress, wrapping his arms around me and pulling me close. He held me without saying a single word.

Exhaustion slinked over me as a tiny voice tapped the inside of my skull.

Hold on while you've got him.

Logan's arms around me felt like the safest place in the world. But as his heartbeat slowed and his breathing evened, my thoughts raced. I couldn't hold on to him forever. The weight of reality crept in, whispering that this was only temporary.

TWENTY-FIVE

MJ

Sometime in the middle of the night, I'd rolled over and leaned into Logan's warmth. He was like sleeping next to a furnace. I also learned that sleepy, middle-of-the-night sex was just as mind-blowing as passionate, take-me-now sex.

Early-morning light slanted through my bedroom window, and I blinked up at the ceiling. Logan's heavy, rhythmic breathing whooshed softly in my ear. I was tempted to cuddle into him when a single thought shot me awake.

Bug.

"Shit," I muttered, easing out from beneath Logan's massive arm.

Yes, I was a full-grown adult woman, but I had zero desire to discuss my sex life with the woman who had raised me.

I glanced at the clock. It was only 5:00 a.m. There was a chance I could get him out the door before she came down for her morning coffee. I sat up, looking around my room.

Dread coiled in my stomach. We'd been so hot for each other that our clothes were still in piles in the kitchen. I stepped out of bed, and when the wood floor creaked, I froze, looking at Logan. He didn't rouse, so I sneaked to my dresser. I tugged on a T-shirt and pajama pants before slipping out of my bedroom.

Bug wasn't just my aunt—she was the voice in my head reminding me of every questionable decision I'd ever made. Sneaking Logan out before she saw him was an impossible mission. It wasn't that I was ashamed of him—I just wasn't ready for the interrogation. Bug had a way of looking at me that made me feel both five years old and a hundred years behind in life.

I listened for any sign of my aunt, but the house was still. I quickly scurried down to the kitchen. It was dark, so I scooped up my clothes.

Where the hell are my panties?

On my hands and knees, I felt around the floor near the island. Halfway across the wood floor, the small scrap of silk was lying in a tiny ball. I reached for it and tucked it into the mess of discarded clothing.

"Morning." Bug's voice startled me and I shot to my feet.

"Oh!" I flicked the hair from in front of my face. "Morning. How are you? You're up early."

My aunt paused, eyeballing me as she pressed start on the coffee maker. Her gaze flicked down to the bundle of clothes in my hand.

I lifted it. "Getting some laundry done early." When her eyebrow only crept higher, I cleared my throat.

Bug's eyebrow arched higher than I thought humanly possible. "Laundry, huh?" she said, her voice dripping with suspicion.

My face burned hotter than the coffee maker. "Yep. Early bird and all that." Bug didn't say anything else, but her smirk spoke volumes. I bolted before she could ask more questions I didn't have answers for. "Okay. Chat with you later."

Without looking at her, I hurried out of the kitchen and back to my bedroom. When I clicked the door shut, I closed my eyes, leaning against it with a deep exhale.

"Morning, Julep," Logan rumbled.

My eyes opened and I flew across the room, planting both hands across his mouth. "Shh! She'll hear you."

His brow furrowed, and I gently removed my hands.

"Your aunt?" he whispered.

"Yes!" I hissed, looking over my shoulder and listening for her.

A soft chuckle rumbled out of him. "I knew you were hiding me," he teased.

I scowled in his direction. "I'm not *hiding* you, but I'm not broadcasting you to my aunt either. She can be . . . tough."

He laughed again. "It's cute you're scared of her."

I scoffed. "I'm not scared of her. I'm scared for *you*." I looked around again, picking up his T-shirt and shoving it at him. "We have to get you out of here."

Logan pulled his shirt on in the sexiest way possible. My hands quickly framed his face, and I kissed him hard. "God, you're handsome."

His wide palm slid around my waist, pulling me closer. "I'll take some more of that."

I climbed off him. "I can't. Not now. Not with her just downstairs."

Logan laughed, completely unfazed by the fact I was shoving him out the door.

After he dressed, I grabbed his hand and pressed a finger to my lips in the universal *shh* gesture. Like a pair of teenagers, we slowly crept down the hallway. The back stairs were our best option, as the front would lead us straight across the entrance to the kitchen. I could still hear my aunt milling around as we made our way to the bottom of the staircase.

Just as my hand reached the doorknob, Bug's voice called out: "Does Logan like cream in his coffee?"

Logan laughed as my mouth popped open.

Bug appeared from the kitchen into the hallway, holding a steaming mug of coffee. "His shoes are by the front door."

Bug's eyes were laced with humor before she disappeared again.

Logan kissed the top of my head. "I got this."

I stared as he sauntered, barefoot and sexy as hell, into the kitchen.

What the heck is happening? Coffee with my aunt was not *the casual, no-strings, no-heartbreak encounter I need right now.*

With a frustrated growl, I padded behind him.

By the time I reached the kitchen, Logan had a mug of steaming coffee in his hand, leaning against the kitchen island and laughing with my aunt.

She was *laughing*.

Do you have any idea how hard it was to make a no-nonsense woman like Bug King laugh? Fucking impossible.

Bug never laughed. Like, *ever*.

Yet there she was, chuckling into her coffee like Logan was some kind of magician. I leaned against the doorway, watching them. Logan's bedhead and sleepy grin should have been disarming, but the way he moved—confident, but not cocky—made my stomach do a weird flip.

How did he make it look so easy?

Mischief sparkled in Logan's eyes as he lifted the mug to his lips. He sighed on the exhale. "Can I pour you a cup?" He moved toward the coffee maker before I could even answer. "Cream and sugar, right?"

I stopped, staring. "Uh—" Noises sputtered out of me, but none of them formed actual words.

Bug walked behind me, reaching for a napkin, when she whispered in my ear. "Close your mouth, dear."

It snapped shut as I watched my aunt be utterly charmed by the man with bed head who was sneaking glances at me and smiling.

~

The Sand Dune Art Barn was just on the outskirts of Outtatowner, nestled between rambling blueberry fields. Lee and Annie had turned a broken-down old barn into a place where tourists and locals flocked to spend an afternoon creating.

The huge doors of the barn were closed, but the parking lot was packed with cars. Next to the barn was Lee and Annie's farmhouse, with creamy yellow paint and white shutters.

Rushing against the cold wind, I slipped inside the barn. Stacks of painted pottery waiting to be picked up lined the shelves. Behind it, the unpainted pieces waited for customers to unleash their creative talents. It was amazing how they'd turned a once-flailing art studio into a place where people spent rainy afternoons and sunny Saturdays.

My hands were buzzing, not from the cold, but from excitement.

I had to tell *someone* about what happened between

Logan and me. Sylvie hadn't answered the phone, and I assumed she was busy with her own life.

Annie would understand.

Behind the counter, Annie's wild red hair was tied in a scarf. She wrapped a glazed mug in white tissue paper. The customer had transformed the white, unfinished ceramic into a riot of greens: earthy moss green mixed with a basily shade. On top, they'd splattered a pale yellow.

The mix of colors reminded me of Logan's eyes, and my stomach did a little flip.

Telling Annie felt like popping the cork on a bottle I'd been shaking for weeks. I wanted to scream about how good Logan made me feel, how right it all seemed. But a little voice whispered, *Don't get used to this. He's not staying.* I shoved the thought aside, focusing on Annie's warm smile.

Impatient, I tapped my foot to release some of the energy building in my body as I waited for the customer to finish. When the customer paid and said their goodbyes, Annie drew her attention to me, and I slapped my hands on the counter.

"I did it!" I leaned forward and practically squealed.

Annie grinned. "Did what?"

I looked around and lowered my voice. "I had no-strings-attached sex. With Logan! And in his jersey too. Oh my god, it was so hot. I'm covering a shift at work, but after that, we're going to get dinner. Eek!"

Happiness and excitement were pouring out of me.

Annie's eyes narrowed as she walked around the cash register to join me on the other side. "So let me get this straight: you've been going to all his games, wearing his jersey, boning, *and* you have plans to go on an actual dinner date later." Her melodic laugh floated into the air. "I hate to break it to you, but I wouldn't call that no strings, babe."

I frowned at her. "I haven't been to *all* his games."

When our eyes met, we both dissolved into a fit of laughter.

Her hand touched my arm. "I'm happy for you, I am. I just don't want to see you get hurt."

"I can handle it," I said, my voice bitchier than I intended.

Annie's smile didn't waver, but her brow crinkled slightly.

"I mean it," I added, softer this time.

She nodded, but the look in her eyes said she wasn't convinced.

My back straightened as I exhaled. "I know what I'm doing. I can handle it."

It was just sex. It didn't have to mean anything at all.

It felt better to remind myself of that before I let my body get ahead of my brain.

"He's only here for the offseason, and we both know that. But oh my god . . ." I leaned in to whisper. "Trent showed up at the field, and they got into an argument. He called me a cunt, and Logan *tackled* him. I think my ovaries exploded."

"Shit, mine too." Annie pressed a hand to her lower stomach. "Sometimes a little unhinged masculine energy is exactly what the doctor ordered."

I shrugged with a smile. "Worked on me, although I did feel bad that Logan got benched for the game over it."

Annie's shoulder bumped mine. "Sounds to me like you made up for it."

Heat prickled my cheeks, and my eyelashes swooped to hide my embarrassment.

I glanced at the clock. "Okay, I need to head to work." I turned to her. "Not that he's tried to call or anything, but do you think you could ask Lee to subtly drop a hint to Kenny that things are . . ."

My hands gestured vaguely in front of me, and Annie nodded. "No worries. Kenny is a big puppy dog, and I think he'll be just fine. But if it comes up, I'll have Lee let him down gently."

I hugged her. "Thanks."

As I said goodbye to Annie, my phone dinged and my chest pinched. I tried not to be too disappointed that it wasn't Logan, but my sister Sylvie.

"Hey," I answered, rushing toward my car.

"Sorry I missed you earlier. Everything okay?" she asked.

"Great," I answered, buckling myself in and giving my car a minute to warm up.

"I've been worried about you." Sylvie's voice took on a worried mothering quality that made me smile.

"Me? Why?" I asked as I drove toward Haven Pines.

"MJ . . . you met Dad's other family. Alone. *They were surprisingly warm and welcoming?* That's all you're giving me?"

A pit opened in my stomach. I didn't want to think about them, let alone tell my sister that just when we thought things with Dad couldn't get worse, they did.

How do I tell them the full truth without causing more pain?

An ugly, jealous feeling grew anytime I let a thought of Bianca and Blair slip in. It wasn't fair. Their *daddy* wasn't the same imposing, frightening man we had been forced to grow up with. I had always thought the generous, benevolent man was a facade. Turned out, he simply reserved that side of himself for *them*.

"I don't know," I answered with an exasperated sigh. "We can talk about it."

"Good," she said. "Why don't you come to the farm for dinner?"

"Tonight? Um . . . I kind of had plans, but—"

"You can bring Logan. I'd like to officially meet him."

My brain stopped. *How did she . . . ? So much for Bug not being a gossip.*

Dinner at the farm wasn't just dinner. It was Duke's grumpy frown, and Sylvie's meddling questions. It was territory I wasn't sure Logan and I were ready to step into. Yet the thought of him meeting them didn't fill me with dread—it filled me with excitement, and that scared me more than anything.

I chewed on my lip. Dinner with my family was flirting with *dating* territory, but I'd be lying if I didn't admit it was a little fun to watch Logan squirm under Duke's hard stare.

"I'll ask him, but count me in." I hung up the phone and gripped the wheel as I made my way toward work.

Once inside, I made quick work of storing my belongings at the nurses' station.

Supposedly it was a full moon, and while I wasn't witchy like my brother's girlfriend, after she'd roped me into participating in a séance that was *very* eerie, I wouldn't put it past the universe to mess with me today.

I looked over my files and headed out on my first set of rounds. When I stopped at Arthur's room, I gently rapped on the door and entered after he greeted me.

"Morning, Mr. Brown," I singsonged.

"Well," he greeted. "Now this is a lovely day, isn't it?"

I smiled. "You sure know how to make a girl feel good, Mr. Brown."

Arthur set down the book he was reading. "You know

you're my favorite. No reason to hide the plain truth. I just hope my grandson is treating you right."

A short laugh shot out of me before I could stop it. "Logan and I are—well, he's been . . . very kind to me. We've developed a friendship."

A sparkle of mischief glittered in the old man's eyes. "If that boy's keeping you just friends, then he's dumber than he looks. If I were forty years younger, I'd court you myself."

I shot him a plain look, trying to hide my smile. "If you were forty years younger, I think I'd have quite the competition."

We shared a smile as I gathered my courage. "I do have a question for you, though. If I were to have dinner at my sister's farm and I wanted to ask Logan to come . . . that wouldn't seem like I was looking for anything *more* than friends, would it?"

"A family dinner is an important thing." Arthur paused, his wrinkled lips pursing as he seriously considered my question. "If it were anyone else, I think it would be a tough sell, but coming from you, I think all you'd need to do was ask."

Pleasure washed over me. "Thanks, Mr. Brown."

As I left, I pulled my phone from the pocket of my scrubs and texted Logan.

> Hey, remember that time you called me a hooker?

LOGAN

Don't remind me . . .

> I thought of how you could make it up to me.

LOGAN

Does it involve my tongue?

My eyes bugged and I looked around. Heat flamed my cheeks as I smiled at the screen.

> Sylvie asked me over for dinner at the farm. Want to join me?

LOGAN

That's easy. I'd love to. But you didn't answer my question.

> About your tongue? I'll think about it.

TWENTY-SIX

LOGAN

I STARED down at her text message and grinned.

I couldn't *stop* thinking about MJ and my tongue. Sex with her hadn't just been good; it had been better than anything I'd experienced. Something about her made me feel centered.

Connected.

"Are you going to pull your head out of your ass or just smile at your phone all afternoon?" Jack's voice had my eyes whipping up.

Still dressed in practice gear, Jack was streaked in mud and was using the cleats brush by the door to wipe off his practice shoes.

Straddling a bench near my locker, I tossed my phone aside.

"You played well out there today. I think if we run the second play a few more times, it'll go a lot smoother." I was intentionally ignoring Jack's dig about my head being up my ass. He wasn't wrong. I had been distracted the entire practice.

I knew better than to let her invade my head like this.

Rugby was my constant, my anchor, but lately MJ had become the thing I couldn't stop thinking about.

And that scared the hell out of me.

We had a few days before we were headed out of town for a match, and the coach was getting antsy about our lackluster performances. I hated to admit that I was part of the problem.

"We're reviewing tape tonight and then getting food. You in?" Jack stripped off his practice jersey and tossed it into the large laundry bin.

I looked at the clock.

Shit.

It was two hours back to Outtatowner. I had just promised MJ I'd get dinner with her at her sister's place.

I had started to come up with an excuse when the locker room door opened. Our assistant coach held the door with his palm. "Brown. Coach wants a word."

I gritted my teeth and stood.

"Oohhh," Jack teased.

"Fuck off," I mumbled, tossing a sweaty sock in his direction.

If Coach wanted to talk with me, it was either to deliver praise or come down on me. Given my lackluster practice, I prepared for the latter as I walked to his office.

Coach's door was open when I reached it, but I rapped my knuckles on the doorframe to announce my arrival. His head lifted and he waved me inside.

"You wanted to see me?" I asked.

Coach removed the cap from his pen. "How's the knee feeling?"

Like shit.

I straightened my shoulders. "I'm not worried about it."

"And your head?"

Besides the ringing in my ear? Perfect.
"Clean bill of health from the doctors."

He nodded and wrote something down on the legal pad next to him. He exhaled and looked at me from across his desk. His hands folded in front of him. "Then what is your excuse for that practice today?"

"Sir?"

He raised his brows. We both knew I knew exactly what he was talking about. I'd called the wrong plays, I'd bobbled the ball, and cement had filled my cleats.

I cleared my throat. "I've been . . . distracted." My hand circled the side of my head. "Just a lot going on right now."

He stared hard. "It's not the yips, is it?"

Fuck, I hope not.

In professional sports, *the yips* could permanently end your career. I'd seen athletes from golf to baseball to hockey suddenly, inexplicably, lose their ability to function. Research said it was purely psychological, but when you lost your ability to perform basic skills, you were done for.

I shook my head. "No, sir. I just need to get my head in the game. Recenter. I'll be fine."

"Distractions happen to the best of us." Seemingly satisfied, Coach leaned back in his chair. "Be certain your head and heart are in it. If you get called up to the Sevens, they'll need you to be ready. This is no joke, Brown," Coach said, his gaze hard. "If your head's not in it, they'll find someone else. This is your chance to remind everyone who you are. Finally put those retirement rumors to rest—don't waste it."

His words resonated, a heavy reminder that rugby wasn't just a game.

It was everything.

I nodded, and he waved a hand toward the door. "That'll be all. Enjoy your evening."

I turned on my heels and left his office.

Called up? Was that even a possibility the head coaches were tossing around?

~

Despite my promise to Coach that I'd get my head back in the game, I ditched my teammates and drove the two hours back to Outtatowner.

MJ made me feel strong and at ease—exactly what I needed if I was going to release the pent-up frustrations I'd been carrying around. I felt bad for using my grandfather as an excuse to not review game film, but I knew my teammates wouldn't understand.

Hell, I wasn't even certain *I* understood why lately I seemed to be able to relax only in MJ's presence.

She had sent me the address to her sister's farm and I enjoyed the quiet ride, listening to music and recalling how MJ's hair fell across the pillow. The bustle of the city eventually gave way to rambling fields and densely forested land.

From its mount on my dash, the phone flashed with a text message.

> **TRENT**
>
> Call me. Don't let a piece of ass get between us.

Piece of ass?

My knuckles whitened around the steering wheel. Trent had a way of reducing everything to the lowest denominator, and right now it made me want to drive to his place and remind him why I broke his nose last time. I ground my teeth together and ignored him completely.

Eventually, GPS brought me to a long path that led to

the entrance of Sullivan Farms. Beyond the small berm that acted as a wind barrier, a beautiful farmhouse came into view. The path veered to the left and led to what appeared to be housing for migrant workers.

I spotted MJ's car, but as I headed in that direction, a hound dog shot out from the bushes.

"Shit." My foot slammed on the brakes, and my wheels skidded across the gravel.

When the dog barked again from the side of my truck, I sighed in relief. The dog continued to bark and circle my car. I realized he was missing a leg, and waddling behind him was a—*Was that a fucking duck?*

"Ed! Get your ass back here!" From the porch, Duke Sullivan appeared. He hollered at the dog again and stomped down the front steps. He waved me forward. "Just drive over his dumb ass."

I stared, frozen.

He gestured again. "Come on. He'll move out of the way once you start rolling again."

Hoping I could trust him, I inched forward. The dog and duck duo continued circling the truck, but thankfully they gave me a wide berth.

After I parked my truck next to MJ's car and climbed out, Ed seemed to lose interest. He ran off toward the large red barn in the distance, the duck waddling behind.

Duke met me with his hand out. "Sorry about that. Three-Legged Ed came by his name honestly, but I swear that hound doesn't want to learn."

I placed my hand in his and gave it a firm shake. "I'm just glad I didn't rename him Two-Legged Ed."

Duke smirked, and I assumed that was as close to a warm greeting as I would get.

"MJ is inside with Sylvie and Gus."

I looked over his shoulder toward the large farmhouse.

Sullivan Farms felt like it was made to last forever. Sturdy, dependable. Not like the hotels and rented apartments I bounced between. It made me wonder—just for a second—what it would feel like to stay. The farmhouse itself looked like it had a soul—strong and steady, the kind of place where generations gathered to share meals and stories. It was everything my life wasn't—rooted, permanent, and filled with warmth.

Not old, but lived in.

Well loved.

The expansive front porch had been decorated for autumn with pumpkins, mums, and dried stalks of corn. A pair of wicker chairs seemed perfect for looking out onto the expanse of the farm. In the distance, beyond the red barn, rows and rows of blueberry bushes were just starting their slow transition from green to reddish-purple.

I nodded to Duke as I stepped past him and climbed the porch steps. I opened the door and stepped inside. Warm smells of something rich cooking in the oven greeted me. I could hear the low conversation coming from the kitchen. Carefully, I slipped off my jacket and hung it on a hook near the door. When I followed the sound of MJ's laughter, I paused in the doorway to the kitchen.

Sylvie had a dish towel flung over one shoulder as she pulled a pan from the oven.

A sleeping child was propped on MJ's hip.

I swallowed hard as I watched her. She moved so easily with the kid on her hip, laughing softly as she whispered something to her sister. It shouldn't have hit me the way it did—like a shot to the chest. For a brief, terrifying moment, I wondered what it would feel like if that kid were ours.

Jesus, what was I thinking?

A deep, hard thump rattled inside my chest.

MJ's lower lip was between her teeth, like she was gathering the courage to ask her sister something. "Is it *always* that good? Like . . . multiple-orgasms good?"

My eyebrows popped up.

"Well," Sylvie responded with a surprised laugh. "It's not common, but when it feels right—certainly when you're with someone who knows what he's doing . . . it can be a lot of fun."

The pair giggled and the awkward feeling grew.

I gently cleared my throat.

MJ's head whipped around as her eyes went wide. "Shit. Hi."

A small laugh burst from Sylvie's lips as she took Gus from MJ's arms. "I'll see if Duke is almost ready to eat." She was grinning as she walked past. "Nice to see you again, Logan."

My eyes were fixed on MJ, who looked like she wanted to melt through the floor. I closed the distance between us. "Sounds like I know what I'm doing."

MJ laughed and buried her head into my chest. My arms wrapped around her and squeezed.

"Can you forget you ever heard that?" she asked, hiding her face.

I held her back so I could look at her. "Absolutely not. In fact, I'm thinking of having it embroidered on a pillow. Or maybe getting it tattooed."

Her eyes rolled. "You're impossible."

I grinned. "Impossible to resist, apparently."

A disgusted sound rattled in her throat, and she turned away from me. "You're the worst," she teased.

I crossed my arms. "That's not what I just overheard."

MJ scoffed with a smile. "Your ego is almost as big as your—never mind."

I cocked a brow. "Careful, Julep. Finish that thought, and I might start believing you've been daydreaming about me."

Her smirk was slow, deliberate. "Who says I haven't? But in my daydreams, you're much quieter."

My eyes drilled into her, remembering how much she liked my filthy mouth. "I seriously doubt that." I grinned. Coming here to tease MJ was definitely a good use of my time, distraction or not.

Without thinking, I looped my arm over her shoulder and pulled her close. Together we walked toward the dining room to find Duke taking Gus from Sylvie's arms and disappearing down a back hallway.

The Sullivan home exuded cozy comfort. From the flowers on the table, to the kids' toys scattered in the adjacent living room, the house was lived in. The large rectangular table was made of sturdy wood. I pulled out a chair for MJ.

Duke returned, without Gus, and took a seat at the head of the table, next to his wife.

"Thank you for dinner. It smells amazing," I said.

"You are very welcome," Sylvie answered. The dinner was served family style, and we all took turns serving ourselves pot roast, mashed potatoes, and roasted carrots. "Any friend of MJ's is a friend of ours." She looked at Duke. "Isn't that right?"

A muscle in Duke's jaw popped, but he finally made a face I imagined was his version of a smile. "Of course."

Conversation was light. They asked about how I'd gotten started in rugby, and I recalled the story of how I'd come up in the sport. I wondered about the farm now that the weather was turning cool. Duke relaxed enough to tell me about the fall preparations they'd been doing and plans for how they overwinter the crops. It was a totally different world than the one I'd grown up in, and I found it fascinating.

To my right MJ smiled, and it was clear how loved she was. My knee brushed against hers, and her soft hand on my knee sent a jolt through my chest.

As I reached for another helping of mashed potatoes, MJ's phone buzzed on the table. She glanced at the screen, and her smile faltered for half a second before she turned it face down. My stomach tightened.

Who the hell was that?

Dinner ended and I stood. "Let me help with that." I grabbed MJ's plate from her hands.

"Oh, we've got it," Sylvie said, but Duke was already taking her plate from her too.

"Go on," he said to his wife. "I know you've been dying to grill MJ over meeting Russell's kids. We'll clean up in here."

MJ chuckled, but something about it told me she wasn't looking forward to the conversation with her sister. I glanced at her and pinned her with a look. I didn't know what I could do about it, but if she gave the signal, I'd come up with something to help her avoid talking about it.

MJ placed her hand just above my elbow and squeezed, silently letting me know she was okay.

She looked between Duke and me. "How about some wine by the fire when you two are done?"

Duke nodded. "You got it."

Content that she'd be fine, I followed Duke into the kitchen. When he placed the dishes into the sink, he turned to me.

His arms crossed over his huge chest. "Is this going to be a problem?"

I looked behind me. "A problem?"

Duke was back to frowning. "I've got to be honest with you. She may not be my sister, but she's my family now."

Ahh . . . the protective older brother.

MJ was not in short supply of those, it seemed.

I opened the door to the dishwasher and waited for him to hand me a dish. "I don't think there's a problem."

"MJ is young. Tenderhearted. I just don't want to see her get hurt."

I nodded, stacking the dishes he handed me. "I can appreciate that. I have no intention of hurting her."

"But no intentions of staying around here either." Duke didn't ask a question. He simply stated it as fact. "She's been let down before, Logan. You leave, and it's just going to prove to her that she's right not to trust men like you."

"Men like me?" I shot back, my voice tight.

Duke held my stare. "The ones who love the game more than they love the people waiting for them at home."

I wanted to tell him he was wrong—that I wasn't the kind of guy who walked away when things got hard. But deep down I wasn't sure I could promise that. Rugby had always come first.

Could I change that for her?

My mouth opened, but I closed it again. I wasn't sure how to explain it to him without sounding like a total dick. "We've talked about my schedule. After the exhibition season, I plan to rejoin my team on the professional circuit."

He harrumphed, and I wasn't sure if he was simply acknowledging me or trying to decide the best way to strangle me without the women noticing.

I didn't like feeling as though I was somehow letting

him down with my answer. We spent the rest of the time cleaning in silence. Something was gnawing at me . . . an emotion I couldn't quite name.

When the tension in the room became too much, I slapped the towel on the counter and leaned against it. "Here's the thing," I said. "I didn't expect to meet anyone here."

I laughed to myself. Who would have ever expected to meet a woman as surprising and special as MJ?

"Right now, things are new and we're enjoying each other's company. The last thing I want to do is hurt her." I looked at Duke, hoping he'd have some nugget of brotherly wisdom he could bestow upon me.

His dark eyes narrowed. "You need to stop lying to yourself."

Now it was my turn to frown. *I'm not lying to myself about anything.*

"When it comes down to it, you can't be half in with anything." His eyes flicked beyond the doorway toward the living room, where Sylvie and MJ were talking. "If my gut is right, you'll come to a point where you're going to have to make a pretty difficult choice."

My own gut turned to lead. I could barely look him in the eye. "And what would you do if you didn't want anyone to get hurt?"

Duke shook his head. "My advice to you is . . . don't let her get attached. It'll hurt her less if you walk away."

Duke snagged a bottle of wine from the countertop and sailed past me. I stayed, rooted to the ground, staring at his back as he left me alone in the kitchen.

The absolute last thing I wanted to do was hurt MJ, but something about Duke's words had me wondering if it wasn't *her* I had to worry about getting attached.

When I joined them on the porch, Duke had started a small fire in a portable fire stove. The wood crackled, and embers slowly rose above the flames.

As the fire crackled in front of us, I looked at MJ and felt the pull again—stronger this time, like gravity itself was conspiring to keep me near her. But gravity didn't care about broken hearts, and it was clear she was the only one with the power to break mine.

"Logan?" MJ's voice was soft, and when I turned, her brows were drawn down like she could sense the storm brewing inside me.

I forced a smile that didn't feel like mine.

"You feeling okay?" she asked, tilting her head.

For half a second, I considered telling her everything. Telling her that she'd completely upended my life in the best way possible. Telling her about the impossible choices ahead of me and how I didn't know how to stop the train before it crashed.

But I couldn't—not until I had it all figured out.

I shook my head. "Yeah, Julep. I'm good."

TWENTY-SEVEN

MJ

The four of us were gathered on the farmhouse porch, cocooned in soft blankets as the firepit crackled and threw a warm, golden glow across the worn floorboards. The air smelled like woodsmoke and autumn, the kind of night that could trick you into believing everything was simple and safe.

Sylvie sat curled up next to Duke on the swing, a glass of red wine cradled between her hands, her head resting lightly on his shoulder. Logan and I were nestled into the wicker love seat, a shared blanket draped across us like it belonged there.

The silence was easy, save for the occasional pop from the fire and Three-Legged Ed snuffling around nearby. I should've been able to relax—cozy porch, good company, and wine strong enough to take the edge off—but my mind wouldn't stop spinning.

"MJ." Sylvie's voice broke through, gentle but pointed. "Are you finally going to tell me what happened, or are we going to sit here pretending you're fine?"

I shot her a look over my wineglass. "We are sitting here perfectly fine, thank you very much."

"Mm-hmm," she replied, unimpressed.

Logan's low voice rumbled beside me as he looked at Duke. "Is this a sister thing I should be concerned about?"

Duke shook his head and chuckled, the sound deep and gravelly, but Sylvie didn't let up.

She nudged me with her toe like we were teenagers again. "Just spill it, MJ. The other Kings. What were they really like?"

I felt Logan go still next to me, though he didn't say anything. I should've known Sylvie wouldn't let this drop—not after I'd been so vague after I'd met Dad's other children two days before.

I stared into the fire, swirling my wine around in the glass. "They were . . . fine. Normal. Nice, even."

Sylvie gave me a look. "MJ."

My jaw tightened. She always saw through me. I took a deep breath, let it sit for a beat, then released it slowly. "They didn't mean to be hurtful. But hearing them call him *Daddy*, like it wasn't poison on their tongues? It was . . . too much."

The words hung in the air, heavy and raw.

Duke glanced at Sylvie, his face unreadable, but his hand slid over hers.

"Did they know anything about . . . ?" Sylvie trailed off, like she didn't want to say the words *what he did to us*.

"They didn't," I said quietly. "They talked about him like he was someone completely different. Like he was a man who showed up to their birthday parties, who drove them to school, who took pictures at graduations." I swallowed hard, the wine not doing much to wash it down. "The kind of dad we never got."

Remembering them talk about him like he was a normal dad—the kind who showed up, cared, and stayed—was like being gutted with a smile. It wasn't their fault, I knew that, but it still felt like they'd been given something I'd never had. And, worse, it made me wonder why he couldn't love us the way he loved them.

I didn't dare look at Logan, but I felt his arm stretch along the back of the love seat, the brush of his knuckles against my shoulder—a quiet, steadying gesture.

Logan had a way of making me feel exposed, like he could see past all my walls without even trying. It was terrifying. But it was also addictive. I wasn't used to someone looking at me like that—like I mattered.

Sylvie was watching me carefully. "God, that must have felt awful."

"It's like being a stranger in my own life," I admitted, the words quiet. I shook my head, a bitter laugh escaping. "It was like listening to a story that belonged to someone else. And maybe that's what we were to him—*we* were the others. Something forgettable."

"That's not true," Logan said softly.

My head turned, meeting his eyes in the firelight. There was no judgment there, only understanding. It made me feel too seen, and I looked away quickly, sipping my wine to hide the lump in my throat.

Sylvie shifted the mood with a forced brightness. "Well, screw him. I hope his other kids inherited his bad teeth and lousy sense of direction."

I snorted. "You're awful."

"Who says?" Sylvie grinned, swirling her wine lazily before glancing at Logan and changing the subject. "What about you, Logan? You surviving the King family circus so far?"

Logan's lips twitched, his gaze flicking to mine before answering. "I think I've been properly initiated. Although I still haven't decided if it's a hazing ritual or just how you show affection."

"Trust me. It's both." Duke chuckled under his breath. "But you're not truly *in* until you get forcibly added to the family group text thread."

Sylvie leaned into Duke's side with a playful bump of her shoulder, a teasing light in her eyes. "It's called quality control. We've got standards."

The banter felt light on the surface, but I could still feel Sylvie's gaze flick to me between laughs. Like she was holding back words she didn't quite dare say—not in front of Logan, not tonight.

Logan tilted his head, his grin softening as his eyes settled on me. "I like it here."

The words were simple, offhand, but they hit me like a jab to the ribs. I opened my mouth to respond, but nothing came out.

Sylvie noticed—of course she noticed—and slid me a look that wasn't quite a smirk. "Well, that's one way to win her over."

"Win who over?" I deadpanned, pretending not to know where she was going with this.

"You." Sylvie shrugged like it was the most obvious thing in the world. "He likes it here. That's gotta count for something, right?"

"Watch it, Sylvie," Duke said, though his voice held no real heat.

Logan shifted slightly next to me, his arm brushing my shoulder through the blanket. I couldn't tell if the movement was deliberate, but I felt it anyway—a quiet reminder of how close he was.

"You're reading too much into it," I muttered, my voice tight as I stared into the fire.

Sylvie didn't respond, but her knowing silence said enough. I felt like the ground beneath me was tilting ever so slightly, pulling me toward a place I wasn't sure I wanted to go.

"I think I hear Gus," Sylvie finally said, rising to her feet and stretching with a yawn.

We all stood, and Duke grumbled good-naturedly, rising to follow her, but not before tossing a look at Logan—something close to a warning, but not quite.

"I think we'll call it a night too." I looked at Logan, who nodded. "Thanks for dinner." I hugged Sylvie, then Duke.

Logan shook hands with Duke and hugged Sylvie.

As their footsteps faded into the house, I stared at the dying embers of the fire. Logan didn't move either. The silence stretched between us, thick and heavy with things we weren't saying.

"You okay?" Logan's voice broke the quiet, low and steady.

"Yeah." I forced a smile and shrugged. "Sylvie just has a way of making everything sound more dramatic than it is."

He didn't look convinced. "Sometimes a little drama is okay."

"Don't start." I turned toward him, trying to keep my tone light, but the words came out harsher than I meant.

Logan studied me, his eyes searching mine. "You don't ever have to pretend, MJ. Not with me."

The low fire crackled, throwing shadows across his face. I swallowed hard, forcing myself to look away.

"Come on," I said, before he could say anything else. "It's getting chilly. Let's not stay out here and freeze to death."

I had started to drop the blanket on the love seat when Logan pulled the edges around my shoulders. "Keep it. You can get it back to her tomorrow."

I pulled the blanket tight around my shoulders and smiled at him. Logan followed me down the porch steps, his presence steady and quiet.

"You've had some wine," he finally said. "I'll drive you home."

A smile bloomed across my face. While I could have driven after only one glass of wine, I liked the fact that he was trying to take care of me.

I'd never had that before.

Logan held open the door, and I climbed into the passenger seat.

He rounded the truck, and I stole a glance at him. Even as the engine rumbled to life, I couldn't shake the feeling that I'd been seen—really seen—and I wasn't sure how I felt about it.

The truck groaned, a low hum filling the space as Logan shifted into gear. Outside, the darkness swallowed the landscape, the farmhouse disappearing behind us as we hit the long gravel drive.

Inside, the warmth of the truck wrapped around me, but it wasn't enough to explain the heat simmering just beneath my skin.

Logan's hand rested easy on the steering wheel, his thumb tapping absently against the leather as his eyes stayed fixed on the road. His other arm stretched across the space between us, close enough that if I moved even slightly, my fingers might brush his.

And I wanted to.

"Your sister's a little intense," he said finally, his voice low, like he didn't want to disturb the quiet.

I huffed a laugh, leaning my head back against the seat. "That's one way to put it."

"She cares, though."

"Too much sometimes." I glanced at him, the faint light from the dash illuminating the edge of his jaw, the angular cut of his cheekbone. "But you handled her well."

"Handled her?" Logan's lips quirked, the faintest grin appearing as he turned his head just enough to look at me. "You make it sound like surviving her was an Olympic event."

"Wasn't it?"

He laughed softly, his eyes lingering on mine a beat longer than they should before he turned back to the road. "If that's the case, I deserve a medal."

"Well," I teased, stretching my legs out under the dash, "welcome to the family. That's your prize."

Logan hummed in response, the kind of masculine sound that sent a shiver down my spine. I squirmed under the weight of it, suddenly too aware of how small the truck's cab felt, how much of him there was in this space—the broad line of his shoulders, the coarse edges of his voice, the way his presence always managed to steady me while unraveling me at the same time.

"You're staring," he said softly, pulling me out of my thoughts as he turned into my driveway and parked.

"I'm not."

"You are."

"I'm not," I repeated, though I knew I was lying. I turned toward the window, crossing my arms under the blanket.

A beat of silence passed before Logan spoke again. "Cold?"

"No."

"Liar."

I ignored him, tightening the blanket around my shoulders as I stared into the darkness.

That's one way to win her over. My sister's words rang in my ears. Sitting next to Logan with the fire crackling, I'd come to the startling realization that Logan had won me over a long time ago.

So much for no strings . . .

Logan didn't let it go. "Come here."

"What?"

Logan glanced at me, one brow raised, as though the words were the most obvious thing in the world. "You're shivering."

"I'm not shivering."

"You're impossible." Before I could argue, he reached across the space between us, grabbing the edge of the blanket and tugging me closer.

"Logan." I protested, but it was weak.

"Relax." His voice was quiet, almost gentle, and when I let him pull me closer, the air in the cab thickened. His arm settled along the back of my seat, so close that the tips of his fingers brushed against my shoulder. I stayed stiff for half a second before I caved, letting my body sink into the warmth he offered.

The space between us was too small, too loaded. I could feel the heat radiating off him, the subtle weight of his eyes on me as the truck idled in the driveway. I risked a glance up, and Logan was already looking at me—his expression unreadable, his gaze heavy enough to make my heart stutter.

"What?" I asked, my voice barely above a whisper.

His lips quirked, slow and deliberate. "Nothing."

"Liar," I shot back, my voice breathless.

The grin faded.

Logan's eyes dropped to my mouth, lingering there long enough that I forgot how to breathe. When they lifted again, something in them had changed—like a line had snapped somewhere inside him.

His gaze dropped back to my lips, and the air in the truck seemed to thicken, charged with a heat that made my skin prickle. Every nerve in my body screamed at me to lean in, to close the impossible inch between us, but my mind hesitated. Letting him in meant risking everything. But then his hand brushed my cheek, and the quiet, steady pressure of his touch silenced every doubt.

The tension in the truck crackled, hot and electric. My pulse thrummed in my ears as I turned to face him fully, ignoring the blanket that slipped from my shoulders.

"Logan." I didn't know if it was a warning or something else entirely, but it didn't matter.

His hand came up, fingers skimming my cheek before threading into the hair at the nape of my neck. The touch was gentle, steady, like he was giving me time to pull away.

I didn't.

"You're killing me, Julep," he murmured, his voice gravelly, like he was holding something back.

I swallowed hard, my heart hammering as I stared at him, gathering my courage. "Then do something about it."

Logan didn't need to be told twice.

His mouth was on mine before I could take another breath—hot, insistent, and utterly consuming. I grabbed fistfuls of his jacket as he kissed me like he couldn't help himself, like he'd been holding back for too long and had finally given in.

I moved toward him, twisting in my seat as his hand slid to my waist, pulling me closer—closer than I thought the space would allow.

"MJ," he breathed against my mouth, his voice strained, his forehead resting against mine. "Tell me to stop."

I didn't.

"Please, don't stop."

Logan groaned softly, the sound vibrating through me as he kissed me again, his hands sliding under the edge of my sweater, wide palms skimming against my skin. My breath hitched, my whole body alive and aching for him as I melted into his touch.

The truck rocked slightly as Logan twisted, his mouth never leaving mine as he pulled me into his lap. The driver's-side door dug into my knee, but I didn't care.

I didn't care about anything except Logan's hands on me, Logan's mouth on mine, Logan—everywhere, all at once.

He leaned back against the seat, his eyes dark and wild as he stared up at me. His hands gripped my hips, steadying me as I scooted over him.

His fingers slid under my sweater again, rough and warm against my bare skin, and the sensation made my breath catch. I clung to his shoulders, the hard muscles flexing under my palms as I adjusted my position, twisting until I was fully settled onto him. The steering wheel was somewhere behind me, but I didn't care. The world outside the truck could have disappeared entirely, and I wouldn't have noticed.

"You're sure?" he asked, his voice almost desperate.

I answered by kissing him again, harder this time, pouring every ounce of frustration and longing and need into it. I ground against his lap, his huge dick hard between my legs.

"Does that answer your question?" I murmured when I finally pulled back, my lips brushing against his.

Logan's grin was slow, dangerous. "Yeah, I think it does."

He kissed me again, and this time neither of us stopped.

The truck cab felt smaller now, the air inside heavy and charged, humming with unspoken words and the heat rolling off both of us. The faint scent of his cologne mixed with the lingering trace of woodsmoke on the blanket, a combination that made my head spin in the best way.

Logan's hands settled on my hips, firm but not demanding, like he was asking permission even as his lips moved against mine, soft and insistent. The scratch of his stubble against my skin sent a shiver down my spine, and I couldn't stop myself from leaning into him, craving more of the way he made me feel—alive, wanted, like I wasn't just some girl from a small town.

Logan pulled back just enough to look at me, his chest rising and falling in heavy breaths, his eyes dark and filled with something I couldn't name. His hands settled on my thighs, fingers curling around the denim, holding me in place.

"You're sure?" he asked again, his voice intense and low, cutting through the silence like a blade.

My answer was immediate, instinctual. "I'm sure." I cupped his face, my thumbs brushing over the strong line of his jaw. "Are you?"

Instead of answering, he kissed me—hard and desperate, like he'd been waiting for this moment as long as I had. His hands slid higher, under my sweater, the warmth of his touch scorching against my skin. My pulse thundered in my ears as he found the small of my back, pulling me closer, until there wasn't a single inch of space left between us.

The truck's cab was filled with the sound of our breathing, uneven and ragged, and the faint creak of the seat as I ground against him. The hard press of his arousal beneath me sent a thrill racing through my veins, my whole body buzzing with the kind of anticipation I hadn't let myself feel in years.

Logan groaned softly, the sound vibrating through me as his lips moved to my neck, his teeth grazing the sensitive skin there in a way that made me arch against him. His hands moved again, one sliding up my spine to tangle in my hair, the other gripping my hip with just enough force to ground me.

"Julep," he murmured against my skin, his voice a low rasp that made my toes curl. "You have no idea what you do to me."

I swallowed hard, my fingers curling into the fabric of his shirt as I whispered, "Then show me."

The challenge hung in the air between us, and for a moment Logan just looked at me—his gaze intense and searching, like he was memorizing every detail of this moment. Then his mouth was on mine again, his kiss deeper, more demanding, his hands guiding my movements until I was rocking against him in a slow, maddening rhythm.

The seat belt buckle dug into my knee, a distant discomfort that made the moment only more real, more visceral. Logan's hands never stopped moving, tracing paths over my skin that left me dizzy and aching for more. He groaned again as I shifted against him, the friction sending sparks of heat through both of us.

"Julep," he said, his forehead resting against mine as he tried to catch his breath. His fingers flexed against my hips, holding me steady. "If we don't stop now . . . I'm going to fuck you in this truck."

I shook my head, brushing my lips over his, soft and

teasing. A wicked smile stretched across my face. "I don't want to stop."

Something in his expression changed, his eyes blazing with a mix of desire and something deeper—something that made my chest tighten and my heart race.

He kissed me again, his movements deliberate and slow, like he wanted to savor every second. His hands slid up my thighs, pushing the fabric of my sweater higher until he pulled it up and over my head. My fingers moved beneath his shirt, tugging it upward, needing to feel the heat of his skin against mine.

The truck rocked slightly as Logan adjusted his position, his hands never leaving me, his mouth never straying far from mine. I felt weightless and grounded all at once, like I could fall apart in his arms and still somehow be whole.

When he finally pulled back, his chest heaving and his lips swollen, he rested his forehead against mine, his voice a harsh whisper. "You're incredible, Julep."

I smiled, my fingers tracing the line of his jaw. "So are you."

Logan's hands gripped my waist, steadying me as I adjusted over him, the heat between us building to a fever pitch. His gaze locked with mine, heavy and intense, and I felt every unspoken word hanging between us.

"You're perfect," he murmured, his voice deep and tight with restraint.

I leaned in, pressing my lips to his, answering him without words. My fingers explored the hard planes of his chest, the heat of his skin searing against my palms. Logan groaned softly, the sound sending a shiver through me as his hands moved lower, his grip tightening just enough to make my breath hitch.

"Tell me what you want," he whispered against my mouth, his tone equal parts reverence and hunger.

"You," I answered without hesitation, my voice trembling with need. "Just you."

His eyes roamed over me, dark and wanting, as his hands explored every curve, every inch of bare skin. "You're so beautiful," he said, his voice raw and honest.

I pushed his jacket off, tugged his shirt over his head, and tossed them aside. My fingers traced the lines of his muscles, marveling at the strength beneath my touch. Logan leaned back slightly, his hands moving to the clasp of my bra. He paused, his eyes searching mine for permission.

I nodded, breathless, and he made quick work of the clasp, the straps falling away to bare me completely. Logan's gaze darkened, his hands cupping me gently as his mouth followed, pressing kisses along the curve of my collarbone, down to the swell of my breast.

I gasped, my head falling back as his tongue flicked over my nipple, sending a bolt of pleasure straight to my core. My hips moved instinctively, grinding against him, and the hard press of him against me made my pulse thunder in my ears.

"Julep," he rasped, his voice thick with desire. "You're going to be the death of me."

I smiled, breathless and emboldened. "Then die happy."

His laugh was low and full of heat, but it was quickly swallowed as I kissed him again, my hands moving to the button of his jeans. Logan stilled, his hands on my hips, his forehead pressing to mine as his breathing grew heavier.

"Are you sure?" he asked, his tone soft but serious.

"Yes," I whispered, my heart hammering in my chest. "I've never been more sure."

That was all he needed. I slid to the passenger seat and clumsily removed my jeans and underwear while Logan unbuttoned his jeans.

When we were both naked, his hands were deft and sure as he guided me back to his lap. Logan spit on his hand, sliding his fingers between my legs to make sure I was ready to take him.

"Look at you," he murmured. "Hot and tight and needy."

God, I am so ready.

The air between us felt electric, every touch, every movement heightening the tension until it felt like we might combust. When he finally guided me down onto him, I gasped. I was stretched and so full the world seemed to stop.

Logan's hands gripped my hips, steadying me as I adjusted to the fullness of him, a hot rush flooding my core. His gaze never left mine, dark and full of awe, and I felt something deep inside me shift.

We moved together, slowly at first, the intensity building as we found a rhythm that made the truck's cab feel too small, too hot. Logan's hands roamed over me, his touch both gentle and possessive, and I couldn't get enough of him—of the way he made me feel seen, cherished, utterly undone.

Every brush of his fingers, every press of his lips, every whispered word of encouragement, sent me spiraling higher until I thought I might shatter. And when I finally did, Logan was right there with me, his own release emptying inside me, his grip on me tightening as he buried his face in my neck.

We stayed tangled together, our breathing heavy and uneven, the warmth of his body grounding me in a way I hadn't realized I needed.

Logan's hands smoothed over my back, his touch soft and soothing now, and he pressed a gentle kiss to my shoulder. "You okay?" he asked, his voice quiet.

I nodded, resting my forehead against his. "Better than okay."

He smiled, his eyes softening as he held me close. "Good."

The world outside the truck was forgotten, the warmth between us chasing away the October chill. I didn't know what would happen next, but for the first time in a long time, I wasn't afraid to find out.

As we sat in the quiet, wrapped in the warmth of each other and the fading heat of the moment, I couldn't shake the feeling that Logan wasn't just someone I wanted. He was becoming someone I needed—and that terrified me more than I wanted to admit.

For the first time in a long time, I felt like I wasn't just existing—I was living.

TWENTY-EIGHT

LOGAN

THE TRUCK CAB WAS QUIET, save for the faint hum of the heater and the sound of MJ adjusting herself in the passenger seat. Her fingers smoothed over her sweater, tugging it back into place, though it still hung slightly off-center, rumpled from where my hands had held her.

Her hair was a mess—soft waves that I'd threaded my fingers through, now spilling wild across her shoulders. She lifted her hips off the seat to tug up her jeans, making her look too small and undone in the dim glow of the dash lights.

I couldn't stop staring.

The silence should've felt awkward, but it didn't. If anything, it sat heavy in the air, a quiet acknowledgment of everything that had just happened.

She caught me watching her as she pushed her hair out of her face, her cheeks flushed. "What?"

My mouth curved. "Nothing."

She arched a brow, her tone teasing but soft. "You look like you've never seen a girl before."

"Not like this," I murmured, surprising even myself.

I've never loved anyone like this.

MJ paused for half a beat, her fingers stilling as her eyes flicked to mine. I felt my thoughts land between us—unspoken, but real—and a dull ache settled in my chest.

With a soft chuckle, I looked away, turning my focus back to the wheel.

The truck idled quietly in MJ's driveway, the engine a low hum beneath us. Neither of us moved to get out, the silence stretching, heavy with everything we weren't saying.

MJ sat in the passenger seat, pulling the edge of the blanket closer around her shoulders. She'd done what she could to hide the fact we'd just fucked in the cab of my truck, but I couldn't stop looking at her—at the curve of her neck, the flush still lingering in her cheeks, the way she seemed smaller but more alive somehow, sitting there wrapped up in a blanket.

She caught me staring again and raised an eyebrow, her voice soft but teasing. "You're quiet."

"Yeah," I admitted, my voice raspy.

"Thinking about something?"

A corner of my mouth lifted, but I couldn't quite meet her eyes. "I'm thinking about a lot of things."

Her gaze lingered on me, like she wanted to press, but instead she smiled faintly and leaned back into the seat, the blanket slipping slightly down her shoulder. I reached across the cab, tugging the edge of it higher, my knuckles grazing her skin.

MJ stilled, her breath catching, and the space between us crackled again—hot and electric. I let my hand linger a second too long before I pulled back.

"You're cold," I said softly, a poor excuse for what I'd just done.

"I'm fine," she whispered, though I wasn't sure she believed it any more than I did.

I leaned back against the seat, dragging a hand through my hair as I tried to gather my thoughts.

What the hell was I doing?

I'd spent years keeping my focus sharp, my head down, my life built around one thing—rugby. The next win. The next tournament. Always moving, always chasing.

Rugby had been my purpose, the thing that kept me moving when nothing else could. But now, for the first time, it felt like a weight. Like every mile I put between me and MJ would pull something loose, something I wasn't sure I could fix.

And here MJ was unraveling me with nothing more than a look.

Rugby had been everything, but now it didn't feel like nearly enough.

Not when Julep would *always* be enough.

My conversation with Coach replayed in my mind. I had a suspicion that a call-up to the Sevens was coming. But I couldn't bring myself to face it, not yet.

Not while MJ was looking at me like that.

I climbed out of the truck and walked around to her side, opening the door for her. She grabbed her purse from the floor, and that was when I saw it—her phone lighting up from the floorboard.

Trent.

The name hit me like a punch to the gut, all the air going out of my lungs in an instant.

I didn't mean to see it, but there it was. A glaring reminder of everything MJ didn't talk about—everything I hadn't asked.

Trent's name glared up at me from her screen like a slap

in the face. I wasn't proud of the way my stomach twisted, how my chest tightened with something dark and possessive. But it wasn't just jealousy—it was doubt. A voice in the back of my mind whispering that maybe Trent had left a mark I couldn't erase.

MJ didn't notice the way I froze, didn't see my fingers flex against the edge of the door as she grabbed her phone and shoved it into her bag.

"Is everything all right?" she asked, looking up at me.

I forced a smile, ignoring the twist in my chest. "Yeah. Just tired."

Her expression softened, and she stepped down onto the driveway, shrugging the blanket closer around her shoulders. I waited until she unlocked the door, lingering a little longer than I needed to.

"Night, Logan," she said softly, one hand on the doorknob.

"Good night, Julep."

Her lips curved faintly, but she didn't say anything else.

The cab of the truck felt colder when I climbed back in. I sat there for a minute, staring at the light glowing faintly through her front window, my knuckles white against the steering wheel.

Fucking Trent.

Of course it was Trent. Like a shadow waiting just offstage, ready to crawl back into a life that didn't belong to him anymore.

The thought made my jaw go tight, and I slammed the gearshift into drive, turning around in the wide driveway with more force than necessary.

I shouldn't care about Trent texting her. It wasn't my place. MJ could handle herself, and I had no right to feel like this—like Trent's name was something I needed to obliterate from her life.

But I did.

As I barrelled down her driveway, a part of me screamed to stop, to go back and tell her everything clawing at my chest. But what could I say? That I wanted her more than I'd ever wanted anything? That I wasn't sure who I was if I didn't have rugby?

She deserved more than half answers and half commitments.

The engine growled as I hit the main road, and I gripped the wheel hard, the words I didn't want to think bleeding into my mind anyway.

My phone buzzed, and I pulled it from my pocket to see that my agent was calling me.

Here it is.

That call was supposed to be everything I'd been working for.

The comeback I had earned.

And yet, as I pictured the empty hotel rooms, the sleepless nights on the road, and the adoring fans—it wasn't enough anymore.

Not when I could so easily recall the way MJ had looked at me tonight—like I was worth something.

The phone buzzed again, the name of my agent lighting up the screen like an accusation. My thumb hovered over the answer button before I let it drop.

Not tonight.

I couldn't fake the excitement he'd expect to hear in my voice, not when the thought of leaving made my chest feel like it was caving in.

Not if it meant leaving her behind.

I drove in silence, the heater doing little to shake the

chill that had settled in my chest. MJ's face flashed in my mind—her laugh, the way she'd whispered my name, the way she'd looked when she said, *Please, don't stop.*

I didn't want to stop.

Not with her.

A prickle of fear rippled through me.

What if she didn't feel the same? She had never made me feel like I was a conquest, but we'd also never discussed the possibility of things being long-term. What if her interest waned once I wasn't some Olympic rugby star, but a has-been?

I didn't know what scared me more—leaving for the Sevens or staying long enough to lose her.

The road stretched ahead, dark and empty, but I couldn't stop seeing her—wrapped in a blanket, mussed and beautiful, standing on her front porch, smiling at me.

I wasn't the kind of man who let people in—not fully. It had always been easier to keep moving, to focus on what was next. But with the vision of MJ, standing on that porch looking at me like what we had was something worth staying for, I felt the ground tilt.

I didn't know how to be what she needed. But god help me, I wanted to try.

And I knew, in that moment, that I was already too far gone.

TWENTY-NINE

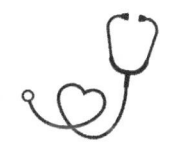

MJ

THE HOUSE WAS quiet when I walked in, the soft creak of the doorframe breaking the stillness. The air inside was warmer than the crisp autumn night, carrying the faint scents of cinnamon and the lemon oil Aunt Bug used to polish every piece of wood in the place.

I dropped the stolen blanket onto the couch, smoothing it down like I could erase the evidence of what I'd just done. The fleece was warm, the faintest hint of woodsmoke clinging to it, but it wasn't the blanket that made me hesitate.

It was *him*.

My pulse thrummed, uneven, as I stood there in the living room, staring at the empty space. He wasn't here, but he might as well have been.

I caught a glimpse of myself in the hall mirror as I turned toward the stairs, and my breath stuttered. My hair was a hot mess—tangled from his fingers. My sweater hung crooked, stretched from the way he'd pulled me close. My lips looked swollen, still tingling from the press of his kisses.

I looked utterly undone.

Like someone who'd just let her guard slip. Like someone who couldn't lie to herself anymore about what this was becoming.

"Late night?"

The voice startled me, and I whirled around to see Aunt Bug standing in the kitchen doorway, holding a steaming mug and her salt-and-pepper hair pulled back at the temples. She was wearing her usual oversize sweatshirt and slippers, her assessing eyes narrowing slightly as she took me in.

I opened my mouth, but no words came out. What could I even say?

Bug's lips curved into a knowing smile, the kind that always made me feel like she could see right through me. "You look like you've been through a windstorm." She took a sip of tea. "Or maybe something better."

My cheeks burned, and I tugged at the hem of my sweater, trying to smooth it out. "It's nothing."

Bug snorted, moving into the kitchen and flicking on the light. "Honey, you're standing in the hallway looking like a cat that got caught in the cream. Don't tell me it's nothing."

I followed her reluctantly, leaning against the counter as she drizzled a bit of honey into the mug.

I gently cleared my throat. "I was out with Logan."

Her eyes flicked up to mine, intense and curious, but she only hummed.

I nodded, suddenly feeling like a teenager again, sneaking in past curfew.

Bug took a sip of her sweetened tea, studying me over the rim of the mug. "You like him."

The words were soft but sure, and I felt something twist in my chest.

"I don't know," I said, my voice quieter than I meant.

Bug set her mug down and leaned on the counter, her gaze steady and warm. "MJ, liking someone isn't the same as trusting them. And trusting them isn't the same as letting yourself be happy."

I blinked, caught off guard by how much her words hit home.

"I understand you've been carrying that fear around for so long, it's like you don't know how to put it down," Bug continued, her voice gentle. "Trust me. I understand that. But recently I have also learned that there comes a point when you've got to ask yourself if holding on to the hurt is worth missing out on something good."

My thoughts drifted to her relationship with Bax. He'd opened something up for her, allowed her to be herself in a way that was truly special. She didn't have to change for him . . . all he ever asked was for a little of her time.

My throat felt tight, and I dropped my gaze to the counter, tracing the veins in the marble with my finger. "What if it's not good? What if it's just . . . temporary?"

Bug shrugged, her expression softening. "Maybe it is. Maybe it's not. But if you spend all your time waiting for the floor to fall out from under you, you'll miss the chance to enjoy standing still. You can trust me on that one."

The room felt quiet again, the weight of her words settling into the space between us. Bug had never married. She'd spent her life raising her brother's children so we wouldn't have to suffer under the weight of his full attention. I paused, wondering whether her advice was speaking from a place of experience. For the first time, I wondered whether Bug had lived a life of regrets.

I swallowed hard, finally glancing up at her. "Thanks, Bug."

She reached out and squeezed my hand, her strong

fingers warm against mine. "Go on upstairs, MJ. You look like you need to sit with yourself for a while."

I nodded, murmuring another thanks before heading for the stairs, grabbing the blanket from the couch on the way.

The old wood steps creaked under my feet, and I moved slowly, my mind still spinning. Bug's words echoed in my head as I reached my room, the familiar space feeling too quiet, too still.

I dropped onto my bed, pulling the stolen blanket around my shoulders again, inhaling the faint trace of woodsmoke and Logan that clung to it. My phone buzzed, and my heart kicked up, hoping for his name.

It wasn't Logan.

It was Trent.

I stared at my phone, the screen glaring back at me in the dim light of my room.

> **TRENT**
>
> MJ, I'm sorry. I messed up, okay? I've been thinking about us a lot. I'm not the same guy anymore. You deserve better, and I want to be that for you. Can we just talk?

The words landed like a punch, harsh and deliberate.

I knew what Trent was doing—this wasn't an apology. It was bait, a carefully crafted mix of guilt and hope, designed to make me second-guess everything I'd worked to leave behind.

And the worst part?

It almost worked.

Not because I wanted him back—*hell*, no. But because his words poked at every raw nerve I hadn't quite managed to numb.

I sank deeper into the bed, my grip tightening around

the phone as I read the text again, my chest tightening with a familiar ache.

Trent had always known how to get under my skin. When we were together, his apologies were always just enough to make me believe him—enough to make me doubt myself when things went wrong.

He'd flash that easy smile, the one that made me forget how cold his words had been the night before. He'd say the right things, just enough to patch the cracks, but never enough to fix them.

And I'd let him. Over and over again until he had gotten what he wanted from me and left for good.

Because I thought that was love.

I swallowed hard, the bitter taste of those memories rising in my throat.

This wasn't love. Not even close.

I shoved the phone onto the nightstand, the screen dimming as I turned away. But the words lingered, curling into the corners of my mind, feeding the insecurities I hated most.

You deserve better, and I want to be that for you.

I squeezed my eyes shut, but it didn't help. Trent's voice in my head mixed with my own doubts—nagging, insidious whispers that sounded too much like truth.

What if you're not good enough for *better*? I had spent my entire life being good, and it wasn't enough for my own father to love me.

What if Logan figures that out too?

His face flashed in my mind, the way he'd looked at me tonight—like I was more than the sum of my mistakes and fears. Like he could love *me* for exactly who I was.

It should've been comforting. Instead, it made the prickle of anxiety worse.

Guys like Logan didn't stick around towns like this. They didn't settle for girls like me.

He was an Olympic athlete, for fuck's sake. A star. Someone with a world far bigger than mine.

And me?

I was just MJ. Small-town MJ with a family full of baggage and a track record for playing it safe.

My phone buzzed again, and my heart twisted, half expecting another message from Trent before I had the chance to block his number.

But, thankfully, it wasn't.

This time, it was Logan and I let a grin take over my face.

> LOGAN
>
> Made it home. Can't stop thinking about you. Sleep well, Julep.

My breath slipped out in a rush.

Logan.

His words weren't elaborate or carefully crafted. They weren't meant to manipulate or guilt me. They were simple, honest, real.

I stared at the message, the lump in my throat easing just a little.

My thumb hovered over the keyboard, the weight of the day pressing down on me as I tried to figure out what to say.

> Tonight was perfect. Good night.

It was short, but it felt like more than enough.

I set the phone down, curling into my blanket as memories of Logan wrapped around me.

For the first time that night, I felt myself start to settle, the ache in my chest softening into something quieter.

But sleep didn't come easy.

I stared at the ceiling, the faint glow of the moonlight outside spilling through the curtains. My mind wouldn't stop spinning, replaying Trent's text, Logan's voice, Bug's words.

Her advice had sounded simple enough—*Don't let fear keep you from something good.*

But what if I wasn't the one keeping it away? What if Logan was just passing through, like everyone else?

What if I wasn't good enough for him to stay?

The last thing I remembered before sleep finally claimed me was the sound of Logan's voice in my head, warm and steady.

And the thought I couldn't shake: I had to figure out how to trust that a man like Logan wouldn't leave.

∼

Bluebird Books always smelled the same—like paper, pine, and the faintest hint of espresso from the coffee maker tucked into the corner. It was comforting in a way I hadn't expected tonight.

The room was buzzing with laughter and chatter, women perched on mismatched chairs and leaning against shelves crammed with paperbacks. Someone had brought a charcuterie board that was already half empty, and there were at least four open bottles of wine scattered across the tables.

This wasn't just a book club. It was a ritual—a midweek reset where we could talk about anything and everything, with only the occasional mention of the actual book we were supposed to be discussing.

I'd barely made it through the door when Annie spotted me. Her eyes lit up, a mischievous grin spreading across her face.

"Well, well," she drawled, crossing her arms and tilting her head. "Look who decided to grace us with her presence—and looking all glowy too."

My cheeks burned instantly. "I'm not glowing."

"You don't just walk into book club looking like that without some juicy details, MJ," another voice chimed in. Emily was already swirling her glass of wine like she was interrogating me.

"I don't know what you're talking about," I muttered, heading straight for the wine.

Annie wasn't having it. She grabbed my arm, steering me toward a circle of chairs near the back. "Oh, you know exactly what I'm talking about. Come on, spill it. What's going on with you and Logan?"

The sound of his name sent a jolt through me, and I fumbled with the corkscrew. "Nothing's going on."

"Liar." Emily leaned in, her grin widening. "That smile says otherwise."

I fixed my face. "I'm not smiling."

"You're totally smiling," Annie countered. "And blushing. God, you're the worst at hiding things. So what's he like? Are the abs as good as they look in the photos?"

Better up close, actually.

I groaned, pouring myself a glass of wine and sinking into a chair. "Can we talk about literally anything else?"

"Fine," Annie said, sitting with a dramatic sigh. "But just know we're coming back to this."

The conversation shifted to more general gossip—who

had pranked whom, the latest drama at the historical society —but the teasing glances didn't stop entirely. As the conversation around me turned from books to town gossip, I found myself zoning out, their voices fading into the background.

Logan had been gone for a few days now, the team gearing up for some big away game. He'd mentioned it before he dropped me off the other night, something about extra practices and being "all in" for the season.

I had nodded, pretending to understand, but the truth was, I hated the way my chest felt hollow without him here.

The thought made me snort quietly into my wine.

What was wrong with me?

He'd been gone for only a few days, and here I was, acting like I didn't know how to function without him. But it wasn't just that. It was the way he'd left—casual, easy, like maybe it didn't weigh on him the same way it weighed on me.

And why would it? Logan had a life so much bigger than this tiny town. He had rugby, a career, a future. Guys like Logan didn't stick around.

I knew that. I'd always known that.

And yet I couldn't stop thinking about the way he looked at me—like I was more than just a woman with fucked up family baggage and a shitty ex-boyfriend.

It terrified me, the way Logan made me feel like I could be myself.

Like that was more than enough.

But then there was Trent's text sitting unanswered in my pocket like a stone I couldn't wait to throw away. It wasn't until later, when the group had splintered into smaller clusters, that I found myself sitting with a few of the women I trusted most.

"Okay," I said quietly, setting my glass down and

glancing around. "I do have something I need to get off my chest."

Emily perked up immediately. "Finally."

"It's not about Logan," I added quickly.

Her face fell. "Boo."

"It's about Trent."

That sobered them up instantly. Annie set her wine down, leaning in closer. "What happened?"

I hesitated. "He texted me the other night. Said he wanted to talk. That he's sorry and he's changed."

The table erupted in groans and expletives.

"Oh, please," Emily said, rolling her eyes. "That man couldn't change if his life depended on it."

"Did you respond?" Annie asked.

"Hell no."

She pointed a finger at me. "Good. Don't."

Emily smirked. "You should send him a list of ex-boyfriend etiquette tips. Rule one: Don't text your ex at one a.m. unless you want a restraining order."

That got a laugh out of me, one I desperately needed.

I'd spent too long letting Trent's words shape me, letting the doubt he planted take root. But with Logan it was different. I didn't need to be a better version of myself. Whatever I already was seemed to be enough.

I felt like two versions of myself were at war.

One was stuck in the past, chained to all the ways I'd been made to feel small and not enough.

The other? The other felt free. Brave, even.

And that unknown version terrified me.

The bookstore was quiet by the time I left, most of the women lingering inside to finish the last of the wine. I wrapped my coat tighter around me, the crisp night air biting at my cheeks as I made my way to my car.

When I pulled into my driveway, I spotted him immediately.

Trent was sitting on the porch steps, his head down, hands stuffed into the pockets of his jacket.

My stomach twisted, freezing me in place.

He looked up when he heard my car door shut, his expression carefully crafted—apologetic, wounded.

Calculated.

"MJ," he said, standing slowly, his voice soft and full of practiced regret. "Please. I just want to talk. Can we do that?"

I didn't move, my heart pounding.

The confidence I'd felt earlier, laughing with the Bluebirds, was on shaky footing.

Trent took a small step forward, his hands raised in mock surrender. "I mean it. No games. No lies. Just . . . let me explain."

I swallowed hard, my feet rooted to the ground as his words curled around me, suffocating. I stared at him as the porch light cast shadows across Trent's face, and the weight of his presence pressed down on me like a storm cloud.

The air seemed to thicken as I stepped closer, my hands tightening around my car keys. The porch light buzzed faintly, casting his shadow long and angular across the wooden steps.

"MJ," Trent said again, his voice low and honeyed, the kind of tone he used when he wanted to win me over.

My stomach twisted, my pulse thundering in my ears.

"What are you doing here, Trent?" My voice came out steadier than I felt, each word a deliberate push against the panic clawing at my chest.

THIRTY

LOGAN

It felt like forever since I'd seen MJ—long days of extra drills, strategy meetings, and barely catching my breath as we prepped for the away game.

Sleepless nights where I'd told myself to focus, to keep my head in the game. But every time I closed my eyes, she was there—messy hair, soft smile, looking at me like I was someone worth trusting.

The snap of the ball, the rush of cleats against turf, the rhythmic hum of breath and muscle—practice felt electric today. Every pass, every run, every play connected like clockwork.

I hadn't felt this smooth in years.

"Nice work, Brown! Nice work!" Coach's voice and claps cut through the cool morning air as I broke through the defense and touched the ball down across the try line. Adrenaline thrummed through my veins.

I jogged to the huddle, my teammates slapping my back, shouting encouragement. The easy camaraderie felt natural, the way it always had when I was locked in like this.

But today was different.

Since I'd met MJ, something had changed.

At first I chalked it up to superstition—a string of good games that started when she showed up, her laugh cutting through the noise in my head, her smile steadying me in ways I couldn't explain.

I had told myself she was a lucky charm. Nothing more.

But now, running drills and pushing through tackles, it didn't feel like luck anymore.

It felt like *her*.

Like she'd slipped into the cracks of my life without me noticing, making everything brighter, more meaningful.

Practice wrapped up with sprints, the kind of grueling, sweat-soaked punishment Coach loved to dish out. By the time we hit the showers, my legs felt like lead, but my head was clear.

"Brown," Coach called as I grabbed my gear bag. "Need a word."

I followed him to his office, the smell of leather and liniment heavy in the air.

"You've been playing like a man on fire," he said, settling into his chair. "Whatever's gotten into you—keep it up."

"Thanks, Coach."

He leaned back, his expression softening into something almost . . . proud. "I got the news. You're getting called up, Logan. Sevens want you back. It's official."

The words hit me like a freight train, the air leaving my lungs in one heavy rush.

Called up.

This was it. The second chance I'd spent months chasing. The dream I'd sacrificed everything for was real.

So why didn't it feel like good news?

Sitting here, staring at his desk, all I could think about was her. The way she smiled, like she didn't know how beautiful she was. The way she kissed me, like I was someone worthy of her light.

What if leaving meant losing that? Losing her?
What if staying meant losing everything else?

I managed a nod, my voice even. "When do they need me?"

"After this week's game," Coach said, his tone light, almost celebratory.

A small sigh of relief escaped me. I still had time to talk with MJ and tell her the news of the call-up and my inkling to decline the offer.

We could figure out what came next—together.

"You'll wrap up this week's game, and then it's straight to training camp with the Sevens squad. They want you ready for the next tournament cycle. Pretty soon, you'll be headed to South Africa."

South Africa. Fuck.

I nodded again, the reality settling over me like a weight I wasn't ready to carry. I'd be facing disappointed coaches, sponsors, and fans. Quitting was essentially setting my entire life on fire and walking away from the blaze.

MJ's face flashed in my mind—her laugh, the way she kissed me in the truck like she trusted me not to break her.

And here I was, on the verge of leaving the only life I knew behind.

I'd spent years chasing this dream, telling myself it was enough. And maybe it was—until her.

Practice had worn me out, but the ache in my chest had nothing to do with the lingering stiffness in my knee or the burn in my muscles.

Back at the hotel, I reclined against the edge of the bed,

phone in hand, scrolling mindlessly through the same notifications I'd already seen twice. The soft hum of the heater filled the silence, but it didn't drown out the restless energy buzzing under my skin.

Practice had been good—great, even—but the high I usually rode after a session like that felt muted. Off.

I couldn't wait to talk to her—tell her I was in love with her and hope like hell she felt the same way.

I pulled up MJ's number, my thumb hovering over the screen. A quick text was all I needed. Something simple to feel like she wasn't so far away.

> Hey. How's book club? Did they grill you about me again?

I set the phone down and waited.

Nothing. Not even the dots that showed she was typing.

She always answered. Even when it was a short, sarcastic reply, she always answered. The silence felt wrong—like a crack forming in something I hadn't even realized I was holding together.

It wasn't like her. My gut twisted as I picked the phone back up, staring at the screen like I could will her reply into existence.

She was probably busy, I told myself. Or tired. Or maybe I was overthinking it.

The thought left a bitter taste in my mouth. I locked the phone and tossed it onto the bed, dragging a hand through my hair.

I paced the room, the carpet soft under my bare feet, but the tension didn't ease. Not even a hot shower had shaken the feeling that something wasn't right.

I sat down again, my phone still stubbornly quiet. Even

as I tried to tell myself not to read into it, the unanswered text sat heavy in the back of my mind.

What the hell was I doing, anyway?

I'd spent years building my life around one thing—rugby. Focus. Discipline. Always moving forward. And now here I was, sitting in a hotel room, letting my head spin over one unanswered text like I didn't know better.

But even as I told myself to let it go, the quiet buzz of unanswered questions stayed with me.

The silence hit me harder than I expected. I stared at the screen, my thumb hovering over her name like just seeing it could give me some kind of answer. I thought about how I would tell her—about the call-up, about everything—but no version of the words felt right.

How do you tell someone you got the second chance of a lifetime and you don't even want to go?

That conversation was one that needed to happen face to face.

Unable to sit still, I grabbed my running shoes and hit the pavement. The night air was crisp against my skin, the rhythmic thud of my feet against the asphalt grounding me.

The cool air hit my lungs like a challenge, painful and unrelenting. My feet pounded against the pavement, each step a heartbeat, each breath a question I didn't have an answer to.

The city lights blurred as I ran, their glow too bright, too harsh. My chest burned, my legs ached, but nothing could outrun the thoughts chasing me down.

MJ was there in every step, every breath, every thump of my heart.

I replayed Coach's words in my mind, the ones he'd said months ago when I'd started on the exhibition squad: "You don't get second chances in this game, Logan. You've got to decide what you want and go after it, full throttle."

I had agreed at the time, nodding like I understood.

This was rugby. This was everything.

Rugby had always been the answer. The thing that gave my life purpose, that kept me moving forward when everything else felt like it was standing still. But now, with MJ in the picture, the edges of that certainty were morphing into something else entirely.

If rugby wasn't everything . . . what was left of me?

I picked up my pace, my lungs burning, my legs screaming for relief.

By the time I made it back to my hotel, my chest was heaving, sweat dripping down my back. I dropped onto the small bench by the front entrance, the glow of the parking lot lights cutting through the dark as I stared at my phone, heavy in my hand.

MJ's number was still pulled up on the screen.

I stared at her name, my thumb hovering over the call button.

I could talk with her tomorrow, but even as I set the phone down, something in my chest twisted.

Why was it when you loved someone, tomorrow always seemed too far away?

THIRTY-ONE

MJ

The night was colder than usual for October, the kind of chill that seeped through your coat and settled in your bones. The faint glow of the porch light stretched out across the yard, illuminating the man sitting on the top step.

Trent fucking Fischer.

He sat there like a ghost from a life I didn't want to remember, his hands shoved deep into his jacket pockets, his shoulders hunched like he wasn't sure he should even be here. But his eyes? His eyes were locked on me, familiar and calculated, the same shade of brown that used to make me think I was safe.

I wasn't.

The wind whispered through the trees, rattling the last of the leaves still clinging to the branches. Somewhere in the distance, a dog barked, the sound barely registering over the pounding of my heart.

"MJ," Trent said softly as he rose, his voice low and steady. "Please. I just want to talk. Can we do that?"

The words froze me in place, the weight of them pressing down on my chest like a stone. He'd said similar words before—too many times. Back when I still believed that talking meant he cared, that smooth words meant he wouldn't hurt me or ignore me again.

This wasn't then. I wasn't her.

"I mean it. No games. No lies. Just . . . let me explain," he pleaded with his hands in the air. "MJ . . ."

My keys bit into my palm. "What are you doing here, Trent?" My voice came out steadier than I expected, cool and clipped, like I wasn't standing there in my own driveway fighting the urge to scream.

I walked toward the steps and gripped the railing so hard my knuckles turned white. "Get off my front porch."

He took a step closer, his hands still out in a mock gesture of surrender. His breath clouded in the crisp air, the faint smell of cologne reaching me as he moved.

"I know I messed up," he began, his tone smooth and practiced, like he'd rehearsed this in his head a hundred times before showing up. "But I've been thinking about us—about you—and I want to make things right."

I laughed, sharp and humorless, the sound cutting through the quiet. "Right," I said, leaning against the railing, forcing my body to stay relaxed. "You've changed. You're different. You're sorry. Let me guess—you didn't know what you had until it was gone?"

His jaw tightened, a flicker of frustration breaking through his carefully crafted expression. "I mean it, MJ. I've grown up. I shouldn't have ghosted you like that. I'm ready to be the guy you deserve."

I shook my head, the anger simmering beneath my skin rising to the surface. "The guy I deserve? Trent, the guy I deserve wouldn't have knowingly taken my virginity and then acted like I never existed."

His brow furrowed, the mask slipping further. "Come

on, MJ. Don't be like this. You were never so . . . difficult before."

There it was. The real Trent. The one who thought he could break me down with just a few words, who thought he still had that kind of power over me.

I straightened and stepped toward him. "You want the MJ who believed your lies? The girl who thought we'd ride off into the sunset together? She's gone, Trent. And the woman standing in front of you? She doesn't care if you've changed, because she has. Now get off my fucking porch before I show you how strong I've become."

His smile faltered, but he didn't back down. "I'm just asking for a second chance. Is that so hard? To forgive someone?"

The door behind him creaked open, and I glanced over his shoulder to see Aunt Bug stepping out, her gaze cutting through the tension like a hot knife through butter. She was wrapped in an oversize sweater, her expression nothing short of utterly unimpressed.

Trent stumbled off the porch and looked up at her. I took the opportunity to climb the steps and stand next to my aunt, looking down at him with my arms crossed.

"You want me to call the sheriff," she said coolly, resting one hand on her hip, "or do you think he can run faster on those bird legs than I can dial?"

Trent's face turned an interesting shade of red, but he held his ground, his hands rising defensively. "I'm not trying to cause trouble. I just want to talk to her."

"Well, it doesn't seem like she wants to talk to you." Bug's tone was flat, unimpressed. "And if you don't want the fire department out here hosing you off this porch, I suggest you leave."

Trent shook his head, a dangerous, defiant glint in his eye. "I'm not going anywhere until she hears me out."

I scoffed at his audacity. The same man who'd called me a cunt was now begging for my forgiveness?

I ground my teeth. "You know what, Trent? I'm actually glad you were my first, because that means, any man to ever come after you is *infinitely* better."

Red splotches bloomed on his neck. "Better?" he scoffed, his tone dripping with resentment. "Who? You think Logan's better?" Fury and resentment marred his features. "He's always been better, hasn't he? The golden boy who takes whatever he wants, leaves the rest of us picking up scraps. You're just another trophy to him, MJ. I can't believe you're the type of girl who would throw her life away to follow him around like a lost puppy."

The words hit like a slap. My breath caught as realization dawned. This wasn't about me—this had never been about me. This was about Trent's ego, about some petty competition he thought he was still in.

An idea struck me like lightning, and before Bug could say more about the fire department, I turned toward the corner of the porch, where the coiled garden hose sat like a beacon of petty justice.

For years, Trent's words had been like hooks, snagging on the insecurities I didn't even know I had. But now, as I stood here with a hose in my hand and his accusations rolling off my shoulders, I realized something important.

I wasn't that girl anymore. And he wasn't strong enough to break the woman I had become.

"MJ . . ." Trent's voice wavered as I grabbed the hose, unspooling it with deliberate calm. "What the hell are you doing?"

I didn't answer, instead twisting the nozzle open just

enough to let the water dribble out in warning. I gave him a once-over, my expression as bored as I could muster. "You're still here?"

He stepped back, his shoes scuffing the driveway. "Don't be a child. You're not serious."

I squeezed the nozzle fully, sending a forceful spray of cold water straight into his tiny dick. He yelped, stumbling backward as I flicked my wrist, water drenching him from head to toe.

Water spurted up his nose. Then the spray hit Trent square in the chest, and for the first time in years, I didn't feel small. I didn't feel powerless. I felt in control, the weight of his words rolling off me like water off the hose's stream.

"MJ!" he spluttered, his arms flailing as he tried to block the spray. "What the hell?"

"I told you to leave," I said evenly, tilting the nozzle to hit him in the face again for good measure. "But I guess you needed a little extra motivation."

His face darkened, his voice dropping to a growl. "You're pathetic. You don't even see he's playing you, MJ. He's only here because it makes him feel like he's better than me."

The words stung, not because I believed him, but because they echoed the doubts I'd been trying to drown out. But then I saw Bug's expression—a mix of pride and something sharper, more protective—and the sting faded, replaced by a surge of defiance.

"Son," Bug drawled, stepping up beside me, "if you really believe that, you're even dumber than you look. Now are you finally going to learn how to leave when a woman tells you to?"

Trent struggled to get to his feet, muttering under his

breath, but I wasn't done yet. I turned the hose on him again, this time aiming lower, the cold water hitting his legs and making him slip slightly on the damp grass. He landed on all fours.

"You're right, Trent," I said evenly, my voice steady. "This isn't about me. It's about you. And your ego. And the fact that you can't stand the idea of someone else being happy when you're not. Well, guess what? That's not my problem anymore."

He glared at me, soaked and humiliated, before finally rising to his feet and storming off into the night like a petulant child.

I stood there, the garden hose still in my hand, water seeping into the grass at my feet. My pulse thrummed in my ears, not from fear, but from the rush of adrenaline still coursing through me.

"And that's how you take out the trash." Aunt Bug's voice was warm but with an edge, pulling me out of my thoughts. She leaned against the doorframe with a smile.

I snorted softly, letting the hose drop to the ground. "Didn't feel like trash when I was with him."

Bug pushed off the doorframe and stepped closer, placing a hand on my shoulder as I climbed to meet her at the door. Her grip was firm, grounding. "Men like him? They don't know how to lose. They twist things around, make you think you're the problem because they can't face their own shortcomings. But you? You're finally learning how to win—your way."

The words hit something deep inside me, a place that had been raw and aching for far too long. I met her steady gaze, feeling a sting in the back of my throat. "It didn't feel like winning for a long time."

"Because you didn't know your worth," Bug said simply. "But you do now, don't you?"

I nodded, swallowing hard. "I think I do."

She gave my shoulder a reassuring squeeze before stepping back. "Good. Now come inside before you catch a cold. I'll make you some peppermint tea."

In the kitchen, the warm light softened the edges of the night. Bug moved around the space with the practiced ease of someone who'd lived here her entire life, setting a kettle on the stove and pulling down two mugs. I sat at the table, staring at my hands, the silence between us comfortable but heavy.

When she slid a steaming mug in front of me, she rested her hip against the counter and tilted her head. "It felt good, didn't it?"

I nodded slowly, wrapping my hands around the mug. "Yeah. I think . . . I think I needed that."

"Not just hosing him down," she said with a small smile. "But standing up for yourself. Owning your strength."

I took a sip of the tea, the warmth spreading through me. "It felt good. Like . . . like maybe I took something back."

Bug's smile softened. "You did. And don't let anyone make you feel bad about it. Not him, not anyone. You think men like him are rare?" Bug said, leaning against the counter with her mug in hand. "Honey, they're a dime a dozen. The real rarity? A woman who knows she doesn't need to settle for them." Her words settled in my chest, warm and heavy, like the tea she'd handed me moments before. "And you're starting to figure that out, aren't you?"

I didn't say anything, but I nodded again, her words nestling into my chest.

The tea's warmth seeped into me, soothing the lingering

edges of my nerves. But it wasn't just the tea, or even the moment with Bug that left me feeling steadier than I had in a long time. It was something deeper.

Logan's face flashed in my mind—the way he'd looked at me the last time we were together, his gaze steady and unflinching, like he saw through all the walls I'd spent years building. He saw me. The real me. And instead of turning away, he stayed.

The thought hit me like a wave, rushing in too fast to stop. I set the mug down, my hands trembling just slightly as the realization settled in my chest, warm and terrifying all at once.

I love him.

Not just because of the way he made me feel—safe and alive—but because when I was with him, I loved the version of myself I was becoming. The version who could stand up to Trent, who could claim her worth, who could trust someone to hold her heart without crushing it.

Bug's words echoed in my mind, soft but steady: *You're finally learning how to win—your way.*

The thought of Logan waiting for me, of seeing his name light up my phone again, sent a jolt of warmth through my chest. Maybe I wasn't ready to say the words out loud—not yet.

But I was ready to fight for what we were building.

For once, I let myself believe it.

THIRTY-TWO

LOGAN

The cool air bit at my skin as I stood outside the hotel, the pavement slick with the sheen of earlier rain. My lungs burned from my run, but it hadn't done a damn thing to clear my head. My legs ached, my knuckles itched, and none of it mattered.

I could still feel the weight pressing down on me, heavy and suffocating. The midweek game loomed like a shadow, but that wasn't what had me tied in knots tonight.

It was that damn call-up. I hated disappointing people.

My chest felt tight, like I couldn't get enough air. It was everything I'd worked for. Everything I was supposed to want, but now it felt hollow.

Dread mixed with excitement. I needed to break the news to Coach and my agent, but not before telling Julep what she meant to me.

Because choosing that meant leaving her behind and there was no way in hell that was happening.

The thought was clear, cutting through the fog like a ray of sweet sunshine.

Julep.

I'd been telling myself this was casual, that what we had was something I could leave behind if I had to. But tonight, staring at the cold reality of what leaving would mean, I knew I'd been lying.

She wasn't just someone I cared about.

She was it for me.

The vibration of my phone snapped me out of the spiral, and I pulled it from my pocket. Her name lit up the screen, and just seeing it was enough to make my heart kick into overdrive.

"Hey," I said, trying to keep my voice steady.

"Hey, yourself," she replied, her voice light, almost giddy. That wasn't what I'd expected, but it was a welcome surprise.

"You sound good," I said, sitting back down on the bench.

"Oh, I'm better than good," she said, her laughter bubbling through the line. "Logan, you are not going to believe what I just did."

There was something in her tone—excitement, pride. "What's that?"

She let out a breathless laugh. "I hosed Trent down. Like, literally. With a garden hose. He showed up at my house like some creepy specter from my past, and I let him have it."

Her words hit me like a sucker punch and my jaw tightened. "Trent was at your house?"

"Yeah," she said, oblivious to the way my pulse was climbing. "He had the nerve to show up on my porch, spouting some bullshit about second chances. Can you believe that? What a moron. Obviously, I sent him packing."

The pride in her voice was palpable, and I grinned like a fool on the other end of the line.

This was her moment, her triumph.

Telling her about the call-up and the imminent implosion of my career would only overshadow that.

So I swallowed the words, burying them deep for later when we could talk face to face.

"That's great, Julep," I said, my voice filled with awe. "You handled it. I am so damn proud of you."

"Damn right I handled it," she said, her laugh softening into something warmer. "You should've seen his face. It was like he couldn't believe I wasn't the same girl he used to know."

The image of Trent standing on her porch, daring to confront her, was enough to make my blood boil. "You really are incredible, you know that?"

"Stop," she said, but I could hear the smile in her voice.

I swallowed past the grit in my throat as my anger toward my former friend built. "I mean it. You're stronger than anyone I've ever met."

Her laugh was quieter now, softer. "Thank you, Logan."

"Listen, I have to go," she added after a pause, her voice still bright and buzzing. "But I'll see you tomorrow. Go Wildhawks!"

The playful cheer in her tone tugged at the corner of my mouth despite the weight in my chest.

We hung up, her voice still ringing in my ears. I stared at the phone in my hand, the anger simmering just beneath my skin. She deserved to feel proud of herself.

But the thought of Trent standing on her porch, spouting lies and poison . . . it was enough to make my vision go red.

Before I could second-guess myself, I grabbed my keys from my hotel room and headed for my truck.

The drive to Trent's house was a blur, my hands gripping the wheel so tight my knuckles ached. It didn't matter that it was late. It didn't matter that I had an important match tomorrow. Logic, reason—none of it factored in. I didn't overthink it—I just acted.

All that mattered was making sure he never came near my woman again.

His house was exactly what I remembered—dark, quiet, unremarkable. I parked haphazardly on the curb, the engine still rumbling as I climbed out. My shoes hit the pavement with purpose, each step heavier than the last as I made my way to the front door.

I didn't knock. I pounded, hard enough to rattle the frame.

The door swung open, and there he was, freshly showered in a white T-shirt and basketball shorts, his face twisting into a smirk that screamed unbothered. He leaned casually against the doorframe, his tone dripping with sarcasm as he drawled, "Well, well. Mr. Amazing himself. What brings you here, Mav? Come to defend your prize? Finally tired of playing house with my leftovers?"

I stepped closer, my voice low and intense. "You showed up at her house. That's your first mistake. Opening this door was your second."

I didn't think. I didn't hesitate. My fist connected with his jaw, sending him stumbling back into the house. Trent recovered quickly, his arrogance fueling his aggression as he threw his first punch, a wild swing aimed at my ribs. I dodged easily, years of training and instinct giving me the upper hand.

"You son of a bitch," I growled, stepping inside and

slamming the door shut behind me. The sound of knuckles against flesh filled the space, the metallic tang of blood in the air as adrenaline coursed through me. "You went to her house?"

"She called you, didn't she?" he said, wiping at his mouth with the back of his hand. His smirk was gone, replaced by something darker. "Of course she did. That's all she knows how to do—run to the nearest man to fix her problems."

"You don't get to talk about her like that," I said, my voice low and dangerous.

"Why not? I knew her first—better than you ever will," he spat, his eyes narrowing. "You think she's some kind of saint? She's a clingy, needy little girl who doesn't know how to let go."

I grabbed him by the front of his shirt, slamming him against the wall. "She's not the girl you used to know. She's a woman who stood up to your sorry ass and sent you packing."

He shoved at my chest, but I didn't let go. "What's your deal, Logan? You playing the hero? Or is this just another trophy for your collection?"

The words hit harder than they should've, but not for the reason he thought. He wasn't wrong about the trophies—that was all my life had been for years. Chasing the next win, the next title, the next shiny thing to make me feel like I was enough.

But MJ? She wasn't a trophy. She was everything.

"You're pathetic," I said, my voice steady as I pushed him back, letting go of his ripped shirt. "You don't even see it, do you? She doesn't need you. She never did. She doesn't even need me. But she chose me. Because I'm not like you. I don't tear her down to feel big. I build her up. That's the difference between us."

I turned, ready to walk out and leave him to his misery. But the next thing I knew, pain exploded across my jaw. The force of his sucker punch made my head snap to the side, a metallic tang flooding my mouth.

For a moment I stayed still, rolling my jaw as Trent stood there, his chest heaving, that cocky smirk already creeping back onto his face. "What's the matter, golden boy? Can't take a hit?"

I ran my tongue along my teeth, making sure none were loose, before turning back to face him, my voice low and steady. "You really should've thought that through."

He didn't have time to respond before my fist connected with his gut, doubling him over with a groan. As he stumbled back, I landed a clean punch to his cheekbone, sending him crashing to the floor in a heap.

I spat blood on the floor next to his face.

"Stay away from her," I said, my voice like steel. "If I hear you went near her again, I won't stop next time."

He glared up at me, his lip split and his breathing ragged. "She'll never stay," he sneered, his voice dripping with venom. "What do you even have to offer? You've got nothing but rugby, and even that won't last forever."

I turned my back on him, his words rolling off me like water. "She's not yours to talk about. Remember that."

My hand gripped the doorknob, and I hesitated, looking over my shoulder one last time. "And don't think for a second this is about us. Whatever we had—friendship, camaraderie—it's done. I see who you are, Trent. And there's no coming back from that."

The drive back to the hotel was quiet, the adrenaline slowly fading as the reality of what I'd done sank in. My knuckles throbbed, and my chest ached, but I didn't regret it.

Ending things with Trent—whatever scraps of friendship we had left—felt like cutting out a piece of my past I didn't need anymore.

All that mattered now was her.

MJ's voice played in my head, soft and teasing, the way she'd sounded on the phone. She was happy tonight, and I'd do anything to keep her that way.

Even if it meant leaving behind everything I thought I wanted.

Because for the first time in my life, I knew what really mattered.

And it wasn't a trophy.

It was her.

THIRTY-THREE

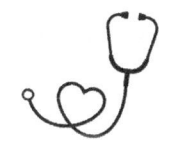

MJ

The stadium buzzed with energy, the kind that seeped into my bones and made my chest hum. I followed Tony the security guard down to the family seating area, followed by Lark, Wyatt, and Penny. We wove through a crowd decked out in team colors, faces painted and voices raised in unison.

It was electric, almost too much, but it was Logan's world.

And this afternoon, we all wanted to be a part of it.

"Hell of a view." Wyatt's deep voice cut through the noise as we found our seats. His calm, commanding presence was steadying, and I appreciated how he kept an eye on Penny while taking in the field with a coach's intensity.

I smiled at him and turned my attention to the field, where the players from both teams were warming up.

"You okay?" Lark whispered beside me.

"I'm good," I said, offering a half smile as I scanned the players for Logan.

"Good, huh?" Lark teased, sliding into the seat next to me. Her scarf fluttered as she adjusted her coat, her movements graceful and practiced, a lingering echo of her former life on-screen. "Because you've been bouncing on your toes since we got here. I think someone's smitten."

"I'm not—" I started, but Penny cut in before I could finish.

"She totally is," Penny said, settling into her seat with a smug grin. Her hair was a wild tangle of braids and curls she'd insisted on doing herself. That girl missed nothing. "You've got googly eyes."

"I do not!" I turned to gape at her, my cheeks heating under her mischievous gaze.

"You do," she said matter-of-factly, popping a piece of gum into her mouth. "But don't worry, MJ. He looks googly when he looks at you too."

My eyes flicked up just in time to see Logan grinning at me from the field. He tapped his chest twice, and I nearly melted into a puddle in the stands. But then I noticed it—a faint bruise shadowing his cheekbone, just visible under the stadium lights. My heart stuttered. Was it from practice? A tackle?

I frowned, a flicker of unease curling through the warmth of his grin. He didn't seem fazed, his focus already back on the field, but the sight of it lingered with me, a question I couldn't quite shake.

Wyatt chuckled, leaning back with a knowing smile. "Go easy on her, Pickle," he murmured, his voice laced with humor. "It's hard enough to rev yourself up for a game without knowing your woman is in the stands watching." He smiled and knocked his shoulder gently into Lark's.

"Can we focus on the game, please?" I muttered, tugging at my scarf to hide the blush creeping up my neck.

"Sure," Penny said, shrugging. "But it's more fun watching you freak out."

Maria arrived, and as she joined in the conversation, I was relieved the focus was off Logan and me and onto the rival team.

The players finally took the field, and the crowd erupted into cheers. My eyes locked on Logan instantly, his broad shoulders and easy stride setting him apart. He looked at ease out there, focused and confident, like he belonged.

And, of course, he did.

This was his entire world.

The thought was both exhilarating and terrifying.

The whistle blew, and the game began.

Logan was incredible, just like I'd known him to be. Every play, every tackle, every sprint, was executed with precision and skill that left me breathless. The crowd roared with every play, and I found myself caught up in the excitement despite my nerves.

When Logan glanced toward the stands, his eyes searching, our gazes locked. My heart did a stupid little flip I couldn't control. For a moment it was just the two of us in the chaos, and everything else fell away.

Penny giggled beside me. "Told you. *Googly* eyes."

"Shut up," I muttered, but I couldn't stop the grin spreading across my face.

"He's good," Wyatt said, nodding in approval as Logan executed a perfect play. "Great instincts. Can't teach that."

"He's an Olympian. I'm not sure why you sound so surprised," Lark said, smiling as she nudged Wyatt's arm. She glanced at me and winked. "Though I do love a man who can command a field."

By halftime, the team was leading, and the energy in the stadium was at an all-time high. Fans were laughing and shouting, the air buzzing with excitement. I leaned back in my seat, letting myself breathe for the first time since we'd arrived.

The announcer's voice crackled through the speakers.

"Let's take a moment to recognize some standout performances tonight," the voice boomed, and the crowd quieted slightly, waiting. "Logan Brown, with his exceptional skill and leadership, has once again proven why he's one of the best in the game. Let's hear it for Logan!"

The crowd erupted into cheers, and I couldn't help but smile, pride blooming in my chest as we stood and screamed from our seats.

But the announcer wasn't done.

"And a special congratulations to Brown, who has officially been called up to rejoin the Sevens squad!"

The cheers grew deafening, but I didn't hear them.

The words hung in the air, sinking into me like a blade.

Called up? Rejoin the Sevens?

My heart plummeted, the warmth and excitement of the afternoon evaporating in an instant. I stared at Logan on the field, his expression frozen in shock as the camera zoomed in on him.

The shock of the announcement was evident, but, as he searched for me, it was clear—he had known.

He hadn't told me.

Lark leaned closer, her voice low and steady. "Did you know about this?"

I shook my head, unable to speak.

"Wow." Wyatt's hand found my shoulder, patting me. "That's great news—"

Maria leaned over. "MJ, I'm—"

"I'm fine," I said quickly, pulling away. But I wasn't fine. Not even close.

The game resumed, but I couldn't focus. The cheers

and whistles and the pounding of feet on the turf blurred into white noise as my thoughts spiraled.

He didn't tell me.

Why didn't he tell me?

Was I just a distraction? Someone to pass the time with until he left?

When Logan glanced toward the stands again, his eyes searching, I looked away. I couldn't bear to meet his gaze, not now. Not when I could feel the tears welling in my eyes and my resolve crumbling.

By the time the final whistle blew and Logan's team secured the win, I was numb. Wyatt and Lark stood, clapping and cheering, while Penny shouted something about Logan being a superhero. I stayed rooted in my seat, staring blankly at the field.

"Hey," Lark said softly, touching my arm.

"I think I'm going to go," I said quickly, grabbing my bag. "I'll see you later. Thanks for coming." I choked out the words and hustled toward the exit before she could stop me.

The cool evening air hit my face as I stepped outside the stadium, but it didn't clear my head. I moved quickly, my steps purposeful, hoping to outrun the ache in my chest.

"Julep!"

His voice stopped me cold.

I turned to see Logan jogging toward me, still in his gear, his hair damp with sweat. The sight of him—so familiar, so infuriatingly Logan—made my chest tighten.

"Wait," he said, his breath coming in short bursts as he caught up to me. "I need to explain."

"There's nothing to explain," I said, my voice trembling. "It's an incredible opportunity—the one you've been waiting for. I'm really happy for you."

"It's not that simple," he said, his voice low and urgent.

"Isn't it?" I shot back, my anger bubbling to the surface. "You weren't going to tell me at all, were you? Or were you just waiting until the last second, so it wouldn't hurt so much when you left?"

Logan's jaw tightened, his frustration evident. "I was never trying to hurt you, MJ. Things happened quickly and I was going to tell you everything in person."

"Well," I said bitterly. "I promise you, I would have rather you told me over the phone than let me find out alongside a stadium full of strangers."

He let loose a frustrated sigh. "I swear I had no idea they were going to announce anything today. I would never—"

I shook my head. "Your team is waiting to celebrate with you." I gestured toward the stadium. "Don't let them down."

The tic of his jaw was heavy and pronounced.

Logan's shoulders stiffened, and for the first time he looked unsure—vulnerable. "Julep, please—"

"I really don't want to do this in front of everyone, you know?" I said, my voice breaking and betraying me. "I need to go. I'll see you later."

I turned and walked away, my vision blurring as tears filled my eyes.

The ache in my chest was unbearable, but I didn't look back.

༄

The hours-long drive felt like minutes. Once I got home, I collapsed onto the couch, the events of the night replaying in my mind like a cruel movie. I had researched the Sevens. Eight separate countries hosted a leg of the tournament, which meant once he left, he'd be gone for a very long time.

The look on Logan's face, the pain in his voice, the reality that he was really leaving—it was too much.

Aunt Bug appeared with a mug of tea, setting it on the table in front of me without a word. She sat down beside me, her hand resting on my knee.

"Everything all right?" she asked softly.

I shook my head, unable to speak.

She didn't push, just sat with me in silence, her presence a quiet comfort. But even with my aunt beside me, the ache didn't ease.

Logan's words echoed in my mind.

I was never trying to hurt you.

I curled up on the couch, pulling a blanket around me as the tears finally came.

And for the first time I let myself feel it all—the anger, the hurt, the uncertainty.

Because as much as I wanted to believe what I had with Logan was different, the truth was undeniable.

He was leaving.

And I loved him too much to beg him to give up his dream and stay. I just didn't know whether I could survive being left behind again.

THIRTY-FOUR

LOGAN

The hotel room was too quiet, the kind of quiet that crawled under your skin and turned every thought into a scream. My rugby jersey hung over the back of the chair, its fabric still damp with sweat. Cleats sat abandoned by the door, the earthy scent of grass and dirt clinging to the air.

I paced, the scratchy carpet scraping against the soles of my feet, the ache in my muscles from the game forgotten under the heavier ache in my chest. My knee screamed with overuse, and every step felt like I was wearing down the threadbare rug—and myself along with it.

My phone sat on the desk, the screen dark, but it may as well have been glaring at me.

I shouldn't have left things like that with her.

Her face haunted me. The way her eyes shone with unshed tears, hard and hurt all at once.

Her voice, trembling but intense: *You weren't going to tell me at all, were you?*

She hadn't even yelled, which somehow made it worse. She had just looked at me, her disappointment hitting harder than any tackle ever could.

I grabbed my phone, desperate for some kind of relief, but the only message waiting wasn't from her. It was from Coach.

> COACH
>
> Congrats again, Brown. You'll be missed, but it's time to focus on what's next.

I tossed the phone onto the bed like it had burned me, the message taunting me.

Focus on what's next? Coach didn't even know what that was. He thought it meant playing for the Sevens again, another Olympic run—rejoining the grind of early mornings, endless travel, and a schedule that never let me plant roots.

Fuck that.

I'd spent my whole life chasing that dream. And once it was in front of me again, it felt . . . different. Hollow. Like the version of myself it belonged to didn't exist anymore.

My hands fisted at my sides as I tried to push away the guilt and disappointment that would inevitably be thrown my way.

I sat down heavily on the edge of the bed, my gaze catching on the jersey draped over the chair. It used to mean everything to me. Every play, every whistle, every moment on the field—it was who I was.

Or at least who I thought I was.

I scrubbed my hands over my face, the stubble on my jaw rough against my palms.

The field used to be the only place I could breathe. She had changed everything.

I should have called her the second Coach pulled me aside. The only dream I wanted to chase was the dream of building a life with her.

MJ had every right to be pissed at me. I should've told her. I should've sat her down and explained everything before the announcement blindsided both of us. But I hadn't. And now she was pulling back before I could explain that I was choosing *her*.

I dropped my head into my hands, the ache in my chest clawing at me.

She was different. She felt like home in a way nothing else ever had. The thought was electric and terrifying all at once.

I had promised her I was nothing like Trent. That I wouldn't hurt her, and I don't plan to. I knew I could be the man she needed.

My phone buzzed again, and for a split second my heart jumped, hoping it was her. Frustration swelled as I stared at the screen, and I didn't even bother reading the message.

I typed out a text to MJ instead.

> Can we talk? I didn't want it to happen like that. I need you to understand.

I stared at the message, my thumb hovering over the send button. My chest felt tight, my breath uneven. I wanted to hit send, but the fear of what her reply might say —or worse, if she didn't reply at all—kept my finger frozen.

I threw the phone down again and raked a hand through my hair, pulling hard until it stung. My frustration bubbled over, and before I could think twice, I picked the phone back up and hit the number I always called when I needed advice.

"Logan," Arthur's voice grumbled on the other end, thick with sleep. "How was the match, son?"

"I screwed up, Grandpa," I said, my voice breaking despite my effort to keep it steady.

He cleared his throat. "You're gonna have to be more specific. Are you hurt?"

"It's MJ," I admitted, my throat tightening. "There was an announcement at the game about me being called up to the Sevens. I hadn't told her first. She thinks I'm leaving—that I'm picking rugby over her. And I didn't get the chance to tell her I want to turn it down. She's pissed and I don't know how to fix it."

Arthur let out a long breath, the kind that usually came before a lecture. "I've always told you that life is about choices. You're certain you're ready to give it all up?"

"I'm sure," I said, my voice thick under the weight of the truth. "Maybe there's a small part of me that doesn't have a clue what comes next, but I know what I want."

"I knew you'd get your head out of your ass eventually," he chuckled. "I know you don't like disappointing people, son, but sometimes it happens. The best you can do is live your life as authentically as you can. The rest will fall into place."

The line went quiet for a beat, his words hitting me harder than I wanted to admit. "You know, you could never have had both, boy—not with a woman like her. You went with your heart. I've never been more proud of you than right now."

Hope unfurled in my chest. "Thanks, Grandpa." I sighed and dragged a hand through my hair. "Now I've got to figure out a way to get her to talk to me."

His soft chuckle floated through the line. "She'll come around. I have a feeling you aren't the only one who's tangled up right now. Maybe try a grand, heartfelt gesture. Greta's books always have someone screwing things up and having to decapitate a rival mafia boss to prove his love."

Jesus.

I shook my head and smiled. "I'll keep that in mind. Thanks again."

When we hung up, I sat in silence for what felt like hours. My gaze landed on the jersey again, the fabric limp and lifeless over the chair. It was everything I used to be. Everything I used to want.

But it wasn't about rugby anymore. I was ready to figure out who I was without the field or the constant noise or the medals.

I stood and moved to the window, my reflection staring back at me in the glass. The city lights blurred behind me, but the voice in my head was clear, low, and determined.

I can't lose her.

My phone buzzed in my hand, pulling my focus back. I turned it over, my chest tightening when I saw her name on the screen.

I immediately answered. "Hey."

"Hi." I could tell she'd been crying, and my hand curled into a fist.

"Listen," I started.

"Logan, I would like to talk."

One corner of my mouth tugged up at her bold self-assurance.

When I was quiet, she continued: "I don't know if you leaving means that whatever we have is done, or if we're talking about a long-distance situation, or what. I love my job. I can't imagine just, what? Following you around while you travel the globe? My family, friends—my *life*—is here. I'm asking for some time to process this and figure out what *I* truly want . . . then we can talk."

The words sent a rush of hope and heavy dread through me, twisting in my gut.

"I understand," I rasped.

Whatever happened next, I knew one thing for sure—I would never go back to the life I had before her.

THIRTY-FIVE

MJ

The steady hum of the fluorescent lights in the hallway matched the monotony of my steps. My sneakers squeaked faintly against the linoleum as I passed the nurses' station, clutching a chart like it was a shield. The smell of coffee hung heavy in the air, tempting me, but I didn't stop.

I didn't need coffee. I needed to keep moving.

"Wow, look at you, always keeping busy like the perfect little nurse." Beth's voice dripped with mock sweetness, each word cutting like a paper-thin blade.

She leaned against the counter, her blond hair perfectly curled despite the early hour. Her black scrubs were always just a little too tight, the neckline tugged down just a little too low.

I didn't even glance her way as I flipped the chart open. "Beth, do you ever get tired of running your mouth, or is this just your cardio for the day?"

Her laugh was short, forced, but she recovered quickly, sidling up beside me. Her perfume—something cloyingly sweet—invaded my space. "Feisty. Trouble in paradise, then?" she said, tapping her nails against the counter.

My grip tightened on the chart, the edges biting into my palm. "I don't know what you're talking about."

"Oh, come on," she said, her lips curving into a smug smile. "You and Logan Brown. I mean, talk about a glow-up for you. A guy like that? Even I'm impressed."

I bit back the urge to snap at her, my chest tightening. Beth had a way of digging in just deep enough to sting without outright drawing blood.

She leaned in conspiratorially. "I always thought he was a little out of your league, but you never know with these rugby types. I mean, a freaking *Olympian*. Must be nice having someone like him around." Her smile curled upward. "Unless, of course, he's not around anymore?"

The words hit like a slap, and I forced myself to stay calm, my voice steady even as my stomach churned. "Logan and I are fine."

"Hmm," she said, drawing the sound out like she didn't believe me. "Well, if you ever get bored of him—or, you know, if he moves on—maybe give me a heads-up? A man like that doesn't come around every day."

I snapped the chart shut and turned to her, my voice cold. "You're right, Beth. He is out of my league—just not in the way you think. See, Logan's kind, intelligent, and actually likes women. Meanwhile, you're stuck here scheming for a hot doctor who's more interested in his chart than you."

Beth's perfectly glossed lips tightened into a thin line, but I wasn't done.

"So here's the deal," I continued, stepping closer. "You can keep your snide comments, your fake concern, and whatever fantasy you have about Logan to yourself. Because I'm not interested in playing games with someone who can't even play nice."

Her expression faltered, just for a second, before she managed to plaster on a smug smile. "Wow, MJ. Who knew you had claws?"

I leaned in slightly, my voice calm but firm. "I've always had them. You just weren't worth the scratch."

Beth's face flushed, and for once she didn't have a comeback. I turned on my heel and walked away, leaving her standing there, speechless.

Every step felt lighter, like I'd finally shed a weight I hadn't realized I'd been carrying.

The chart in my hand felt heavier than it should, the weight pressing into my palm like a reminder of everything I was trying to forget. I scanned the notes for the fifth time, the words blurring together. Mrs. Bernard's blood pressure was stable. Mr. Freemont had finally eaten his lunch. Nothing had changed since the last time I checked.

That was the point, though, wasn't it? If I kept moving—kept doing—then maybe I could outrun the negative thoughts that had been chasing me since the game.

Logan's face flashed in my mind, his expression a mix of shock and something else I couldn't quite place when the announcer revealed his Sevens call-up. The crowd's cheers had drowned out the sound of my heart cracking wide open, but only for a moment. Now the echoes of that afternoon followed me everywhere.

I shoved the chart into its slot and grabbed another, my hands trembling. When I flipped it open, my stomach dropped.

Arthur Brown.

The letters blurred as a fresh wave of unease settled over me. My fingers tightened on the edge of the chart before I closed it quickly, the weight of his name heavier than all the others combined.

The faint sound of laughter carried down the hallway, tugging my attention. A group of residents gathered in the common room for their morning coffee. Sylvie must have caught word about the unexpected announcement, because when I'd arrived at work, the break room was overflowing with blueberry crumble muffins, chocolate orange scones, and enough hot coffee to drown a village—or in this case, my heartache.

My coworkers' voices were warm and familiar, weaving together like an old quilt. I wanted to join them, to lose myself in their easy conversations and forget for a while, but I couldn't.

Not when I felt like a frayed thread, ready to snap.

My phone buzzed in my pocket, and I pulled it out without thinking, my heart clenching for a moment before I saw the name.

> **SYLVIE**
> How are you holding up?

> Just another day in paradise. Thanks for the treats.

> **SYLVIE**
> The Sugar Bowl sends their love. Dinner tonight? Gus wants to see his favorite aunt.

The offer was tempting, but the thought of sitting at her table, dodging questions about Logan, was enough to make me type out a quick excuse.

> Can't. Double shift. Rain check?

I hit send before the guilt could set in and shoved the phone back into my pocket. The lie felt like a pebble in my shoe—small but sharp, and impossible to ignore. I turned toward Arthur's room, determined to find something, anything, to keep myself busy.

I took a deep breath before knocking on his door. Arthur's room was dark when I peeked in, the bed neatly made and his chair conspicuously empty. My pulse quickened as I stepped inside, flipping on the light. The little table by the window was untouched, his mug still sitting there from last night, and the faint scent of the sandalwood lotion he swore helped his knees lingered in the air.

But no Arthur.

I closed the door behind me and glanced up and down the hallway. Empty. The tightness in my chest ratcheted up a notch as I thought through the possibilities. He wasn't in the common room or the library—I'd just come from there—and if he were outside, someone would've noticed.

Unless he sneaked out.

No, Arthur wouldn't just disappear without telling someone. Right?

The memory of him grinning like a mischievous kid flashed through my mind, his voice playfully defiant: *Rules are more like suggestions around here, don't you think?*

Oh, hell.

I didn't want to make a scene. The thought of calling Logan and admitting that his grandfather was AWOL? That was a spiral I wasn't ready for. And alerting the staff would just lead to panic and half the team mobilizing. No, I could find him. I just needed to think.

Arthur was a creature of habit. He had his favorite spots: the front porch, the sunroom, sometimes the garden when the weather wasn't too miserable. I'd start there.

I retraced my steps to the common areas, scanning the

faces of the residents and staff as I passed. "Seen Arthur?" I asked Carol, one of the nurses on duty.

She frowned, shaking her head. "Not since breakfast."

Great.

The garden was empty except for a pair of robins hopping through the flower beds. The sunroom was filled with chatting residents, none of whom were Arthur. The front porch? Nada.

My pulse thrummed louder as I headed back inside, my sneakers squeaking against the tiles. Where would he go?

Then it hit me.

Red Sullivan.

Arthur had mentioned visiting him more than once, and it wasn't like I hadn't seen the two of them plotting over coffee before. Red's condo wasn't far—it was on the Haven Pines property in the semi-independent living section. If Arthur had gone anywhere, that was my best bet.

I detoured to the break room, grabbing a box of coffee and a couple of pastries from Sylvie's spread. If I was going to barge into Red's place to drag Arthur back, I figured I'd better come bearing gifts.

The box of pastries balanced precariously on one arm as I juggled the coffee. My keys clinked against the box, my footsteps quick and purposeful. The chill of the morning air hit me as I stepped outside, the bright scent of pine and damp earth grounding me for a second.

"I swear, if you two are sitting there debating pie crusts again . . ." I muttered under my breath, the corner of my mouth tugging upward despite my frustration.

The path to Red's place was quiet, lined with bare trees that swayed in the gentle breeze. By the time I reached the condo, my nerves were buzzing, half with irritation and half with relief that I might have solved the mystery of Arthur's disappearance.

The familiar sight of Red Sullivan's residence eased some of the tension in my chest. The white shutters were gleaming, and the flower beds had faded with autumn's chill, but it was homey in a way that felt unshakable.

I pounded on the door, balancing the coffee box against my hip. "Arthur? Red? If you're in there and you've kidnapped one of my residents, now's your chance to surrender peacefully!"

The door opened a crack, and Red's familiar face appeared, his expression a mix of amusement and suspicion. "Well, look who's here."

The condo smelled like fresh coffee and something faintly sweet—probably the remains of whatever breakfast Red had whipped up. Arthur sat at the kitchen table, looking entirely too pleased with himself as he stirred sugar into a mug of coffee.

"MJ!" Arthur greeted, like he hadn't just caused my blood pressure to spike. "What a happy surprise. Come in, come in."

"I'm not here to stay," I said, setting the coffee and pastries on the counter with a clatter. "Do you have any idea how much trouble you're causing me?"

Red leaned against the counter, crossing his arms. "He's not causing trouble. He's having coffee with an old friend. What's the harm in that?"

I shot him a look. "The harm is that I thought he was missing. You couldn't have called? Sent a carrier pigeon? Smoke signal?"

Arthur grinned, entirely unrepentant. "Didn't think it was necessary. You're always saying I need to socialize more."

"You can't go wandering off without telling someone, or we'll have to put a bell on you like a cat."

Red chuckled, motioning toward the coffee I'd brought. "You came prepared, though. Good instinct."

I sighed, plopping down in a chair across from Arthur. The weight of the morning lifted just slightly as I watched the two of them bicker about which flavor of pie was superior.

Red slid me a mug of coffee without a word, and the warmth seeped into my hands as I sipped it.

"You two are going to be the death of me," I said, but there was no heat behind it.

"Us?" Arthur said, feigning innocence. "You've got enough spirit to handle us just fine, MJ."

"Barely," I muttered, shaking my head.

Despite my swirling feelings about Logan, we fell into an easy rhythm, their voices filling the quiet corners of my mind. They debated pies, shared a few football and rugby stories, and even teased me about my sour mood. I let their laughter wash over me, the heaviness in my chest easing—just a little.

Arthur was smart, and he wasn't about to let me off the hook. His gaze narrowed as he leaned back in his chair, a muffin balanced in his hand. "You're quieter than usual. What's got you stewing, MJ? Never seen a good stew that didn't need stirring."

I hesitated, my fingers tightening around the thermos. "It's nothing," I said quickly, but the words sounded hollow even to me.

Red snorted. "Girl, you're a terrible liar. Spill it."

My gaze drifted to the shelf in the corner of the room, where an old football sat next to a box filled with knick-knacks. The sight of it brought back a memory I'd been trying to bury—the box I'd handed over to my father's family, filled with ashes and expectations I hadn't been able to name.

"I met my dad's other family. I thought I'd feel relief after meeting them," I murmured, my voice barely above a whisper. The admission slipped out before I could stop it. "But I just felt . . . hollow. Like the man they described wasn't the same one I grew up with."

Arthur set his coffee down, the mug clinking softly against the table. "Let me guess—they painted a picture that didn't match the one you lived with every day."

I nodded, my throat tightening. "They said he was loving, patient. Warm. Like we're talking about two completely different people."

Red leaned forward, his weathered hand resting over mine. "People can be many things, MJ. Sometimes the good parts only come out for certain people, and the bad parts . . ." He trailed off, shaking his head. "Well, the bad parts can cast a hell of a shadow."

Red knew. He had known my father for a long time, and Red's late wife, June, was a catalyst in revealing the truth about what he'd done.

Arthur nodded in agreement. "Doesn't mean their experience wasn't real. And it doesn't mean yours wasn't either."

I swallowed hard, my chest pinching with the weight of their words. "I guess I thought meeting them would . . . fix something. But it didn't. It just made me realize how much I don't want to carry him with me anymore. I gave them his ashes, thinking that would be enough, but . . ." I exhaled sharply, my voice trembling. "I don't know how to let the rest go."

Red's grip on my hand tightened gently, grounding me. "You let it go by living your life, girl. By loving the people who matter and not letting the ghosts of the past tell you what you're worth."

Arthur added with a soft chuckle, "And by realizing that letting go doesn't mean forgetting. It means making space for better things."

I blinked back tears, the ache in my chest loosening, if only slightly. Their words were like sunlight breaking through a storm. I wasn't sure I had all the answers, but maybe I didn't need them. Maybe letting go wasn't about fixing the past, but about making peace with it.

Arthur sighed. "I just hope my grandson is smarter than he looks." He looked at his friend and shook his head. "I don't know how you survived all your kids getting wound up by love. It's hell on the old heart." He tapped his chest, and I couldn't help but smile.

Red's brow furrowed, his eyes growing glassy with uncertainty. "Did something happen?"

A sheepish smile spread across my face. "I've sort of been seeing Arthur's grandson." I swallowed hard. "He's actually gotten called back up to the Sevens, so now . . ."

Arthur's sharp gaze softened, his head tilting slightly. "Love's tricky. It'll knock you down and leave you wondering if you can get back up. But when it's the real thing, it's worth every bruise. Give the boy a chance to speak his heart. He may surprise you."

Red leaned forward, his hand patting my knee. "Don't be afraid to fight for what you want, young lady. Even if it means getting a little dirt under your nails."

I swallowed hard, their words wrapping around my heart.

"I don't even know if he feels the same," I admitted quietly. "What if I'm fighting for something that's already gone?"

"Did he tell you he was leaving?" Arthur asked, his brows lifting with a mischievous glint in his eye.

My brows tipped down. "Well . . . no. I didn't exactly give him the chance to say it." I huffed. "But come on. Why wouldn't he go? It's the opportunity he's been waiting for."

Red shook his head, his voice steady. "The best things in life are messy, MJ. You just have to figure out if they're worth the cleanup."

Arthur's laugh rumbled low and warm. "And if they're not, there's always pie."

The two of them dissolved into hearty laughter, and for the first time in days, I felt a flicker of something that might've been hope.

The drive home was quiet, the soft hum of the radio filling the car as their words echoed in my mind.

Maybe Red was right—love was messy. It certainly had been for my siblings.

But I'd been hiding behind work, avoiding the mess instead of facing it and *talking* with Logan.

I pulled into my driveway and sat there, the engine ticking softly as it cooled. My thoughts drifted to him, to the way his voice had cracked when he'd tried to explain, to the way he'd looked at me like I was the only thing tethering him to the ground.

Either way, it was time for me to stop hiding.

With a deep breath, I grabbed my bag and headed inside, determination settling into my chest. If Logan wanted to talk, I'd listen. And if he didn't, well . . . I would just have to figure out how to get back up.

THIRTY-SIX

LOGAN

The cool air bit at my skin as I stood in the parking lot of an old warehouse, nestled on the outskirts of Outtatowner. The building loomed ahead of me, its weathered brick and high windows softened by the pale light of the late afternoon. The air smelled like rain lingering on rust, damp earth mixing with a faint metallic tang. The acreage behind it was dull and grayed from autumn's chill.

It certainly wasn't much to look at—yet. But standing there, with the cool autumn breeze biting at my face, I could almost see what it could become.

A home for something new. Something real.

I walked toward the warehouse with my hands in my pockets. Inside the building, the echoes of my boots on the concrete floor filled the vast emptiness. The warehouse had good bones: sturdy beams, wide-open space, and the potential to be more than just a building. I ran my hand over a weathered column, its surface cool and solid under my palm. It felt steady, grounded—a noticeable contrast to the mess in my head.

I paced the length of the room, imagining it filled with

kids running drills, the sound of laughter, and the thud of a rugby ball against the walls. Young athletes learning to love the game as much as I had. The thought gave me a strange kind of hope—a flicker of something steady in a life that had always felt like it was in motion.

But was it enough?

The question echoed in my mind, louder than my footsteps. Competing had been my whole life—my anchor. It had defined me, shaped me, and given me a purpose. But it had become an anchor dragging me down rather than holding me steady. This wasn't about giving up. It was about finding balance.

Building something better.

For the first time in years, the thought didn't terrify me. It felt like breathing after holding my breath for too long.

I pulled out my phone, the screen cold against my fingertips as I typed.

> Meet me. I need to show you something.

I stared at the message, my stomach twisting. She might not come. I wouldn't blame her if she didn't. But she deserved to see this—deserved to know what she meant to me.

~

THE CRUNCH of gravel reached me before I saw her car pull up. My pulse rose as MJ stepped out, her arms crossed tightly against the chill. The late-afternoon light caught the caramel strands in her hair, turning them to fire. She looked unsure, her guarded expression matching the stiffness in her movements, but she'd come.

That was enough for now.

I waited as she approached, my hands shoved deep in my pockets to hide their shaking.

"Surprise," I said, my voice steady despite the nerves churning inside me.

She arched an eyebrow, her lips quirking in that way that always knocked me off balance. "Dragging me out to the middle of nowhere? If this is a kidnapping"—she looked around the abandoned property—"that's more of a *King* move..."

A laugh escaped me, unexpected and soft. Leave it to her to find humor in the tension. "No ransom notes, I promise. Just trust me."

Her smile softened, her walls slipping just a fraction. "All right," she said, her voice quieter now. "What did you need to show me?"

"Not yet." I hesitated, rubbing the back of my neck. "There's something I need to tell you first."

Her expression changed, curiosity giving way to caution. "Okay..."

I took a deep breath, the weight of my next words pressing down like a vise. "That night at the ramen place, Wyatt offered me a coaching position at his university."

Her eyes widened, the flicker of hope breaking through her guarded expression like sunlight through clouds. "Wow, that's... that's great, Logan. Are you considering it?"

"I turned him down." The muscles in my jaw worked. "Twice."

The flicker disappeared, replaced by confusion and something that looked a lot like hurt. Her lips parted, but no words came. The disappointment in her eyes hit me like a punch to the gut.

"You turned it down?" she said finally, her voice barely

above a whisper. "So that's it, then? You're going to rejoin the team?"

I stepped closer, the raw edge in her voice cutting deeper than I'd expected.

Her brows knit together, her lips trembling as she searched my face. "I can't—I have had enough time to think, Logan. I'll fight for us. If it means doing long distance while you're playing with the Sevens, we can figure that out. I choose you, but I'm also choosing myself. That means I am not afraid of what might come next. I'm *excited* for it. I only hope it's still with you."

I surprised her with a laugh, soft and full of relief, pulling her hands to my chest. "Julep."

Her gaze shot up to mine, confusion flickering across her features.

"I'm not leaving. I was never leaving. I've been everywhere, done everything, but there's nothing I want more than to be right here with you." I tightened my grip on her hands, my voice steady and sure. "You're not fighting for us alone."

She gazed up at me, her lips trembling as a shaky laugh floated out of her. "Then what the hell are we doing standing in front of this dilapidated building?"

"I figured it was better than decapitating a mafia boss." A nervous chuckle escaped me.

Her eyes went wide. "*What?*"

"It's nothing. Something my grandfather said, I—" I laughed and gestured toward the warehouse. "I'm doing this."

My voice was quieter, but full of conviction. "I'm building a rugby training facility here. Something lasting. A place for the game, for the town . . . for us."

She blinked, her walls cracking as my words sank in. "Logan . . ."

I reached for her hands, holding them tightly in mine. The feel of her skin—cool, soft, real—grounded me. My voice softened, every word carrying the weight of what I'd been too afraid to say until now.

"I love you, Julep. I love you in a way I didn't ever think was possible. You make me want to be better, to do better, because for the first time, I don't want to win alone. I want to build something real—with you."

Her breath hitched, her lips trembling as tears filled her eyes. "I . . . I don't know what to say."

I cupped her cheek, my thumb brushing away a tear as it fell. "Just say yes. Say yes to us. Say yes to a future where we figure out the messy stuff together. Because I'm not giving up on you, and I'm not giving up on us."

A tear streaked down her cheek, a shaky laugh and smile breaking through the tears. "Yes," she whispered, her voice cracking but sure. "Yes, Logan."

Relief flooded through me, my body lighter than it had been in years. I bent down and kissed her, my hands framing her face as our lips met.

The kiss was soft at first, hesitant, like we were testing the boundaries of something fragile. But then she leaned into me, her fingers curling into my jacket, and the world tilted. Everything—her warmth, her taste, the feel of her against me—crashed into me all at once, and for the first time in what felt like forever, I stopped thinking.

When we finally broke apart, her forehead rested against mine, her breath mingling with mine in the cool air. "That was unexpected," she murmured, her voice shaky but full of warmth.

I grinned, brushing a strand of hair from her face. "Good surprise?"

"The best," she said softly, her smile widening. "What now?"

I stepped back, my hand still wrapped around hers as I led her toward my truck. "There's one more thing."

I opened the tailgate, revealing the red bicycle I'd spent the past month finding and restoring. The frame gleamed in the fading sunlight, the vivid color bold and unmissable.

Her hands flew to her mouth, a soft sob breaking free. Tears spilled down her cheeks as she reached out, her fingers brushing the handlebars. "Logan, I . . ."

"You told me once that seeing your father teach Bianca to ride a bike hurt because it was something he never did for you. I can't fix the past, MJ, but I can try to give you something better. We'll make all new memories if we have to."

She turned to me, her tear-filled eyes brimming with something I hadn't seen before—hope. "You didn't have to . . ."

"Yes, I did," I said softly. "Because you're the strongest person I know, but even the strongest people deserve someone to steady them when they're learning to ride."

She let out a shaky laugh, her hand sliding into mine. "We're really doing this? Choosing us."

I grinned, my thumb brushing across her knuckles. "Every damn day."

"I love you." Her lips quirked into a soft smile, the kind that made my chest pinch. "For the record," she murmured, stepping closer, "I already know how to ride a bike."

I chuckled, the sound low and easy as I tugged her gently toward me. "Good," I said, my voice dipping. "I can plan on keeping you steady in a thousand other ways."

Her breath hitched, her gaze flicking to my mouth before locking back on my eyes. "Logan . . ."

I didn't let her finish. My lips found hers, soft at first, testing, tasting, until her arms slid around my neck and she pressed closer. The kiss deepened, the air between us heating as her fingers curled into the fabric of my jacket.

The world around us blurred—the fading light, the cool bite of the breeze, the looming husk of the old warehouse—and all that remained was her.

Us. This.

When we finally broke apart, her forehead rested against mine, her voice barely a whisper. "You're really not going anywhere, are you?"

I smiled, brushing a strand of hair from her cheek. "Stuck with me. I go wherever you are."

Her answering smile was a kaleidoscope of warmth, like the last vibrant colors of a setting sun spilling across the sky, soft and breathtaking enough to make the world stand still. She tugged me by the front of my jacket, her voice soft but sure. "Then shut up and kiss me again."

And I did—losing myself in her completely, knowing this was just the beginning of everything we were about to build—together.

EPILOGUE

MJ

The sun hung low in the sky, its golden summer light casting long shadows across the indoor training field of Anchor Point Rugby. The faint sound of rugby balls thudding against turf and laughter carried through the air, mixing with the hum of conversation from the gathered crowd. The facility buzzed with life, a symbol of everything Logan had worked so hard to create.

And, in a way, everything we'd built together.

I stood at the edge of the building, watching young athletes show off passing drills under the watchful eye of one of Logan's assistant coaches. My heart swelled as I took it all in—the warehouse turned training facility, the bustling community Logan had brought together, and the unmistakable sense of purpose that filled the air.

It wasn't just his dream anymore. It was ours.

A familiar voice cut through my thoughts. "Lost in your thoughts again, MJ?"

I turned to see Arthur, making his way toward me with

a mischievous glint in his eyes. He held a cane, though he barely leaned on it, and the corners of his mouth quirked in a wry smile.

"Just taking it all in," I said, smiling back. "It's hard to believe it's been over a year."

Arthur nodded, his gaze sweeping the field. "He did good, didn't he?"

"More than good," I murmured, the lump in my throat catching me by surprise. "He built something incredible."

Arthur chuckled, his hand patting my elbow. "And he wouldn't have done it without you. Don't let him sell you short, miss. You're as much a part of this as he is."

Before I could respond, a burst of laughter drew my attention to the far side of the field, where my siblings and their families had gathered. Ben and Tillie darted between Abel's legs while Gus attempted to tackle Royal, much to Sylvie's exasperation. Whip was wrapped up in Emily, whispering something in her ear that made her blush. Hazel and JP stood off to the side, laughing at the chaos as Veda rolled her eyes at Royal's antics. Bax was fussing over Bug, and while she tried to pretend she hated it, her soft smile gave her away.

My heart tightened, the sight both familiar and surreal. We had found our peace.

This is where we belonged. Together.

Logan caught my hand as the family celebration continued at the edge of the field. "Come with me for a second," he said, his tone light but his eyes giving away something deeper.

"You're acting weird," I teased, narrowing my eyes.

He grinned, brushing a hand through his hair. "You'll see. Just trust me."

He led me through the quiet halls of the facility, the

noise of the celebration outside fading behind us. My curiosity peaked as he guided me toward the outdoor training field, now bathed in the warm hues of the setting sun.

He stopped at the edge of the grassy field, turning to face me with an intensity that made my breath catch. "I've been waiting for the right moment to do this," he said, his voice low but steady. "And it feels like everything has led to this."

"Logan . . ." I started, my heart pounding as his hands took mine.

"You walked into my life and turned everything upside down in the best way," he continued, his gaze never leaving mine. "You made me see that rugby wasn't my only home. You were."

Tears pricked my eyes as he dropped to one knee, pulling a small velvet box from his pocket. He opened it to reveal a stunning ring that sparkled in the golden light. It was a huge, oval-cut ring set with an intricate vintage-inspired design that wove all around the band. Tiny white diamonds sparkled from the band, and when it moved, even more diamonds surrounded the center stone like a peek-a-boo halo. The ring was the perfect combination of simple vintage chic and subtle glamour.

Logan peered up at me. "You've been my anchor, my inspiration, and my everything. Marry me, Julep. Let's keep building this life together."

"Yes," I whispered, my voice trembling. "Yes, Logan. Of course, yes."

Relief washed over his face as he slid the ring onto my finger and rose to his feet, pulling me into a kiss that stole what little breath I had left.

Cheers erupted behind us, and I spun to see the entire

crowd pouring onto the field. "What . . . What is this?" I stammered through a watery laugh.

"They all knew," Logan said, grinning. "I wasn't sure which of your brothers to ask, so . . . I kind of asked all of them. I wanted this to be more than just a proposal. I wanted it to be a celebration of you—the way you deserve to be celebrated."

As the crowd surged forward, my siblings enveloped me in hugs and laughter. Sylvie teased me about how massive the ring was, while Abel tried to wrangle Ben and Tillie. Royal clapped Logan on the shoulder, muttering something about "finally," and JP's warm smile felt like a silent affirmation that everything had fallen into place.

Arthur raised his cane in a mock toast. "To Logan and MJ—already a team to be reckoned with."

The warmth and love radiating from everyone filled me with something I'd never quite felt before. I wasn't just part of this family—I was at its center, and for the first time I let myself believe I deserved to be here.

Later that evening, Logan's office door clicked shut behind him. My pulse jumped as I turned, his dark gaze locking with mine.

"Hiding out?" he asked.

I grinned, looking around his tidy office and down at the ring on my finger. "I just needed a quiet minute to wrap my head around everything."

"You know," he said, his voice low and teasing, "you're going to have to get used to being celebrated."

I smiled, my heart thudding as he crossed the room in a few strides. "And if I don't?"

"Then I'll remind you. Like this."

His lips crashed into mine, stealing my breath and flooding me with heat. His hands slid to my waist, pulling me closer until there was no space between us. My fingers tangled in his hair as I pressed against him, needing more.

When he lifted me onto the desk, the cool surface beneath me sent a shiver up my spine, but his heat consumed me. His lips trailed fire down my neck, his hands sliding beneath my shirt to explore bare skin.

"Logan," I breathed, my voice breaking on his name, knowing there was a building full of people just beyond the door.

"I've got you," he murmured, his fingers tugging at the waistband of my pants. He made quick work of them, his eyes darkening as he took in the sight of me.

His mouth followed the path of his hands, kissing and nipping until my hips bucked against him. Heat coiled low in my belly as he touched me, his fingers stroking until I was shaking, gasping, begging for more.

"Please," I whispered, my voice raw.

Logan's lips curved into a wicked grin, and he rose to his full height, his hands steadying me as he unbuckled his jeans. "Please, what?"

Heat radiated to every corner of my body. "Please fuck me like I'm yours."

When he slid inside me, the stretch was exquisite, the feeling so intense I couldn't hold back the moan that escaped.

"God, MJ," he groaned, his forehead pressing against mine. "You're perfect."

Our bodies moved together, the rhythm building as we both lost ourselves in the moment. His name tumbled from my lips as pleasure crashed over me, and he followed, tightening his grip and burying himself deep.

Afterward he pulled me into his arms, his lips brushing against my temple.

"You're mine, Julep," he whispered, his voice low and certain. "And I'm yours. Always."

I grinned at him, breathless and happy, as we both fumbled to fix our clothing. Logan peeked out the door with an exaggerated seriousness that made me laugh before assuring me the coast was clear. His hand found mine as we stepped out together, the quiet hum of the facility wrapping around us like a warm embrace.

As we walked back to the party, my thoughts drifted to my father's other family. Their kindness had stung, their warmth a reminder of what I hadn't had—but it had also been the catalyst for letting go. For the first time, I felt at peace with the past and with myself.

Royal's booming laughter greeted us as we rejoined the celebration. Sylvie's sly smile slid over me as she leaned close. "Your hair is a disaster," she whispered knowingly, her eyes twinkling with mischief.

A hot blush crept up my face as I tried to smooth the strands, but before embarrassment could take hold, Logan's arm slid around my waist, grounding me with his steady presence.

I looked out at the scene before me, my chest tightening in the best way. My siblings—Sylvie, Whip, Abel, Royal, JP—surrounded by their spouses, children, and the unshakable love we'd built together. Kings and Sullivans, laughing and mingling as though the past had never kept them apart. The Bluebirds, in the background, sipping wine and tittering as they no doubt gossiped about all of us.

This was my family. My home. The life I'd never dreamed possible but now couldn't imagine living without.

We had found our peace. This was where we belonged. Together.

Logan's lips brushed my temple again, his voice a soft, comforting rumble. "Penny for your thoughts?"

I smiled up at him, threading my fingers through his, holding on tightly to the man who had turned my world upside down in the best way. "Just thinking about how far we've come," I said softly, my words meant for him alone.

His answering smile was like the sunrise—warm and endless, casting light on every dark corner I'd ever known. "Only the beginning," he murmured, pulling me closer, his lips ghosting over mine. "And we've got a lifetime to go."

As the sound of laughter and children playing surrounded us, I leaned into him, knowing with certainty that I was exactly where I was meant to be.

And for the first time in my life, I was no longer afraid to say yes to all of it.

ACKNOWLEDGMENTS

Giving MJ the happily-ever-after she deserved was the only way I knew how to end this series. For so long she was a beacon of light and love—despite the feud, despite her father, despite all of the obstacles in her way. I hope you loved her story as much as I did!

To my husband who is my listening ear and warm hug at the end of every day. I couldn't do any of this without your unwavering support.

To Elsie & Kandi, thank you for not letting me give up on this one. Ending a series is always tough and I couldn't have done it without your love and support.

To Paula who has become the voice in my head. Any time I *think* something might not work, you confirm what I already knew. My books are better because of you!

James, every book feels more natural than the last. I am so thankful we're still working together. You push me to be better in many ways and I am so grateful for you!

Anna and Trinity, we did it! Having your beta feedback on this series has been incredible. I am so grateful for your encouragement and insights into my world!

To Ashely, I couldn't keep the day-to-day running without your help. You keep me sane and the Lena machine running! Thank you for all you do.

And most importantly, to you, my readers! I wouldn't be able to do what I do without your enthusiastic love and support. THANK YOU! 🖤

HENDRIX HEARTTHROBS

Want to connect? Come hang out with the Hendrix Heartthrobs on Facebook to laugh & chat with Lena! Special sneak peeks, announcements, exclusive content, & general shenanigans all happen there.

Come join us!

ABOUT THE AUTHOR

Lena Hendrix is a *USA Today* and Amazon Top 5 Bestselling contemporary romance author living in the Midwest. Her love for romance stared with sneaking racy Harlequin paperbacks and now she writes her own hot-as-sin small town romance novels. Lena has a soft spot for strong alphas with marshmallow insides, heroines who clap back, and sizzling tension. Her novels pack in small town heart with a whole lotta heat.

When she's not writing or devouring new novels, you can find her hiking, camping, fishing, and sipping a spicy margarita!

Want to hang out? Find Lena on Tiktok or IG!

ALSO BY LENA HENDRIX

Chikalu Falls

Finding You

Keeping You

Protecting You

Choosing You (origin novella)

Redemption Ranch

The Badge

The Alias

The Rebel

The Target

The Sullivans

One Look

One Touch

One Chance

One Night

One Taste (prequel novella)

The Kings

Just This Once

Just My Luck

Just Between Us

Just Like That

Just Say Yes

Printed in Great Britain
by Amazon